There is nothing conventional about WHEN EVIL WAKES. It is edited by a master in his field, and packed with gruesome contributions, few of which have appeared in book form before.

The publishers would like to think this is the perfect bedside book – but perhaps, on reflection, it is not! What it is, undoubtedly, is superb entertainment for the price of a handful of coffin nails. . . .

EDITED BY
August Derleth

When Evil Wakes

AN ANTHOLOGY
OF THE MACABRE

CORGI BOOKS
TRANSWORLD PUBLISHERS LTD
A National General Company

WHEN EVIL WAKES

A CORGI BOOK 0 552 08737 8

Originally published in Great Britain
by Souvenir Press Ltd.

PRINTING HISTORY
Souvenir Press edition published 1963
Corgi edition published 1965
Corgi edition reissued 1971

This book is set in Monotype Times

Corgi Books are published by Transworld Publishers Ltd.,
Cavendish House, 57–59 Uxbridge Road,
Ealing, London, W.5.
Made and printed in Great Britain by
Hunt Barnard Printing Ltd., Aylesbury, Bucks.

Contents

Acknowledgments

The Eye and the Finger, by Donald Wandrei, copyright 1936, by Esquire, Inc.; copyright 1944, by Donald Wandrei. By permission of Arkham House.

The Feasting Dead, by John Metcalfe, copyright 1954, by John Metcalfe. By permission of Arkham House.

Death Waters, by Frank Belknap Long, copyright 1924, by The Popular Fiction Publishing Company; copyright 1946, by Frank Belknap Long. By permission of Arkham House.

An Invitation to the Hunt, by George Hitchcock, copyright 1960, by the *San Francisco Review*.

The Tsanta in the Parlour, by Stephen Grendon, copyright 1948, by Weird Tales; copyright 1953, by August Derleth.

Moonlight—Starlight, by Virginia Layefsky, copyright 1959, by the Curtis Publishing Company; copyright 1963, by Virginia Layefsky. By permission of Anne Curtis-Brown.

The Kite, by Carl Jacobi, copyright 1937, by Beacon Magazines, Inc.; copyright, 1947, by Carl Jacobi. By permission of Arkham House.

Sweets to the Sweet, by Robert Bloch, copyright 1947, by Weird Tales; copyright 1960, by Robert Bloch. By permission of Arkham House.

A Thin Gentleman with Gloves, by Simon West, copyright 1943, by Weird Tales; copyright 1945, 1953, by August Derleth. By permission of Arkham House.

The Horror at Red Hook, by H. P. Lovecraft, copyright 1926, by The Popular Fiction Publishing Company; copyright 1939, 1947, by August Derleth and Donald Wandrei. By permission of Arkham House.

The Triumph of Death, by H. Russell Wakefield, copyright 1949, by August Derleth; copyright 1961, by H. Russell Wakefield. By permission of Arkham House.

The Lips, by Henry S. Whitehead, copyright 1929, by The Popular Fiction Publishing Company; copyright 1944, by August Derleth and Donald Wandrei. By permission of Arkham House.

A Cautionary Word

Nothing in the imagination of man equals the horrors of Belsen and Dachau and those of nuclear war, all of which prove that—as Dorothy Sayers pointed out some decades ago—we have progressed from the evil outside of us to that inside; but nothing in those dreadful examples of man's inhumanity to man has diminished very much the individual reader's predilection for fictive shudders on a less grandiose scale than the very real horrors of our age.

Anthologies of macabre fiction are published with fair regularity, and repeat themselves with sad frequency; the best stories of the modern masters in the genre have been reprinted scores of times, while many splendid examples of the macabre tale at its most entertaining have lain neglected in the pages of magazines or in books of very limited circulation.

The macabre tale reached its peak of excellence during the early decades of the present century, in both England and America—in the work of Dr. Montague Rhodes James, A. E. Coppard, Walter de la Mare, Arthur Machen, William Hope Hodgson, May Sinclair, M. P. Shiel, Lord Dunsany, E. F. Benson, H. Russell Wakefield, Thomas Burke, W. F. Harvey, L. P. Hartley, Lady Cynthia Asquith, John Metcalfe, Saki, Marjorie Bowen, and a few others, in England; in that of Henry James, Edith Wharton, Mary E. Wilkins-Freeman, F. Marion Crawford, H. P. Lovecraft, Clark Ashton Smith, Henry S. Whitehead, among others, in America. There is not so substantial a group of writers devoting the best of their creative energies to the macabre tale in English today. H. Russell Wakefield, John Metcalfe, Roald Dahl, John Collier, Margery Lawrence, John Wyndham, L. P. Hartley, Arthur C. Clarke, for example, are still writing in the domain of the uncanny in England; while in America Ray Bradbury, Stanley Ellin, Charles Beaumont, Jack Finney, and Theodore Sturgeon are pre-eminent in their ability to satisfy those readers who take pleasure in being given a bit of a turn, agreeable or disagreeable, and who want to be made to feel what it is like to come face to face with something shatteringly horrible where one has been long accustomed to expect the familiar.

The stories in this book are not elsewhere represented in any anthology, and the majority of them—indeed, all but two—have never been anthologized at all, though some of these tales have appeared in collections under their authors' by-lines. There are stories here of supernatural vengeance and sorcery; there is a very modern *conte cruel*; there are tales of pure grue and hauntings—and many more. The horrors in these pages are of various kinds—from the psychiatric problem of Donald Wandrei's *The Eye and the Finger* to the physical torment of George Hitchcock's *An Invitation to the Hunt*; from the fatal mental torture of David Keller's *A Piece of Linoleum* to the frankly supernatural terror of H. Russell Wakefield's *The Triumph of Death*; from the demoniac possession of John Metcalfe's superb novella, *The Feasting Dead* —surely a tale with few peers in contemporary literature, such as might be expected of a story by a longtime master of his craft, to the poignant graveyard tale, *Moonlight—Starlight*, Virginia Layefsky's first published story; from the deceptively glib witch-craft of Robert Bloch's *Sweets to the Sweet*, to the lingering fright-fulness of *The Horror at Red Hook*, by H. P. Lovecraft, who is in a very real sense *sui generis*, for in his horror fiction he evolved an entire mythology which has drawn a dozen other writers to con-tribute to it and continue it.

This anthology has been assembled for no other purpose than to entertain those readers who like to experience an occasional frightening feeling of psychic insecurity, be it because of a monster in the garden, a ghost in the attic, a mouldering corpse in the cellar, or, worse, a sudden brief dislocation in space or personality. Let us, therefore, accept the authors' premise that there *is* indeed something outside in the dark—or inside in the dark—and turn to a pleasant variety of chilling horrors.

7 February 1963

AUGUST DERLETH

The Eye and the Finger

DONALD WANDREI

He was neither contented nor unhappy as he plodded up the five flights of stairs towards his room. His eyes felt weary. They always ached a little at evening after he had finished his day's work, for the bright lights of the department store bothered him. Not the shrill voices of women, which swept into his ears for eight hours like a thin, far scream. Not the mask of calmness that rules compelled him to wear. Not the standing on his feet, the smirking, bowing, directing, explaining, and approving. He had long become used to these. They varied. Their relative values changed. But the glare of the lights was a tireless, implacable enemy.

He reached the second floor. The half-gloom of the staircase-well soothed him.

Tomorrow he would draw his salary cheque. The twenty-five dollars would guarantee his existence a week longer. If the fatal pink slip came with his salary, he could last about three weeks by scrimping and letting the rent slide. He was vaguely conscious of these possibilities, but they didn't prey on his mind. Five years of steady employment had fitted him into routine.

Passing the third floor, he smiled politely at a woman. He had seen her before, and was often on the point of speaking, but didn't know her name.

At the fourth floor he hesitated. He had a notion that he had forgotten something. He checked off the evening newspaper under his arm, the toothpaste in his pocket, the laundry that would arrive later. Halted there under the bulb on the landing, he showed no distinguishing features. No one would notice him in a crowd. Away from the store he was diffident, mild-mannered, and he himself found it hard to characterize his appearance whenever he faced a mirror.

He climbed on to the fifth floor. His room had an old lock on the door, which he had never yet succeeded in opening on the first try. He worked the key back and forth until the lock turned.

As soon as the door stood open he felt for the wall switch, and when the light came on, he closed the door with a backward kick of his foot.

An eye was lying on the top of his bureau.

He saw it instantly, for the eye was staring at him.

11

He grew ill at ease, for he had few friends and did not like practical jokes. Or perhaps one of the children in the building had thoughtlessly played a prank upon him. That must be the explanation. He felt relieved, though he couldn't imagine how the locked door had been overcome. He walked over to the bureau and picked up the eye.

A strange, colossal silence all at once enveloped him, in which he distinctly heard the tiny paws of a mouse scampering through the walls. Then a great roaring swept up, so that his eardrums throbbed to the hammer of gigantic poundings.

The eye was living, humid, and horrible to feel.

He dropped it. The eye made a soft, dull plop as it hit the bureau. It rolled and came to a stop staring unwinkingly at him. A moist film clung to his thumb and forefinger.

He backed away from the bureau, his gaze glued to the eye. Surges of thunder and blankets of incredible silence alternately shook him and numbed him.

The eye watched him retreat.

He backed into a chair and jumped nervously from the contact. The room whirled. Among the shifting objects, a cup crossed his vision. He remembered a piece of cardboard in a box of stationery.

He got the cup and the cardboard, but was loath to approach the eye. It continued to look at him with a singularly intense, compelling, and mournful fixity, as though it wished to convey a message.

He turned the cup upside down and dropped it over the eye. The cardboard rustled as it slid across the cloth spread that covered the bureau, and slid under the cup. Something rolled around inside the small area of the prison. He lifted the cup and cardboard, walked to the door, and went out, down to the street. A terrifying motion, like the slow progress of a slug, took place between the pasteboard and the cup. The faint warmth that seeped through seemed searing flame upon his palm.

He deposited the cup in a waste-can, and weighted it with a brick so that whatever was on the inside of it could not escape.

He returned to the main entrance of the building where he lived. The threshold blocked him by an invisible barrier that he could not force himself to cross. Walking on, he felt better when the doorway receded behind him.

Passers-by did not register upon his consciousness. He had no memory of streets, nor of pavements flowing beneath his measured tread. It startled him to discover that he walked indeed with solemn paces, instead of strolling at random as he had planned. He was tramping through night, but the street lamps at spaced intervals broke the darkness with rings of light. They measured in time to the beating of his footsteps, in rhythm with the far roaring and alternate silences that divided his ears.

If he had been walking in a funeral procession, he could not have chosen a more appropriate gait.

He paid no attention to the lapse of hours, until he looked up and found himself again in front of the entrance. Aching weariness made him realize the miles he must have covered during his half-stupor. The shock, the grip of horrific nightmare, only now waned. And as it passed away, he began to wonder what had caused him so vivid an illusion of living through an experience that had no connection with any previous part of his life.

He began climbing the stairs, the five flights. His hand, clutching the banister, helped pull him along. The wood felt clammy as though sweating to damp air. The atmosphere must have been saturated, for beads of moisture collected upon his forehead.

The heavy pounding of his heart commenced upon the third floor. He went on, a sense of constriction and of doom accompanying him.

Arrived at last in front of his door, he listened, and heard the creaking sounds of the building. What else could he have heard? he wondered, breathing audibly.

The key wouldn't work, until he remembered that he had forgotten to lock the door. He pushed it open, slowly, and the light in the room gave him a moment's panic until he remembered that he had forgotten to press the switch when he carried the eye out.

He entered. Frozen into immediate paralysis, he jerked only when the door swung shut, of its own accord, upon its ill-balanced hinges. The click came to his ears like a detonation in the midst of a desert of solitudes.

A hand hung in mid-air, a hand that pointed at the open window.

Where it should have been attached to an arm, he clearly saw blood, veins, flesh, muscular tissue, and bone. But it did not bleed. And there was no body. And the nap of the rug underneath it remained erect.

He stared at the hand with blind, unreasoning, raging horror. The hand curled, so that the forefinger pointed directly at him. It curled in no haste, but as inexorably as the tick of time.

His first instinct, to flee forever from the room, he suppressed. He heard the rumble of wheels upon a street, and in the presence of that familiar reality, he could not yield to this visitation that had no right to afflict him. For if he rushed out, not to return, he could never through all years to come efface the haunting of events that he could not explain.

His breath came in deep gulps, and trembling fits of exhalation, as he advanced.

The hand, hanging without support, pointed straight towards him. He drew nearer, and nearer, but could detect no change in its position. The room fell away from his vision, light and darkness

13

departed, leaving to him a universe composed only of a disembodied hand, and himself.

He seized the hand, intending to hurl it far out the open window. The fingers instantly curled around his own, not fiercely, but tugging him along, pulling him towards the window. For a step he followed, hypnotized and unnerved. The hand felt neither living nor dead, neither hot nor cold. Its touch brought unrelieved terror, because it resembled nothing that he knew. It seemed most like the clasp of some fantastic alien, not of this or of any other imaginable world, but of a solidity beyond. It felt like a marginal thing, trapped midway between stone oblivion and tissue of life.

He pulled, and the hand reluctantly, with heavy drag, yielded, drifting away from the window as upon the surface of an unseen ocean. The fingers retained their firm clasp, all save the forefinger which opened like an unfolding worm. He fought the hand. He seized the forefinger with a tug that tore the other fingers loose. The forefinger began to curl inward upon his left palm. His right fist hit and hammered it. He freed himself wholly from that corrupt touch, and backed away, a salt taste upon his lips.

The hand relaxed. It drifted over to the spot at which he had first observed it. His own hands were shaking, shaking incessantly, and yet all the rest of him seemed ice. Not until the marginal thing had resumed its former position did he manage to overcome his paralysis, but the palsy of his hands continued. If the marginal thing had only attacked him—if it would try to overtake him, track him down, hound him deliberately—he could have coped with physical, tangible horror in action. The fiendish element was the thing's confidence. It urged, without threatening him, and waited because it had the whole of time till doomsday.

A towel caught his glance. Not once letting the hand out of his sight, he took the towel from its rack by the washbowl.

The forefinger curled up in a dreadfully wagging gesture as he drew near again.

The towel trembled even before he flung it over the marginal thing. He grabbed the four ends, wondering if the prisoner had escaped. With the corners of the towel clutched, he distinctly felt a weight, heard and saw a gruesome scrabbling within the bulge.

His descent was nightmare. He twisted the ends of the towel, and held the bag that imprisoned the creature under his arm. There it squirmed, nudging him with fingers that prodded inquisitively. Towards the ground floor the forefinger began a diabolic tapping in measure with the beating of his heart, and when his heart skipped, the tap did not come.

At the refuse receptacle, he had a compulsion to lift the cup, and find if the eye had escaped. But the fear of knowing proved greater than the fear of not knowing. He knotted the towel to a mass of iron. He walked away rapidly, then, to escape the scuttling flurry that threshed the cloth.

The one man who could help him was Dr. Behn, the psychiatrist, who lived nearby. The psychiatrist did not like being called from bed. At first gruff, then sceptical, impatient, soothing, and interested in turn, he finally agreed to accompany the patient.

"It will at least help to settle your nerves for the night when I've proved that nothing unusual is present," said Dr. Behn reassuringly. "The hallucination may return, of course, but you'll be better prepared because you'll understand that it is a hallucination. I almost wish you were right, though. What an uproar it would create among my colleagues! But, of course, such things simply can't be, can they?"

"No, they can't be, but they are. Why do they happen to me? Why not somebody else? Why not you?"

Dr. Behn did not answer.

The street, now dark and long deserted, echoed their tread as they entered the building. The echoes had a dismal, reverberating sound as forlorn, as final, as footsteps towards the grave.

The psychiatrist breathed a trifle more heavily by the time he had reached the fifth floor. He was not used to such effort. He waited for the door to be opened.

His companion, however, had difficulty with the key and the lock, partly because of the palsy, partly because he had again forgotten that the door was merely closed. When he finally opened it, the light in the room likewise made him rigid for a moment. The pattern of his life had been swept away. Twice he had forgotten to extinguish the lights and to lock the door.

The eye—an eye—was lying on top of the bureau.

He saw it instantly, for it was staring at him. He pointed at it, cried out—but not even a whisper issued from his lips. He tried once more to speak, but the breath rattled around in his throat below the level of an audible murmur.

Dr. Behn half-turned his head, a strange expression on his face. He seemed to be looking at his patient, but his pupils remained fixed upon the eye.

The psychiatrist strode forward positively, and yet with a frown. "Hmmm!" he exclaimed. "I don't wonder you got a shock. That's the most convincingly real artificial eye that I've seen. Whoever made it is a remarkable craftsman."

He picked the eye off the bureau.

An expression of utter loathing altered his features until they were as dustily grey as those of a corpse. He felt the eye quiver. A sickness, a nausea added itself to the grey. He opened his fingers mechanically. The eye fell with a dull plop. Its pupil returned its gaze towards the other man, ignoring Dr. Behn.

The psychiatrist stood dazed, his glance crawling towards the eye and back to the film of moisture on his thumb and forefinger. His breathing became more rapid. All at once he turned, began walking, hurrying, running for the door.

A voice harried him. "Wait! *Wait!* What is it?"

The psychiatrist paused briefly, his face twisted into detestable ferocity and hatred. "What is it? I don't know. I don't want to know.

"My province is psychology and mental hygiene. This is wholly outside my field. I know nothing about it. I do not care to have anything more to do with it. When I leave I shall forget that I listened to you. I shall forget that I came here. I shall forget that anything happened. I shall leave instructions with my secretary that under no circumstances will any appointment whatsoever be made with you at any time hereafter. I refuse to accept your patronage. My practice is, and will be, confined to mental cases, not physical impossibilities.

"I can't help you. There's nothing that anyone can do to help you. This is your own problem. Work it out any way you see fit. Good night, and good-bye."

The door slammed.

Even through the walls, he could hear Behn's receding tread, hurrying farther and farther below. The sound, fading swiftly, died away among the remote world.

When he turned around, he uttered a whistling sigh.

The eye upon the bureau still watched him unwaveringly.

And in mid-air hung the hand, forefinger pointed towards the open window.

He took a step in the direction of the hand. It began to swing towards him, leisurely. Its supreme indifference, the impersonal confidence of that horrible, marginal thing obsessed him even more than the eye. And the eye with its cold, implacable stare had already initiated him into the brotherhood of the blind.

The curtains gently swayed as he walked towards them. He did not look behind at the hand or the eye.

The drapes rippled from the eddy of his plunge through the open window.

The Feasting Dead

JOHN METCALFE

I

Our boy, Denis, had at no time been very strong, and when his mother, whom he had adored, died suddenly, I fetched him from his boarding school by Edinburgh and let him stop a while at home.

Poor little fellow! I had tended previously perhaps to be a trifle stern with him, but we needed each other now, and I did all I could to make up to him for anything of harshness in the past and soften, for his tender sensibilities, the blow I myself felt so sorely.

No doubt, I had become a thoroughly "indulgent" father, and would not, I think, have rued it but for that train of circumstances to be narrated. We were living, then, in the big pleasant old place "Ashtoft," near Winchester, which I had bought on my retirement from the army, and when Denis asked still to stay from school for one more term and "keep me company" I was secretly flattered I expect as well as comforted. The milder southern air, and his daily rides over the downs, would do him good and he would take no harm from missing a few months of Greek and Algebra.

There was, that May and June, a French family—or rather, a father with his young son and daughter—spending part of the summer in the neighbourhood, and that Denis should like them and they him I found altogether fortunate. Cécile, my wife, had been half French, and when it transpired that our new acquaintances were not only residents of her native province but must actually (as we compared notes and worked it out together) be some sort of distant cousins, this chance encountering seemed more than ordinarily felicitous. Cécile had never tired of talking to Denis of Auvergne—its history, scenery, and above all its legends, some of them she admitted rather shocking—and we had frequently regretted that, as yet, he had not seen it for himself. He could however, read and speak French very tolerably— putting me to a total shame—and now, in a variety of loyalty, I fancy, to his mother's memory, was doubly prejudiced in favour of anything or anyone of Gallic origin.

As for these Vaignons, the father, who cultivated us with considerable assiduity, was, I believed, a landowner of consequence, with a château not far from Issoire. He was a lean, somewhat nervous yet taciturn man, with sunken cheeks and an unhappy brooding manner which I set down to his recent bereavement.

17

The fact that he, too, had lost his wife last year was an added, if unspoken, reason for sympathy amongst us, and I was wholly glad that Denis had the orphaned Augustine and Marcel for his playmates. Truth compels me to confess that they weren't very prepossessing little scamps—being undernourished-looking, swarthy, narrow-eyed and quarrelsome!—but for Denis their society evidently had charm.

"This shall be *au revoir* and not good-bye, M. le Colonel," said M. Vaignon upon leaving. "For Denis, at the least. Denis shall come to see me in Auvergne, if you can spare him, in his holidays, while, to be quits, my own Marcel and Augustine might visit you."

Here was a new idea! But, when I questioned him, Denis, it seemed, knew all about it.

"And would you care to go?" I asked, surprised.

"Oh, yes ... I may, mayn't I?"

"We'll see. ... Yes, I daresay," I temporized. "Wait and we'll see."

The notion had been rather sprung upon me, yet such holiday exchanges were constantly advertised in the Press, and in the present instance there was an already-existing acquaintance between the families, to say nothing of a degree, if slender, of relationship. As for "holidays"—Denis had had plenty of *them*, lately, but he *would* be off to school again, nearer home, before so long. He had been falling behind, inevitably, in his studies, and now, I thought, he had a golden opportunity of picking up his French.

Next August I went over with him to Foant, saw him installed in M. Vaignon's château, where I stopped one night, and returned placidly enough to Hampshire with Marcel and Augustine the following day.

This arrangement remained in force for well over a year till Denis was thirteen, being renewed, after he had re-started his schooling, through several successive holidays, or parts of them. My boy's persistence and perseverance with the business, I must say, somewhat astonished me. What kind of fun could he have there, I wondered, that so attracted him? Marcel and Augustine, when they came to me as they usually did, could largely amuse each other, but Denis had no one of his own age to play with. Cécile had had a young nephew, Willi, her brother's child, but he had died two years ago, or else, I thought regretfully, my Denis might have looked *him* up and found him, possibly, congenial company. Now, even Willi's parents, who had lived within easy drive of the château, had moved to Dijon, and Denis was reduced, as I have said, to M. Vaignon for the supply of entertainment. I was perplexed and, maybe, a shade jealous.

Thus far, I had had but that one glimpse of the château, since it was either M. Vaignon or his major domo Flébard who, on the

18

next few occasions, took the children to and fro; and now, still wondering, I tried to recall the place more clearly.

The château was old, and generally in somewhat poor repair, though its interior was pleasing. Its exterior, and the immediate approaches, had been dusk-shrouded when we arrived, but before that I had had to hire a taxi, at an exorbitant fare, from the nearest station, a dozen miles away, and had had some chance of viewing the countryside between. It was austere, and grimly forbidding, with a burnt-out, cindery quality I found depressing. However, that didn't matter particularly, and our effusive welcome from M. Vaignon, coupled with repeated apologies for the breakdown of the car that should have met us, had reassured me, if I needed it. After Denis was in bed, my host and I had chatted till midnight, over some superlative brandy. There had been, from him, some laughing allusion to a "haunted" turret room, but the story attached to it seemed confused and I could not subsequently recollect it.

"Do you still want to go to Foant *every* holiday?" I had asked Denis once. "Why don't you give a trial to Uncle Michel and Aunt Bette instead? They'd love to have you there with them, at Dijon."

"Oh *no* . . . I like it so at Foant, yes I *do*. . . ." A quick anxiety in his tone surprised me.

Till then, I had acquiesced in the arrangement somewhat luke-warmly, though certainly without misgiving; and even now it would be exaggeration to say I was at all uneasy. Simply, I felt that, from such slight and casual beginnings, the thing had some-how become too important or endured too long.

"But surely, you must be terribly dull there sometimes. What do you do with yourself all day?"

"Oh . . . there's a lot to do. We——" He faltered, embarrassedly, and I experienced a faint, disquiet qualm. His delicacy had always caused his mother and myself concern, and at her death I had feared seriously the effect upon his health. But he had borne his share of grief for her manfully enough and, for a while, had seemed to benefit from exercise and a respite from lessons. At the moment, however, he was nervously flushed—maybe dreading my vetoing his further visits—and his eyes had an odd strained look, as if, the idea curiously struck me, he were carrying some sort of burden.

No more was said, at that time, on the subject, and the appearance, the next week, of escort Flébard—a decent, sober fellow who seemed propriety incarnate—temporarily allayed my doubts.

Yet after Denis was gone they naggingly revived. What *was* it, at the château, I could not stop wondering, that held this strong continuing attraction for my boy? Without, exactly, scenting any-thing amiss, I recognized that here was an affair or situation which I had been to blame in not exploring thoroughly, and which, at least, would bear more careful scrutiny.

I resolved that, on Denis's next trip, if there should be one, I would again accompany him, or perhaps bring him back, myself, and possibly, in either case, remain with him at Foant for a day of so before returning.

That visit I remember very well. I remember, at its close, concluding that no, there was really nothing after all to worry about, and then, as a wave of unaccountable depression overcame me, feeling as vaguely puzzled and undecided in my mind as ever.

M. Vaignon, pressing me to stop longer than the three days I did, had been almost too attentive a host, scarcely indeed permitting me out of his sight. With his own children (of whom, next year he would see less, one being entered for a lycée at Bourges, the other for a convent school in the same town) he seemed stricter than in Hampshire, and I reflected wryly that, while it lasted, this exchange-system certainly gave him the better of the bargain, for there could be no comparison between my handsome, graceful Denis and his two "replacements"—queer, cryptic little monkeys that they were.

For my sojourn at the château it had turned out more convenient to choose not the beginning but the end of a stay there, by Denis, of four weeks. The hours passed, not disagreeably and till my final night quite unremarkably, in talking, eating, card-playing, sheer loafing, and a short series of amiably conducted tours of the estate. Upon these rambles Denis would go with us, not ill-pleased to assist M. Vaignon in the part of showman, and yet, I thought, a trifle distrait and subdued, his bright head glinting on before us in the sun. It was extremely sultry, the middle of August, and the scorched country frowned quivering around us through a heat-haze. Towards Foant, the turmoiled landscape was a gross tumble of smirched rocks, like something caught in the act of an explosion or—a more fanciful comparison occurred to me—as if these riven slabs, seared spires and pinnacles and blackened ingots of fused earth had been the "men" which sportive devils had hurled down upon the gaming-table of the puys in some infernal tourney, and then left in disarray. I told myself I would be very thankful when my boy and I were home.

But what had chiefly struck me during my three days at the château was a peculiar faint change—for all his courtesy—in M. Vaignon. Once, when I referred casually to Denis's next visit, a strange hesitating and constrained look crossed his face.

"Yes," he replied, without conviction "Ah well, we all grow up, and the best of things come to an end. . . ."

That night—the eve of our return to England—I was restless. My feather-bed stifled me, and I remembered that a winding stair outside my room, adjoining Denis's, led to a small garden. To snatch a breath of fresher air I began, in my dressing-gown, to descend the stairway, but stopped short at the sound of voices.

It was M. Vaignon, talking, I rather guessed, to Flébard.

"No, no," the disturbed half-whisper reached me. "We can't ... I tell you, *hélas*, it has *come again*. ..."

Hastily but softly I retreated. M. Vaignon's last words had been spoken with a curious emphasis—of fear or of a kind of despairing disgust—and for an instant I regretted not having waited for a sentence or two more. Undecidedly I regained the landing, and saw a crack of light under Denis's door. I gently opened it, and entered.

"Hello," I said, "so you can't get to sleep either."

"No. ... It's so hot. ..."

He was sitting up in bed, a candle burning in a wall-sconce beside him. In some way he seemed apprehensive and excited.

"It's not as quiet as you'd suppose, out here in the country," I remarked, less from an interest in the fact than to conceal my own continuing agitation. "I thought just now I could hear those old cows moving in the barn,——or it may have been the horses in the stables. ..."

"—Or the ghost," said Denis, "in the tower room."

I smiled, as I presumed he expected me to smile. "Oh, does the ghost make noises?" I inquired, preoccupiedly, and with my mind still running upon M. Vaignon.

"Yes. ..." Denis paused, smiling, too, then added, oracularly: "Rinking noises. I—I make it make them."

" '*Rinking*' noises?" I came out of my brown study, startled, somehow, both by this odd description and by a peculiar intonation in his voice.

"Like roller-skating," he exclaimed. "Ever so funny. We——"

He had checked himself abruptly; though the smile lingered on his lips. It was a smile, I had the unpleasant intuition, that saw musingly beyond what *I* could see—a smile of some superior intimacy and acquaintance, real or fancied. But I considered it wiser not, at this time, to pursue the subject. "Good night," I said presently, and went back to my room.

After all this, I had reckoned gloomily on further wakefulness, yet, actually, fell very soon asleep, arousing with my spirits lightened and refreshed. If it were nothing worse, I remember thinking, than some absurd superstition that was afflicting M. Vaignon, then most of my anxiety was groundless. Merely, I was now tired of the business. Just one more visit, possibly, and then this holiday-exchange arrangement must begin to die a natural death.

However, as we were leaving, I had a mild resurgence of my previous qualms. M. Vaignon's looks were wan and the hand that shook mine trembled. Suddenly, a word to characterise his altered manner—the word I had been seeking, unsuccessfully three days—flashed disconcertingly into my brain. "Guilty." But how preposterous. . . ! What had he to feel *guilty* over? And yet,

... A shadow seemed to darken round me and round Denis too as we entered the car and waved our farewells through its windows.

But in the train and on the boat I managed temporarily to re-dismiss my bothersome forebodings. Perhaps M. Vaignon had privately decided that he had seen enough of us, had resolved gradually to drop us, and yet had found it hard frankly to tell us so. Well, *I* had felt for my part that the Vaignons latterly were bulking too oppressively and largely on our own Habgood horizon, and if the break did come eventually from their side rather than from mine, so much the better and the easier for me! I was in cheerful mood as we returned to "Ashtoft."

Two days had passed when the postman delivered to me a registered envelope, postmarked Foant. The enclosed letter from M. Vaignon read:

"DEAR COLONEL HABGOOD,

"It is with infinite distress that I am driven to inform you that it has become advisable for the hitherto so pleasant intimacy between our families to cease; nor can I, I am afraid, give any explanation of this deplorable necessity that could satisfy you. I am the victim, it appears, of a fantastic persecution or visita-tion with which it would not be fair that you should any longer be remotely and even unknowingly associated. This is the most that I am able to tell you in condonation of a gesture that must seem so brutal; but, in effect, I have to draw a *cordon sanitaire* around myself—not for my own protection but for that of those outside it! I can only hope, with my most extreme regrets that one whom I esteem so highly may accept this fact as it unfor-tunately stands, and grant me, henceforwards, the privliege of silence.

"Yours,
"V. DE LA F. VAIGNON."

I replaced this amazing missive in its envelope. A little while ago I had been meditating just such a development—but not in this style, no indeed! Was the man mad? Oddly, my predominant emotion was not of hurt, or any anger with him. It was, rather, of bewildered consternation, and even a sort of fear, as if, instead of ending, as it seemed, the real trouble were just beginning.

Somehow, the thing hit me in the face.

I did not immediately tell Denis of M. Vaignon's letter, and for over a week I was considerably exercised as to how I could best and most wisely do so. Finally, I let him know of it, saying that the Vaignons were going through some kind of private domestic crisis which would probably prevent his staying again at the château, for some while at least.

Admittedly, this was putting a mighty gloss on the affair, yet how else was I to phrase it? Probably, as I had surmised, M. Vaignon had been brooding this step for several months, and failed to muster courage to declare it verbally—but now its absurd written, black and white, announcement was, in all conscience, blunt to crudity (whatever its excuses, and whatever the dickens "persecution" and "visitation" might be held to mean!)—and I could hardly show Denis *that*.

He received the news quietly, though I felt it a false and deceptive quiet. It must have been a serious matter to him, and, as I see it now, he was inwardly and desperately trying to measure its gravity and to decide how far this set-back might be neutralized or remedied and still accommodated to his own desires. I was extremely sorry for him, and cast about in my mind for anything that would render the blow less wounding, and leave him a little happier.

Oddly and soon enough he himself sought to help me out of this difficulty, but in a fashion I by no means relished.

"I think it'll be Raoul I'll miss most," he said as if reflectively, yet with a certain patness that did not escape me. "I told you about him, didn't I?"

" 'Raoul'? No, you didn't."

"*Didn't* I? Not Raoul Privache? Surely I——"

"No, you never spoke of him. Who is he?"

"Why, he was my greatest friend over there, in a way. I *must* have told you. . . . We caught moles and bats together, and went up the puy. He's—well, he's a sort of odd-job man I suppose you'd call him. He gardens, and fells trees, and looks after horses, and— Oh, *I* know!" Denis paused, as though struck by a sudden inspiration. "He could come *here*. He could work for *you*. You need someone like that! Oh, if we had Raoul here I wouldn't mind not going again to the château. . . ."

"Nonsense!" I answered brusquely. "Now, *really*. . . . How many licences d'you think I'd have to get for importing an article like *that* from France?"

What made my tone momentarily bitter had not been the bizarre character of the suggestion so much as the recognition, in my own boy, of a species of duplicity. For he had never mentioned this Raoul previously, and must have known it.

While most emphatically I wanted no more Vaignon echoes, of any sort, size or description.

Denis's brows had contracted in a kind of secret defiance.

"Oh, well," he said glumly, "I expect we'll see him here anyhow. . . . I expect he'll turn up, one day, just the same."

And, the devil of it was, he did. We had finished breakfast, and I was lighting my pipe in the morning room when I heard a light tap at the window. Glancing up, I saw a man outside. He was short and rather shabby, but his face I could not then properly discern.

In an instant, heart-sinkingly, I realised who it must be. The fellow was gesturing, and I, in turn, found myself echoing his signals, and pointing sidewise towards the front door, which I opened for him.

He stood there, in the porch, and again, with vague nonplusment, I had the incidentally worried feeling that, somehow, I could not make out his features as plainly as I should. But at that moment there was a scamper of footsteps behind me, and Denis all but flung himself into the figure's arms. "Raoul! Raoul!" he exclaimed ecstatically. "Oh, I *knew* you'd come!"

"*Bonjour, m'sieu.*" Our visitant had put out a hand, which I mechanically shook. The hand wore a mitten leaving only the fingers exposed, and in clasping them I experienced a strange repugnance. They were cold, and lifeless as a dummy's.

But the man could speak, it soon appeared, and volubly. Denis had led him to a back room giving on to the lawn, and there the creature began to chatter, presumably in French of sorts, though too quickly for my comprehension. Denis translated sketchily. "Raoul," it seemed, was offering me his services as general handyman. He had always wanted to live in England, and to have my son for his young master would be bliss indeed. His manner, as he waited while Denis was interpreting, was an odd mixture of deference and sly assurance.

"But, good heavens!" I protested. "*I* can't employ him. What about his labour-permit? He can't just plant himself on us like this and——"

The man sat there, impassive, his shadowed face averted. Denis was talking with him again, conveying, I supposed, the substance of my objections.

"He's staying here, in the village anyhow," Denis announced, "though it would be nicer if he could use our loft over the old coach-house while he was looking around. . . ."

"He shall *not* use our loft. . . !" I remember almost spluttering in my dumbfounded indignation.

But, in the end, he did.

Whether a greater, and a prompter, firmness on my part would have prevented or, later on, ejected him I do not know. I believe now that it would not, and, in a sense, that what was had to be.

Since Cécile's death I had denied her child nothing, and if such "pampering" were weakness it had at least been, hitherto, a natural and perhaps pardonable weakness. But my acceptance, or toleration, of this creature, this object, this ambiguous knot-in-a-board, with whom Denis's infatuation seemed quite inexplicable, was a capitulation to my boy's half tearful and half sullen importunities surpassing any previous indulgence.

Be that as it might, "Raoul" took up his abode in the loft, and, thus confronted with the *fait accompli*, I realized gloomily that

24

it would mean, now, a lot of unpleasantness and fuss to shift him. So, for the time being, and the time being only (as I tried to make it plain), he stayed.

There were nearly three weeks still to run of Denis's summer holidays, and he spent their waking hours, to my chagrin, almost entirely in his idol's company. I felt bewildered. Why, actually, had the man come here, and had there been a prior secret understanding between him and his admirer in the matter? Was his passport in order (though I presume it must be, for him to have arrived at all), and what would the neighbours, and my own servants, think?

However, superficially and for a while, there was less trouble than I had anticipated. The fellow, to grant him his due, was unobtrusive to the point of self-effacement and indeed appeared anxious to keep out of people's way. He insisted on some pretence of working for me and occasionally was to be seen polishing boots and harness, clearing dead wood from the shrubbery, and the like. His meals he ate, usually, apart, fetching them from the kitchen, and consuming them in his loft. How he got on with my cook, Jenny, or with my maid Clara I was at first unable to find out. Probably they decided that the curious importation represented merely one more whim of the young master's and for the present let it go at that. As for my regular groom and gardener, Dobbs, he, as it happened, was in hospital, so his reactions were not yet available.

Just the same, the position was bizarre. Denis would shortly be returning to school, and then of course there could be no excuse for Raoul's remaining. I half thought, once or twice, and despite the "silence" so mysteriously enjoined on me, of writing to "sound" M. Vaignon on the subject, but, as may be imagined, I was pretty much on my dignity in that quarter, and had, besides, no right whatever to assume that *he* was implicated or involved in any way with Raoul.

I was on edge and out of sorts, living it seemed unreally in a kind of semi-dream. More and more I became sensible of this man Raoul's presence, irking me in a manner I could not describe. And one small item in particular still teased me. The fellow had been here, now, close on two weeks, and yet for some reason, I had never formed a clear idea of his appearance. Either his features struck me differently at different times or had a queer indefiniteness that amounted, as it were, to nullity. It was not till later that I discovered that this little difficulty of his facelessness had bothered other people too.

One day, less than a week before the end of his holidays, Denis had started a slight cold. It seemed nothing much—and hadn't stopped his going out all morning, as was now his rule, with his obnoxious playmate on the down—but was enough, in view of the nearness of his return to school, to worry me. I remembered telling him to take it easy indoors for the rest of the afternoon and then retiring myself, to my study with the intention, I also recall, of settling, finally, my future course of action in this whole exasperating "*affaire Raoul*."

But my deliberations had not got very far when they were interrupted by a visit from a Mr. Walstron, a local farmer to whom I was arranging to lease a meadow. Terms having been agreed to mutual satisfaction, the old man went on to gossip amiably of other things.

"Your boy misses his mother, sure-*ly*. Up there on the Winacre I met him this morning, looking right poorly, and chattering away like that, all to himself. . . ."

"To himself? Why he——" I faltered, confused and apprehensive.

"Well, yes. . . . Talking, or it might have been singing, you know, and—funny thing—my two dogs, they—oh, you should 'a seen 'em. Such a snarling and a snapping. . . I Never seen 'em act that way with *your* young lad before. . . ."

Presently Mr. Walstron wished me good day, leaving me, certainly, with plenty to think over.

It was extremely strange. Denis, I knew, had gone out, not alone but with Raoul. And then—those dogs. . . . For, oddly, it had been with dogs that Raoul had achieved, as yet, his summit of unpopularity. My own setter, Trixie, could not abide him, shivering and growling quite dementedly whenever he was by, and evidently undecided whether to fly from or at him.

I was still trying to digest the implications of Mr. Walstron's story when the form of Raoul himself darkened the panes. Outwardly and otherwise well conducted, he had an annoying habit of coming round to the windows and tapping to attract attention. This time, perceiving I had ready observed him, he did not tap but simply held up a hand. To my disgusted consternation I saw that the wrist and forearm were bloody.

Hurrying out, I examined his hurt. The flesh was badly lacerated. "*Chiens*," I understood him to mutter. "*Chiens*. . . ."

Here was a further complication! Dog bites can be mischievous and I would not risk attempting to treat such wounds myself. So far, I had shirked bringing the man's residence to any official or even semi-official cognizance, but now, if the doctor were called, my precious piece of contraband must be declared and I foresaw all sorts of tiresome queries as to the fellow's position under the Health Insurance Act and any amount of stupid fuss . . . .

In the event, I summoned my old friend and adviser, Goderich, who had attended Cécile during her last illness. He dressed Raoul's arm and, while on the spot, looked at my boy as well. Denis's cold had got worse. He was running a temperature, and Goderich promised to come again next day.

Reports, then, on the two patients were discouraging. As for Raoul, he had had to be moved to a small attic bedroom. His wound was an ugly one, and I somehow gathered an impression that Goderich was puzzled by the case.

Denis, it seemed probable, would not be fit to return punctually to school and for a time I half suspected him of shamming in order to postpone the parting with his friend. He, Denis, had been told of Raoul's misadventure and pleaded, vainly, to be allowed to see him. The pair were upon different floors, and in different wings, the farther from each other, I had thought, the better.

Raoul's accident (and he could or would not state which dog or dogs it was that had attacked him) had been upon a Thursday, and by the Sunday his arm still showed no improvement. The following morning, Goderich rather surprised me by asking me to "see for myself," and I watched him unwrap the bandages. I caught, I fancied, an expression of something approaching astonishment on his face when the torn flesh was bared. The entire limb below the elbow was swollen and had a repulsive livid hue. Goderich motioned me to go. "I'll see you afterwards," he murmured.

"Well," he said, rejoining me downstairs, "I'll confess I'm a bit foxed. The latest wonder-drug's proved a flop and—it's—it's quite extraordinary, but the whole fore-arm seems——"

"Yes, what?" I pressed impatiently.

"Why, to have mortified. But it—it *couldn't* have, to that extent, without other associated symptoms, gross symptoms, which just aren't there. Yet—well—pah. . . ! Well, the damn thing almost stinks. . . !"

I stared at him, and he went on. "I'm speaking unprofessionally, Habgood, and not merely being nosey. Precisely how you came by this odd customer I'm not inquiring, but——"

Our talk was interrupted by a scurrying commotion in the passage. The door burst open and Clara entered with scarcely a preliminary knock "Oh . . . excuse me, sir, but—Master Denis——"

Behind her, at that instant, Denis himself appeared, tearfully distraught.

"What is it?" I said, pushing Clara aside and catching him up in my arms. "What's happened?"

But for a while, after I had carried him back to bed, he refused to tell us. It was only, at first, from Clara that we discovered that Raoul must have stealthily crept from his room, traversed the intervening corridors, and visited the boy. Clara had heard a cry from within the bedroom and seen Raoul emerging just as she arrived upon the scene.

Furious, I was starting off there and then for Raoul's attic, but Goderich restrained me. "Let me," he said. "I'll go."

27

He was away a long time, and when he returned his words further amazed me.

"Well . . . I give up. I'm not a doctor. Doctors don't see such things. . . . Call me a bald-headed Belgian and be done with it . . . . I give it up!"

"What do you mean?"

"Why, when I got there, the fellow was smiling—by the way, has he a face to smile with? I'm never sure .. . was sort of smiling and holding out his arm and saying '*guéri, guéri*,' like a cheshire cat . . . if they do . . . I—I'm a bit overcome. . . ."

"You mean——?"

"I mean that it *was* cured, *is* cured. A little swelling, and he's a normal slight fever. Here, gimme a tot of your Glenlivet. . . . I tell you, I give up."

This episode, itself grotesque, marked the beginning of a fresh, more ominous phase in my relationship with Raoul, and brought into my mind's open a host of doubts and until then but dimly realized fears. Just as the startled eye may all at once perceive the latent shapes of horror in the far, nobly drifting clouds and summer leaves, or as the meek familiar pattern of a wallpaper may spring into a sudden tracery of hell, so now the course of these events revealed a darker trend. The unaccountable affair of Raoul's arm had left me quite uncertain what to believe or disbelieve or what might happen next.

Circumstances had forced me to admit Goderich to my confidence, yet for a while we each fought shy of a direct discussion. What had occurred was so fantastically out of line with ordinary experience that we had, I suppose, to try somehow to deny and to discredit it a little even to ourselves.

Raoul made a complete recovery, and my determination to evict him was renewed. Denis however remained by no means well and I still shrank from distressing him. As if guessing what I meditated he had grown louder than usual in his companion's praises.

"You don't like him," he accused, reproachfully yet with a suppressed tight smile that had about it—how shall I express it? —a sort of odd repugnant coyness.

"I—well, I just don't see anything much *in* him. . . . He can't stay here forever."

"Why, what harm does he do? I *wish* you liked him. . . ."

I did not answer and we turned presently to other topics, but I continued baffled and, in some deeper sense, dismayed. It might be, as Denis said, that Raoul appeared to do no active harm, but it was this very negativity that partly was the trouble and made his evident attraction for my boy so utterly incomprehensible. The fellow, in his coarse labourer's clothes and ridiculous mittens, was an incongruity and an excrescence on the English countryside— and yet his most outstanding characteristic, to be paradoxical, was his characterlessness. He seemed as sinisterly unresponsive and empty of emotion as a robot.

The date when Denis should have returned to school was passed. He had got better, then had a relapse, developing a variety of low undulant fever. An X-ray of his chest reassured me as to the state of his lungs, but the symptoms did not abate.

I was disappointed also in finding it, now, the harder to give Raoul his *congé*, and I could not but connect the two things in my mind. Raoul, I was certain, was somehow the cause of Denis's poor appetite, his wan and wasted look, and alternating fits of nervous stimulation and depression. Denis slept in a room close to mine, and once or twice I fancied I heard noises of bumping and what I could then only describe as a kind of dull sustained metallic humming coming from it. A dark suspicion visited me. Could Raoul be there? But on softly opening the door I found Denis alone and apparently asleep. The noises, if there had been any, had entirely ceased.

However, and recalling the anomaly—or prodigy—of the instantaneously healed arm. I remained still convinced that Raoul must be, ultimately, their author.

This instinct or persuasion—that Raoul was the source of some pernicious influence destructive of my boy—gained steady strength. Denis's manner to me had changed, and his constant terror that I should part him from his strange playmate was obvious. While, more specifically, the noises I had heard *were* noises, I would swear it. They increased towards midnight but for a time, whenever I approached, died down.

Goderich, up to a point, did what he could, but was, I felt, as well aware as I that tonics and cough mixtures did not touch the matter's root. At last, after I had told him of the odd sounds, he remarked, mildly: "If I were you, Habgood, I *would* consider getting rid of that chap 'Raoul,' you know . . . I really would."

The restraint of this recommendation was almost comical, but I did not smile.

"Do you know anything *about* him? I was just wondering if, by any chance, he had ever had anything to do with your wife's family—worked for them once maybe, and used that as an introduction to you? I'm only guessing. . . ."

"Oh, no," I replied confidently enough. "Denis chummed up with the beauty in the Vaignon's village in Auvergne, that's all."

"These noises—is there ever anything broken or disarranged as well, after you hear them?"

"No, I've—wait a bit though. . . ." Yes, I remembered, I *had* found a vase smashed once, and more than once had noticed drawers pulled out, and a general air of untidiness or confusion. I told Goderich so.

"Well, pass the word if that sort of thing hots up. And, seriously,

I *should* give that chap the boot. It'll upset the lad, but—I should risk it."

When Goderich had gone I pondered his indubitably sound advice lugubriously. I could readily guess what had been at the back of his mind in asking, as to the noises, whether anything had been broken or moved about, yet the notion of poltergeist activities, while certainly sufficiently unpleasant, did not appear, entirely, to fit the case. They might, for all I knew, be present but, even so, would fall short of providing a complete explanation.

For, possibly, the hundredth time I vowed that Raoul *must* go; and indeed, quite apart from my own resolutions, matters were coming to a head. The commotions in Denis's room increased, being heard now by the servants, and were at last admitted by Denis himself. He denied all responsibility for them—in which I fully believed him—but did not seem afraid of, or disturbed by, them.

"But don't they wake you up and spoil your rest?"

"Oh . . . sometimes. But I don't care. I go to sleep again."

He looked restive under my interrogation. Nowadays, he was dressed and intermittently able to stroll out of doors if it were sunny, but spent much of his time in a *chaise-longue*, either in his room or, latterly, with Raoul, on a glass-roofed veranda. The pair would sit there, conversing softly, the man whittling sticks which he would fashion into a variety of uncouth doll, and my boy watching him, fascinatedly, as if the world's fate hung upon these operations.

Denis glanced up at me appealingly. "Promise me something."

"What?" But I guessed what it would be.

"That—that you won't send Raoul away."

"Well, as I've said already, he can't stay forever. Why do you think I shouldn't send him away?"

Denis's eyes, wide in some secret conjuring of disaster, met mine squarely. "It would kill me," he said simply.

As well as I might, although, I felt, evasively and with some sacrifice of honesty, I pacified him, and then left him. What *could* I do? Denis, of course, had been exaggerating and distraught, but such words, from a child. . . !

Of late, he had grown appreciably thinner, and I had only to contrast these waxen cheeks and pallid lips with his comparatively vigorous appearance a short month ago to realize the alarming swiftness of the change. To say I could not *prove* this due to Raoul was idle. It was from Raoul's arrival that the symptoms dated, and it was from him, I was certain, that they sprang. This lay-figure—this *fantôche*, this hollow puppet—was the unhallowed instrument of a vile infestation that had assaulted Denis's whole physical and moral organism. . . . Watching the two together (as I was often able from a window overlooking the veranda) I would be driven into a kind of agony of speculation as to the nature of the bond between them. My boy's face, raptly brooding or wearing that charmed smile I loathed even more, was usually averted, but I caught on it, sometimes, an enthralled abandon or absorption that would chill my blood. The creature Raoul, meanwhile, in his adorer's presence, would seem re-animated, made less neuter and less negative, as if his very being was enhanced and—how to put it?—as if it were at Denis's expense, by Denis's depletion of vitality, that he existed or that his actuality was heightened, as if, as the one waxed, the other shrank and waned. . . . Scarcely troubling to hide my agitation as such ideas possessed me, I had tried, once or twice, to break in upon the pair in these ambiguous intimacies, but, I soon recognized, to no avail. The two would fall momentarily silent, Denis looking half guilty and half angry; then, as I knew, the instant that my back was turned their curious *tête-à-tête* would recommence.

Nevertheless, despite its accumulating worry and distraction, my life had still preserved a surface ordinariness and normality. Friends would occasionally drop in on me, or I on them, as heretofore, and I do not think, now, that they noticed much amiss. To be sure, they commented upon Denis's exhausted, drooping air and sympathised with my anxiety about him, but they can have seen little of Raoul, and probably the "gossip" I had tended to imagine rife was confined chiefly to my own household.

There, certainly, there must have been some. Clara and old Jenny, even while not appreciating its significance, could not be blind (and deaf) to a good deal of what was happening under their noses, and their refusal to spread tales or "fuss" was testimony to their loyalty and long-suffering discretion.

As for Raoul's outward or official status, this had been regularized with less ado than I expected. A week or so after his arrival, on the insistence as I learned surprisedly of Denis, he had gone into Winchester and, Denis acting as interpreter, registered at the police station as an alien.

"What did he put himself down as?" I had asked disturbedly. "Not as my employee, I hope." And "Oh, no," Denis reassured me. "Just as a visitor. Just as your guest." That sounded well enough and I had grudgingly had to give Denis credit for his enterprise, but to confirm it I went in myself next day to Winchester. Yes, everything, I was told, was quite in order; oh yes, perfectly. . . . I would have been interested to see the passport which must have been produced by Raoul, but had not pressed the matter.

I was recalling this piece of compliance with legalities—comfortingly factual and satisfactory-seeming so far as it went—to Goderich.

" 'M . . ." he mused dubiously. "The blighter's an infernal incubus whatever else he is or ain't, and I wish you could just show him the door. As I've confessed, I'm a finger or so out of my depth. . . . The case is fairer game I fancy for a psychical researching bloke, or a psychiatrist. You're prejudiced, I realize, against *them*, and I'm not insisting, but—I'm worried about *you*, as well as Denis. I'll have two patients here, instead of one, directly. . . ."

It was true that the business was wrecking me. Each day, I felt that I could stand no more and that, to end it, I should be driven to some act of violence.

When I, eventually, *was* so driven it appeared, for a short time, almost a relief.

The situation had continued to deteriorate. Denis, after a session with his dear, would wear an aspect veritably of the grave, and the idea which had been shaping in my mind before besieged me now with an increasing force. He is losing something, giving something, I thought, but he would not *want* to do that, do it deliberately, more or less voluntarily, for nothing. He must get something, be tempted by something, in return—but what—ah, what?

I lived in a waking nightmare, and the idea's hold on me grew stronger. That Denis's delicately nurtured boyhood should fall prey to the appetites of an amorphous doll and become the meat of this uncanny zany seemed of all things the most abominable. The details and precise technique of such infernal commerce were beyond my fathoming, but that the ghastly trade existed and that Denis was its dedicated victim I felt positive. *Who* was this "Raoul"? When he had first arrived I had attempted, if simply in grudging "common courtesy," to engage him in conversation, but his thick Auvergnat dialect (as I presumed it) had defeated me, and nowadays I did not try to talk with him. As I watched him through the window, whittling his sticks and looking rather like a well-fed scarecrow, a speechless rage possessed me. Was the man knave or loon? For hours on end, complacently yet dully and only his hands moving, he would squat there, with the bland corpulence and mindless sedentary persistence of some gigantic blow-fly and my own hands would writhe in fury. "If I could catch him at it," I thought chokingly, "—if I could catch him at it I would strangle him. . . ."

"*If* I could catch him. . . ." Yes . . . I had, emotionally, a very vague and general notion or suspicion of what might be going on, but that was all. While, as for "evidence". . . . If this dumb, gangrened oaf were a variety of psychic leech as I surmised, able to tap and suck away my boy's vitality, his health and spiritual stamina, how was it done? It was probably, I realized, a vain or at least not ordinarily answerable question, yet the business, I argued, must have some sort of "rationale," some sort of place and time. During a good part of the day the pair were under—or liable, if I chose, to come under—my observation, and I hardly believed that Denis received his consort in his bedroom, or vice versa. Latterly, Raoul had returned to his old sleeping-quarters in the loft, and in any case I had taken, I considered, adequate precautions against a nocturnal meeting. It was, however, then—between dusk and midnight—that the "noises" and other disturbances were most troublesome; and this too, I reflected, fitted in with my "theory" to some extent. Poltergeists, I had heard, were regarded as the prankish play of a surplus vital force or energy; and it was just after this force's flow, from Denis, had been stimulated but yet deprived, temporarily, of its accustomed receptacle in Raoul that the impish manifestations, centring round my boy, were commonest. As to the poltergeists themselves, if poltergeists they were, I was not primarily concerned about or bothered by them, and it was commentary enough upon the situation, as I saw it, that such a matter should be reckoned a mere minor and subsidiary nuisance.

Could it be only—how long?—barely five weeks today, since "Raoul" appeared. . . ?

At this time, my nights were as a rule dark stretches of tormented wakefulness, and when—not, often, till towards early morning—I did fall asleep, my rest would usually be broken, and haunted by appalling dreams.

One of these I especially remember.

I was in France, and Cécile was still with me. She had been recounting, it seemed, a legend of her native province and, with an unexplained urgency, was directing my attention to a particular passage in a book. We were both standing by a wide window, and the diabolically piled Silurian landscape of Auvergne stretched from us, for many leagues, under a breathless summer heat. But the odd thing was that Cécile was holding the book up in front of her face, and expecting me to read it *through* its covers and all the intervening pages! This, in some miraculous manner, I was able, in my dream, to do, though with difficulty and a sense of growing apprehension and oppression. Of one sentence, which she was extraordinarily anxious I should read, I could make out four words only: ". . . shall feast upon thee . . ." I was on the point, I thought, of deciphering the rest when suddenly the book slipped from my wife's hands, revealing, not her face, but—empty air. With a cry of terror, I awoke.

The dream *was* only a dream, and probably, just before I fell asleep, my mind had again been running on Goderich's query, once, as to a possible connection between Raoul and Cécile's family; yet its tense, loaded flavour clung to me, and had the quality, somehow, of a presentiment.

I felt I had no need to ask of what. For a good while now I had been scarcely capable of keeping up the pretence of normal living, and a crisis would not be long delayed. "If I could catch him at it," I found myself always repeating, "If I could catch him. . . ."

And then, one day, I did.

It was an afternoon in October and Denis had been sitting, with his inseparable companion, on the sun-porch. Occasionally, he would desist from his talking and take up a book. It was a child's book from the shelves of his old nursery, and I was mildly surprised that he should still be interested in what I thought he had outgrown.

The veranda, as I have said, was glass-topped, and there was a glass-paned wind-break at one end too. Branches of a wistaria tree at the side had been persuaded to straggle irregularly over part of the roof, and there were pots of hydrangeas along the front. The blooms, now, were past their best, but the place retained a faded greenness and a, to me, pleasantly shabby, half-neglected air which I should have been sorry to see give way to greater trimness.

A window, as I have also said, commanded a restricted view of this semi-enclosed space, and it was through this window (the high french window of a small spare parlour) that I had often, with an uneasiness that had mounted, as the weeks dragged by, to anguish, watched my boy and his companion. Yet what was the good of that, I asked myself? They must realize, by this, my bursting suspicions and antagonism, and, to them, my harrowed glances would be merely "spying." Denis was alienated from me—from his own father—and there was nothing I could do.

On this afternoon I quickly abandoned such entirely fruitless surveillance. I must find something to occupy my thoughts and hands or else go mad, and I had remembered a broken fence by the apple orchard that needed mending. But, having collected hammer and nails, I had scarcely started on my job before a fearful premonition of disaster gathered in my brain. I was aware, as if by a direct insight, of something enormously, incredibly evil. I must go back. . . . This recognition of sheer calamity was so overpowering that I instantly dropped my tools and actually started running towards the house.

However, an instinct of discretion slowed my steps and I approached more cautiously. I could not, where I was, be seen from the veranda but, to make doubly sure, I took a devious route around a hedge of macracarpa. Mingled with my apprehension was a swelling rage. How could I have been so blind, I remember thinking, to what was going on under my nose? For that was what it had amounted to. Why had I fancied that this infernal traffic necessarily required a set "rendezvous," or any physical propinquity? "I will strangle him," I heard myself saying. "He deserves it and I shall do it." It was as if my fingers were upon the creature's neck, as if time were foreshortened or in some fashion telescoped, as if what was to happen had already happened and I was already there. . . .

The October day was waning as, very quietly, I re-entered the parlour, tip-toed across the room, and looked.

34

Raoul, from where I stood, was invisible, but I could see Denis plainly, still sitting, as I had left him, in a battered old wicker chair, reading his book. Or rather, he was not so much "sitting" as crouching, hunched forward in an odd stiff posture on the edge of the chair-seat. A last shift of reddening light drew frail fire from his blonde hair, but his face was hidden by the book.

An intimation of horror and of an unnameable corruption filled my heart. Something in Denis's queer locked attitude, in his whole appearance, utterly dismayed and sickened me.

Hardly breathing, I stole nearer. My movement was very soft, but Denis must have caught or have divined it, for he started violently. The book slipped from his hands.

Upon his suddenly revealed face was an expression I will not describe. It was open before me, like a dreadful flower. Evil, we know, exacts its dues of ruin from the tenderest transgressors, but the reverse side of the matter is less willingly admitted and more shocking; and now the swift unveiling for me of sin's fleeting wage to my unhappy boy was beyond words appalling.

I would, if I could, have shut my eyes on what I had surprised. Denis's features, fixed in their long enchantment, wore a look that was a travesty of boyhood and a blasphemy of all my memories of him. The face, in its ecstasy, was laced and hemmed, and old, with an oldness that had nothing to do with years. Watching him, while the running sands of his being received their frightful recompense, I too was a prisoner to an unreal eternity, though in my case of anguish.

Then, instantaneously, the spell was broken, as Denis gave a low despairing cry. I flung apart the french windows and dashed on to the veranda.

Where was Raoul? Denis, I must subconsciously have told myself, would recover presently from his half-swoon and my first business was with his despoiler. Had the thing vanished? Not altogether. Below the veranda, in the direction of the shrubbery, I indistinctly glimpsed it, already in lumbering flight.

I caught it up beside the hedge of macracarpa, making for the coach-house. The figure, shadowy in the fading light, had turned at my approach and in an odd ineffective way put up a fumbling arm to keep me off.

My hands closed round its throat and for a while we struggled, swaying. Some seconds passed, and as yet the loathsome ninny had remained quite silent, but, all at once, I heard a little noise. It is said that certain creatures, ordinarily voiceless, may in extremity, find feeble tongue—that, in the agony of boiling, wretched lobsters compass a last faint unexampled squeak—and it was, now, of such a puny cry that I was put in mind. The sound filled me with revulsion.

My fingers pressed more strongly, Raoul, as we grappled, was being forced slowly backwards towards a tree-trunk, against which it was my idea to pin him and. . . .

Either he had managed to trip me, or I had slipped and stumbled. The two of us crashed heavily, I uppermost. For some seconds longer I was still aware of him beneath me, writhing and battling, yet, somehow, eluding me; but the next moment, he had gone.

Dazedly, I picked myself up and gazed round me in search of the thing that had melted into vacancy from my grasp; and there was no sign of it, anywhere at all.

II

They were black days that followed—I cannot convey *how* black. Though, with the exit of Denis's sinister playfellow, the worst seemed over, I felt in my heart, chilly, that this was only an uneasy breathing-space and that the story, yet, was far from done.

"Breathing-space"—no, it was not really even that. Raoul, I hoped, was banished, but his work remained. Denis was ill. Staring at me with horror and aversion, as if *I* were the sole author of his misery, he could scarcely bear that I should speak to him or go near his bed. The loss, I recognized with anguish, of his frightful parasite and paramour had virtually prostrated him, and he had ceased to be the boy Cécile and I had loved.

As to the eerie lummox who had plagued us, I concluded that he had succeeded, somehow, in wriggling free from me and fleeing, that he would probably make his way back to France, and that, at least in person (if he *were* a person) he would trouble us no more. Or rather, this was what I tried to tell myself I had concluded. Truth is not necessarily or always "sober," and there was something here, I realized inwardly, of which all ordinary "sane" explanations and conjectures failed to take account.

Denis, when I had re-entered the house after Raoul's flight, had been in a half-faint. The servants, roused by my running footsteps along the veranda, had found him lying by the chair, and carried him to his room. Reviving, he had set up a low continuous moaning which did not abate till Goderich, whom I had at once rung up, had given him a sedative. That had secured him a night's sleep; but next day, as I have said, he would hardly suffer my approach, and once had even barricaded his door against me. I was at my wit's end, and terrified less he should do himself an injury.

Goderich shared my anxiety.

"Have you discovered any more about this unholy creature, now he's gone?" he asked.

" 'Any more?' Why, how——"

"I mean that, now he *has* gone, tongues might wag a bit more freely. Your servants', for instance. . . ."

"Oh yes," I agreed. "Yes . . . plenty of that!"

It was a fact that Jenny and Clara had unbosomed themselves to me of a good deal as to Raoul and their sentiments towards him which they had hitherto repressed—though without adding materially to my actual information. I told Goderich so.

"How did you explain the fellow's sudden disappearance to them?"

"I didn't. In any detail. They must have guessed that I—well, chased him off. I don't think they cared how he went, as long *as* he went."

" 'M . . . well, honestly, I feel I can't do much. I wish you *would* try a psychiatrist. . . ."

But I was not ready for that, yet. And was there, possibly, an ever so slightly hurt or reproachful tone in my friend's voice? If so, it must have been because he could divine that with him too, in my description of the final scene, I had been reticent of what I had called "details". . .

Denis recovered to the extent of leaving his bed and room and occasionally loitering, alone, about the orchard and the meadow; but we were strangers to each other. My acquaintance, or partial acquaintance, with his dreadful secret made me a terror to him, and there seemed something pathetically horrible in the evident efforts of this child to wrest the situation to his own partisan, extenuating view of it—to digest, modify or soften it so as to render it more tolerable to him, and to see me, not Raoul, as his enemy.

It could not, I would think, go on like this. How, if I lived to be a hundred, could I forget—or *he* forget that I must still remember? I would remind him always. As he grew up, if not already, in a shame so poignantly embarrassed, he would wish my death. . . .

Thus, for a week or so, matters continued. My uncertainty as to what had really happened to Raoul prevented my finding much consolation even in his absence, and soon after his disappearance I had a visit from the Winchester City police. "Privache," they said (at first I barely recalled the fellow's surname) had failed to report at the expiration of one month's residence—and was he still with me still? I could only reply, with a modicum of truth, that he had run off suddenly, I had no notion where. "Run off?" "Yes." I explained that the defaulter was a friend of my boy's of whom I had practically no knowledge; and I could see that my worthy—and, to me, very respectful—constable was dissatisfied and puzzled. "He should 'a checked out properly," he grumbled. "If 'e went back to France, now, there'd be trouble and an 'itch, you see, o' some kind, at the port."

Meanwhile the improvement in Denis's condition had been, at least superficially, maintained. That was, he looked a shade less pale and had a better appetite. The nightly thumpings, hummings and (a new ingredient) derisive hootings had, however, increased, the racket finally attaining such proportions that, out of consideration for my domestics' rest, I had his bedroom changed to one as far from theirs as possible.

To me, his manner remained stubbornly hostile. I had pleadingly attempted to get him to speak openly, frankly and give me his own version of affairs, but quite in vain. It seemed but too apparent that he had suffered a veritable bereavement and was still pining for his vanished mate. Reluctantly, I was beginning to resign myself to taking Goderich's advice and trying a psychiatrist. This course would pretty evidently expose me, as well as the patient proper, to a good deal of awkwardness and incredulous silly catechisings, but I must shirk no measure that might restore my boy.

The leaves were falling and the October days growing colder when I happened to receive a note reminding me of the approaching anniversary dinner of my old regiment. I had never missed attending it, and the formal invitation card was enclosed, but now I had no heart to go, and besides it would be out of the question. On the other hand, it was from Winchester, barely six miles away, that Mayfield, who had been my adjutant and was organising the affair this year, had written me. He chanced, he told me, to be spending the inside of a week there on business—and he was probably expecting, I surmised, that I should ask him to stay with me instead of at his hotel, at any rate for Saturday and Sunday.

This too, as matters were, was scarcely practicable, but the least I could do, I thought, was to run over to Winchester and see him. I decided to risk leaving Denis in Jenny's and Clara's care, and drove off after lunch.

My chat with Mayfield, to whom I explained the position so far as necessary, was as pleasant as anything could be in my state of worry about Denis, but I hurried home from it so as to arrive by tea-time.

Clara and Jenny, to my dismay, were both waiting for me at the porch, and their first words, as I jumped out of the car, told me the worst.

Denis had gone.

Self-reproach was as useless as unavoidable. I had to act.

"When did you miss him?" I asked.

It had been only twenty minutes ago. He had been on the veranda, and then, no longer seeing him there and wishing to reassure themselves, they had looked for him. His room was empty, and fairly tidy, but a small suit-case was undiscoverable, likewise some socks and a shirt. The most conclusive piece of evidence, however, which seemed to rule out hope that he had merely set off for a walk and might return, was the fact that Jenny's room also had been entered, and her money stolen.

"How much?"

"Four pounds ten, sir. I—I had it in a little china box and was going to bank it Tuesday."

Expecting me at any moment, they had not as yet given an alarm to the police, and I decided, rather than telephone, to drive back again myself to Winchester. Meanwhile, Jenny could ring me at the police station if my poor truant did, after all, return.

The desk sergeant knew me well and listened attentively to my story. "It's early yet," he encouraged, "and he *may* be just—just larking. But of course we'll notify it and alert other stations round about. Five-fifteen now. . . . He can't be very far."

"And watch the ports too," I reminded him. My first thought, naturally, had been of Raoul, and my first fear that Denis was rejoining him.

"Oh, yes, we'll do that, as routine—although he couldn't get across, you know, without a passport."

As to that I had, privately, my doubts. Given sufficient determination, there *were* ways of doing it, as a recent instance happened to have shown.

After a further consultation—this time with the local superintendent in his adjoining sanctum—I drove home.

"No news, I suppose, Jenny?"

"No, sir."

With what fortitude we could we resigned ourselves, as remorseful empty hours passed, to the wretched, and in my case almost sleepless, night.

Feeling that the emergency had more than justified my breaking any rule of silence, I sent a wire of inquiry to M. Vaignon. An answer arrived, fairly promptly: "Not here yet."

This left me more "up in the air" than ever, and in vain did I strive to supply, as it were, the real and un-telegraphable intonation of the word "yet." It sounded as if M. Vaignon rather expected that Denis *might* come, later—but I could not be sure.

I returned to the question of the passport. Denis *had* had a passport—an individual one, to allow of his escort sometimes by Flébard and sometimes by myself. But I had locked it up after his last trip, and had it locked up still. In any case, I thought, he must have realized that, before he could possibly reach the coast, the dock police would have been warned, so that the document would be useless to him.

The Winchester district, I was told, had been combed thoroughly without result and, as time passed, it surprised me that a boy could elude the police net for so long. It argued, certainly, either a degree of ineptitude on the one side or considerable adroitness and resource upon the other. Perhaps, whatever official incredulity might say, Denis had succeeded, by walking only at night and spending each day up a tree (in a manner I had read of) in striking

39

a place where French fishing-boats put in, and then bribed some sailor into smuggling him across. . . .

This notion was if anything strengthened by a discovery made by Clara when the hunt was six days old. She ran excitedly to me in my study one morning, crying: "Oh, we've—we've found something!"

It transpired that, in cleaning out the loft, she had come upon two loaves, two tins of sardines and a can-opener, a jar of marmalade *and* the suit-case, which was empty—a veritable *cache!*

These objects, which I went with her to inspect, had been hidden under sacking near a back door giving on to a short outer stair by which access could be gained to the loft without first passing through the coach-house below. Close by, I noticed with aversion, was a collection of the grotesque wooden dolls, something like ninepins, which Raoul had been used to whittle and—most significantly—an empty opened tin and scattered crumbs showed that one meal at least had been consumed up there already.

However illogically, this find, and particularly the abandoned suit-case, established as an emotional certainty in my mind the belief that Denis had managed to reach France, or was upon his way there. He had been clever enough, I told myself, to lie hidden in the immediate vicinity while the search was most intensive, and then to slip off by night as I had supposed. Yes, that was it—that must be it! I came to a prompt decision.

That very afternoon, having rung Goderich to tell him what I contemplated, I set off for Southampton, calling in at the Winchester police station *en route*. I could see that my plan to "pursue" (they would not admit that it *was* that) my boy to France had met with official scepticism and disfavour, but—though I did concur in the suggestion that a watch be set, if all too tardily, around the loft—I would not allow the cold water thrown on it to weaken my resolve.

And, as it happened, while I was not to know it then, I had only as it were anticipated matters by a single night. A second wire from M. Vaignon, I learned later, "Denis here," arrived for me the morning after I had left.

Once more, the prosaic and accustomed train, my gentle heaving bunk upon the almost as accustomed channel packet, and the familiar harbour of Le Havre at misty dawn. The same, yes all the same, and yet how different! Many times had I made this crossing, but with a heart unracked, as now, by care.

Eating my *petit déjeuner* in the station buffet when I had passed through the customs, I bought a newspaper and a further supply of brioches and again boarded the train.

Paris and lunch, then southwards—on to what? As we began to breast the gradual ascent towards the *massif* a vague but

40

dreadful apprehension grew upon me. I had dashed off from England, I realized, largely because inaction had become intolerable—yet here, in France, I quailed. It was as if, while I approached that black and tortured landscape of Auvergne, I were adventuring foolhardily into some citadel of evil powers, pitting my puny strength against a host of devils.

I took up my newspaper and tried to read—in vain. Denis, I thought, where are you? What are you doing now—and why?

With an effort, I forced myself to re-examine, as critically and calmly as I might, the chain of circumstances that had led to my being where I was, and upon such a quest.

Vaignon—and Raoul. . . . The whole business of the holiday exchanges had been so casual, so benign, and yet—yes. . . . There must be some connection, beyond mere coincidence, between the two.

I recalled M. Vaignon's brooding and half-guilty looks—and that peculiar scrap of conversation I had overheard. "It has *come again*," he had said then to Flébard. What had "come again?" Could it. . . .

Suddenly my mind snapped on something, and deliberately, for a second, I made it blank, as if afraid of the light that threatened all at once to flood it. I even grabbed my paper and feigned a furious engrossment in its long columns of advertisements. Next moment, however, I gave up the pretence, and a sigh escaped me— a sort of cold sigh of recognition and admission. "Could it. . . ?" Why yes, of course it could. The "It" of M. Vaignon's terrified lament was—Raoul.

How this lurking while fairly obvious conjecture had managed to get itself hushed up in the recesses of my brain (as I am sure it had) for such a time before issuing forth at last to startle me I did not know. But I found it, now, a highly disturbing one. Without, as yet, being able to appreciate all its implications I felt, dimly, a kind of spreading illumination, as though the contours of some formidable truth would presently emerge.

To reach Foant I had, directly, to change to a slower train, with a number of stops. The countryside remained, on the whole, placidly pastoral, but I fancied I began to detect in it, here and there, faint earnests or intimations of that sinister quality which the Auvergne whither I travelled had always held for me. M. Vaignon would be prepared for my coming, since I had telegraphed him from Le Havre, but what sort of welcome he would accord me I had no idea. I had not, it must be remembered, received the wire from him that would arrive at "Ashtoft" the next morning, and I had nothing, at the moment, but my impulsive intuition to lead me to suppose Denis at the château.

The sun was westering as we slackened speed for Foant, and before that, of course, the scenery had assumed the intimidating gigantism and cataclysmic look of violence which, every time I visited the place, had sent a shiver up my spine.

Alighting, I stared round me but could see no one, on my own island platform or on either of the other two, except the ticket collector and a couple of peasant women. Perhaps M. Vaignon was so indignant at my flat defiance of his previous virtual prohibition that he was not sending anyone to meet me! Owing to his strange imposition of silence I had felt unable to write to him—or question him maybe concerning Raoul—and though I now suspected him of knowing more about it than he might confess his official state was one of ignorance, and he might not appreciate the seriousness of the case.

For a quarter of an hour I waited impatiently in the little *salle d'attente*. Had M. Vaignon actually resolved to deny me his hospitality? But no; he *had* answered my first wire, and surely, in common humanity, he couldn't be such a bear—and such a brute!

I was however on the point either of telephoning the château or, without doing so, of hiring, if I could, a taxi, when a car hurtled furiously into the station yard. It hurtled in *so* furiously that I experienced a curious start of anticlimax at sight of the form that crawled feebly out from the driving-seat.

The figure advanced immediately, with a sort of frenzied impetuous hobble, towards me.

Yes, it was M. Vaignon.

III

Question and answer between us tumbled over each other, standing on no ceremony of greeting. "Is he with you?"

"Yes . . . but you could not have my telegram so soon."

"Is he—all right?"

"He—you will see. . . ."

We got into the car. "Flébard," M. Vaignon explained interjectorily, "has left, and it is I who am chauffeur. I fear I am late."

I mumbled something, to which he paid no attention. We had shot out of the station yard into the gathering dusk of the highway, M. Vaignon still driving like a maniac. His manner, notwithstanding, had a kind of distrait, debonair moroseness, and the conditions generally, as we careered wildly onwards, were unfavourable to conversation. Yet I did, once, attempt it. "Denis has been terribly ill," I said. "He is not himself, or he would not have run away, and I would not have had to trouble you. How does he seem, now?"

M. Vaignon's nearer shoulder gave me an absent shrug. "I cannot tell you. . . . We are all bedevilled, *n'est-ce pas*, and the evil days are on us. They are on your boy, who does not know you are here but won't, I bet you, let you talk to him, or get within ten feet of him. . . ."

My heart sank, but despair goaded me to a flare of anger too. "We shall see about that!" I said.

The château, when we entered it at nightfall, was a place of dark, uneasy stillness. A man whose face was unfamiliar had admitted us and he immediately retreated again from us.

"Where is Denis?" I asked M. Vaignon. "Where is he?"

We had passed, from the hall, into a small *salon* to the left, wherein, I remembered, it had once been promised that Denis should devote a daily hour to the study of De Musset, the Dumas and Victor Hugo. Whether he had ever done so I doubted, but two walls of the room were book-lined.

"Where *is* he?" I repeated, but at this very instant, hearing a step along the hall, I glanced up towards the door, and there, staring back frozenly at me, was—Denis.

It was a glimpse only that I had of him for with a kind of indignantly affrighted "*Ah . . .*" he vanished. I rushed out after him into the hall, calling his name.

A man—it was he who had let us in—stood there. "Dinner will be——" he was beginning.

"Where is my boy, *le jeune garçon*?" I interrupted him. "Which way did he go just now? Which is his room?"

The fellow regarded me consideringly as he replied, slowly: "The same . . . but——" He stopped, then, with a quick and as if guilty or surreptitious movement, crossed himself.

Denis's old room was on the first floor, by the stairhead. Having run up to it, I tried the door, but it was locked and there was no answer to my knocks. "Denis!" I cried. "Denis, are you there?"

Not a sound. It was just possible though most unlikely that the door had been locked from the outside. I knocked and called again, in vain.

Descending to the *salon*, I debated, wretchedly. It appeared but too evident that M. Vaignon had spoken truly and that Denis had not ceased to regard me as his enemy. I recalled, in misery, the intonation of his "*Ah . . !*" when he caught sight of me some moments since. It had been an "Ah!" not merely of disconcertment and dismay but, I realized, of actual execration.

M. Vaignon had come out into the hall. "You see," he murmured dryly, "I was right. . . ."

At dinner, no place was laid for Denis, and M. Vaignon must have noticed my disappointedly inquiring glances. In the presence, however, of the ever-attendant Dorlot (as, I gathered, was his name) nothing of any importance could be said, and our talk was of trivialities.

Meanwhile, my mind ran feverishly on what I had so far dis-

43

covered. I had already seen, alas, enough to recognize that matters could not be adjusted offhand, or hurried, and that the home-bringing of my poor prodigal would prove no simple and probably no brief procedure. There would be difficulties, especially in a foreign country, about compelling him, forcibly, to go with me, and, in consulting with M. Vaignon and striving to come at the inner truth of the whole business, I must do what I could to practise greater patience and restraint.

After the meal I again followed M. Vaignon into the *salon*, where he motioned me to a seat by the fire.

"As you will doubtless have observed," he began immediately, anticipating one, though certainly not the most pressing, of the questions that burned upon my tongue, "Marcel and Augustine are gone. They were in all benevolence snatched from me by an aunt, my sister-in-law, who considered the atmosphere here not —not altogether sympathetic to young children. . . . *Mon dieu*, ha, ha . . . how very right she was. . . !"

My good resolutions, at such words, broke down, and I burst out: "And *my* child, *Monsieur*, what about *him*? He wasn't at dinner with us. Where is he *now*? Is he safe *now*, this minute. . . ? When did he come here, and why? You have told me nothing yet. There is a person, a creature, 'Raoul,' who——"

"*Ah, ça. . . !*" M. Vaignon had raised a nervously, or it may only have been contemptuously, deprecating hand to check me. "Let us not speak that name too loudly! It is a name, to me, of ridicule and of annoyance; to others, many people, whose sus-ceptibilities one must regard, of—well, of something infinitely worse. It——"

He paused, continuing presently: "You are bound, now that you are here, to hear of this—this nonsense—anyhow, and I may just as well prepare you and forewarn you. . . . *Enfin*—it was of that, in fact, I wrote to you, or anyhow of that that I was thinking when I advised you in my letter not to send me your boy again. When I told you I was the victim of a persecution, as, in a mood of some exasperation, I recall I did, I was hardly exaggerating, and——"

"But," I broke in, "I don't understand how——" I hesitated, for my most urgent question would not be repressed. "Is he—is it—here now?"

M. Vaignon considered me warily. "It—if we are to call this damnable old wives' tale an 'it'—is not here, or active, now. That is to say—*enfin*, it is not here now. . . ."

After a moment he went on, morosely: "As for 'understand-ing'. . . . There are things of which one can perceive the effect, upon oneself and others, but which one may not altogether 'under-stand,' and may indeed, in a sense, entirely repudiate. As I have just told you, this—this nuisance, this most supreme and con-summate nuisance—is not with us, *actuellement*, but your boy—

your boy arrived here late last night, in—in search of it. He is trying—he will do his best, to get it back. . . ."

It would be hard to describe the unhappy confusion into which these words had thrown me. What was I to believe? M. Vaignon had alluded almost scoffingly to Raoul as if to a sort of troublesome but relatively minor notifiable disease or garden pest—much as he might have spoken of some curiously periodic scarlatina or potato-blight!—yet underneath his shrugging air I could divine a genuine and continuing apprehension.

He rose abruptly, with an access of agitation. "This thing—this kind of molestation, or superstition of a molestation—is not entirely unexampled if one may credit certain authors, certain bogeymongers, of—oh, of at least two centuries and more ago . . ." He had moved to the bookshelves, ran a finger along the tops of a few heavy-looking tomes, and half pulled one out. "No matter . . ." he said, pushing the volume into place again. "It is there . . . and duly catalogued, though under an evasive appellation. They called these—these preposterousnesses, or the cast of mind that fostered and engendered them, 'san noms'— simply that. The 'nameless'. . . ."

Undecidedly, he resumed his seat. "I—I give you my word of honour that, when I first met you and until recently, this particular—'nameless' had not, to my recognition, bothered us, or at all events . . . I do not deny that it, or the—the rumour of it, was supposed to *have* bothered us in the past, but it was presumed to be gone. *Tant même*, there was a technical, an academic risk of which I might no doubt have warned you earlier. . . ."

A tide of bewildered anger swelled in me. "Yes," I said bitterly, " 'rumour' or not, whatever the thing was, and whether we are mad or sane, you might indeed! You certainly should have warned me!"

"Yet you would have laughed, and rightly or *au moins* most excusably, at such a history. You would have derided it and me."

"And what would that have mattered if I *had*?" I almost shouted, unable longer to contain the explosion of impatience. I had had to wait, on tenterhooks, all through the drive from Foant and then through dinner to ask anything of what I had been bursting desperately to ask—and now, when I could at least demand straightforward answers, I was treated to nothing but side-steppings and prevarications.

M. Vaignon was silent, his head bowed. I was entirely convinced that he knew very well he had not told me the whole story and was still keeping something back.

"This—this 'nameless'," I insisted. "What *is* it? I mean this particular specimen. . . . We are just beating round the bush about it all and I can't in the least follow what it really is you think you are telling me—if you *are* telling me. What *is* it? That's what I've got to know! But whatever it is you surely could have stopped my boy from—from meeting it. *He* told me it was someone he—

45

chummed up with in the village. A kind of semi-vagrant, it sounded, but. . . ."

My words trailed away. M. Vaignon, his face white under my accusation, twirled his brandy of which a glass was before me too, untasted.

He raised his own glass all at once and drained it. His expression showed an almost morbid exaltation.

"*Ah, bah!* 'It', you say, '*it*'. . . *! Eh bien.* . . . 'It' is something, if you please, that ebbs and flows and that refuses to be satisfactorily dead, something that crops up and comes and goes, and is reputed to have plagued my family through three generations; something that has nourished itself, at intervals, so the tale runs, at our expense and owes its very being and persistence to its victims. All that—ha, ha!—is in the text book. . . . Oh, we are not unique in this affliction. 'The So-and-so's,' you will hear, '—ah yes, a fine old family, *but*—they have a *sans-nom.* . . .' As for this— this particular example, as you say, it has a human shape, which you have seen. It eats, drinks, sleeps as other men, while it exists. *Mon dieu* . . . 'it' has even mended my hedges, and bought soap or tea or salt at the *épicerie*, before I suspected it and till it was recognized. . . . And then, when it *was* recognized—oh what a how-d'ye-do. . . ! But, *to* exist, it must, they say, have an—an attachment. And—its attachment must be young. If and when its victim, its *petit ami*, dies, the pest transfers its—its attentions, we are to believe, to the children of another, and the nearest, branch. The thing is amorous and—and rapacious. *Ah, nom d'un nom, quelle histoire! Quel fumisterie! Quelle imbécilité! C'est ridicule, fantastique, incroyable. . . !*"

His voice had risen wildly on a note, it might be equally of scorn or terror as a knock, at first soft, then louder, was repeated on the door. The man Dorlot entered, wearing a look of remonstrance.

"*Monsieur* should know that such excitement, of which the noise has penetrated to the kitchen, is very bad for him. Go to bed, *Monsieur*, I advise it. Go to bed, where you may forget our troubles possibly in sleep."

Meekly accepting the rebuke—and, I imagined, rather welcoming the excuse to escape further questioning—M. Vaignon said, to me: "Dorlot is right, and, if you will forgive me, I shall leave you now. My health, latterly, is precarious. . . . Dorlot will give you anything you require. But first"—he turned to the man —"where is the young *monsieur*? Is he in his room, and—and quiet?"

"Yes; he is in his room, as is to be inferred from the very fact that his room is *not* entirely quiet. The noises are there again, while not, as yet, excessive."

My heart sank at these words, though they conveyed nothing

new. The 'poltergeist' disturbances, however, were connected in my mind with Raoul, and their continuance depressed me.

"Good night . . ." said M. Vaignon.

I was desperately tired, but lingered a little longer in the "library."

What, honestly, could I believe, and what try, still, to disbelieve? Ordinarily, of course, the recital which my host had just concluded would be dismissible as a farrago of lurid and unpleasant nonsense—but I had had experience, alas, myself, of what too plainly contradicted this consoling view.

As I was going over what M. Vaignon had said, and sipping my brandy at last, my eye fell on the volume he had started to pull out from the shelves. It protruded slightly still, and I got up and took it to my seat.

Légendes d'Autrefois the tome was entitled, tritely, but I had scarcely flicked over a haphazard page or two before I read, as if my glance had been directed to the spot: "... *et, c'est à dire, les morts se régaleront des vivants. . . ."*

I experienced a cold grue of that sort of surprise which is not surprise at all, but eerie confirmation, and immediately restored the volume. "The dead shall feast upon the living". . . . There it was, and I did not want, at present, to read more. It was the completion of the passage in that dream that I had had, some weeks ago, about my wife, holding the book before her non-existent face. . . .

I don't know what had made me so optimistic, in leaving England, as to the prospect of an early return there with my boy. No doubt I had the legal right to compel him to come home, but if he still repulsed me and offered physical resistance the practical difficulties would be, to put it mildly, formidable. On the morning after my arrival and throughout that day and the next I had tried again to speak with him, but either his room would be locked and silent or, if I caught sight of him at all upon the stairs or in the grounds, he would take literally to his heels.

"Where does he eat?" I asked—for he continued absent from our meals—and it appeared that sometimes he would raid the larder and carry off his plunder to the fields. Neither M. Vaignon nor his domestics had any control over him, and, even if they had, I could not have relied on them to exercise it upon my behalf. As to the servants, they were in all respects so unco-operative as to be almost obstructionist, while, in particular, their extraordinary reticence caused me to think that they had probably been forbidden to "gossip" with me, upon this or any other subject.

How fervently I wished that Goderich were here! But of course he could not desert his patients at short notice, nor, obviously, was M. Vaignon's hospitality in my gift.

Denis, I found, had done as I had thought and managed to stow away upon a fishing-boat at Brixham. It had been evidently useless for him to pretend that his visit had my sanction and he must have known I would eventually pursue him—but, beyond his infatuated determination to be reunited with Raoul at any cost, I doubted whether he could have had much of a settled plan of action and campaign. He had steered as clear as possible, it seemed, of M. Vaignon and so far as I could gather had confided the manner of his crossing only—half inadvertently—to Dorlot, who had retailed the story subsequently to his master.

Well it was a beautiful kettle of fish all round. I sent a wire to the police at Winchester, reflecting what slight satisfaction it had brought me thus to have proved them wrong.

In my anxiety, I had little or no help from M. Vaignon. Either he was genuinely ill, or feigned it to avoid my "badgering." Never joining me at breakfast, he would retire, though with excuses, immediately after lunch and dinner; and, since our talk on the first evening, had said nothing to me of the least seriousness, sincerity or moment as to what should have been our common problem.

Left to my own devices, I would wander wretchedly around the estate and nearer villages, exchanging a "*bonjour*" occasionally with some peasant, but often meeting no one, as I chose the less frequented paths. The autumn days were dull, but now and then a brighter spell invited me to extend my rambles towards a puy that topped a line of rocky hillocks to the north.

One afternoon—it was the fourth or fifth since my arrival—I had set out thither at about three o'clock. I paid no particular heed to where I was going, and walked on. I suppose, with my head bent in gloomy thought, for which I certainly had food enough.

Yes, the position was fantastic, and a description of it, given baldly, would provoke only pitying disbelief. And yet the history was *true*. That was, I knew that as much of it as I had seen with my own eyes was true. As for the rest—for M. Vaignon's wild while half-contemptuous elaborations on the theme—I reserved judgment. He was a sick man, whatever the cause, and his troubles seemed reflected in the unprosperous, depleted and decayed condition generally of his estate and household. The château was in disrepair and its staff, whether by flight or by dismissal, reduced to an uneasy remnant. Why, for example, had the trusted Flébard left? My heart was leaden with misgiving. Could M. Vaignon—a diabolic suspicion flashed into my brain—could he, initially, have asked Denis to the château, or anyhow have gone on having him there, in order to—to safeguard *his* children? Could he, at one time, to protect *them*, to divert something from them and fasten it on Denis, have actually been tempted to promote and foster the disastrous intimacy between Raoul and my boy... ? But I rejected such a vile hypothesis as altogether too far-fetched. *My* mind, as well, must be infected to have harboured it, and....

Suddenly, rousing from my reverie, I looked about me. The country was unfamiliar and very lonely, and a small half-ruined—church or chapel, with a graveyard attached, added to its general air of desolation. In that indifference of purpose which is born of mental exhaustion rather than of any, even "idle," curiosity. I entered the graveyard and wandered aimlessly among its tombs. Some distance off, I noticed, a man was wending towards me down the road ahead.

I loitered absently round the inside of the boundary wall. The burial-ground was evidently disused and the graves were untended, many overgrown with bramble or rank grass. Now and then a date caught my eye—1830, 1813, 1770.... Possibly the —all at once I stopped, transfixed, as in the silence, a name stole, staring back at me. It was inscribed upon a headstone slightly taller than the rest, though lichen-coated, tilted, cracked and weather-worn as they. "Privache".... And, just decipherable below—yes. "*Raoul. Mourut 1873.*"

A footfall made me start. It was the man I had seen on the road and whose approach, over the grass, had been noiseless. He seemed a respectable, decent fellow of the sturdy "bon-homme" type, probably a small tradesman or petty farmer—but he was regarding me, and the grave, with a frown of sombre disapproval.

He gave a significant upward jerk of the head and pointed to the tomb. "*Monsieur* knows perhaps of whom that is the grave?"

In a double disconcertment I stammered, faintly: "Yes, I—I know the—no, I cannot, I—I mean it is the name, the same name as somebody's I know."

The man took a step backward, crossed himself, and said coldly: "Enough ... then it is to he hoped that *Monsieur* knows also that it is a bad name.... *Alors, bonjour, Monsieur.*"

He was going slowly away from me but, on an impulse, I detained him.

"Why, who—who was he?" I asked. "Was he a—a criminal, or——"

My tongue faltered, and, as the man's glance met mine searchingly, it was as if a thousand things had passed wordlessly between us.

"No, *Monsieur*, in life he was not a criminal but——" He paused, then, stooping, traced with a forefinger the date, 1873. "That, *Monsieur*, was when he died. It is there, cut in the stone, and is, so far as it goes, correct. My father was *maire* of the *commune* and could remember all about it. I have even, myself, seen the burial record, which was in the register of the parish before the amalgamation. I can tell you no more than that, if you please, *Monsieur*—that he died almost eighty years ago, in 1873. ..."

Again he crossed himself, and this time, as he withdrew, I did not stay him. I was thrown, momentarily, into a kind of panic. In a sense, my talk several evenings since with M. Vaignon should have prepared me for this further shock, yet I had still tended then, I think, to discount a good deal of his discourse as crazy ranting—which he had not repeated and, probably, repented. But now the story, borne out in another mouth, had gained fresh substance and solidarity. Something—a mortuary breath of evil—had addressed me, subverting reason and defeating sanity. "Raoul"—if it were he . . . dead eighty years ago. . . . Or what would lead this steady countryman and sober citizen thus to accost me so suspiciously and reprehendingly?

Waiting only until he disappeared across a field, I walked quickly back to the château.

That same evening I got M. Vaignon's consent to my begging Goderich, if he could possibly arrange it, to join me at the earliest opportunity. I had spent six days here, quite uselessly. My boy remained obdurate in avoiding me, keeping out of doors as much as he could and eating his meals I knew not when nor precisely where. This could not go on indefinitely, and he must be removed somehow, but I did not feel confident of my ability to hale him home single-handed, or wish, either, to invoke police assistance, French or British. I worded my letter to Goderich very strongly and, having posted it, was slightly easier in mind.

Otherwise, I was more tortured by anxiety than ever, and my discovery of the lonely grave had had a horrible effect on me. Coupled with the queer manner of the honest fellow who had spoken to me beside it—his doubting, fearful looks and his ambiguous reticence—it left me prey to a complete bewilderment and cold dismay.

Of Denis, meanwhile, as I have just said, I caught only fleeting glimpses. M. Vaignon, who had warned me that he, Denis, would "try to get it back," pretended to have interceded with him, but on this I placed no least reliance. I had little real idea of what my boy did with himself all day, of whether he still slept in the same room (though I was assured this was so) or of when he fed, or bathed, or changed his clothes. As to this last point, I had brought with me for him some clean shirts, socks and underwear, which I had handed to Dorlot and were now, I was informed, in use. But, generally, it seemed to me, his condition was one almost of semi-vagabondage, the château being for him not much more than a base or headquarters from which to "forage" in the countryside.

However, the next morning I did have news of him which, while unreassuring, was somewhat more detailed than previous accounts. Denis, Dorlot remarked, had latterly been spending a good deal of his time in the east wing "near the tower." But on my asking what my boy was doing there the man had shrugged "*Qui sait, Monsieur?* I have seen him reading, or carving wood with his knife. . . ."

"Is he there now?"

"*Non, Monsieur.* It was yesterday and the day before. This morning he has gone out."

This conversation had been at my *petit déjeuner*, which I always had alone, my host preferring his brought to his bed. After the meal I busied myself in writing a short note to my faithful Jenny, from whom I had heard two days ago. She had reported all well at home, and that she and Clare were hoping, poor things, to welcome us *both* back very soon.

I went out to post my reply to her, struck, as I passed beneath the *porte-cochére*, by the château's latterday appearance of neglect. It was as if it lay under a spell—as if some blight, of doom and galloping decay, attacked it. Yes—and assailed its inmates too, I thought—one Colonel Walter Habgood not excepted! *I*, to be sure, was only a temporary occupant of the place, a guest, yet I was conscious, whenever I walked abroad, that something of its ill-repute attached to me. With the local peasantry I, too, was in bad odour, the carrier of an aura, an aroma, of the dimly sinister and menacing. And when I had mailed my letter to Goderich yesterday at the little office three kilos up the road to Foant whither I now again was on my way, the postmistress had eyed me balefully, touching her scapula as I was leaving. Go where I might, a species of anxious hostility attended me, expressed in covert stares, in sullen glances, crossings and avoidances. Even the children scattered from my path.

What *was* the truth, I demanded for the hundredth time, about this whole fantastic business? These yokels (*and* M. Vaignon, I suspected) were abjectly superstition-ridden. You might suppose a recent world-war would have knocked such nonsense out of them, but—suddenly, and wryly, I laughed at myself—though it wasn't at all funny. Yes, that was rich! Talk of the pot and kettle. . . ! For *I* was equally in thrall to a grotesque myth with any of the folk I was deriding.

It was exasperating not to know quite what I did believe or disbelieve. Everything and everybody seemed to be conspiring to throw dust in my eyes and keep me ignominiously in the dark. Here was I, Denis's own father, thankful when I could pick up, as just now, a few crumbs of second-hand intelligence about him from a conceited surly menial like Dorlot! More than once, latterly, I had been tempted to question the fellow bluntly, about many things, but hitherto my pride had not allowed me to interrogate the man behind his master's back. As for the master aforesaid, M. Vaignon, since his first outburst, had retired completely into his shell and been as cordially informative as any oyster.

I felt I could endure this mystifying and maddening secretive-

51

ness no longer. I must request from someone—anyone—a forth-right explanation of the whole enigma and see, at least, what sort of answer was provoked. Accordingly, when I had posted my letter to Jenny, I asked the postmistress to direct me to some person of responsibility—the *maire*, perhaps, or schoolmaster—with whom I could discuss a private matter.

The woman regarded me dirtily enough, replying only after a suspicious pause. "The *maire* is ill," she said, "but there is M. Boidilleule the *garde champêtre, qui était de la résistance* and is ill likewise, or M. Tanvy the *pharmacien*. M. Tanvy," she added more amiably, "is very clever, and of a great discretion, having been a quartermaster in the army. . . . Then there is too, of course, Père Puindison, the *curé*. . . ."

Rejecting the belauded M. Tanvy, I decided on the *curé*—an obvious choice which it was strange had not occurred to me before. There was no difficulty in locating him. He had just returned from Mass and welcomed me into his *vicairie* politely.

Somewhat haltingly I outlined as much as necessary of my story, including, particularly, my discovery of the grave. Was, I inquired, the "Raoul" from whom my boy had this unfortunate infatuation a grandson, possibly, of the deceased?

The *curé's* face had darkened and at my final question wore a look of, as it were, a scandalized discomfiture. I was quite sure he had known all about me in advance.

"*Franchement, Monsieur*, it is not easy to reply. This is a district *assez superstitieux* and. . . . *Enfin*, the individual whose grave you saw up there at Saint Orvin had no descendants. He was, it would appear, a butler at the château Vaignon, where, actually, he died. But that was eighty years ago, and. . . ."

"Yes, yes," I said. "But—but this other fellow, that my boy met. . . . Who is *he*?"

The good father blinked at me morosely. He was an elderly, florid-visaged man, with eyes that were worldly but, at the moment, troubled and unsubtle.

"*Monsieur*," he said, reproachfully, "you come to me, like this, and ask me—what? To confirm and to endorse a doubt that has, beforehand, been implanted in your mind—or maybe to deny it. I can state to you only that the Privache we *know* of died in 1873. The rest is—is merely superstition.'

"And the superstition is——?"

He shrugged weakly, uncomfortable and disdainfully apologetic under my pressure. "*Evidemment*, the superstition you insist that I enunciate so clearly is that the Privache who died in 1873 and he for whom, you say, your boy has this *engouement* are one and the same. . . . *C'est ridicule! Alors*. . . . And I have told you, *absolument*, all I can. . . ."

His manner, while still courteous, showed the beginnings of a self-protective frostiness, and again, marvelling, I felt defeated.

All these folk, when you tried to tackle them and pin them down upon the subject of this preposterous myth, affected superiorly to scoff at it—yet all of them, in their hearts, were really scared of it!

Thanking the *curé*, I took my dissatisfied and disappointed leave.

I had been at the château just a week—an utterly, completely useless week!

Each day, I had sought every chance of pleading with my boy, so far quite unavailingly. Must I then drag him home a literal captive and so make him hate me worse than ever? Possibly, if need be, but not till I had tried every other, more persuasive measure. Denis was like a wild thing, a wild thing piteously spellbound and enchanted, and it would profit little, I thought, to trap and pinion the poor body if the spirit still eluded me. I wished to snare him—yes—but to snare the whole of him, and lovingly; and bonds and handcuffs seemed an unhappy way of doing this.

Yet if he would not voluntarily come with me there was nothing for it but a degree of force, and it had been with this necessity in closer prospect that I appealed to Goderich, whose sympathetically auxiliary convoy, at the pinch, would certainly be less humiliating than that of a police escort!

In this pass, M. Vaignon was a broken reed, his nerve-racked inanition now, indeed, almost amounting to a kind of passive, undeclared resistance. And why, after exploding as violently as he had about his blessed "*sans-noms*," had he stopped short there? the *curé* had grudgingly enlightened me to the limit that his scruples or timidity allowed—but why couldn't M. Vaignon have told me all this, and more, himself?

I walked to the window of my breakfast room and surveyed the autumn fields. From here, they were visible, in brown or sallow squares, stretching irregularly up a saucer's rim to misty hillocks, and in one of them, far off, I fancied, with a start, that I saw Denis. But no, the figure was motionless, and I remembered now that it was only a scarecrow, lingering purposelessly in the stubble.

My letter should reach Goderich today, and, if and when he came, we could hold some sort of council of war. How glad I would be of his refreshing sanity and clearer judgement! My own ideas had become quite chaotic and my affronted reason hurled itself hour by hour against brick walls of contradiction. It was a veritable antinomy. On the one hand, here was the mid-twentieth century, with (even in this backwater) the trains, post, newspaper and radio (should M. Vaignon but elect to buy a set) and an occasional avion droning overhead; while, on the other, equally compulsive of assent, there lay—sheer mediaevalism, rank mythology, a weird anachronism of fantastic horror.

The two worlds, though interpenetrating, were irreconcilable—and each was true.

I went undecidedly towards my room and then, passing it, along a series of corridors. I had often roamed unchallenged up and down the château's twisting stairs, beneath its faded tapestries and seigneurial banners and across its echoing halls; and now, uneasily while unpremeditatedly enough, my steps trended in the direction of the east wing and its tower.

Nothing in particular rewarded my reconnoitre, if it were one, though in a chamber just below the so-called "haunted" room I did find a few chips and shavings of the sticks, presumably, that as Dorlot informed me, Denis had been whittling. It was not till I had redescended that a speculation springing from my recent conversation with the *curé* crossed my mind. "Raoul." Père Puindison had stated, had died in the château—and Denis, long ago, as I could now also remember, had said, in speaking of the turret room, that "someone died there."

Was the "someone" Raoul, and was it actually in the tower that he had died? It seemed more than probable.

I spent the rest of the morning and most of the afternoon in desultory "mooching," too anxious and distracted, till at least I had Goderich's reply, to settle definitely to anything.

My visit to the east wing and my ensuing conjecture about Raoul had, admittedly, disturbed me, but, beyond that, I seemed dimly conscious of some other cause of a vague apprehension or dissatisfaction. It was something—I had the feeling—that had happened, or that I had briefly noticed, during the course of the day, but which I could not quite lay finger on—something of which the impact had been oblique and that now tapped irritatingly, with an obscure persistent warning, at my mind. For a time, I tried vainly to recall it, whatever it had been, then gave it up.

I wandered, restively, into the "library" again and took out the volume of "Legends," despite a kind of contemptuous repugnance, to consider, more attentively, what it might have to say.

Presently I found the passage I wanted. It was in a long section entitled, simply, *Auvergne*, and its immediate context was rather mystifying—too occult or too rhapsodical in diction for me to follow clearly. Regretting the inadequacy of my French, I read on, puzzled. ". . . exceptional tenacity of life . . . enabling the said nameless to withdraw vital force . . ." (a line of two here that I could not make head or tail of). ". . . so to rebuild itself around the mammet as around a nucleus of focus and . . ." (again a string of unfamiliar words defeated me). ". . . or other homely object, so be it have the semblance of a man. But woe to all who do adventure thus, and whether child or woman, if the right fixative be not supplied. . . ." And then some sentences of what appeared to be a sort of general description: ". . . their chief weakness being in the

54

wrists and wattles. Yellow above all they joy in, and a certain tint of bluish grey they do defy, wherefore, in extirpating them. . . ."

Disappointed at my stumbling translation, I rested the volume, open, on my knee, and pondered. In a sense, what I *had* managed to translate relieved me, because it seemed such arrant, puerile nonsense. Why yes, I thought, in a delighted welling of, as it were, half-hesitant astonished thankfulness, it *was* all nonsense. Sheer, utter nonsense, and I *could* laugh at it. How had I ever—my fleeting elation ebbed. But Denis—I remembered. . . . Yes Denis. . . . That was the trouble. "Nonsense" or no, my boy's plight was actual enough, and. . . .

My host entered—suddenly and brusquely. Owing, ostensibly, to his continued indisposition, we had scarcely encountered for the last several days, and his face now wore a slight frown. "*Bonjour*," he greeted, peevishly. "I—I regret to see you so poorly entertained. You will hardly derive much profit, or even amusement I should think, from *that*. . . ." To my amazement he swooped upon the volume and replaced it smartly in the shelves.

Really, M. Vaignon was very trying; and it was now, all in an instant, that, as the result of this comparatively trivial incident, I found myself having an outright, first-class row with him. No doubt, on each side, nerves were frayed to breaking point, and it had needed but this spark to set our tempers in a blaze.

I had stood up. "You might, *Monsieur*, at least have had the courtesy not to *snatch* from my very knees a book that I was actually reading. . . !"

He glared at me, out of eyes swimming with tears. "It is my book. It is *my* book," he repeated childishly, "and I shall do, as I believe you say, what I bloody well like with it! I am going to bloody-burn it. There *Monsieur!* Can you advance any argument against my bloody-burning my own property, including the entire château, if I see fit? And should anybody still insist on lingering—on *lingering* I say—in this so-charming château of mine *when* I burn it, he will be burnt too, neck and crop, along with it, unless. . . ."

Staggering, he had clapped a hand to his breast. "Forgive me. . . . I am desolated to have made such an exhibition of myself and caused you to think me like—like a stage-Frenchman, *n'est-ce pas*, but—but certain things in this establishment are not quite as they should be. . . . A large—an infinitely large—bluebottle has got loose in my bedroom and kept me awake all night, and I, too, am as your *sans-noms*—weak in the wrist and wattles. . . !"

Was he going mad? Or shamming mad? "*My*" *sans-noms!* I was really completely disgusted with him, the more so perhaps because he had somehow succeeded, in this ridiculous fashion, in taking the wind out of my sails.

"This creature of yours, whatever it is," I was startled to hear myself shouting, "this precious *sans-nom* of *yours*, I say, that has attacked my boy and that for some reason you'll tell me nothing more about—he died here, didn't he? Up in the tower room, or under it. . . ."

M. Vaignon regarded me, at first uncomprehendingly and then almost as if pityingly. "My poor friend," he said slowly. "My poor friend—all this has been too much for you and—and, ha, ha, you are going crazy. *Mon dieu, c'est le comble, ça!*" He approached nearer, with a curious dancing step and, to my utter dumbfounding, snapped a finger and thumb beneath my nose. "I repeat it, *Monsieur*. I repeat, with inexpressible regret, that you are quite demented!"

I had backed from him, far too bewildered to feel insulted by the taunting words and gesture, and it was at this instant that, as at a previous, somewhat similar, crisis, the tall form of Dorlot filled the doorway.

"*Calmez-vous, mon maître*," he remonstrated. "*Calmez-vous!* It is this heavy weather that surcharges the nerves, but to yield to your temperament in this manner and with these antics is unseemly. *Calmez-vous!* Thank heaven," he added in a lower tone, "it cannot last much longer now."

M. Vaignon looked at us wildly. "Forgive me," he murmured again, "forgive me. . . ." A strange expression, a sort of leering, still half-impudent despair, flickered over his features as, turning, he let Dorlot lead him unsteadily away.

I stayed motionless where I was a full minute. The whole scene had been incredible, and bedlam had flowered, unashamed, before my eyes.

At length, dazedly, I walked from the house.

Outside, I recovered. That was, my immediate emotional disturbance gradually died down, but I felt exhausted, as if I had been through a fight or in a mêlée, and my fundamental apprehension and confusion were increased.

It is a nightmare, I thought, a nightmare. That is why everyone appears mad and why you yourself behave like a madman. All at once you will wake up—perhaps when Goderich comes. . . .

The air, as Dorlot had observed, was close and muggy. It was mild, but with a treacherous intimation of tenseness—of I did not quite know what. The fields stretched round me passively—too passively I fancied oddly, as if conspiring, or abandoned, to a gathering sly enchantment. They rolled, in their meek rectangles of ochre, dun and beige, up to unstirring foothills, dreaming a guileful dream. Crossing one of them, I remarked, idly, that the scarecrow I had noticed earlier from the *salon* window seemed to have altered its position slightly.

M. Vaignon . . . Good heavens! "*Sans-noms*". . . . *His*, if you please, not mine! I wished him joy of them! "*Sans-noms*"! Ye gods. . . ! Who would invent such bogeys such farcically loathsome things, unless . . . I raised my eyes to the grey bated sky, and shivered. No, I was not, to word it temperately, much enamoured of this devil's nook, this baleful twelfth- or thirteenth-century pocket of provincial France, where superstitions and obscene mythologies, instead of just remaining quaintly decorative, had the unpleasant trick of springing suddenly alive and driving mad all those who brooded on them overlong. If only. . . .

My disjointed ruminations petered out. Once more I raised my eyes, with a faint shudder. All about me, as I walked, the hills, the waiting fields, kept quiet pace with me. I was aware—how shall I put it?—of a bland banking-up, of a demure stealth, a kind of tiptoe ripening of something. . . . My head ached and I had an indescribably oppressive feeling. The château, from the spot where I had now come rather giddily to a halt, was visible, maybe a kilo off, but partially obscured by a dip and by a thin belt of trees. I would get back to it as quickly as I could in case my disagreeable symptoms should increase.

Slowly, I proceeded, conscious, upon my mental palate, of some recrudescent flavour that was dimly nauseous and half-familiar. I had covered perhaps a third of the distance to the château when a dog ran up behind me, whining. It was one of the three or four dogs of the house, an amiable enough little creature, mainly poodle, called Zizi. Denis had been fond of it, and I supposed it still companioned him in his present, gipsyish style of life. But now it appeared distressed or frightened and slunk whimpering and cringing at my heels.

We went on together, skirting a field of stubble. It was the field containing the useless scarecrow, and again, puzzled, I had the impression that the object had moved slightly, in the direction of the château. Hang it! I thought querulously in a sort of mildly annoyed perplexity, this was preposterous, and I must previously have misjudged the confounded thing's position. Zizi, beside me, cowered closer and gave, very low, a series of curious suppressed yelps.

The day had grown overcast and my headache was no better. I had a sense of something brewing, something "making"—a kind of dumbly guarded watchfulness or wakefulness—in the dull air, the trees, the hilltops and the whelming sky, as if they too were, like myself, alerted and upon some strange and semi-animate *qui-vive*. The dog, while we passed opposite the middle of the field, darted for a moment from me and through the hedge, venting two stiff little barks, of actual terror or of a variety of canine scandal.

Gradually, as we neared the house, my head ached less, yet a conviction of uneasy imminence, a presentiment of swiftly gathering evil, knocked still at my mind's door, and again, more fervently, I longed for Goderich.

I entered the château, and there, on a tray in the hall, lay an answer to my prayer. Yes, said the telegram, he could come on Tuesday, that was, in three days' time.

IV

This heartening news was confirmed in a letter from him the next morning, explaining that he would have joined me instantly had not his partner been somewhat indisposed and hardly capable, till the promised Tuesday, of shouldering the extra work. Well, it was more than I had had the right to hope that my friend should have been able to arrange to get away at all, and, heaven knew, I blessed him.

During the week-end, however, my feeling of tension increased, and was appreciably heightened, as it happened, by my host's ill-humour. M. Vaignon, after our recent row, had offered me a somewhat grudging apology for his rudeness—but now he was exasperated again upon a different score. While *I* had had, from Goderich, a cheering and reassuring letter, *he* had received, it seemed, a violently upsetting one. The aunt, he told me, with whom *les petits* had been staying had written saying she was compelled to visit Tunisie on business, it might be for several months, and must accordingly send her brother-in-law's children home.

"It is an excuse!" he fumed. " 'Business'. . . . Pah! They *cannot* come here yet—not yet!"

My sympathy for him, when I remembered the plight of my own boy, was not excessive, and privily I blamed no aunt for getting sick of young Marcel and Augustine, but the matter set my mind running, with a revival of curiosity, on the connection (or in the case of Denis actual relationship) between our respective families, for it was through the sister of this same discredited and disobliging lady that it existed. She had been, before her marriage to M. Vaignon, a Mlle. Drouard, and, by a common ancestor three generations back, a cousin (though I do not think they knew each other) of my wife's.

This train of thought led naturally to a re-consideration of the whole question of M. Vaignon's conduct and attitude throughout; and here I was as far as ever from a satisfactory conclusion. He had blown hot and cold and been, by turns, solicitous and callous, courteous and grossly impolite. He had been contrite enough (if it were that) to break off the "holiday exchange" arrangement, yet insufficiently honest to warn me, plainly, about Raoul. He had had the grace, later, to wire me twice after Denis had run away to France, but then, when I arrived for the retrieval of my truant, had given me no help. There was no making the man out. . . .

I had been puzzling, alone, upon the Saturday evening, over these and allied problems when I heard a confused noise of angry shouting. The sounds seemed to come from the direction of the stables, suggesting by their volume and persistence that several persons, possibly a dozen or so, were engaged in a violent fracas. But by the time I had gone out to look, just as the hubbub had rather suddenly subsided, the disputants must evidently have stopped their fight, and scattered. Crossing the *basse cour*, however, I saw a man, limping painfully and holding a bloodstained rag to his face. I recognized him as a fellow I had noticed driving one of the wagons that carried hay, or milk and butter from the *laiterie*, and might have asked him what the trouble was had I not at that moment caught, from somewhere within, the shrilly furious tones of M. Vaignon.

As to this incident it was again from Dorlot that I received enlightenment, incomplete though it was. His master (who made no allusion to the matter) having retired immediately after dinner, he, Dorlot, brought me my customary glass of lonely brandy in the library and said: "That parcel of rascals from Saint Orvin were after Batiste and your boy this afternoon, and nearly had them too. . . .!"

"What!" I exclaimed, alarmed. "After my boy? What for? Is he all right?"

The man replied, coldly, addressing the ceiling, it appeared, rather than me.

"The young *monsieur* is entirely unharmed since they were unable to catch him, but Batiste—that one, he certainly got a scratch or two. . . ."

"But why—why should they be attacked?"

Dorlot shrugged, spreading his hands. "People here, *Monsieur*, are superstitious. They are believers in all kinds of nonsense, and possibly the young *monsieur* had been doing something, quite inadvertently, which caused them to suspect him, *sans dire* most wrongfully, of dealing in—in such matters. I cannot tell. . . . *Enfin*, the two of them, he and Batiste, were pursued by this band of ignoramuses and ruffians into our very yard, where they found refuge. It is unfortunate," he added as if meditatively, "that certain, even, of our own servants, too, should take sides with this rabble. . . . Enough—it is no longer my affair or properly my concern. I leave this place tomorrow. . . ."

I was exceedingly disturbed, not only by Dorlot's story and its implications but also, if to a less degree, by his announcement of departure. It would have been foolish to regard him as an ally, yet he had not been actively hostile and latterly had constituted almost my only source of news concerning Denis.

As to the tale itself—more lay behind it, obviously, than Dorlot would disclose, but of this I could guess at a good deal. Amongst the peasantry Denis would but too naturally be a prime object of suspicion, and it was really a wonder he had evaded molestation (if he had) till now. The man Batiste, surmisably, had been his friend or his associate and fallen, consequently, under the same stigma. . . . Evidently, the business had attained the proportions of a feud, and M. Vaignon's ranks, within the château, had been split. Dorlot, I fancied, would not lack company upon the train tomorrow. . . .

While I was counting the hours to Goderich's arrival with a fresh sense of urgency I renewed, vainly, my efforts to lessen Denis's hostility. I no longer hoped, now, for a full reconciliation so speedily, but, short of that, I would have liked, before Goderich lent me what help he could, to be at all events on speaking terms with my own child.

Twice I tried to talk with him through his locked door, receiving on the first occasion no reply and on the second the response: "Oh, go away! I *hate* you!" And twice, also, I got within undignified hailing distance of him in the grounds, only to be humiliated by his almost offhandedly contemptuous flight. Obviously, at any time, I might probably have rallied M. Vaignon's odds and ends of still faithful retainers (a further couple had left with Dorlot in the morning!) to round up my quarry, and then forced him, as my prisoner, to parley—but such trappings or waylayings would have been very much against the grain and, as I saw it then, have done more harm than good.

What, I would wonder could be his view of the position? How, in his own opinion, was he faring? Pretty evidently he had expected, or at least hoped, to find his odious playmate here—and had not M. Vaignon told me that he, Denis, would do his best to get Raoul back? In that, however, so far as I could judge, he had been disappointed. What had become of the physical "Raoul" —of the physical "aspect" of him—I had no idea. Presumably, after my half-throttling of him, he had returned somehow to France, but had not yet (I trusted) reappeared in his old haunts. Upon this point I could have, to be sure, no certainty, but, whoever or whatever the creature was, its headquarters seemed to lie on this side of the Channel, and the next step of minimum precaution was to transport Denis to the other.

Monday—and tomorrow Goderich would be here. Indeed, a letter for him, *aux soins de* M. Vaignon, had rather surprisingly preceded him already, arriving together with one for me from Jenny. The weather was still gloomy, rainless but boding, and again I strolled dejectedly around the nearer fields.

The landscape, as before, was sere and sullen, but its mood, to my imagining, had subtly changed. The sense of stealthy ferment and evil quickening had departed, and the drab acres had an empty look, as if delivered or relieved of something. Loth to accuse myself of being over-fanciful, I stared about me, seeking for anything that might account, more factually, for this impression, but could find nothing. Merely, the scarecrow I had noticed formerly had gone, having been removed and set up for whatever none too obvious reason, as I subsequently discovered, in another field considerably closer to the house.

I wandered slowly back to the château. Help was at last at hand —for Goderich should be here tomorrow evening—yet my heart was curiously unlightened. The countryside, louring and secret, with that discharged and voided aspect of an ominous fulfilment, seemed to wear a mien of hidden ridicule, of some kind of deceptive somnolence and inward mockery, as though it were laughing at me up its sleeve. Nonsense! I tried to think. What utter nonsense. . . ! With a derisive apt theatricality a trio of stage-property bats, encouraged by the dusk, skimmed past me as I turned by the corner of a barn.

And then, suddenly, I had a shock.

"Hello, Daddy . . ." said Denis.

He was there, in front of me, shyly smiling and addressing me in this form he had discarded for some years, as "babyish." His clothes were stained and torn and his cheeks wan under their grime. I did not believe he had washed properly for days.

But it was far less his ragamuffin air that horrified me than his manner. It was flat and almost bored, yet confident; casual and unconstrained in some utterly wrong way, as though he were so tired out with whatever he had been up to that he had forgotten, even, what it was. How could he, else, have carried it off with this weary, this to me actually hideous, aplomb? He stood, gazing at me in a sort of forlorn and rather vacant friendliness, as if nothing had happened, as if he were completely unconscious of my misery, or his own.

"Come in," I think I said to him. "And—and talk things over, shall we. . . ?"

"Yes . . ." he replied absently. "All right. I'm hungry too." He paused, then added, reconsideringly and as a careful qualification, "That is, you know, not really *very*. . . ."

We had begun to walk on, from the barn, and the fading light shone, briefly, on his face, discovering there a look that sickened me but is not easy to describe. It was at once wily and exhausted, an expression so to speak of a supreme irrelevance or imperviousness to the situation, of a precocious unconcern and hard frivolity or falsity—a falsity all the worse for being undeliberate and still childish. My gorge rose as at something odious. Rage filled me and, to my dismay, I found my fist clenched to strike him. It was with the greatest effort that I controlled the impulse.

"Denis . . ." I heard myself saying. "*Denis. . . !*" My anger had turned suddenly to yearning and I had him, unresisting, in my arms. He was light as a feather, limply yielding, and weighing nothing, almost nothing. I felt, while I strained him to me, as if

61

he were liable at any instant to melt away from my embrace into thin air.

At the château, when we entered, M. Vaignon had just come into the hall, gaping at us as though quite confounded.

I do not really know how the next few hours passed, what words were said or what was done in them. I do know and remember that they were not happy or triumphant hours—alas, far from that. A deep emotional conviction of impending sorrow or calamity persisted and I could not banish it. Superficially, it was to the good that the pursuits, the trappings and lassoings I had envisaged were dispensed with—yet what had I instead? *Not* Denis. That was the trouble. It was only the curious shell of him I had. He was a wanling, almost a changeling—something that most horribly denied each trait and feature of the Denis I recalled, and of which the contemplation could but be agonizing.

None the less, as I say, this unexpected turn of events was a practical simplification. Presumably, Denis would "come quietly" and not have to be dragged home a prisoner. Goderich, when he arrived, would have nothing to do but go back with us again. And then. . . ?

"Are you tired?" I believe I asked once, "after all the—the camping-out. . . ?"

He regarded me queerly, head cocked, with the suspicious, quasi-intelligent incomprehension, the notion visited me dreadfully, of a parrot. "A—a little. Yes, a little. . . ."

That was all; but the manner if not the matter of the reply had remained vaguely hostile—and violently unsatisfactory. His tone held a deplorable sort of cunning, or a fancied cunning—as if, despite his sudden yielding, he still had an ace hidden somewhere in the pack, or thought he had.

What had prompted his surrender? Had he merely wearied of roughing it and craved the ordinary home comforts he had missed, now, for three weeks? Had his designs, whatever was their nature, been frustrated, or miscarried, so that at last he had had to give them up? Or had he, possibly, decided that my reinforcement by Goderich (of whose coming, apart from servants' gossip, he could have got wind in any case from the letter in the hall) would be too much for him and that he might as well cave in to me right away?

I must wait to find out all that, for the time was not propitious yet, I felt, for direct catechisings. Fortunately, perhaps, for that evening at any rate this question did not arise, as Denis professed himself so drowsy that, as soon as he had had his tea, and then a bath, he went to bed.

Of M. Vaignon, save for his startled apparition in the hall, I had seen nothing since lunch. I dined alone and, after a couple of pipes in the *petit salon*, was glad to get up to my room.

Denis and I, I reflected, had forgotten, or at least—perhaps on both sides semi-deliberately—omitted, to say good night to each other. I wondered whether he were yet awake, or (if his sleep were half as troubled as I feared likely in his father's case) what dreams would visit him.

Next day, I was in two minds about taking Denis with me to the station to meet Goderich, deciding finally against it. I did not think he would slip off again, and if he did it would only prove his capitulation no real capitulation after all. As to that, indeed, I still felt something disquietingly planned or spurious in it; but my misgivings did not include, now, any apprehensions of his renewed and literal bolting.

Nothing much had happened during the morning. M. Vaignon, encountering me just before lunch, congratulated me, with a deathly simper, on my improved *entente* with Denis and made no difficulties over lending me the car, which I was mightily relieved he did not propose to drive, this time, himself. Goderich would stay one night at the château, and tomorrow the three of us would return to England.

I pictured my friend's surprise when he learned of the fresh development. In a sense he would have had his journey for nothing, but I didn't think he would mind that. A wire yesterday evening might just have caught and stopped him, but, actually, Denis's unexpected "surrender" had put everything else out of my head, and I was selfishly glad, now, that it had.

At the station, I had still ten minutes to wait, and outside the yard entrance to the baggage-office I noticed a wagon drawn up, and a long box being unloaded from it and then carried in to the clerk. The wagon I could recognize as from the château, and the fellow awkwardly shouldering the box was, I was pretty sure, that same "Batiste" I had seen limping, with the bloodstained kerchief to his face, in the *basse cour* two days ago. As he climbed again into his seat, the *chef de gare* himself came out to confer for a few moments with him in an undertone.

But here at last was Goderich's train. It had scarcely clanked puffing to a standstill before he leaped out and clasped my hand in his.

"Well," he was saying, "it's rather like one's toothache fleeing on the dentist's doorstep. If I hadn't 'come for nothing,' as you are so kind as to suggest, you and your young jackanapes would probably still be at loggerheads."

We were approaching the château, and I wondered. Goderich's hearty vigour, his very tone of cheerful lightness, was a gust of health and hope from another world—and yet, I doubted, and was even, somehow, shocked.

"If we're *not* still at loggerheads, as it is," I remember answering. "You'll see for yourself presently."

We drove under the *porte-cochère*, and alighted. M. Vaignon was there to greet us, all politeness. A small, dim figure hung back, hugging the shadows.

"Hello, scallywag!" called Goderich. "Hi, come out of that!"

Denis moved forwards undecidedly. His face, again, horrified me by its hollow wanness.

" 'M . . ." Goderich commented. "Not altogether a walking advertisement of anything I must say. That's the deserts of being A.W.O.L. . . . Nineteen days adrift, eh? But we won't clap him in the glass-house this time, sergeant-major. . . ."

Once more, I gave a mental gasp. I did not know whether to admire or be scared out of my wits by Goderich's breeziness. Wasn't it, I misdoubted, a trifle overdone? It jolted me, I think, not so much through a fear of its effect on Denis as by appearing almost *too* temerarious a defiance of the evil gods.

But Denis did not seem to mind this "joshing." He even smiled faintly, as Goderich persevered with his hardy badinage, and ate, under the friendly bombardment, a reasonably good tea.

None the less, I could divine, beneath his fun-poking, that Goderich was concerned. When Denis had gone off, "to see the horses fed" he said, with Zizi, my friend's expression became grave.

"What do you make of this, Habgood?" he surprised me by inquiring.

"*I* . . . ? Why, I—I want *you* to tell *me!*"

"Of course. But first I'd be interested in your opinions, so far as you have any. Do you, for instance, really——" He broke off: "Wait a bit. Are we likely to be disturbed here? Our perfect host isn't liable to butt in, is he?"

"I shouldn't think so. He's completely haywire these days, and we probably won't see him again this evening."

"Suits me. . . . And if——"

But at this moment, to falsify my prophecy, M. Vaignon *did* "butt in," insisting upon "entertaining" us, with the most oddly vapid small talk, until and throughout dinner; and it was only when he had at length proffered his excuses and retired that I and Goderich could continue our discussion. Denis himself, as on the previous night, had gone early to his bed.

"Well," Goderich resumed, "what *is* your feeling, about the whole thing now? For example—and putting a conceivable crack-brained 'impersonation' out of it, as I think we may —do you actually believe that the pernicious loon we both knew down in Hampshire is the same Privache whose grave, you've said, you saw near here last week?"

"It—it certainly *sounds* nonsense," I replied.

" 'Nonsense'—yes, naturally it does. But even nonsense can be dynamic. In its proper realm, where its writ runs and it holds sway, it *isn't* nonsense. And it can, often, effectually intrude into a sphere beyond its own. It has become at least *mentally* real for Denis, and also, up to a point, for you. I just wanted to know how real."

"I tell you, I don't know. It simply doesn't add up."

"All right. It doesn't. If it *did*, for instance, this damned sally-dore could eventually be traced, and be run-in for something. But for what, exactly? In what terms could you prefer a charge? I'd hate to see you trying! The notion would be quite absurd—which just shows you that it *can't* 'add up' for us in any ordinary way. But the next obvious practical step anyhow is to get your boy as clear of it all as we can and pray that later he'll—well, respond to treatment."

"But what do *you* think, honestly? Is . . . ?" I faltered.

"I know what you're going to ask. Well, *is* it? Or again, *is* it? How can *I* tell? It was *there*, that precious gaby was, and it appeared to be more or less passably a man—and, for some revolting reason, it wore mittens. Also, it had an arm which acted up pretty unorthodoxly. . . . What I *don't* see is how a mere throttling, a semi-throttling, could have snuffed it out and kiboshed it, at all events temporarily, as it seems to have done. . . . No doubt, that rubbed in the fact that it wasn't too popular, and would be a deterrent to some extent, but. . . ."

Goderich, too, hesitated; then went on: "I don't fancy we can get much forrarder along those lines. It's easy enough to say the whole thing's farcical—and if you could *feel* that as well as say it, it would be fine. What about the 'poltergeist' noises? Do they still go on?"

"I was told so. I've not heard them here myself."

"And the 'haunted' room, where you're persuaded the original fee-faw-fum demised. How does that come into it? Did our host admit definitely that Privache No. 1 *had* died there?"

" 'Definitely'. . . ! No indeed. He's never said anything definite or straightforward. When I did as it were challenge him to deny that the—the first Privache had died where I felt he had, he just behaved quite weirdly, was abominably rude, and accused *me* of going mad. . . ."

For some while longer our talk continued without leading us to any more concrete conclusion than we had reached already—that our sole hope for Denis lay in getting him away immediately and that, when this was done, it would be only in the nick of time.

We had thought, Goderich and I, that we were bringing Denis home, and that morning we treated our precious freight as if no precaution for its safety could be excessive. Denis was, actually and in literal truth so worn and wasted that such an attitude would have been natural in any case, and I think we both felt that, unless the greatest care were exercised, he might as it were collapse in our hands or be blown away by a puff. His eyes were lustreless and his skin dry, and his manner held some ingredient I could not define, at once apathetic and expectant, or perhaps apprehensive.

The day had broken cloudily after, for me, a restless night. I had had dreams, but could not recall them clearly. Mostly, they had been of absurdities—of M. Vaignon addressing a meeting of puppets in the library, of Dorlot roller-skating somewhere overhead, and even of the ridiculous scarecrow, shifting from field to field in a continued march towards the house—but their persisting savour was oppressive, and I had woken from them with nerves jangled.

Our train was to leave Foant at about ten-thirty, and we had risen, we realised, rather unnecessarily early. Denis, glancing at us distraitly from under lowered brows, ate an extremely sketchy breakfast. Once, he appeared lost in a kind of reverie, and then, arousing from it with a start, upset his chocolate bowl. The slight mishap caused him to open his mouth, aghastly, in an unuttered scream.

This time, we wouldn't need our host's car. I had arranged, yesterday, for a taxi to come out for us from Foant, and now I prayed it might be punctual. Our luggage was stacked in the hall; I had tipped the servants, and M. Vaignon, dressing-gowned, had made a grisly mountebank descent to say goodbye. Bowing, and stiffly shaking hands, he muttered something else that sounded like: ". . . if it will let you. . . ."

At last the three of us drove off. For a while, my spirits lightened and I breathed more freely.

"Are you all right?" I asked Denis.

"Oh yes. . . ."

He was next me and facing Goderich, gazing dreamily—or raptly—out of the window. His expression was remote, as though he were attending to something we could not see, or not appreciate. His hair, I noticed, had grown long and wanted cutting.

Suddenly, from under his seat, issued a low bark. Zizi! How he had managed it I did not know, but the little creature must have leaped in after Denis, and we should now have to ask the station-master to restore him to his owner.

This, on alighting from the taxi, we did, and presently the train drew in. Denis, for a second or two as Goderich and I were about to board it, was not to be found, and my heart froze. But next moment he came scurrying from the direction of the *consigne* and clambered in with us just in time.

I was so thankful at retrieving him! A passion of yearning sympathy for my poor darling rose in me, and I pressed his arm. The train gathered speed and I remember sighing in relief and thinking that every mile now was a mile further towards his safety. Actually, I had hardly expected or quite dared to hope we *would* ever do it—ever get away. I had feared, all the while, that something—though I couldn't guess how or what—would happen or put out a hand to halt us or detain us—some sort of accident or hitch—and. . . .

But my satisfaction ebbed, and died. Denis's manner suddenly alarmed me. He was distressed, I could not tell why. "The—the scare——" He seemed to be trying, unsuccessfully, to say something; then, changing to French, at length got out: ". . . *l'épouvantail, c'est dans*. . . ." He paused, and added, with an urgency I could not understand, the one word: "Zizi. . . ."

Sure enough, to my annoyed confusion, the dog was there, and with us still, whether or not with Denis's abetting I did not know. But it was not the dog's presence I was bothered over: it was the curious looks and bearing of my boy.

Another train, which must be an express, was overtaking us, coming up rapidly upon a parallel track. Our own train, as if inspired to a race, increased its speed, and the express gained on us less swiftly. Zizi had burst in upon us, at first delightedly, from the corridor, wagging his tail, but now appeared strangely subdued. With a short bark of half-hearted challenge he slunk cowering under the seat, by Denis.

"What *is* it, Denis? What's the matter?" I implored.

Goderich had pulled out a brandy flask and held it to Denis's lips. They moved slowly and bewilderedly. "*L'épouvantail*. . . . The—the scarecrow . . . *c'est*. . . ."

Suddenly he broke from us, moaning, and dashed into the corridor. Both I and Goderich had grabbed at him, ineffectually. The dog, as though torn between its fear and a kind of loyalty, had emerged from under the seat and stood whimpering in the doorway.

Thrusting it aside with my boot, I followed Denis. The express was quickly overhauling us. I could just see, at the moment, the front of its locomotive showing level with the corridor's end, then creeping foot by foot along our windows.

"Denis, Denis!" I repeated. "What *is* it? What are you *doing*?"

He was hunched oddly, staring out at the other train with a quite indescribable look of terror on his face. His eyes were round with fright and his body was pressed desperately against the corridor's inner wall as if, despite his fascinated interest, he were trying to get as far from the pursuing coaches as he could.

What followed has an *outré* horror and grotesqueness which puts such a strain on ordinary credence that even I who witnessed it still find it hard if not impossible at times to reconcile with, or accept as, "literal" truth. I cannot, in any way, explain it, but I believe, now, that something, then, went hideously wrong— went wrong from Denis's and Raoul's point of view, I mean— and that whatever sort of ghastly schemes and machinations may have been afoot were, at the last moment, bungled. What I did see, or what at all events I seemed to see, was the result, I feel, of some bizarre and odious miscarriage. . . .

I had caught Denis's arm, and shook it, but he paid no attention to me. Two men, on the farther side of him, stuck curious heads out of their compartment, and gaped foolishly at us. Behind me, squeezed up in the narrow passage, Goderich was shouting over my shoulder, above the uproar of the trains: "Come on, young man, snap out of it! Come back!" His voice was cool, but he added, in my ear: "For heaven's sake get hold of him somehow!"

Denis had wedged himself against the jamb of a half-open door, and it was now, as I was struggling, in the cramped space, to wrest him from it, that our own pace abruptly slackened, so that the express began to flash by our windows at a rush. I learned later that it was then that Goderich had pulled the communication cord. Meanwhile I still could not drag Denis free. I was aware that he was in some awful danger but tugged at him in vain. As in a nightmare, I strained till the sweat stood on my forehead, praying that the dream would break.

It never did, or has. For an instant I had looked out of the window. The guard's van of the express was just passing us. Something, a long box like a coffin, cocked lewdly up and protruded slowly from it, flew out of it towards us, and crashed against us. The corridor was littered with shivered glass.

The train had stopped with a violent jolt. People were running along the track, and already I caught, from somewhere, amazed exclamations: "*Un épouvantail.* . . ! It was, in that box there, solely a scarecrow. . . !"

I turned again to Denis, thinking I heard his call. "Zizi . . ." I fancied he had said. But what had happened to the dog I did not, then or later, know or care.

My boy's face was seamed and wizened as that of an old man, and the starkest terror was graven on it. His body now was quite limp in my hands.

Goderich and I carried him back to the compartment and laid him on a seat, and it was then I saw that, before his last cry, his hair, which had changed to elf-locks, had gone white.

Death Waters

FRANK BELKNAP LONG

We were seated in the pilot house of the *Habakkuk*, a queer little tug which carries daily passengers from New York steamers south along the coast of Honduras, from Trujillo to the Carataska lagoon. We were a chatty, odd group. Shabby promoters elbowed enthusiastic young naturalists (botanists from Olanchito, and entomologists from beyond Jamalteca) and tired, disillusioned surveyors from the Plateau. The air was thick with unwholesome bluish smoke from fantastic pipes, which formed curious nimbuses about the heads of the older men. No one had a reputation to lose, and conversation was genial and unaffected.

One of the veterans stood in the centre of the cabin and pounded with his fists upon a small wooden table. His face was the colour of ripe corn, and from time to time he nodded at his companion. His companion did not return his salutations. The face of his companion was covered; and he lay upon the floor in an oblong box six feet long. No word of complaint issued from the box, and yet, whenever the veteran brought his eyes to bear upon the fastened lid, tears of pity ran rapidly down his cheeks and dampened his reddish beard. But he acknowledged to himself that the tears were blatantly sentimental, and not quite in good taste.

Everyone else in the cabin ignored the existence of the man in the box—perhaps intentionally. A man's popularity depends largely upon his attitude. The attitude of the man in the box was not pleasing, since he had been dead for precisely four days. The veteran choked out his words fiercely between ominous coughs.

"My dear friends, you must be sensible of my embarrassment. It is my opinion that I am not an orator, and it is impossible for me to make you understand. I can explain, but you will never understand. There were millions of them, and they came after *him*. They attacked me only when I defended him. But it was hard—to see him collapse and turn black. The skin on his face shrivelled up before he could speak. He never left me a last word. It is very hard—when one is a devoted friend! And yet his perversity was absurd. He brought it upon himself. I warned him. 'The man has a warm temper,' I said. 'You must be careful. You must humour him. It is not good to provoke a man without

69

morality, without standards, without taste.' A little thing would have been sufficient, a small compromise—but Byrne lacked a sense of humour. He paid horribly. He died on his feet, with the nasty things stabbing him, and he never emitted a shriek—only a gurgling sob."

The veteran looked reproachfully at the six-foot box, and the ceiling.

"I don't blame you for thinking me queer—but how do you explain this?—and this?" he added, rolling up his sleeve and baring a scrawny brown arm.

We pressed forward and surrounded him. We were eager and amused, and a sleepy Indian in the corner ran his fingers through his fragile black beard, and tittered.

The veteran's arm was covered with tiny yellow scars. The skin had evidently been punctured repeatedly by some pin-like instrument. Each scar was surrounded by a miniature halo of inflamed tissue.

"Can any of you explain 'em?" he asked.

He drummed on the taut skin. He was a tired, nervous little man, with faded blue eyes and eyebrows that met above the arch of his nose. He had an amusing habit of screwing up the corners of his mouth whenever he spoke.

One of the young men took him solemnly aside and whispered something into his ear. The man with the punctured arm laughed. "Righto!" he said. The young man closed his eyes, and shuddered. "You—you shouldn't be alive." The youth had great difficulty in getting his lips to shape the words properly. "It isn't reasonable you know! One bite is nearly always fatal, and you —you have dozens of 'em."

"Precisely!" Our man of the scars screwed up his lips and looked piercingly at us all. Some faces fell or blanched before him, but most of the young men returned a questioning gaze. "You know that the culebra de sangre is more certain than the taboba, more deadly than the rattler, more vicious than the corali. Well, I've been bitten ten times by culebras, five times by rattlers and thrice by our innocent little friend, the boba.

"I took great pains to verify these facts by studying the wounds, for each snake inflicts a slightly different one. Then how is it that I am still alive? My dear friends, you must believe me when I say that I do not know. Perhaps the poisons neutralized each other. Perhaps the venom of culebra de sangre is an antidote for that of the rattler, or vice versa. But it is enough that I stand here and talk to you. It is enough that I find within me the strength of youth—but my heart is dead."

His last comment seemed melodramatic and unnecessary, and we suddenly realized that the veteran was not an artist. He lacked a sense of dramatic values. We turned wearily aside, and puffed

70

vigorously on our long pipes. It is difficult to forgive these little defects of technique.

The veteran seemed sufficiently conscious of our reproach. But he kept right on, and his voice was low and muffled, and it was difficult to follow the turnings and twistings of his disconcerting narrative. I remember distinctly that he bored us at first, and spoke at great length about things that did not interest us at all, but suddenly his voice became gritty, like a raucous blundering of an amateur with a viol, and we pressed closer about him.

"I would have you bear this constantly in mind: We were alone in the centre of that lake, with no human being except a huge black savage within a radius of ten miles. It was risky business, of course, but Byrne was devilishly set on making a chemical analysis of the water just above the source of our spring.

"He was amazingly enthusiastic. I didn't care to parade my emotions in the presence of the black man, and I longed to subdue the glitter in Byrne's eye. Enthusiasm grates upon a savage, and I could see that the black was decidedly piqued. Byrne stood up in the stern, and raved. I endeavoured to make him sit down. From a tone of suppressed excitement his voice rose to a shout. 'It's the finest water in Honduras. There's a fortune in it—it means——'

"I cut him short with a cold, reproachful look that must have hurt him. He winced under it, and sat down. I was level-headed enough to avoid unnecessary enthusiasm.

"Well, there we were, two old men who had come all the way from New York for the privilege of sitting in the sun in the centre of a black miasmal lake, and examining water that would have shocked a professional scavenger. But Byrne was unusually shrewd in a detestable, business-like way and he knew very well that the value of water doesn't reside in its taste. He had carefully pointed out to me that whenever water is taken from the centre of a lake directly over a well it can be bottled and sold under attractive labels without the slightest risk. I admired Byrne's sagacity, but I didn't like the way the cannibal in the front was looking at the sky. I don't mean to suggest that he actually was a cannibal or anything monstrous or abnormal, but I distrusted his damnable mannerisms.

"He sat hunched in the bow, with his back towards me, with his hands on his knees and his eyes turned towards the shore. He was naked to the waist, and his dark, oily skin glistened with perspiration. There was something tremendously impressive about the rigidity of his animal-like body, and I didn't like the lethal growth of crisp black hair on his chest and arms. The upper portion of his body was hideously tattooed.

"I wish I could make you perceive the deadly horror of the man. I couldn't look at him without an inevitable shudder, and I felt that I could never really know him, never break through

71

his crust of reserve, never fathom the murky depths of his abominable soul. I knew that he had a soul, but every decent instinct in me revolted at the thought of coming into contact with it. And yet I realized with jubilation that the soul of the monster was buried very deep, and that it would scarcely show itself upon slight provocation. And we had done nothing to call it forth; we had acted reasonably decent.

"But Byrne lacked tact. He wasn't properly schooled in flattery and the polite usages of rational society. He somehow got the queer notion into his head that the water should be tasted then and there. He was naturally averse to tasting it himself, and he knew that I couldn't stomach spring water of any sort. But he had a weird idea that perhaps the water contained a septic poison, and he was determined to settle his doubts on the spot.

"He scooped up a cupful of the detestable stuff and carried it to his nose. Then he gave it to me to smell. I was properly horrified. The water was yellowish and alive with animalcules—but the horror of it did not reside in its appearance. Hot shame flushed scarlet over Byrne's face. I was brought sharply and agonizingly to a sense of spiritual guilt. 'We can't bottle that. It wouldn't be sportsmanship; it wouldn't be——'

" 'Of course we can bottle it. People like that sort of thing. The smell will be a splendid advertising asset. Who ever heard of medicinal spring water without an excessive smell? It is a great feather in our cap. Didn't you suppose that a smell was absolutely necessary?'

" 'But——'

" 'Let us have no "buts." That water has made our fortune. It is only necessary now to discover its taste."

"He laughed and pointed to the black man in the bow. I shook my head. But what can you do when a man is determined? And, after all, why should I defend a savage? I simply sat and stared while Byrne handed the cup to our black companion. The black sat up very stiff and straight, and a puzzled, hurt expression crept into his dark eyes. He looked fixedly at Byrne and at the cup, and then he looked away towards the sky. The muscles in his face began to contract—horribly. I didn't like it, and I motioned to Byrne to withdraw the cup.

"But Byrne was determined that the black should drink. The stubbornness of a northern man in equatorial latitudes is often shocking. I have always avoided that pose, but Byrne never failed to do the conventional thing under given circumstances.

"He virtually bifurcated the savage with his eyes, and did it without a trace of condescension. 'I'm not going to sit here and hold this! I want you to taste the water and tell me precisely what you think of it. Tell me whether you like the way it tastes, and after you have tasted it, if you feel somewhat out of sorts and a bit dizzy it is only necessary for you to describe your feelings. I don't want to force it upon you, but you can't sit there and refuse to take part in this—er—experiment!'

"The black removed his eyes from the sky and gazed scornfully into Byrne's face. 'Na. I don't want this water. I didn't come out here to drink water.'

"Perhaps you have never seen the clash of two racially different wills, each as set and as primitive and as humourless as the other. A silent contest went on between Byrne and that black imp, and the latter's face kept getting more sinister and hostile; and I watched the muscles contracting and the eyes narrowing, and I began to feel sorry for Byrne.

"But even I hadn't fathomed Byrne's power of will. He dominated that savage through sheer psychic superiority. The black man didn't cower, but you could see that he knew he was fighting against fate.

"He knew that he had to drink the water; the fact had been settled when Byrne had first extended the cup, and his rebellion was pure resentment at the cruelty of Byrne in forcing the water upon him. I shall never forget the way he seized the cup and drained off the water. It was sickening to watch his teeth chatter and his eyes bulge as the water slid between his swollen lips. Great spasms seemed to run up and down his back, and I fancied that I could discern a velvety play of rebellious muscles throughout the whole length of his perspiring torso. Then he handed the cup back without a word, and began to look again at the sky.

"Byrne waited for a moment or two, and then he commenced to question the black in a way which I did not think very tactful. But Byrne imagined that his spiritual supremacy had been firmly established. I could have pointed out to him—but I cry over spilt milk. I can see Byrne now, knee-deep in questions, with his eyes scintillating and his cheeks flushing red. 'I made you drink that water because I wanted to know. It is very important that I should know. Have you ever tasted a bad egg? Did it taste like that? Did it have a salty flavour and did it burn you when you swallowed it?'

"The black sat immobile and refused to answer. There is no understanding the psychology of a black man in the centre of a black lake. I felt that the perversity of nature had entered into the wretch, and I urged Byrne to ease up. But Byrne kept right on, and then finally—it happened.

"The black stood up in the boat and shrieked—and shrieked again. You cannot imagine the unearthly bestiality of the cries that proceeded out of his revolting throat. They were not human cries at all, and they might have come from a gorilla under torture. I could only sit and stare and listen, and I became as flabby as an arachnid on stilts. I felt at that moment nothing but unutterable fright, mixed with contempt for Byrne and his deliberate tempting of—well, not fate exactly, but the inexcusable phenomena of cannibalistic hysteria. I longed to get up, and shriek louder than the savage, in order to humiliate and shame him into silence.

"I thought at first, as the screams went echoing across the lake, that the black would upset the canoe. He was standing in the bow and swaying from side to side, and with every lurch the canoe would ship some water. One cry followed another in maddening succession, and each cry was more sinister and virulent and un-natural, and I observed that the devil's body was drawn up as taut as an electric wire.

"Then Byrne began to tug at his shoulders in a frantic effort to make him sit down. It was a hideous sight to see them strugg-ling and swaying in the bow, and I even began to pity the black. Byrne hung on viciously, and I suddenly became aware that he was pommelling his antagonist fiercely on the back and under the arms. 'Sit down, or you'll wreck us! Good heavens! To create such a rumpus—and for a triviality!'

"The canoe was filling rapidly, and I expected her to capsize at any moment. I didn't relish the thought of swimming through a noisome cesspool, and I glared incontinently at Byrne. Poor chap! Had I known, I should have been more tolerant. Byrne deserved censure, but he paid—paid horribly.

"The black devil sat down quite suddenly and looked at the sky. All of his rebellion seemed to leave him. There was a genial, almost enthusiastic expression upon his loathsome face. He leered beneficently and patted Byrne on the shoulder. His familiarity shocked me, and I could see that it annoyed Byrne. The black's voice was peculiarly calm.

" 'I didn't mean anything, now. It's just the weather, I guess. I liked the water. I can't see why you shouldn't bottle it, and sell it. It's good water. I have often wondered why no one ever thought of bottling it before. The people who come out here are rather stupid, I guess.'

"Byrne looked at me rather sheepishly. The savage possessed intelligence and taste. His English was reasonably correct, and his manners were those of a gentleman. He had indeed acted out-landishly, and given us good reason to distrust him; but Byrne's tactics had been scurrilous, and deserving of rebuke.

"Byrne had sense enough to acknowledge his error. He grumbled a bit, but in conciliatory mood, and he asked the black to row to shore with a geniality that I thought admirable.

"Byrne put his hand over the side and let it trail in the water. I lit a cigarette and watched the greenish tide swirl and eddy beneath us. It was some time before I glimpsed the first of the little obscenities.

'I tried to warn Byrne, but he suddenly drew his hand up with a shriek and I knew that he would understand. 'Something bit me!' he said. I fancied that the black scowled and bent lower over his oars.

" 'Look at the water,' I replied. Byrne dropped his eyes, rather reluctantly, I thought. Then he blanched. 'Snakes—water snakes. Good Lord! Water snakes!' He repeated it again and again. 'Water snakes. There are thousands! Water snakes!'

" 'These are quite harmless. But I never saw anything like this before!' And I was indeed shocked. Imagine an unexpected up-heaving of a million nasty little pink river snakes, from dank depths and without rhyme or reason. They swam about the boat, and stuck their ugly little heads in the air, and hissed and shot out hideous tongues. I leaned over the boat and looked down into the greenish water. The river was alive with myriads of sway-ing pink bodies, which writhed in volatile contortions, and made the water foam and bubble. Then I saw that several had coiled themselves over the side of the canoe and were dropping down inside. I felt instinctively that the black devil had something to do with it.

"Such indignities were unthinkable. I stood up in the boat, and stormed. The black lifted his sleepy eyes and grinned broadly. But I saw that he was making directly for the shore. The snakes were crawling all about the boat, and they were attacking Byrne's legs, and their hissing sickened me. But I knew the species—a harmless and pretentious one. Still, the thought of taking them up by the tails and throwing them overboard was repugnant to me. And yet I knew that the noisome things horrified Byrne. He shrieked with the pain of their aggressive little bites and swore immoderately. When I assured him that they were innocuous he eyed me reproachfully and continued to mash them with the heels of his boots. He ground their loathsome heads into a pulp, and blood ran out of their tiny mouths and fairly flooded the bottom of the boat. But more kept dropping over the sides and Byrne had his hands full. And the black rowed fiercely towards the shore and said nothing. But he smiled, which made me long to strangle him. But I didn't care to offend him, for his methods of retaliation were apt to be unsavoury.

"We finally reached the shore. Byrne jumped out with a shout and waded through several feet of black, sluggish mud. Then he turned about on the shore and looked back over the water. The whole surface was covered with swimming pink bodies, and they crisscrossed, and interlaced on the top of the tides, and when the lurid sunlight fell upon them they resembled unctuous charnel worms seething and boiling in some colossal vat.

"I got out somehow and joined Byrne. We were furious when we saw the black push off and make for the opposite shore. Byrne was upset and nearly delirious, and he assured me that the snakes were poisonous. 'Don't be a fool,' I said. 'None of the water snakes hereabouts are poisonous. If you had any sense——'

" 'But why should they have attacked me? They crawled up and bit me. Why should they have done that? They were scions of Satan. That black ensorceled them! He called them, and they came.'

"I knew that Byrne was developing a monomania, and I sought to divert him. 'You have nothing to fear. Had we rattlers or culebras de sangre to deal with, but water snakes—bah!'

"Then I saw that the black was standing up in the canoe and waving his arms and shrieking exultantly. I turned about and looked up towards the crest of the hill in back of us. It was a savage hill and it rose wild and bleak before us, and over the crest of it there poured an army of slithering things—and it is impossible for me to describe them in detail.

"I didn't want Byrne to turn about. I sought to keep him interested in the lake, and in the black devil who was standing up in the canoe and shouting. I pointed out to him that the black had made himself ridiculous, and I slapped him soundly on the back and we congratulated each other on our superiority.

"But eventually I had to face them—the things that were crawling upon us from over the sombre grey crest of the hill. I turned and I looked at the deep blue sky and the great clouds rolling over the summit, and then my eyes went a little lower, and I saw them again, and knew that they were crawling slowly towards us and that there was no avoiding them.

"And I gently took Byrne by the arm, and turned him about and pointed silently. There were tears in my eyes, and a curious heaviness in my legs and arms. But Byrne bore it like a gentleman. He didn't even express surprise, although I could clearly perceive that his soul had been mortally wounded, and was sick unto death. And I saw shame and a monstrous fear staring at me out of Byrne's bloodshot eyes. And I pitied Byrne, but I knew what we had to do.

"The day was drawing to a close, amidst lovely earth-mists, which hung over the hill; and blue veils made the water gorgeous and hid the canoe and the gesticulating savage. I longed to sit calmly down there by the water, and to dream, but I knew that we had something to do. Near the edge of the water we found a gleaming yellow growth of shrubs and of stout vegetation, and we made stout clubs and strong cutting whips. And the army of reptiles continued to advance, and they filled me with a sense of infinite sadness, and regret and pity for Byrne.

"We stood very still and waited; and the mass of seething corruption rolled down the hill until it reached the level rocky lake shore, and then it oozed obnoxiously towards us. And we cried out when we counted the numbers of rattlers and culebras and bobas, but when we saw the other snakes we did not cry at all, for the centres of speech froze up in us, and we were very unhappy.

"My dear friends, you cannot imagine, you cannot conceive of our unhappiness. There were charnel reptiles with green, flattened heads and glazed eyes, which I did not attempt to identify, and there were legions of horned lizards, with blistered black tongues, and little venomous toads that hopped nervously about,

76

and made odd, weird noises in their throats; and we knew that they were lethal, and to be avoided.

"But we met them face to face, and Byrne fought with genuine nobility. But the odds were overwhelming, and I saw him go down, panting, suffocated, annihilated. They crawled up his legs, and they bit him in the back and sides, and on the face, and I saw his face blacken before my eyes. I saw his lips writhe back from his teeth, and his eyes glaze, and the skin on his face pucker and shrivel.

"And I fought to keep them from him, and my club was never idle. I flattened innumerable heads that were round, and I rounded heads that were flat, and I made sickening crimson pellets out of quivering gelatinous tissue.

"My dear friends, they went away at last, and left him there. And the blue calm of the hills seemed inexplicable under the circumstances, but I was thankful for the coolness and quiet, and the deepening shadows. I sat down with peace in my soul, and waited. I looked at the tiny punctures on my arms, and I smiled. I was reasonably happy.

"But my dear friends, I did not die. The realization that I was not to die amazed me. It was several hours before I could be certain, and then I did a shocking thing. I took my beard firmly between my two hands and pulled out the hair in great tufts. The pain sobered me.

"I tramped for two days with the body. It was the decent, the proper thing to do. I waited in Trujillo for the fashioning of the coffin, and I personally supervised its construction. I wanted everything done properly, in the grand manner. I have very few regrets—but my soul is dead!"

There was an infinite misery in the veteran's eye. His voice grew raucous, and he stopped talking. We noticed that he shivered a little as he turned up his collar and went out through the cabin door into a night of stars. We pressed our faces against the glass of the one window and saw him standing before the rail, with the rain and moonlight glistening upon his beard, and the salt spray striking against his incredibly chastened face.

An Invitation to the Hunt

GEORGE HITCHCOCK

His first impulse upon receiving it had been to throw it into the fire. They did not travel in the same social set and he felt it presumptuous of them, on the basis of a few words exchanged in the shopping centre and an occasional chance meeting on the links, to include him in their plans. Of course, he had often seen them—moving behind the high iron grillwork fence that surrounded their estates, the women in pastel tea-gowns serving martinis beneath the striped lawn umbrellas and the men suave and bronzed in dinner jackets or sailing togs—but it had always been as an outsider, almost as a Peeping Tom.

"The most charitable interpretation," he told Emily, "would be to assume that it is a case of mistaken identity."

"But how could it be?" his wife answered, holding the envelope in her slender reddened fingers. "There's only one Fred Perkins in Marine Gardens and the house number is perfectly accurate."

"But there's no earthly reason for it. Why *me* of all people?"

"I should think," said Emily, helping him on with his coat and fitting the two sandwiches neatly wrapped in aluminium foil into his pocket, "that you would be delighted. It's a real step upward for you. You've often enough complained of our lack of social contacts since we moved out of the city."

"It's fantastic," Perkins said, "and of course I'm not going," and he ran out of his one-story shingled California ranch cottage to join the car pool which waited for him at the kerb.

All the way to the city, like a dog with a troublesome bone, he worried and teased at the same seemingly insoluble problem: how had he attracted their notice? What was there in his appearance or manner which had set him apart from all the rest? There had been, of course, that day the younger ones had come in off the bay on their racing cutter, when by pure chance (as it now seemed) he had been the one man on the pier within reach of the forward mooring line. He recalled the moment with satisfaction—the tanned, blonde girl leaning out from the bowspirit, with a coil of manila in her capable hand. "Catch!" she had cried, and at the same instant spun the looping rope towards him through the air. He had caught it deftly and snubbed it about the bitt, easing the cutter's forward motion. "Thanks!" she had called across the narrowing strip of blue water, but there had been no sign of recognition in her eyes, nor had she, when a moment later the yacht was securely tied to the wharf, invited

78

him aboard or even acknowledged his continuing presence on the pier. No, that could hardly have been the moment he sought.

Once at the Agency and there bedded down in a day of invoices, he tried to put the problem behind him, but it would not rest. At last, victim of a fretful pervasive anxiety which ultimately made concentration impossible, he left his desk and made his way to the hall telephone (years ago a written reproof from Henderson had left him forever scrupulous about using the Agency phone for private business) where he deposited a dime and rang his golf partner, Bianchi.

They met for lunch at a quiet restaurant on Maiden Lane. Bianchi was a young man recently out of law school and still impressed by the improbable glitter of society. This will give him a thrill, Perkins thought, he's a second generation Italian and it isn't likely that he's ever laid eyes on one of those.

"The problem is," he said aloud, "that I'm not sure why they invited me. I hardly know them. At the same time I don't want to do anything that might be construed as—well—as——"

"Defiance?" Bianchi supplied.

"Perhaps. Or call it unnecessary rudeness. We can't ignore their influence."

"Well, first let's have a look at it," Bianchi said, finishing his vermouth. "Do you have it with you?"

"Of course."

"Well, let's see it."

Poor Bianchi! It was obvious that he was dying for an invitation himself and just as obvious from his slurred, uncultivated English and his skin acne that he would never receive one. Perkins took the envelope from his notecase and extracted the stiff silver-edged card which he lay face up on the table.

"It's engraved," he pointed out.

"They always are," Bianchi said, putting on his shell-rimmed reading glasses, "but that doesn't prove a thing. They aren't the real article without the watermark." He held the envelope up against the table lamp hoping, Perkins imagined, that the whole thing would prove fraudulent.

"It's there," he admitted, "by God, it's there." And Perkins detected a note of grudging respect in his voice as he pointed out the two lions rampant and the neatly quartered shield. "It's the real McCoy and no mistake."

"But what do I do now?" Perkins asked with a hint of irritation.

"First let's see the details," Bianchi studied the engraved Old English script:

The pleasure of your company at the hunt
is requested
on August sixteenth of this year.

R.S.V.P.   *Appropriate attire ob.*

"The 'ob.,' " he explained, "is for 'obligatory'."

"I know that."

"Well?"

"The problem is," Perkins said in an unnecessarily loud voice, "that I have no intention of going."

He was aware that Bianchi was staring at him incredulously, but this merely strengthened his own stubbornness.

"It's an imposition. I don't know them and it happens I have other plans for the sixteenth."

"All right, all right," Bianchi said soothingly, "no need to shout. I can hear you perfectly well."

With a flush of embarrassment, Perkins looked about the restaurant and caught the reproving gaze of the waiters. Obviously he had become emotionally involved in his predicament to the extent of losing control; he hastily reinserted the invitation in its envelope and returned it to his notecase. Bianchi had arisen and was folding his napkin.

"Do as you like," he said, "but I know a dozen men around town who would give their right arm for that invitation."

"But I don't hunt!"

"You can always learn," Bianchi said coldly and, signalling for the waiter, paid his bill and left.

Meanwhile, word of the invitation had apparently got round the Agency, for Perkins noticed that he was treated with new interest and concern. Miss Nethersole, the senior librarian, accosted him by the water-cooler in deep thrushlike tones.

"I'm so thrilled for you, Mr. Perkins! There's no one else in the whole office who deserves it more."

"That's very sweet of you," he answered, attempting to hide his embarrassment by bending over the tap, "but the truth is, I'm not going."

"Not going?" The rich pearshaped tones (the product of innumerable diction lessons) broke into a cascade of rippling laughter. "How can you say that with a straight face? Have you seen the rotogravure section?"

"No," Perkins said shortly.

"It's all there. The guests, the caterers, even a map of the course. I should give anything to be invited!"

No doubt you would, Perkins thought, looking at her square, masculine, breastless figure, it's just the sort of sport which would entertain you, but aloud he merely said, "I have other commitments," and went back to his desk.

After lunch he found the rotogravure section stuck under the blotter on his desk. Aware that every eye in the office was secretly on him, he did not dare unfold it, but stuck it into his coat pocket and only later, after he had risen casually and strolled down the long row of desks to the men's room, did he in the privacy of a locked cubicle and with trembling hands spread it out on his knees. Miss Nethersole had been right: the guest list was truly staggering. It filled three columns in six point type; titles gleamed like diamonds in the newsprint; there were generals, statesmen, manufacturers and university presidents; editors of great magazines, movie queens, and polar explorers; broadcasters, regents, prize-winning novelists—but Perkins could not begin to digest the list. His eyes ferreted among the jumbled syllables and at last, with a little catch of delight, he came upon the one he had unconsciously sought: *Mr. Fred Perkins.* That was all, no identification, no Ll.D. or Pres. Untd. Etc. Corp. He read his own name over four times and then neatly folded the paper and put it back into his pocket.

"Well," he said with a thin-lipped smile, "I'm not going and that's that."

But apparently Emily, too, had seen the paper.

"The phone has been ringing all day," she informed him as soon as he entered the house and deposited his briefcase on the cane-bottomed chair by the TV set. "Of course, everyone is furiously envious, but they don't dare admit it, so I've been receiving nothing but congratulations."

She helped him off with his coat.

"Come into the dining-room," she said mysteriously. "I've a little surprise for you." The telephone rang. "No, wait, you mustn't go in without me. It will only be a minute."

He stood uneasily shifting from one foot to the other until she returned.

"It was the Corrigans," she announced. "Beth wants us to come to a little dinner party on the seventeenth. Naturally," she added, "the date isn't accidental. They expect to pump you for all the details before anyone else in the subdivision hears about it. Now come on——" and like a happy child on Christmas morning she took his hand and led him into the dining-room.

Perkins followed her with mumbled protestations.

"Isn't it gorgeous?"

There, spread out on the mahogany table (not yet fully paid for) were a pair of tan whipcord breeches, a tattersall vest, and a bright pink coat with brass buttons. In the centre of the table where the floral piece usually stood was a gleaming pair of boots.

"And here's the stock," she said, waving a bright bit of yellow silk under his eyes. "You can wear one of my stickpins, the one with the onyx in the jade setting I think would be best. And I've ordered a riding crop with a silver handle; it's to be delivered tomorrow."

"You're taking a great deal for granted," Perkins said. He picked up the boots and felt the soft, pliable waxed leather. "They must be very expensive. Where did you get the money for them?"

Emily laughed. "They're on time, silly; we have twelve months to pay."

"I'll look ridiculous in that coat."

"No, you won't. You're a very handsome man and I've always said you'd cut a fine figure anywhere."

"Well," said Perkins hesitantly, "I suppose we can send them back if I decide not to go."

After dinner Bianchi drove by in his old Studebaker and obviously a bit fuzzy from too many cocktails. Emily opened the door for him.

"Fred is in the bedroom trying on his new hunting outfit," she said. "He'll be out in a moment."

"Who is it?" Perkins shouted, and when she answered he hastily took off the pink coat (which was a bit tight under the arms anyway) and slipped on his smoking-jacket. He remembered the scene in the restaurant and felt ashamed to let Bianchi see that his resolution was wavering.

"Look, Fred," Bianchi said when they were seated in the living-room over their Old Fashioneds, "I hope you've finally changed your mind—about——" He glanced at Emily to see how much she knew of the invitation.

"Go ahead. I've told her everything," Perkins said.

"Well, you can certainly decline if you feel strongly about it," said Bianchi in his best legal manner, "but I don't advise it. If they once get the idea you're snubbing them, they can make things pretty unpleasant for you—and in more ways than one."

"But this is ridiculous!" Emily interrupted. "He's not going to decline. Are you, darling?"

"Well," Perkins said.

She caught the indecision in his voice and went on vehemently, "This is the first social recognition you've ever had, Fred; you can't think of declining. Think what it will mean for the children! In a few years they'll be ready for college. And you know what that means. And do you seriously plan to remain in this house for the rest of your life?"

"There's nothing wrong with this house," Perkins said defensively, reflecting that the house was not yet paid for, but already Emily was finding fault with it.

"Suppose the invitation *was* a mistake," Emily continued. "I'm not saying that it was, but suppose it just for a minute. Is that any the less reason why you shouldn't accept?"

"But I don't like hunting," Perkins interjected weakly. "And I'll look ridiculous on a horse."

"No more ridiculous than ninety per cent of the other guests. Do you suppose Senator Gorman will exactly look like a centaur? And what about your boss, Mr. Henderson? He's certainly no polo player."

"Is *he* going?" Perkins asked in surprise.

"He certainly is. If you had paid the slightest attention to the guest list you would have noticed it."

"All right, all right," Perkins said, "then I'll go."

"I think that's the wisest course," said Bianchi with a slightly blurry attempt at the judicial manner.

He wrote his acceptance that evening, in pen and ink on a plain stiff card with untinted edges.

"It's all right for them to use silvered edges," Emily pointed out, "but they're apt to think it shows too much swank if you do." She telephoned a messenger service, explaining, "It's not the sort of thing you deliver by mail"—and the next morning a uniformed messenger dropped his acceptance off at the gatekeeper's lodge.

The ensuing week passed swiftly. Emily fitted the pink coat and the tan breeches, marked them with chalk and sent them out for alterations. The yellow stock, she decided, would not do after all—"A bit too flashy," she observed—so it was replaced by one in conservative cream. The alteration necessitated a change in stickpin and cuff links to simple ones of hammered silver which she selected in the village. The expense was ruinous, but she overrode his objections. "So much depends upon your making a good impression, and after all, if it goes well, you'll be invited again and can always use the same clothes. And the cuff links will be nice with a dinner jacket," she added as an afterthought.

At the Agency he found that he basked in a new glow of respect. On Monday Mr. Presby, the office manager, suggested that he might be more comfortable at a desk nearer the window.

"Of course, with air-conditioning it doesn't make as much difference as it did in the old days, but still there's a bit of a view, and it helps break the monotony."

Perkins thanked him for this thoughtfulness.

"Not at all," Presby answered. "It's a small way of showing it, but we appreciate your services here, Mr. Perkins."

And on Friday afternoon Henderson himself, the Agency chief, reputedly high in the councils of Intercontinental Guaranty & Trust, stopped by his desk on his way home. Since in a dozen years he had received scarcely a nod from Henderson, Perkins was understandably elated.

"I understand we'll be seeing each other tomorrow," Henderson said, resting one buttock momentarily on the corner of Perkins's desk.

"Looks like it," Perkins said noncommittally.

"I damn well hope they serve whisky," Henderson said. "I suppose hot punch is strictly in the old hunting tradition, but it gives me gas."

"I think I'll take a flask of my own," said Perkins, as if it were his longstanding habit at hunts.

"Good idea," Henderson said, getting up. And he as left the office he called back over his shoulder, "Save a nip for me, Fred!"

83

After dinner that evening, Emily put the children to bed and the two of them then strolled to the edge of Marine Gardens and gazed across the open fields towards the big houses behind their iron grills. Even from that distance they could see signs of bustle and activity. The driveway under the elms seemed full of long black limousines and on the spreading lawns they could make out the caterer's assistants setting up green tables for the morrow's breakfast. As they watched, an exercise boy on a chestnut mare trotted by outside the fence, leading a string of some forty sleek brown and black horses towards the distant stables.

"The weather will be gorgeous," Emily said as they turned back. "There's just a hint of autumn in the air already."

Perkins did not answer her. He was lost in his own reflections He had not wanted to go; part of him still did not want to go. He realized that he was trembling with nervous apprehension; but of course that might have been expected—the venture into new surroundings, the fear of failure, of committing some social *gaffe*, of not living up to what they must certainly expect of him— these were causes enough for his trembling hands and the uneven palpitations of his heart.

"Let's go to bed early," Emily said. "You'll need a good night's sleep."

Perkins nodded and they went into their house. But despite the obvious necessity, Perkins slept very little that night. He tossed about envisaging every conceivable social humiliation until his wife at last complained, "You kick and turn so that I can't get a bit of sleep," and took her pillow and a blanket and went into the children's room.

He had set the alarm for six—an early start was called for—but it was long before that when he was awakened.

"Perkins? Fred Perkins?"

He sat bolt upright in bed.

"Yes?"

It was light but the sun had not yet risen. There were two men standing in his bedroom. The taller of them, he who had just shaken his shoulder, was dressed in a black leather coat and wore a cap divided into pie-shaped slices of yellow and red.

"Come on, get up!" the man said.

"Hurry along with it," added the second man, shorter and older, but dressed also in leather.

"What is it?" Perkins asked. He was fully awake now, and the adrenalin charged his heart so that it pumped with a terrible urgency.

"Get out of bed," said the larger man and, seizing the covers with one hand, jerked them back. As he did so, Perkins saw the two lions rampant and the quartered shield stamped in gilt on the breast of his leather coat. Trembling, and naked except for his shorts, he rose from his bed into the cool, crisp morning.

"What is it?" he repeated senselessly.

"The hunt, the hunt—it's for the hunt," said the older man.

"Then let me get my clothes," Perkins stammered and moved towards the dresser where in the dim light he could see the splendid pink coat and whipcord breeches spread out awaiting his limbs. But as he turned, he was struck a sharp blow by the short, taped club which he had not observed in the large man's hand.

"You won't be needing them" his attacker laughed, and out of the corner of his eye Perkins saw the older man pick up the pink coat and, holding it by the tails, rip it up the centre.

"Look here!" he began, but before he could finish the heavy man in black leather twisted his arm sharply behind his back and pushed him out of the french doors into the cold clear sunless air. Behind him, he caught a glimpse of Emily in nightclothes appearing suddenly in the door, heard her terrified scream and the tinkle of glass from one of the panes which broke as the short man slammed the door shut. He broke loose and ran in a frenzy across the lawn, but the two game-keepers were soon up with him. They seized him under the armpits and propelled him across the street to the point where Marine Gardens ended and the open country began. There they threw him onto the stubbled ground and the short one drew out a whip.

"Now, run! you son of a bitch, run!" screamed the large man.

Perkins felt the sharp agony of the whip across his bare back. He stumbled to his feet and began to lope across the open fields. The grass cut his bare feet, sweat poured down his naked chest, and his mouth was filled with incoherent syllables of protest and outrage, but he ran, he ran, he ran. For already across the rich, summery fields he heard the hounds baying and the clear alto note of the huntman's horn.

The Tsanta in the Parlour

STEPHEN GRENDON

After seven years of profound silence—surely a length of time sufficiently long to have encouraged hope for the worst—Ernest Ambler made it plain to his uncle, Theophilus, that he was not, after all, dead—"lost in the wilds of South America," as he put it, but not permanently. His letter was followed by his peace-offering, and no doubt, the old man reflected pessimistically, his peace-offering would in all probability shortly be followed by Ernest himself, and there would then begin once more the problem of waiting upon Ernest's better nature just long enough to allow his real self to assert control, after which Ernest would need to be packed off to some remote place all over again.

Full circle. Circles, rather.

"I may very well be a crusty old curmudgeon," said Theophilus to the single servant who waited upon him in his gloomy old house on Main Street in the Southern town of Euphoria, "but naturally, *I* couldn't believe it, could I? No, of course not," he went on, replying to his question precisely as he had replied to his own questions for half a century gone by, "nor do I need Ernest to remind me. What a curse on my old bones! To have to deal with Ernest once, twice, thrice—and God knows how many times! Get his room ready, Fulton. And what was in that box? I noticed you took the stamps off for your cousin's girl—I hope her collection is growing."

"It is, Mr. Ambler. Very much. Thanks to you partly."

"The box, Fulton."

"Yes, sir. A small object."

"Yes, it was, wasn't it! Oh, forgive me—you meant its contents. I referred to the box. My error. A small object, eh? What kind of object?"

"It was a shrivelled something. Rubbery."

"Where is it?"

"Over on the mantel. I thought perhaps it was meant to belong with your collection of ivory and ebony pieces."

Theophilus Ambler meandered over to look at his nephew's peace-offering. He was a tall, thin man, but not cadaverous so much as anaemic-looking, still able despite his seventy-odd years, and only a little absentminded. He put on his pince-nez and peered.

The peace-offering stood between an ivory elephant and an ebony rook, looming larger than either. Brown, shrivelled, rubbery indeed, with a resemblance to a monkey's head; it was not nice to touch. He swept it off the mantel in the palm of his hand and held it forth into the sunlight streaming through the french windows.

"Ernest will never change," he said. "I suppose he would call in a sense of humour."

"What is it, Mr. Ambler?"

"Damn it, man—you might have seen it for yourself. It's a human head, shrunken of course. Propably Jivaro in origin. They call these things tsantas. There are still head-hunters down there, I suspect. It doesn't seem to be Ernest's head, though. Much too dark. An Indian, probably."

"It's an odd gift, isn't it?"

"Only Ernest would think of it. And what the devil I'm to do with it, I don't know."

"No one would notice it among those pieces, sir. That's why I put it there."

Ambler smiled and replaced it. "Good enough. Now let me have his letter again."

"I think it's in the pocket of your robe, sir."

"Oh, yes. So it is." He took it out and read it slowly, aloud, while Fulton stood in almost obsequious attention. " 'Dear Uncle Theophilus, Like a bad penny, I am turning up again. It now seems quite possible that I may be in the States again within a few weeks or months—events will determine that—and I should like to see you, naturally. I hope all is forgiven. Under separate cover, I am sending you a little curio which you might like. I picked it up not long ago and thought of you immediately. My best wishes.' Humph! Best wishes, indeed. That is an ambiguous letter, in my opinion. But, of course, Ernest never wrote anything straightforward in his life—or spoke it, either. How long ago was it written? Three weeks. I suppose we can expect him any day."

"I'm afraid so," agreed Fulton.

Fulton drifted out of the room and Theophilus was left alone. He made a determined effort to put the unpleasant thought of his nephew from his mind, and settled down to read. But Ernest persisted. Ernest, who had never been a very pleasant child, and who had made life miserable for practically everyone, relative or friend, with whom he had been associated. And how long will it be before I have to get him out of another scrape? he wondered. He was really getting too well along in years for that sort of thing, he felt. Not really doddering yet, of course, but still—no longer young. And Ernest, who must now be well into his forties, was old enough by this time to know what responsibilities meant. But he knew in his heart that Ernest would never be old enough for that.

In the night the house creaked and groaned in the wind; rafters cracked and the bushes around the old building whispered in the hushing night air. Theophilus Amber went to his bed not long after sundown, and Fulton went shortly thereafter. The old house was thus quickly lulled in darkness, and the sounds it made were long familiar. Mice scuttered in the attic, making their intimate small patterings; Theophilus had come to welcome them; he slept to their footsteps, and no creak or crack or groan invaded his sleep.

But this night a new sound flowed through the house.

Theophilus woke to it at last. He lay for a while listening, and decided finally that it must be Fulton talking in his sleep. Or grumbling. He sighed and waited for the sound to subside.

But it did not subside. So Theophilus dragged himself out of bed, got into his slippers and dressing-gown in the dark, puttered over to a candle, lit it, and held it before him to light his way into the hall. He went down to Fulton's room, opened the door, and looked in. Fulton's face caught the flickering candlelight.

Theophilus listened.

No sound. Nothing whatever from Fulton.

Fulton lay in peaceful sleep, as quiet as a tired child. And a child he is sometimes, reflected Theophilus wearily, withdrawing again and closing the door.

He stood there in the shadowed hall, listening.

Certainly there was a voice somewhere. Since it was not Fulton's, it must belong to someone else. A faint prickle of perturbation made itself evident. No one else should be in the house, and the sound came from inside; the wind would have whipped breath away from anyone beyond the walls.

Thoughtfully, Theophilus blew out the candle. He felt somewhat more secure in darkness without the light to offer himself as a target for any possible invader. Ah, but who would invade the house? And for what? For there was nothing of value in any part of it. And what potential burglar would announce himself so carelessly?

The darkness enfolded him, the darkness enclosed him in an uncertain security.

He went noiselessly back along the hall to the head of the stairs. The sound came from below, steadily. Ah, but what was it? A muttering—or a tittering—a shrill gibberish—or an incoherent series of mouthings, scarcely human. And yet, now and then, it seemed, there were guttural words.

Ambler listened, straining himself to detach and isolate recognizable sounds.

And presently, slowly, word by word, fragments of a sentence fell into his consciousness, and he put them together painstakingly, while the darkness pressed about him with false security.

"Een . . . thees . . . house . . . ees . . . Meestaire Amblair. . ."

The darkness concealed menace, the terrible muttering from below gave birth to alarm. Ambler was not afraid, but he was not inclined to dare the unknown without weapons and without

88

some knowledge of what he might face. He felt instinctively that something dreadful lurked in the darkness below.

"Bite," said the gibbering voice. "Bite," came the muttering. "Bite," rose out of the incoherent sounds from below.

"Een . . . thees . . . house," it said again.

And what a horrible tittering sound! How primitive! thought Ambler in some confusion. His confusion was, however, controlled. He made no betraying sound; whatever it was, menaced him, he was sure.

The silence which fell was as sudden as it was unexpected. It made Theophilus Ambler even more uncomfortable than the sounds. But what came after was even worse in that sentient darkness.

A new sound now, an incredible sound.

Someone weeping, someone sobbing!

Ambler stood there listening unbelievingly. What in God's name had got into the house? He felt his skin scrawl; he felt something gnawing at the pit of his stomach; he felt in turmoil, in a wretchedness of undefined fear and a kind of sick loathing, for the sound was so piteous that it was revolting.

The sound of grief diminished, fell away, was gone, and the silence came.

In a little while the familiar signatures of the old house began once more, serenely—the creaking and cracking and groaning, the wind's hush-hush at the eaves, the comfort of mice scampering above overhead.

Theophilus Ambler retreated noiselessly to his room, where he sat for a long time listening, listening and wondering, before he brought himself to put off his slippers and dressing-gown and return to bed.

He considered inquiring next morning to Fulton whether he had heard anything in the night, but thought better of it. If Fulton had heard, he would find some opportunity to mention it; if he had not, there was no need to alarm him. That would come soon enough, if the experience persisted.

Nevertheless, Theophilus Ambler made a thorough search of the old house. He turned up several articles which had been lost for years, but nothing at all to show that anyone had got into the house during the night. Every door and every window remained locked, just as they had been at bedtime the previous night. Moreover, nothing whatever was in any way disturbed. Could it have been that one of the Negroes from the other side of town had got drunk and wandered into the neighbourhood, finding himself a corner somewhere outside the house from which the sounds, despite the tearing wind, had reached into and through the walls? But no, hardly; that was stretching the bounds of probability too far. Yet it was undeniable that the sounds he had heard in the night might very well have been made by a black.

89

Theophilus sat for some time in the horsehair-furnished parlour, ostensibly reading, but secretly pondering the problem. With each hour that passed, his perplexity grew. More than once, he gazed meditatively over at that curious peace offering of Ernest's, and at last he went to bring it out into a strong light so that he could examine it closely. Was it his imagination, or was the thing damp?

He looked at it closely.

It had once been a fine head, he decided. Almost Nordic, save for its dark skin and the cut of the mouth. He fingered it judiciously. It seemed that some kind of teeth had been put into it. Very sharp, too. The jaws seemed firm enough. He replaced it on the mantel; his improbable theory was clearly untenable, and he was left more puzzled than ever.

Several times during that day, he found himself regarding the Jivaro head with mixed emotions, uppermost among which was the impulse to rid himself of the object with summary dispatch.

He waited for night with some apprehension.

That night he lay in his dark bedroom at the head of the stairs waiting for untoward sounds, for no wind filled the old house with the familiar noises to which Theophilus had been so long accustomed. The clock struck nine, the clock struck ten, the clock struck eleven. Outside, the town grew quiet towards midnight as the streets emptied and the last late crowd from the last picture-show dispersed.

Inside the old house on Main Street the voice began again.

Theophilus rose at once; he had not undressed, but had only put on his gown, in one pocket of which he had taken care to place a small pistol. He had put out a strong-beamed flashlight, feeling more secure with it in his hand than candles; and, so armed, he set out from his room, walking with every caution to the head of the stairs and slowly, slowly down, step by step, careful to make no sound.

The voice gibbered in the darkness; the voice complained, argued, cried—a horrible cacophony in the black well below.

Near the bottom of the stairs, Theophilus paused. The atmosphere of menace around him was thick, unpleasant, cloying. Once again, there were audible words, disjointed, almost meaningless.

"Head . . . of . . . stairs . . . room . . . een . . . these . . . house . . . een . . . third . . . night. . . ." And again gibberish, horribly intermingled with sounds of grief.

And what was to be made of that?

The sounds came from the parlour, beyond any question.

Mustering his courage, Theophilus tiptoed down the hall towards the old-fashioned portieres which marked the entrance to the parlour. In the silence which held the house, the sounds seemed twice and three times as loud as they were, so that at any moment Theophilus expected a distraught Fulton to appear at the head of the stairs. But there was no betrayal from above.

He stood before the closed portieres listening. He heard a constant muttering, and, paying careful attention, he detected a pattern of gutturals. Words, certainly. But not English. Words in some alien language. Phonetic, he decided; probably primitive, with now than then an English word. It struck him as very odd that the heavy accent of the English words so similar to the less obvious accent Ernest had affected when last he had visited in Euphoria.

His impulse was to retreat, but he would not yield to it.

He did the second-best thing; he effected a compromise. Rather than enter the parlour, he made a small parting of the portieres at the level of his eyes, thrust his flashlight into the opening and, focusing the beam on the mantel, switched it on.

The ivory and ebony figures sprang into being—and the dark brown head, agleam as with perspiration there. It seemed to Theophilus Ambler that there was a burning of tiny eyes, a movement of the shrunken lips. But the instant the light flashed forth, the sounds from within the room ceased.

There was nothing.

But wait—! The head was not where he had put it. When last he had put in down, it was left standing next to an ivory knight; now it stood before a teakwood box—fully a foot and a half away. Could Fulton have moved it? Hardly. Even if he had taken it up, he would have replaced it precisely where it had been.

What then? The possibilities which occurred to him were not comforting. Theophilus was not unimaginative, but he was not inclined to accept the products of his imagination too readily. He looked across the room to the figures illuminated by his flashlight's beam. He could not rid himself of the conviction that one among them gazed back, with malevolence.

He snapped off the light and withdrew, allowing the portieres to close before him. He waited.

Nothing happened.

He was vaguely disconcerted; he had expected the gibbering and muttering to begin again, but no, no untoward sound came out of the parlour. Indeed, the room and the house were as one might expect them to be in the dead of the night.

Theophilus walked back to the stairs. There he waited a while longer. Nothing took place, no unaccountable sound invaded the darkness.

He went slowly up the stairs in the dark, with every step expecting to hear that weird voice again. But he heard nothing; all was as before, except that Fulton was snoring. He's lying on his back again, thought Theophilus. He turned at the head of the stairs and looked back down into the well of black. He had a momentary feeling that someone watched him; he thought he saw a vague, shadowy figure, neck to toes—without a head; but he blinked and it was gone.

More shaken that he cared to admit to himself, he re-entered his room. He considered blocking the door with the heavy easy chair in his room, but stoutly refused to give way to a fear so nebulous as that he now entertained. Just to be on the safe side, however, he slipped his pistol under his pillow, and presently he slept after a fashion.

The morning brought more than another day. It brought Ernest Ambler, looking, if possible, more dissipated than ever, with bags under his eyes, and smoulding fire, like a fever inside. He was of medium height, stoop-shouldered, and, one might have said, hawk-like in his appearance, except that it did injustice to a noble family of birds. His face was not so much prepossessing as it was fascinating in a revolting way. He looked, and often acted, like a character out of a painting by Felicien Rops, quite as if he had practised every known major vice and quite a few minor ones.

Theophilus found his nephew at breakfast when the old man descended.

Ernest shot him an unsteady glance. "Hello, Uncle Theo," he said with false heartiness. "You're looking uncommonly well."

Theophilus growled an acknowledgement. "And you're looking seedy, if I must say so. Puffy."

"It was a long trip."

"I'll bet it was. How'd you make it? In steerage?"

Ernest set forth his trip in patience. He made it commendably short. He had been working among the Jivaro Indians. He had sent a sample of their work, but apparently it had not yet arrived.

"I got it," said Theophilus shortly.

Ernest seemed manifestly surprised. "Oh," he said. "Oh, you did." He licked his lips. "But surely, not very long ago, eh?"

"Two days ago."

"Then this is actually the . . . the third day you've had it, isn't it?"

A stupid question, though Theophilus. Small wonder he tittered after it. Still had that disgusting accent too.

"How the devil did you get along with the Indians, Ernest? Or can you speak their language?"

"I learned it. And I taught some of them English. Oh, I taught them a lot of things, and they taught me. That head I sent you— I can do that sort of thing myself now. And a lot of others."

"Equally reprehensible, no doubt."

Ernest frowned angrily. "You would think so."

"I know the precedents," answered Theophilus curtly. "How long are you planning on staying?"

"Oh, not too long. A week or two, maybe. Then I must go back. I've got quite a reputation among those Indians."

"I can imagine."

92

"You'll find it hard to believe, but they think I'm a big medicine-man—the equivalent of an African witch-doctor, no less."

He was gloating. He was actually proud of what the Jivaros thought. Theophilus repressed a shudder.

"Congratulations," he said dryly. "And tell me, Ernest, that head you sent me. Did it take you very long?"

"Oh, no, just. . . ." Ernest caught himself and glared at the old man. "What do you mean?"

"What did you think I meant?" countered Theophilus blandly.

Ernest swallowed. "You always think the worst of me," he muttered.

"Ah, and whose fault is that?" Theophilus got up, leaning above his nephew. He had scarcely touched his coffee, but he no longer had any appetite for it. "If you're staying, Ernest, you take the room next to mine. I have to tell you, though—there appears to be somebody else in the house, besides Fulton and me. You'll find out about that in good time."

Ernest stared after him with narrowed eyes.

Theophilus was profoundly disturbed. He read his nephew's eyes. He read hope, hate, avarice; he read more. And how curiously Ernest had spoken! He was not cringing, as he had formerly done; he was not apologizing or begging; his was an attitude of watchful waiting, an almost irrepressible gloating straying from behind his feverish eyes.

Theophilus continued to be upset at intervals throughout the day. So did Fulton, what with the way in which Ernest presumed to order him about. Ernest managed to surcharge the already troubled atmosphere of the house on Main Street with an explosive chaos. Moreover, as evening approached, Ernest began to get extremely fidgety, and at last, immediately after supper, rose and left the house, mumbling that he would be back later, and no one needed to be waiting up for him—as if anyone intended to do so.

"The front door will be left open," said Theophilus. And it would be just like Ernest to come in in the midst of a soliloquy from that thing in the parlour, he thought. He half hoped he would do so.

But that night advanced without the disturbance of the past two nights. Theophilus listened for hours. When at last the clock struck eleven, he was tense with listening. He heard the murmur of wind in the trees, the creaking of the house, the scuttering of mice—and, a quarter past the hour, a terrific clatter on the front porch, followed by an assault on the door, which opened and closed, and permitted Theophilus to hear a succession of unsteady footsteps advancing down the hall.

Ernest—and drunk. Theophilus sighed. He might have expected that. He got up, pulling on his dressing-gown. He opened the door of his room and stood there, waiting, listening to Ernest stumbling through the hall, up the stairs. He hoped that Ernest would find his own room.

That hope, however, was not destined to be fulfilled. Seeing the open door, Ernest came into his uncle's room, lurched across to the bed, and flung himself on it. Disgusted, Theophilus walked over and touched him on the shoulder. Ernest looked warily around, bleary-eyed. Seeing Theophilus, his eyes, opened wide and closed again, tightly.

"Go 'way," he muttered thickly. "Never wash 'fraid 'v you 'live, n' 'fraid 'v you dead. Go 'way."

Was it worth it? Theophilus wondered. If left alone, Ernest might go to sleep in a matter of seconds; if not, he might become obstreperous and insistently difficult. He stood there for a moment, feeling the chill of the night through his dressing-gown; then he gave up, and went out, leaving the door ajar, so that he might hear if Ernest got up again. He could as easily sleep next door, in the room assigned to Ernest, as in his own, much as he disliked being routed from his own warm bed.

He got into Ernest's bed, profoundly hoping that he might be able now to sleep without interruption for what remained of the night.

He was.

He woke up just as Fulton found him. Fulton, much agitated, his hands almost palsied. He woke quickly.

"Mr. Ambler, sir—Mr. Ernest's on your bed."

"Yes, of course. I let him."

"I'm afraid he's ill, sir."

"Drunk, damn him! Just plain beastly drunk."

Fulton looked apologetically dubious. "But the blood," he said faintly.

"Blood?" echoed Theophilus.

He got up, forgetting his dressing-gown, and walked in his nightshirt as fast as he was able down the hall to his own room.

Fulton had not exaggerated. There was quite a bit of blood emanating apparently from some puffy wounds on Ernest's neck. Ernest himself was dead; of that there was not the shadow of a doubt. His neck was torn and lacerated but not fatally, to Theophilus Ambler's untrained eye.

"Call somebody," he said to Fulton.

"The undertaker?" ventured Fulton.

"And the sheriff, too. They'll want to ask questions. They always do."

The sheriff came and asked a good many questions, particuearly after a report from the county coroner was in. Ernest Ambler had died of poison, evidently administered through the wounds in his neck. Curare. A poison well-known to certain Indian tribes of South America. As for the wounds in his neck—clearly bites of some kind. Perhaps rats. What did Mr. Theophilus Ambler know about it?

Theophilus was not of much help. But for the fact that he had not a shred of motive for wanting his nephew out of the way, it might have gone very badly for him and for Fulton. As it was, the absence of evidence failed to constitute anything positive. Two or three times it was on the tip of his tongue to say something about that strange tsanta on the mantel, but he wisely forebore; he might escape a barred cell for a padded one.

At the first opportunity, however, he examined the bloodstains on the stairs which the men from the sheriff's office had found; there were not many, and they ended half-way down the stairs. He went into the parlour. The tsanta stood on the very edge of the shelf. There was a red-brown smear at one corner of its mouth. Theophilus had not a doubt but that, if he sent away the pointed "teeth" from that monkey-like head, he would find the source of the curare which had killed Ernest.

He had an understandable reluctance to do so.

But something would have to be done about the thing on the mantel. For the time being it could stay where it was—but not for long.

Within a fortnight the mail brought in a letter sent to Theophilus Ambler by the American consul at Cuenca, Ecuador. Did Mr. Ambler have in his possession a shrunken Jivaro head, recently acquired? And if so, would he send it post-haste to the consulate? The consul was sorry, but he had been plagued by a Jivaro woman who had told him a long rigmarole and given him no rest until he sent to inquire. Her husband, whose headless body had been discovered in the garden behind a small house once occupied by Ernest Ambler, who had gone from there, had been murdered by someone—according to her, by Ambler, who had—so she told the consul she had learned from her husband's spectre—performed certain ancient rites in sorcery over the head and dispatched it to a place in America to do a deed, after which the head would be returned. Now the ghost of the dead Indian appeared nightly to his wife, weeping and clamouring for his head. It was absurd, it was ridiculous, but the consul hoped that Mr. Theophilus Ambler knew how difficult a consul's life could be and might understand.

Theophilus understood very well indeed. The tsanta had been sent to do a deed—on the third night in the room at the head of the stairs. The incorrigible Ernest had counted on the tsanta's earlier arrival. Fortunately, Theophilus was in a position to appreciate the irony of the situation, however incredible.

He took no chances with the tsanta. He packed it carefully and sent it by air to the American consulate at Cuenca.

Moonlight—Starlight

VIRGINIA LAYEFSKY

The genesis of the idea for the party was in an old Halloween costume Anne Carey found packed in a box in the attic. It had been made thirty years ago for a seven-year-old Anne by her mother. She had been a woman who threw nothing away.

After Anne inherited the large Victorian spaces her mother had swept and garnished most of her life, she often came upon pieces of her own life—up until her marriage at least—neatly labelled and stored here or there. She was apt to find them on those first days of her husband's occasional absences when she used house cleaning as a balm for initial loneliness.

The costume she found that day was so beautifully sewn and carefully packed that its state of preservation was remarkable. When she shook out its folds, the coins which her mother had sewn individually on the bodice long ago clinked with a special sound that set up a painful little echo of disappointment in her forgetful heart. Though she remembered clearly then the smell of chrysanthemums and sewing-machine oil in her mother's room the day the costume was fitted, she could not have said why the sound of the coins oppressed her with such a profound sense of loss.

It had to do with the party she had lost, of course. It was to have been her very own. The games had been planned and the decorations made. Invitations had already been sent when, due to the death by drowning of two small cousins in upstate New York, the party was cancelled. The accident had happened the day before they were to leave to visit Anne. She had been broken-hearted, not for the cousins whom she had never seen but for the party which was cancelled. In time she was able to forget everything about it but the sense of loss, which persisted unacknowledged up to today when she opened the box to find the costume still waiting there.

And that was the reason why Halloween became the occasion for the only really large children's party Anne Carey ever gave. She made a costume, less carefully done, for her nine-year-old son and dressed her daughter in the gypsy outfit she herself was to have worn long ago.

The party was a resounding success. Children, remembering it, asked her for months afterwards to give another, but she never did. Nor did she tell the reasons why it became the last children's party of any kind that she ever gave. . . .

The arrangements seemed so simple at first. She told her son Bobby he could invite the entire fourth grade with all its younger brothers and sister.

Games and refreshments were no problem. Now that Anne thought of it, she remembered the entire programme of the beautiful party planned long ago. The bobbing for apples, followed by pin the tail on the donkey and musical chairs, marched through her mind in a succession almost as orderly and magical now as then. There would be none of the professional entertainment that had figured recently in some of the more ambitious neighbourhood parties. What she wanted was a real, old-fashioned Halloween party.

It was something she was to repeat often during the week to the friends who called her with warnings and advice.

Had she a first-aid kit? She would probably need one. And be sure to omit the booby prizes—children who won them were apt to weep, considering them a disgrace.

The warnings began to include, unpleasantly often, the names of the Usher children. Everyone hoped they had not been invited, although on being questioned no one seemed able to tell Anne more than that they were considered strange, the rather menacing unknown quantity in the local algebra of human relationships. They were not much liked by other children.

And then, everyone knew how strange the parents were, living off by themselves as they did, never associating with anyone.

Had she seen the father's work? Gruesome decadent stuff that no one who hadn't a morbid streak would think of painting. And according to rumours, it was just as well they did keep to themselves. It seemed Usher had a sense of humour that, to say the least, was sardonic. It could be, they had heard, very ugly at times.

By that time, however, it was too late. The older child—the girl—was in the fourth grade. She and her brother had been invited along with the rest.

On Halloween Anne with her two children stood in the golden porch light welcoming their guests. The children, in various disguises, began to come shortly after dark. They all seemed to arrive at the same time, coming out of the gloomy, old-fashioned lane like a small army of faceless grotesques. Every child was masked.

For an instant Anne felt invaded by a force of nameless, not necessarily friendly strangers. Only the shadows of parents coming from the obscurity into familiarity assured her that beneath the grinning skull or monstrous face was a dimple or a freckled nose she knew.

The party had become a reality at last. Each adult whispered instructions of various sorts to each small mystery at his side before setting it free to join its wriggling, hopping contemporaries. As they took leave of Anne with compliments and thanks, there was an unmistakable look of relief on most of their departing faces. She had said she could manage alone, even with her husband absent on business for his firm.

By eight o'clock, when the party hats had been passed out, and the last parent had gone, almost everyone who had been invited was there.

The party began in good order. They all pinned the tail on the donkey. Waiting patiently, good-children-all-in-a-line, each child was blindfolded and sent with cardboard tail in hand towards the donkey on the wall. Only one very young black cat—anonymous to Anne—cried because it had pinned its particular tail to the donkey's nose. It was quite easily comforted.

The second game passed gaily, even hilariously. The children unmasked as they went to the big tin washbowl full of apples floating on top of the water that filled it. At the sight of laughter on small faces freed so recently from the horrors which had hidden them from sight, Anne was charmed with a sudden feeling of felicity.

The children, hands held behind their backs, bobbed for the apples. She watched them, holding to her moment with the sweet satisfaction of fulfilment.

Down to the last detail, from the sound of the children's shrill, excited voices to the orange-and-black crepe paper and balloons, the festive smell of candle wax heating the pulpy pumpkins, she had her party at last.

It was well that she held to the moment, listening to the laughter, seeing the children's warm cheeks and tender, perspiring necks, her own daughter's thrilled awareness of her multicoloured petticoats. For shortly after that the party began to change.

It started during the next game, which was musical chairs, and at first it was almost imperceptible. Perhaps because it was the third rather strenuous game of the evening, Anne noticed some of the children showing signs of being overtired. Some of the smaller ones' cheeks were too flushed or pale.

They had put the chairs in a row themselves, working rather wildly with some petty wrangling. There were quarrels in the air before they even started. And at the same time, something else, an odd feeling of restlessness and distraction as though their minds were somewhere else.

Watching them march around the chairs, and the way each scrambled for a place once the music stopped, Anne decided she never had liked the game. It demanded a ruthlessness in the end that she found unpleasant, disliking the ultimate winner.

She was glad when it was over and she had settled the children to making funny men and animals out of the marshmallows, gumdrops and toothpicks she had set out on card tables.

A drooping rabbit's ear, a cat's tail hanging from its owner down the back of a chair, a worn sneaker sticking out beneath a ghost's shroud seemed charming to her still. And yet, she felt less delighted than before.

The room became quiet enough for her to hear the children's laboured breathing as they concentrated on their efforts. As they reached for the coloured candies to fit them awkwardly on the toothpicks, Anne was not able to get rid of the slight depression settling over her. There was that furtive, restless quality creeping about the room as though all the small figures bending over their nonsense were less intent than they pretended to be. There was a sense of shifting, of lifting the head to listen, though no child did these things.

In the near silence she heard the wind rising outside. It was then, too, that she heard the front gate creak as it opened.

No child looked up. As Anne listened for the footsteps which should have sounded on the porch afterwards, each child seemed to concentrate more obliviously than before.

When Anne crossed the room to the entrance hall, she felt she was being watched. It was such a strong feeling she turned to look back. No one had even seen her go.

Nothing but the wind, rushing into the hall like some belated guest, met her at the open door. Behind it, in darkness that crept away from the porch light, she could see no one.

It was when her eyes searched the old garden at the side of the house that she saw them. They were standing by a small stone sundial Anne's grandfather had set there years ago. A boy and a girl, hand in hand, they stood looking at her, motionless as it was.

Not until she called to them inviting them inside did they move forward. As they came through the dark, up the porch steps, Anne felt at last how truly starless the night was, how like these particular parents to send them out alone.

They passed in silence through the door she held open for them. Once inside the hall, they waited, making no move towards the living-room, standing always together in their peculiar stillness. Anne, for some reason unknown, not only closed but bolted the door.

They were staring wordlessly up at her when she turned back to them. She found herself struggling with a feeling of aversion for them, since now that they had arrived she realized how relieved she had been earlier at their absence.

The girl was a head taller than her brother, though both were identically costumed. Neither of them was masked, yet it was only one face that both turned to her, the boy's being simply a smaller version of the girl's.

To Anne they had the look of having been drawn by their father instead of procreated in the usual way. She thought she even recognized Usher's personal style in the deliberate exaggeration of line and the faintly corrupt, half-graceful proportions of that face with its twofold glance.

The eyes, in particular, were as overly large as the ones he painted. They were a flat, tobacco brown. It was to the expression in them that she owed her feeling of aversion. For both pairs held a fixed, impersonal intentness that was less unchildlike, she thought, than inhuman.

Still, they were only children, just come to a strange house. Anne, feeling slightly guilty, pointed the way to the living-room.

They walked ahead of her, docilely enough, not seeming to notice when Anne, following them, suddenly stopped still. She had noticed at last what they were wearing. She felt a sense of affront, of somehow being publicly insulted. If friends had called Usher's humour unpleasant and sardonic, she had not known up until then what those words could mean. For even to Anne, no authority on such matters, it was obvious he had sent them dressed in costumes representing the grave-clothes of children of a past generation. Both wore on their heads wreaths of stiff formal leaves, and were dressed in folds of white cloth from shoulder to foot. The costumes were draped delicately and, from a distance at least, looked as beautifully sewn as her own child's dress. That each detail had the stamp of conscious artistic effect only added to the cynical horror of the idea.

Though the other children looked up as they entered the room, they remained sitting at their tables. Anne, sensing the general withdrawal on their part, came closer to her new guests, intending to reassure them. Close enough to the boy, in fact, to feel she had seen the worst, ultimate point of the joke. For the material of their costumes had the limp suppleness of age. The hand-sewn lace on them was yellow.

After their initial drawing back the children began to speak again, to laugh, get up from the tables and show her what they had made.

They began a game of blindman's buff. It was not one of the games planned for the evening, but Anne took advantage of it to go away to privacy for a few moments.

She stood alone in the gaily decorated dining-room with its rows of shining, waiting plates. She frowned, moving her lips slightly like a child over a mathematics problem, wondering uneasily how the children of such a father might be expected to behave. A need to see what was happening, as urgent as the need for privacy had been a few minutes before, sent her to the door of the room.

What she saw reassured her. The two children, along with the others, crouched, hiding from the blindfolded child who groped after them with outstretched hands. She saw the boy shrink away in his turn from the blindman, giggling softly. His eyes were shining childishly. She reproached herself.

Yet the party was changed. The mood of it began to resemble more nearly the wild "play-outs" of her childhood's summer nights, when the long, soft dusk encouraged a feeling of lawlessness, of perilous emotions, a sort of childish debauch. There was a feverish, tense look on some of their faces.

Anne had gone to the kitchen before the party went out of control. The children had begun to choose their own games by that time, and had been playing a comparatively quiet one when she left the room. It was an ancient game, a sort of ritual she remembered having played herself, known as old witch.

> *"I'm going downtown to smoke my pipe*
> *And I won't be back till Saturday night*
> *And if you dare let the old witch in*
> *I'll beat you red—white—and blue!"*

A small voice chanted the words behind her as she entered the kitchen. For a time she busied herself pouring cider, warming plates, mentally counting heads, as she concentrated on her own activities.

Until the lights went out.

The entire house was suddenly dark. Someone, she knew, had pulled a switch. When she called out anxiously she was answered by her son's cheerful voice.

They had decided, he called, to play moonlight-starlight.

The name, heard aloud, made a chill run over Anne. She hadn't thought of it for years. As a child it had been the only game she had feared and hated. She felt intolerable anxiety as she wondered, while knowing at once, who had suggested it. The party was out of hand.

She groped across the kitchen to the drawer that held her husband's flashlight, disguising her unreasonable fear with irritation at her son for pulling the switch without permission.

Someone had taken and forgotten to return the flashlight. As she turned away, trying to think where she had put candles, she was remembering against her will the way the game was played.

For moonlight-starlight was an outdoor game, another part of the summer nights. Children played it only after dark.

Anne remembered it well. The child who was "it," the ghost, hid in some dark and secret place. Each child, separate and alone, had to wander in search of it. On finding it they, too, became ghosts. Until at last only one child was left to wander alone, watched by all the secret ghosts, who would, in the end, pounce upon it.

There were no candles. She set out in darkness.

The switch box was located across the living-room in an alcove which had been built as a small conservatory with french doors opening into the garden. Even in the blackness of the hall, Anne knew exactly where it was.

The house, except for small sounds and sudden scamperings,

was silent. It seemed to take a long time to walk the length of the hall. In darkness the house grew larger, as large as she had thought it as a child. And now, more nearly child than adult, she walked forward with dread.

At any time now "it," changed from the familiar playmate to some nameless horror, could jump suddenly upon her from its hiding place. For, like it or not, she, too, was a player now.

Her hand touched the living-room wall and she groped forward, angry with herself for the way she shrank against it. She had reached the doors leading to the conservatory before she heard the whispering. It came from inside the room and there was a quality in it that froze her motionless, hardly breathing.

For a few seconds her faculties were turned inward on her own pounding heart. It was only gradually, as she realized she had not been noticed, that she calmed somewhat. She found she was able to see dimly the three small figures standing inside. The white garments of two of them even shone slightly, though so little light came from the night which waited outside in the garden.

When she was able to hear something besides her own pulse she listened to the phrase the two in white whispered again and again, distinguishing, at last, the words.

"Come out . . . come out into the dark . . . come with us. . . ."

They whispered it together, excited, persuasive, with an urgent, secret sibilance that held an increasing seductiveness at each repetition.

The third child, so enticed, whimpered once and stood quiet between them after that. It had been the small sound of an animal so full of fear as to be beyond outcry.

It released Anne from the fear that held her. For the voice had been her daughter's.

Though she leaped forward she made no attempt to reach her child. Her urge was the primitive, overwhelming one for light to chase away the darkness. The hands that had fumbled so often before moved with the speed and sureness of fear which is beyond panic.

And if the taller of the two, the girl, swayed gently towards her with smiling teeth at the same second lights blazed throughout the house and her own child was in her arms.

They stood alone in the glass-enclosed room. Other players who had been wandering about downstairs blinked their eyes in the sudden light, calling reproachful questions.

Every child had come back into the living-room before Anne, with trembling hands, shut the french doors which had been swinging open in the wind from the garden. No child asked where two of the guests had gone.

No one mentioned them at all through the final stages of the party. Anne, having had to choose between illness and anger, chose rightly. It was anger that sustained her through the refresh-

102

ments, the collecting of coats and the arrival, thanks and good-byes of parents.

It was faithful through the night. She went to bed angry and it was with her when she woke the next morning. She guarded it carefully as she planned the call she would make to Usher that day, since if she lost it she feared what might take its place.

In the end, it was Mrs. Usher who called Anne first. She had a pleasant voice, crisp and courteous though rather impersonal sounding.

She called, she said, to explain why her children had not been able to attend the party. They had had fever all day and she believed it might be developing into a light case of chicken pox. Both she, and they, had been so disappointed. She had made their costumes herself; they were to have gone as a cat and a mouse.

The voice seemed to fade out on the next few sentences. At the first words Anne heard there had been a slight, sickening wrench somewhere inside her. It was a relatively mild one, considering that it was the displacement of whatever held her being secure in its particular place in the universe.

The voice wanted to know if most of the other children had been able to make it. Some of them, it knew, had had to come a long way.

The invitations had been on orange paper. She remembered them. Her mother had let her cut out and address them herself, guiding her hand as it made fat wavering letters on the envelopes. She had been so proud that they were to go all the way to upstate New York.

Anne's voice, when she answered, was steadier than the room, still wheeling crazy around herself and the telephone.

Yes, she said, some of the children had had to come a very long way.

Children would do almost anything not to miss a party, the voice said.

Yes, Anne said. All the children had come.

The Kite

CARL JACOBI

Tuesday being Christmas, I slept late, worked until noon on my paper for the *Batavia Medical Journal*, then headed for the waterfront to arrange passage on the next K.P.M. boat for Singapore. It was the anniversary of my six years' practice in Samarinda, and I was glad to be leaving Borneo for good.

I returned to my quarters in the European district and began immediately the long job of packing. At 2 p.m. suddenly and without warning a strange nervousness seized me. At the very moment the last strokes of the clock died into silence a nameless fear swept through my brain, quickening my pulse.

I lay no claim to being psychic. Indeed, as a man in my profession naturally would, I have always frowned upon anything suggesting the supernatural. But I have learned by past experience that such a feeling as I now experienced invariably presaged some black event, some tragedy within my own circle of acquaintanceship.

A quarter of an hour later I received that strange message from Corlin. The message was delivered by a Cantonese boy, and it read as follows:

DEAR DR. VAN RUELLER:

Since Alice was to see you last, her illness, which you diagnosed as a touch of fever, has grown steadily worse. If you can possibly make the trip upriver before you leave Samarinda, I would be much indebted to you.

I must warn you of one thing, however. If you do come and you see a kite flying over the jungle near my place, on your life make no attempt to pull it down.

Faithfully,

EDWARD CORLIN.

I read that letter twice before I looked up. I hadn't known Corlin long. A year ago he had wandered down from British North Borneo where he had held the post of Conservator of Forests. Following him on a later steamer had come his lovely wife, Alice, and his daughter, Fay.

There were ugly stories about Corlin. Rumour had it that the

British Government had requested his resignation after his cruelty to the Dyaks had caused a native outbreak in one of the forest preserves.

Shortly after his arrival in Samarinda, the man took over an old rest-house a short distance up the Mahakam river. There he had made his home, and there his wife and daughter were forced to accept the loneliness and the jungle with him.

As the Cantonese boy stood there I felt a strong desire to refuse the call. Frankly, I didn't like Corlin. But what I didn't understand was the mention of the kite.

"Kang Chow," I said, for I had spoken to Corlin's "boy" several times before, "have the Dyaks in your district taken over the Malay practice of kite flying?"

The boy shook his head.

"The Malays are doing it then?"

"No Malays there. Only one Dyak village. You come?"

I hesitated.

"Yes, I'll come," I said at length. "Have your boatmen and sampan ready in half an hour. I'll meet you at the river jetty."

My usual procedure during a trip upriver is to sit back in the shade of the thatch-cabin, puff a pipe and wait until the chanting Dyaks pole the sampan to my destination. Today, however, I squatted tense in the bow, under the hot sun, and gazed at the steaming shores.

For two hours nothing happened. Then, as we approached the last turn before Corlin's place, Kang Chow pointed up into the sky, said:

"See? Kite. Big kite."

The kite was there, and I could see it clearly from the river. There was nothing strange about it—an enormous cross fashioned of two pieces of bamboo and red rice paper, the tail cut to resemble a dragon.

But suddenly I caught the sunlight at a new angle, and I gave a sharp exclamation. The line which held the kite was not native hemp but wire. Copper wire! I could see it glinting like a slender strand of gold. The wire slanted down from the sky and disappeared in the jungle.

"Inshore, Kang Chow," I snapped. "Inshore."

Minutes later I was fighting my way through the bush, fighting off a horde of insects. The wire ended abruptly at a large *palapak* tree. It was wound several times around the bole and spliced.

What was a kite doing here, flying without human guidance? A native kite and yet held down by white man's wire.

Troubled, I headed back for the sampan. Ten minutes later the boat slipped to a mooring beside the Corlin wharf, and I followed Kang Chow to the clearing and the house.

Corlin met me at the door, shook hands and ushered me into the central room.

"Glad you could make it, Doctor," he said. "It's been hell waiting to see if you'd come. Alice is in the back room. My daughter, Fay, is attending her."

"How is the patient?" I asked.

"She's no better," Corlin replied. "I've kept her dosed with quinine, as you suggested. But it isn't fever that's troubling her. It's . . . In God's name, Doctor, did you see the kite?"

I stared at the man. Corlin was hawk-faced with little pig eyes and a skin insect-bitten from years in the tropics. But something was troubling him.

"Perhaps you'd better look her over first," he said. He led the way to a room in the rear.

It was a small chamber with a single bed, the window shutters partially closed, and a definite smothering odour of sickness. Corlin's wife lay motionless on the bed. In a chair by her side sat the daughter, Fay.

I felt the woman's pulse, took her temperature. The heart action was rapid, but the thermometer showed below normal.

Abruptly Corlin stepped forward and drew me to the window. He pointed out into the sky.

"Look!" he whispered hoarsely. "Do you see it?"

My gaze followed his hand, and again I saw that kite. It was still as high, but much closer, blown by the rising wind. The red rice paper glowed like a fever spot against the blue.

"Yes, I see it," I said. "A kite. But what. . . ?"

Corlin snapped at me before I could finish. "I want you to watch that kite, Van Rueller. Keep looking."

Staring upwards, I felt my own heart begin to hammer in my throat.

"Now feel her pulse and keep watching that kite," Corlin directed. He lit a cigarette with shaking hands and leaned against the wall.

For a long time I kept my hand pressed to the limp wrist, while I watched the kite, motionless, high over the jungle. Abruptly the dragon tail sagged in a slackening of the wind, and the kite settled fifty feet downward.

I whirled to the woman in the bed. Her breath was coming in short gasps. Her pulse was only a feeble flutter.

But even as I ripped open my case and reached for a capsule of amyl nitrite, the sinking spell passed. The heart returned to normal. Outside the kite was leaping, climbing like a frightened bird to new altitudes.

But it was a quarter of an hour before I realized the hideous significance of it. With shaking fingers I gave the woman a dose of strychnine. Stepping to the door I motioned Corlin to follow.

Back in the central room I poured myself a glass of whisky and faced the ex-Conservator across the table.

"Corlin," I said, trying to control my voice, "I've been in Borneo six years. I've treated everything from yellow jack to the bite of a hamadryad. But I never came upon anything like this before. It's—it's—Good Lord, it isn't possible!"

"I'm not crazy then?" Corlin drummed his fingers.

"You saw——?"

"I saw," I replied, "and impossible as it may sound, it's true. In some unholy way your wife's physical condition is linked with the movements of that kite. When the kite is stationary or climbing, her pulse is normal.

"But the moment the thing begins to fall, her heart slows, and death is close. How long has it been there?"

"Since yesterday afternoon," Corlin replied. "I noticed it shortly after Alice became so weak she was forced to bed. The first thought that came to me was to pull the kite down.

"I tried it, and I almost killed her. Went over to that tree and began to pull it in slowly. Fay was to fire a revolver the moment she noticed any ill-effect. The shot came almost at once."

He paced over to me. "In heaven's name, what are we up against?"

I moved towards another doorway leading into a side chamber. Inside I could see several cases, an array of curious objects on the wall.

"Show me your collection," I said at length. "Perhaps it will give me time to think."

Corlin's collection was well-known through the district. Gathering it had been his one intense interest for many years. The man turned his head now, called:

"Kang Chow. Here, damn you. Chop-chop."

The Cantonese boy came on the run, surmised Corlin's orders and quickly drew the shades in the other room.

"Someone broke in here a couple of nights ago," Corlin said. "Tried to steal my things. I fired a shot at the sneak, but I missed."

Most of Corlin's collection was Borneo stuff from the deep interior. There was also articles from Java, the Celebes and China. I saw *parangs*, blow-pipes and pottery. But my eyes lingered on a case in a corner within which was an enormous piece of crimson silk.

"That silk is pure Tibetan work," Corlin said, noting my interest. "Comes from the forbidden temple of Po Yun Kwan, the headquarters of the Nepahte sect in North India. When I obtained it, it was adorning the Supreme Fire Altar in what was known as the Sacred Flame Room.

"I—er—well, to be frank, I climbed up an outer wall, sneaked through an unbarred window and lifted it when the priests were sleeping."

"You stole it?" I exclaimed.

Corlin nodded. "One has to do such things if he's going to have a collection. This silk has some mystic significance to a

Tibetan. The priests called it the cloth of the Fire-God, and all the terrors of seven hells are supposed to follow anyone who defiles it.

"The beauty of the piece is the dragon design in the centre. I don't know for sure, but I understand all sorts of evil obscene rites have been practiced in its name. This is the least understood religion of Asia. It is steeped in Black Magic and. . . ."

I stepped closer and examined the cloth. The lower right corner ended in a ragged edge where a section had been torn off.

"The thief who broke in here did that," Corlin snarled. "I surprised him before he could rip it completely out of the case, and he got away in the darkness—What is it, Fay?"

The Conservator's daughter had entered the room. Her face was white as lime.

"Quick, Doctor," she cried. "My mother. . . ."

In ten strides I was into the other room. But the moment I knelt at the woman's side I realized she was beyond human aid. There was practically no pulse. An instant later the death-rattle sounded. Alice Corlin was dead!

Still holding the lifeless wrist I looked through the window up into the sky. My eyes filled with horror. Even as I watched, the kite slowly settled downward. It fell into the jungle and disappeared.

Impatient as I was to leave Samarinda, the curious facts surrounding the death of Alice Corlin led me to postpone my departure. My certificate attributed her death to congestive malarial fever. But I knew—only too well—the cause went deeper than that.

I had the kite. River Dyaks near Corlin's house had brought it to me in return for a quantity of tobacco. It was made of bamboo sticks and rice paper, as I had suspected. But glued to the surface was a small remnant of red silk—a fragment from Corlin's Fire-God altar cloth.

Exactly a week later Corlin came to my quarters. He entered my veranda and faced me with haggard eyes.

"Van Rueller," he said. "There's another kite."

"What?" I cried.

He nodded. "Exactly like the first. Same size, same colour, same kind of wire. It's been up two days now, but it seems to disappear each night. And my daughter Fay. . . ."

"It isn't affecting her too?" A feeling of helpless horror swept over me.

Corlin clenched his fists.

"Not physically the way it did Alice, but mentally. Something unspeakably evil is slowly claiming her soul."

By this time I was tense with excitement. Dislike Corlin I did, but the events combined to draw me on with a hypnotic attraction. I told Corlin I'd go upriver in an hour.

It had rained during the night, and as we paddled up the Mahakain the sky was a leprous grey. Again Kang Chow sat stiffly in the stern directing the Dyak boatmen.

The kite came into view in almost identically the same spot I had seen its predecessor. I watched it until the sampan thumped against the wharf, but I made no comment.

A moment later in the house I came upon Fay Corlin. She sat in a chair in the centre of the room, rigid, eyes fixed ahead. There was a drawn look of terror in her face; her lips were white.

For five minutes I spoke to her soothingly. She did not respond. Instead, abruptly and without warning, she leaped to her feet gave a choking cry. Then like a lifeless thing she slumped to the floor. Even as I bent over her I knew my worst fears were realized.

The kite was working again!

But this time I had no intention of standing by without intervention. The girl's physical condition was linked with the movements of that kite. Impossible as it seemed, I knew that was true. The kite could not be pulled down, or Fay Corlin would die. *It must be destroyed in mid-air*.

I seized my medicine case and ran out. I dashed along the jungle path and down to the jetty. I leaped into the sampan and paddled furiously for the opposite shore.

Overhead low-bellied storm clouds were racing in from the horizon. The sky to the east was a slickly green. Following the copper wire, I reached the far bank and plunged into the bush.

The wire was fastened to the same *palapak* tree. I opened my case and fell to work.

From one compartment I drew forth a quantity of pyroxylin, spread it before me. Forty grams of pyroxylin mixed with ether and alcohol make collodion, which is useful in treating small wounds. But pyroxylin is nothing more than gun cotton.

I had in my case also a brass tube, capped at both ends to carry matches. Tearing off the caps, I inserted the gun cotton. Next, from an inner pocket I drew forth a large piece of paper, then ripped free my watch chain.

You've seen a boy send a message up a kite string, driven upward by the wind? I was doing much the same, only my "message" was a charge of inflammable gun cotton.

The slightest charge of lightning from the oncoming storm would be sufficient to ignite the pyroxylin and destroy the kite in mid-air. I re-fastened the wire to the tree again, then threaded the paper up the wire.

As I worked, the storm raced nearer. The kite rode high above the undulating roof of the jungle.

I released it. For a moment the message hung motionless. Then with a low hum it began to mount upward along the wire. I rushed back to the sampan and paddled back across the river.

Back in the house I found Fay unconscious on the cot in the

collection room where Corlin had carried her. At the far side of the room, peering out the window, stood the Cantonese boy, Kang Chow.

I waited. One hand clamped to the girl's wrist, I knelt there. Corlin paced back and forth across the room. If he saw Kang Chow, he gave no sign. The room was half-masked in shadows.

In the corner the crimson silk, the Fire-God cloth from the Tibet temple shone luridly in its bamboo case. Its scarlet surface seemed enlarged a hundred times.

The storm drew nearer. From out of the east a blacker cloud raced over the jungle. And then, knifing down, a jagged fork of lightning shot towards the kite. A roar of thunder trembled the very piles of the house.

Five seconds later a sheet of flame burst out into the sky, high above the open window. The fire swept down the dragon tail like a devouring monster, and the wire dropped earthward like a writhing snake. The kite was gone!

Instantly a violent tremor shot through the stricken girl. A gasp came to her lips. The pulse became a pounding hammer. Then the beats slowed to normal, and I leaned back with a cry of exultation.

But at that instant any thought of success was thrust from my mind. A muffled cry from Kang Chow spun me round. The Cantonese boy stood rigid, eyes fastened on the crimson silk in the case beside him.

And it was that silk that held my own gaze. Even as I watched a streamer of smoke appeared over the design of the Fire-God. A tongue of flame shot outward.

Corlin whirled. One instant he stood motionless. Then the door of the case shot open. And slowly, a fraction of an inch at a time, the flaming silk began to move outward. Of its own accord, without support, it moved, lifted into the air, began to float across the room.

Relentlessly it closed in on Corlin. The Conservator's face was ashen. He tried to turn, but seemed riveted to the spot. Horrified, I watched the flaming silk lessen the intervening distance. Then was a final jerk it leaped forward.

The burning mass dropped over Corlin's head, tightened like a shroud.

I swear I was powerless to move. For an instant I vow some outer power prevented me from taking a single step.

Screaming hideously, Corlin fell to the floor. A curtain of smoke rolled over him. Into my nostrils swept the odour of burning flesh.

I broke the spell then, ran forward. I snatched at the cloth with both hands. It resisted all efforts. I seized a rattan rug, attempted to smother the flames. But the fire only flared higher.

At last Corlin's hands flailed wildly in a last death agony. He sank downward and lay still.

Fay Corlin left Samarinda on the 29th of January. My own passage to Singapore and thence to home was scheduled for a week later. But Kang Chow disappeared.

I might have explained the Cantonese boy's part in the death of Edward Corlin to the Dutch authorities. Or I might have asked for an inquest and testified to all that I knew. Yet somehow those facts, if brought to light in a colonial court of law, would have seemed even more impossible.

I can offset the whole thing by cataloguing a few of my subsequent findings. There was for example, the can of petrol which I discovered under Corlin's house.

There was the spool of wire, a section of which had been stretched across the collection room, presumably as a supporting line for a bamboo curtain. Such a wire might conceivably have served as a track for the floating, flaming silk.

And there was my own knowledge that the Chinese will sacrifice anything to attain the proper theatrical effect. For Kang Chow, as was later revealed was not a Cantonese coolie.

He was a Tibetan, a former priest of the forbidden temple of Po Yun Kwan, from which the cloth of the Fire-God had been stolen!

And yet there was the kite, the death of Corlin's wife and the strange effect on the life of the daughter, Fay. Perhaps it was fever that caused these things. But I do not think so.

Sweets to the Sweet

ROBERT BLOCH

Irma didn't look like a witch.

She had small, regular features, a peaches-and-cream complexion, blue eyes, and fair, almost ash-blonde hair. Besides, she was only eight years old.

"Why does he tease her so?" sobbed Miss Pall. "That's where she got the idea in the first place—because he calls her a little witch."

Sam Steever bulked his paunch back into the squeaky swivel chair and folded his heavy hands in his lap. His fat lawyer's mask was immobile, but he was really quite distressed.

Women like Miss Pall should never sob. Their glasses wiggle, their thin noses twitch, their creasy eyelids redden, and their stringy hair becomes disarrayed.

"Please, control yourself," coaxed Sam Steever. "Perhaps if we could just talk this whole thing over sensibly——"

"I don't care!" Miss Pall sniffled. "I'm not going back there again. I can't stand it. There's nothing I can do, anyway. The man is your brother and she's your brother's child. It's not my responsibility. I've tried——"

"Of course you've tried." Sam Steever smiled benignly, as if Miss Pall were foreman of a jury. "I quite understand. But I still don't see why you are so upset, dear lady."

Miss Pall removed her spectacles, and dabbed at her eyes with a floral-print handkerchief. Then she deposited the soggy ball in her purse, snapped the catch, replaced her spectacles, and sat up straight.

"Very well, Mr. Steever," she said. "I shall do my best to acquaint you with my reasons for quitting your brother's employ."

She suppressed a tardy sniff.

"I came to John Steever two years ago in response to an advertisement for a housekeeper, as you know. When I found that I was to be governess to a motherless six-year-old child, I was at first distressed. I know nothing of the care of children."

"John had a nurse the first years," Sam Steever nodded. "You know Irma's mother died in childbirth."

"I am aware of that," said Miss Pall, primly. "Naturally, one's heart goes out to a lonely, neglected little girl. And she was so

We love life

If you enjoy life now you'll still want to do so when you retire. And you'll need the money to enjoy it with.

£10,000 when you retire
by taking out now a Prudential Endowment Assurance. For more details, complete and return this card.

Some examples
The value of Prudential policies has been amply demonstrated over the years, as is shown by these examples of payments on claims under Ordinary Branch with-profits endowment assurances for £5,000 taken out in the U.K., and which matured at age 65 on 1st January, 1971.

Age at entry	30	40	50
Sum assured	£ 5000	£ 5000	£5000
Bonuses*	£ 6325	£ 5065	£3360
Total payable	£11325	£10065	£8360

*Bonuses·on future maturities cannot be guaranteed

1

The Chief General Manager
THE PRUDENTIAL ASSURANCE CO. LTD.
(Incorporated in England)
142, HOLBORN BARS
LONDON, EC1N 2NH

terribly lonely, Mr. Steever—if you could have seen her, moping around in the corners of that big, ugly old house——"

"I have seen her," said Sam Steever, hastily, hoping to fore-stall another outburst. "And I know what you've done for Irma. My brother is inclined to be thoughtless, even a bit selfish at times. He doesn't understand."

"He's cruel," declared Miss Pall, suddenly vehement. "Cruel and wicked. Even if he is your brother, I say he's no fit father for any child. When I came there, her little arms were black and blue from beatings. He used to take a belt——"

"I know. Sometimes, I think John never recovered from the shock of Mrs. Steever's death. That's why I was so pleased when you came, dear lady. I thought you might help the situation."

"I tried," Miss Pall whimpered. "You know I tried. I never raised a hand to that child in two years, though many's the time your brother has told me to punish her. 'Give the little witch a beating' he used to say. 'That's all she needs—a good thrashing'. And then she'd hide behind my back and whisper to me to protect her. But she wouldn't cry, Mr. Steever. Do you know, I've never seen her cry."

Sam Steever felt vaguely irritated and a bit bored. He wished the old hen would get on with it. So he smiled and oozed treacle. "But just what is your problem, dear lady?"

"Everything was all right when I came there. We got along just splendidly. I started to teach Irma to read—and was surprised to find that she had already mastered reading. Your brother dis-claimed having taught her, but she spent hours curled up on the sofa with a book. 'Just like her,' he used to say. 'Unnatural little witch. Doesn't play with the other children. Little witch'. That's the way he kept talking, Mr. Steever. As if she were some sort of— I don't know what. And she so sweet and quiet and pretty!

"Is it any wonder she read? I used to be that way myself when I was a girl, because—but never mind.

"Still, it was a shock that day I found her looking through the *Encyclopaedia Britannica*. "What are you reading Irma?' I asked. She showed me. It was the article on Witchcraft.

"You see what morbid thoughts your brother has inculcated in her poor little head?

"I did my best. I went out and bought her some toys—she had absolutely nothing, you know; not even a doll. She didn't even know how to *play*! I tried to get her interested in some of the other little girls in the neighbourhood, but it was no use. They didn't understand her and she didn't understand them. There were scenes. Children can be cruel, thoughtless. And her father wouldn't let her go to public school. I was to teach her——

"Then I brought her the modelling clay. She liked that. She would spend hours just making faces with clay. For a child of six Irma displayed real talent.

113

"We made little dolls together, and I sewed clothes for them. That first year was a happy one, Mr. Steever. Particularly during those months when your brother was away in South America. But this year, when he came back—oh, I can't bear to talk about it!"

"Please," said Sam Steever. "You must understand. John is not a happy man. The loss of his wife, the decline of his import trade, and his drinking—but you know all that."

"All I know is that he hates Irma," snapped Miss Pall, suddenly. "He hates her. He wants her to be bad, so he can whip her. 'If you don't discipline the little witch, I shall,' he always says. And then he takes her upstairs and thrashes her with his belt—you must do something, Mr. Steever, or I'll go to the authorities myself."

The crazy old biddy would at that, Sam Steever thought. Remedy—more treacle. "But about Irma," he persisted.

"She's changed, too. Ever since her father returned this year. She won't play with me any more, hardly looks at me. It is as though I failed her, Mr. Steever, in not protecting her from that man. Besides—she thinks she's a witch."

Crazy. Stark, staring crazy. Sam Stever creaked upright in his chair.

"Oh you needn't look at me like that, Mr. Steever. She'll tell you so herself—if you ever visited the house!"

He caught the reproach in her voice and assuaged it with a deprecating nod.

"She told me all right, if her father wants her to be a witch she'll be a witch. And she won't play with me, or anyone else, because witches don't play. Last Halloween she wanted me to give her a broomstick. Oh, it would be funny if it weren't so tragic. That child is losing her sanity.

"Just a few weeks ago I thought she'd changed. That's when she asked me to take her to church one Sunday. 'I want to see the baptism,' she said. Imagine that—an eight-year-old interested in baptism! Reading too much, that's what does it.

"Well, we went to church and she was as sweet as can be, wearing her new blue dress and holding my hand. I was proud of her, Mr. Steever, really proud.

"But after that, she went right back into her shell. Reading around the house, running through the yard at twilight and talking to herself.

"Perhaps it's because your brother wouldn't bring her a kitten. She was pestering him for a black cat, and he asked why, and she said, 'Because witches always have black cats'. Then he took her upstairs.

"I can't stop him, you know. He beat her again the night the power failed and we couldn't find the candles. He said she'd stolen them. Imagine that—accusing an eight-year-old child of stealing candles!

114

"That was the beginning of the end. Then today, when he found his hairbrush missing——"

"You say he beat her with his hairbrush?"

"Yes. She admitted having stolen it. Said she wanted it for her doll."

"But didn't you say she has no dolls?"

"She made one. At least I think she did. I've never seen it—she won't show us anything any more; won't talk to us at table, just impossible to handle her.

"But this doll she made—it's a small one, I know, because at times she carries it tucked under her arm. She talks to it and pets it, but she won't show it to me or to him. He asked her about the hairbrush and she said she took it for the doll.

"Your brother flew into a terrible rage—he'd been drinking in his room again all morning, oh don't think I don't know it!—and she just smiled and said he could have it now. She went over to her bureau and handed it to him. She hadn't harmed it in the least; his hair was still in it, I noticed.

"But he snatched it up, and then he started to strike her about the shoulders with it, and he twisted her arm and then he——"

Miss Pall huddled in her chair and summoned great racking sobs from her thin chest.

Sam Steever patted her shoulder, fussing about her like an elephant over a wounded canary.

"That's all, Mr. Steever. I came right to you. I'm not even going back to that house to get my things. I can't stand any more —the way he beat her—and the way she didn't cry, just giggled and giggled and giggled—sometimes I think she *is* a witch—that he made her into a witch——"

Sam Steever picked up the phone. The ringing had broken the relief of silence after Miss Pall's hasty departure.

"Hello—that you Sam?"

He recognized his brother's voice, somewhat the worse for drink.

"Yes, John."

"I suppose the old bat came running straight to you to shoot her mouth off."

"If you mean Miss Pall, I've seen her, yes."

"Pay no attention. I can explain everything."

"Do you want me to stop in? I haven't paid you a visit in months."

"Well—not right now. Got an appointment with the doctor this evening."

"Something wrong?"

"Pain in my arm. Rheumatism or something. Getting a little

115

diathermy. But I'll call you tomorrow and we'll straighten this whole mess out."

"Right."

But John Steever did not call the next day. Along about supper time, Sam called him.

Surprisingly enough, Irma answered the phone. Her thin, squeaky little voice sounded faintly in Sam's ears.

"Daddy's upstairs sleeping. He's been sick."

"Well don't disturb him. What is it—his arm?"

"His back, now. He has to go to the doctor again in a little while."

"Tell him I'll call tomorrow, then. Uh—everything all right, Irma? I mean, don't you miss Miss Pall?"

"No. I'm glad she went away. She's stupid."

"Oh. Yes. I see. But you phone me if you want anything. And I hope your Daddy's better."

"Yes. So do I," said Irma, and then she began to giggle, and then she hung up.

There was no giggling the following afternoon when John Steever called Sam at the office. His voice was sober—with the sharp sobriety of pain.

"Sam—for God's sake, get over here. Something's happening to me!"

"What's the trouble?"

"The pain—it's killing me! I've got to see you, quickly."

"There's a client in the office, but I'll get rid of him. Say, wait a minute. Why don't you call the doctor?"

"That quack can't help me. He gave me diathermy for my arm and yesterday he did the same thing for my back."

"Didn't it help?"

"The pain went away, yes. But it's back now I feel—like I was being crushed. Squeezed, here in the chest. I can't breathe."

"Sounds like pleurisy. Why don't you call him?"

"It isn't pleurisy. He examined me. Said I was sound as a dollar. No, there's nothing organically wrong. And I couldn't tell him the real cause."

"Real cause?"

"Yes. The pins. The pins that little fiend is sticking into the doll she made. Into the arm, the back. And now heaven only knows how she's causing *this*."

"John you mustn't——"

"Oh what's the use of talking? I can't move off the bed here. She has me now. I can't go down and stop her, get hold of the doll. And nobody else would believe it. But it's the doll all right, the one she made with the candle-wax and the hair from my brush. Oh—it hurts to talk—that cursed little witch! Hurry, Sam. Promise me you'll do something—anything—get that doll from her—get that doll——"

Half an hour later, at four-thirty, Sam Steever entered his brother's house.

Irma opened the door.

It gave Sam a shock to see her standing there, smiling and unperturbed, pale blonde hair brushed immaculately back from the rosy oval of her face. She looked just like a little doll. A little doll. . . .

"Hello, Uncle Sam."

"Hello, Irma. Your Daddy called me, did he tell you? He said he wasn't feeling well——"

"I know. But he's all right now. He's sleeping."

Something happened to Sam Steever; a drop of ice-water trickled down his spine.

"Sleeping?" he croaked. "Upstairs?"

Before she opened her mouth to answer he was bounding up the steps to the second floor, striding down the hall to John's bedroom.

John lay on the bed. He was asleep, and only asleep. Sam Steever noted the regular rise and fall of his chest as he breathed. His face was calm, relaxed.

Then the drop of ice-water evaporated, and Sam could afford to smile and murmur "Nonsense" under his breath as he turned away.

As he went downstairs he hastily improvised plans. A six-month vacation for his brother; avoid calling it a "cure". An orphanage for Irma; give her a chance to get away from this morbid old house, all those books. . . .

He paused halfway down the stairs. Peering over the banister through the twilight he saw Irma on the sofa, cuddled up like a little white ball. She was talking to something she cradled in her arms, rocking it to and fro.

Then there was a doll, after all.

Sam Steever tiptoed very quietly down the stairs and walked over to Irma.

"Hello," he said.

She jumped. Both arms rose to cover completely whatever it was she had been fondling. She squeezed it tightly.

Sam Steever thought of a doll being squeezed across the chest. . . .

Irma stared up at him, her face a mask of innocence. In the half-light her face did resemble a mask. The mask of a little girl covering—what?

"Daddy's better now, isn't he?" lisped Irma.

"Yes, much better."

"I knew he would be."

"But I'm afraid he's going to have to go away for a rest. A long rest."

A smile filtered through the mask. "Good," said Irma.

117

"Of course," Sam went on, "you couldn't stay here all alone. I was wondering—maybe we could send you off to school, or to some kind of a home——"

Irma giggled. "Oh, you needn't worry about me," she said. She shifted about on the sofa as Sam sat down, then sprang up quickly as he came close to her.

Her arms shifted with the movement, and Sam Steever saw a pair of tiny legs dangling down below her elbow. There were trousers on the legs, and little bits of leather for shoes.

"What's that you have, Irma?" he asked. "Is it a doll?" Slowly, he extended his pudgy hand.

She pulled back.

"You can't see it," she said.

"But I want to. Miss Pall said you made such lovely ones."

"Miss Pall is stupid. So are you. Go away."

"Please, Irma. Let me see it."

But even as he spoke, Sam Steever was staring at the top of the doll, momentarily revealed when she backed away. It was a head all right, with wisps of hair over a white face. Dusk dimmed the features, but Sam recognized the eyes, the nose, the chin. . . .

He could keep up the pretence no longer.

"Give me that doll, Irma!" he snapped. "I know what it is. I know *who* it is——"

For an instant, the mask slipped from Irma's face, and Sam Steever stared into naked fear.

She knew. She knew he knew.

Then, just as quickly, the mask was replaced.

Irma was only a sweet, spoiled, stubborn little girl as she shook her head merrily and smiled with impish mischief in her eyes.

"Oh Uncle Sam," she giggled. "You're so silly! Why, this isn't a *real* doll."

"What is it, then?" he muttered.

Irma giggled once more, raising the figure as she spoke. "Why, it's only—candy!" Irma said.

"Candy?"

Irma nodded. Then, very swiftly, she slipped the tiny head of the image into her mouth.

And bit it off.

There was a single piercing scream from upstairs.

As Sam Steever turned and ran up the steps, little Irma, still gravely munching, skipped out of the front door and into the night beyond.

A Thin Gentleman With Gloves

SIMON WEST

At first glance you would have thought Corbin Bellaman an old duffer who had long ago run to seed. At second, you might have considered him a benign and harmless fellow who was somebody's grandfather. As a matter of fact, Bellaman was distinctly on the shady side; he was a crafty barrister in his late fifties who had for better than twenty years been the last resort of fences, petty thieves, murderers, embezzlers, and eccentrics—like Alonzo Potter. Bellaman had done very well for himself in those two decades plus, but Alonzo Potter was his downfall. Not at all in the way one might suspect, however. He got along very well with Alonzo alive; but Alonzo dead was a different matter entirely.

Alonzo Potter, almost alone among Bellaman's clients, was not a criminal. That is to say, he was not obviously one; the fact is, no one knew very much about him, except that he had once written a book which a great many people had burned with a lot of public and private to-do, since it was a book purporting to tell the secrets of black magic, necromancy, sorcery, and the like. At the time Bellaman first knew his client, Potter was already an old man, a wizened, stooped figure of a man who got around with the aid of a cane, and was never without a tall, gangling companion, who walked a little behind him and to one side, like a mendicant, holding his head bowed and saying nothing. This might have occasioned considerable comment if Potter had gone out much; but he did not; he kept to his out-of-the-way house in Soho, living quietly, despite the queer stories that got around about strange happenings in his house, and eventually dying quietly, leaving Bellaman to execute his will, which revealed that there was a little matter of fifty thousand pounds to be bestowed upon Miss Clarice Tregardis, an old flame of Potter's.

Despite his dealings with the underworld, Bellaman had never in his life seen fifty thousand pounds all in one lump, and the prospects of having so much money under his control was an exciting one. However, it was not until he had seen Miss Clarice Tregardis that any thought of appropriating the money entered his head. He had supposed that Miss Tregardis was most likely a chorus girl with a dubious past and a questionable present; but when she came to his office in response to his request, she turned out to be a pleasant old lady who was rather vague about the reason she had been sent for, and remembered Potter as an unsuccessful suitor—"A nice boy, to be sure, Mr. Bellaman, and for a long time we were very dear friends, *very dear*—but, time and events! Well, you know how it is, I'm sure, Mr. Bellaman."

"Well, he's left you all his money, Miss Tregardis," said Bellaman.

"Dear me! How surprising! But then, he always used to do such queer things! Is it very much?"

It was then that the idea of appropriating some of Potter's money for his own use occurred to Bellaman; he had been telling himself all along that he would charge a nice fat fee for acting as executor of the will; but now he realized that Miss Tregardis had no idea at all how much Potter might have left, and, since she was obviously in poor circumstances, virtually any sum at all would be satisfactory. A chorus girl might have raised an immediate outcry and demanded to see the papers, but this old lady would be only too happy to leave it all in Bellaman's hands and take whatever he cared to hand out to her.

"The exact sum hasn't been computed as yet, Miss Tregardis," said Bellaman cautiously, "but when the tax to the Crown has been deducted, I have no doubt it will leave you fairly comfortable for a while."

That was putting it nicely, he thought.

"Oh, really!" she said. "Then perhaps I could buy myself a few new dresses, and a coat, and perhaps I could even have my apartment refurnished. Yes. perhaps I could!"

"I think you could," agreed Bellaman—she might as well be assured of that much; it would not take a large percentage of the total sum left in his predatory hands. "Would you care to retain legal representation, Miss Tregardis, or are you content to leave the matter in my hands?"

"Oh, if Alonzo trusted you, I'm sure I can, too," she said naïvely, and departed.

Bellaman had not expected it to be that easy.

He set about laying his plans at once. Of course, he did not intend to take any unnecessary chances; the old lady might, like as not, have some inquisitive relative who might poke his nose into the affair and demand a full accounting; so, to take care of any such contingency, Bellaman determined to rig up dummy papers and a plausible account of doctored expenses in connection with the disposal of the money for anyone to see on demand. He toyed with the idea of just decamping with the entire sum, but then there would be the tax collectors for the Crown, and besides, he was comfortable where he was, and there was no need of leaving his routine or his business, which was drawn largely from Whitechapel, Limehouse, Soho, and Wapping along the Thames; more unsavoury areas of London could hardly be imagined.

His plans were laid, with the care of an old master.

He began by abstracting a modest sum—a thousand pounds—with which to play the races; he did this with the idea that if he could make a goodly sum by so doing, he need not deduct as much as he had planned from Potter's hoard. Gambling was Bellaman's weakness; he might have been the owner of a comfortable nest-egg if he had not insisted upon trying to double or triple every fee he took in, with the result that he was constantly living from hand to mouth.

He lost the thousand pounds.

Moreover, he had a most disgreeable experience at the races. Just after he had placed his money, he fancied that someone tapped him on the shoulder, and, turning around to look, he did not immediately see anyone he knew; but then saw, standing a little distance away, a tall, thin gentleman wearing a bowler hat not unlike that Alonzo Potter had worn, and with a certain familiarity about him. He turned away, wondering where he could have seen him before; but in a flash he remembered. It was the silent companion who had always appeared with Potter, and who had vanished completely on the day that Potter was found dead. He looked back, but the fellow had gone. The disagreeable aspect of this trivial event lay not in the event itself but in the uncomfortable twinge it gave to his vestigial conscience, particularly after he had lost the money.

Before he dipped further into Potter's funds, he determined to conduct an inquiry into the identity of Potter's one-time companion, to discover for himself whether he might have any knowledge which would be brought to the attention of Clarice Tregardis.

He worked at it for a week, utilizing every source of underworld information that was his.

At the end of that time he was not one whit better informed than he had been before. No one knew anything whatever about Potter's companion save that he was never known to speak, no one had ever seen his face, the fellow habitually wore gloves, he was thin to emaciation, and he shuffled along after Potter more like a dog than a fellow human being. That he had disappeared completely after Potter's death, everyone was agreed. While the lack of information annoyed Bellaman, nevertheless, the unanimity of opinion about the fellow's disappearance was reassuring.

He closed the incident by coming to the conclusion that he had mistaken someone else for the cadaverous companion of Alonzo Potter.

After the lapse of a week, he tried the races once more, this time with two thousand pounds, in that sublime confidence which always obsesses the gambler and leads him to believe that he can recoup previous losses as if by a magic windfall, convincing him each time he ventures anew that his luck must turn by that mythical law of chance, and that this is the time.

But this was not Bellaman's time. Far from it.

He lost not only Potter's two thousand, but also ten and six of his own. Moreover, all the way back to his office he could not shake himself of the conviction that he was being followed. Naturally, being guilty of such peccadilloes, he imagined that the police might be keeping an eye on him, and kept looking for anything resembling an officer; but of course, the ludicrousness of this presently impressed him, and his range of vision became more general. It was then that he saw the thin man, with his gangling arms and his gloved fingers, shuffling along as unobtrusively as possible half a block behind him.

He stopped the first passer-by to whom he came, caught him by the arm, and said, "Pardon me. I've lost my glasses, and I've been expecting a friend. He's a tall, thin fellow, who shuffles along, wears gloves, holds his head down so that his face is practically invisible. I thought I heard him behind me, but I can't see well enough to be sure. Is there anyone fitting that description walking along behind me?"

After a moment of careful scrutiny, the passer-by, looking askance at Bellaman, as if the barrister had been drinking, assured him that there was no one even remotely answering that description in sight.

His forehead beaded with cold perspiration, Bellaman went directly to his office and took out Potter's will, thinking that perhaps he might have missed some reference to that mysterious companion in it, and hoping against hope that he would discover it without delay.

He did.

"As for Simeon Brown, who has been my constant companion for several years, he shall be considered released from the bondage I have put upon him, when the terms of this will shall have been carried out."

That was all, nothing more. After he had read it a dozen times, Bellaman was more mystified than ever. No matter how one looked at it, it did not make sense. What bondage? How could the dead Potter exercise any choice in the matter of "releasing" Simeon Brown—the thin gentleman with gloves who had manifested himself so curiously on these two occasions? No, the whole thing was fantastic.

All except the thin gentleman with gloves—Simeon Brown. Bellaman might have made a mistake the first time, but not the second. Bellaman was no fool. Clearly, there was more to this than met the eye. With a vague sense of uneasiness, the barrister laid his plans to go away for a while—in the company of as much of Miss Tregardis's legacy as he could make away with.

He paid the tax to the Crown, made out a preposterous bill, and converted certain of his own securities into more cash—just in case he should take it into his head not to come back at all. Then he prepared, when the time was ripe, to send a cheque for a thousand pounds to Miss Tregardis, supremely confident that she would be completely satisfied with this amount in lieu of what, unknown to her, she had coming.

However, he reasoned, before he did anything rash, there would be no harm in looked into the matter of Simeon Brown. Since that last disturbing glimpse of him hurrying down the street in his wake, Bellaman had seen nothing more of him; he did not connect with this fact the incident that he had kept his hands off Potter's money throughout this time.

He pursued a careful inquiry, investigating Potter's papers to the last of them. He came upon a great many extremely strange references to subjects which Bellaman thought properly belonged in the Middle Ages, when people still had a healthy respect and fear for witches, warlocks, and the like, and when spells and enchantments and potions were the order of the day. Curious, how old recluses, male and female, seemed to go in for spiritualism, table-rappings, ouija, and the like.

The late Mr. Potter's activities, however, did not come under any one of these heads.

He had been a warlock; in his modest way, he had been a good warlock. He knew how to adapt even the most difficult of the old spells to his own uses; and he had left behind him a great many of these old spells, most of them in Latin, so that Bellaman did not take the trouble to decipher them. However, it was among them that Bellaman caught sight of the name of Simeon Brown, and after it, what appeared to be an address: *37, 213 Upper Leshaway*. At least, that is what it appeared to be; Bellaman could not be sure, for Potter's writing was spidery and small and not very certain. There was nothing else.

And even this turned out to be a false lead, Bellaman thought, when he tracked down the address, for 213 Upper Leshaway was not a house address at all, but the number of the gate post of a cemetery. Obviously Potter's script had been beyond Bellaman. There was a Latterby Lane, and there was also a Leshly Street —it might have been one of those; but both were at such a distance from his office that Bellaman was loath to go there.

However, before taking his final drastic step, he made careful note of his findings, together with his suppositions as to where he had made a mistake, and set out for a meeting with three of his old cronies, two of whom were medical men of a sort and had known the late Potter. With a directness singular for him, he told them about his experiences with Simeon Brown.

Peter Benfield, who was the oldest among them, opined that this may have been the same Brown with whom Potter had once had so much trouble.

"No, Sim died years ago," offered Pearson.

Benfield smiled oddly, and turned to Bellaman. "You know,

Bellaman—you might be dealing with Potter's familiar."

The others took up the theme at once, making sport of the barrister. There was no doubt of it, they averred, with many a wink and sly joke, Bellaman was being hounded by Potter's familiar. Stung, Bellaman suggested that someone might explain the meaning of the jest which was amusing them at his expense.

Oh, said Benfield, a familiar was just halfpenny magic for an old wizard like Potter. A familiar was a companion summoned from outside somewhere, to attend the wizard and obey his commands. A spell was put upon him by the wizard—if you went in for that sort of thing.

"A ghost?" asked Bellaman, with a poor attempt at concealing his ire at his companions.

"Well, I don't think I'd call it a ghost exactly," conceded Benfield. "But then, it might be that—or a skeleton, an imp, maybe even a corpse."

He cackled mirthfully, much to Bellaman's disgust, so that the barrister did not know whether Benfield was joking or not. Wouldn't it have been just like old Potter, Benfield went on, to command Simeon Brown? It certainly would. But Pearson, who had a literal mind, reflected again that poor Brown had passed on some years ago.

Instead of clarifying the matter, it seemed that Bellaman only got himself more perplexed. This was annoying to a man of his calibre, and it was inevitable that he should chuck the whole thing and go ahead with his plans.

The tax to the Crown had been straightforward enough.

The carefully doctored bill, preposterous as it was, Bellaman put into his files, for any curious person to see if any kind of investigation should follow in the wake of his absence from his usual haunts.

Then he dispatched the cheque by the late post, and that evening he set out for Paddington to entrain for Aldershot, from whence he would cross the channel and lose himself somewhere in France or Switzerland.

Alas! for plans of mice and men!

Bellaman had scarcely stepped from the building which housed his office when he was conscious of someone walking along behind him. It was a dark night, and he was not at first listening, being busy with a reconsideration of his plans; only when he had passed the street light did he become aware of the fact that the sounds coming along behind him were rather a steadily mounting shuffling than orthodox footsteps. He looked back.

It was the thin gentleman with gloves!

A kind of panic seized Bellaman. He did not for an instant believe anything of the conversation he had had with Benfield and Pearson, but there was undeniably something uncanny about the appearance of old Potter's companion at moments such as this.

He felt frantically for the money which he carried in a stout wallet in the inside pocket of his coat; it was safe, for it bulked large there and filled his questing hand. He increased his pace, his agile mind concerned now with some way of escape from Potter's companion.

There was an alley which led out into a brightly lit street where he might take the underground to the Praed Street station; it was a short cut, and by vanishing into its dark maw, Bellaman's chance of outdistancing his pursuer was much greater. Accordingly, he slipped across the street, keeping to the shadows, and, at the appropriate moment, he darted skilfully into the alley.

If he had had the proper kind of imagination, he would have thought twice about doing what he did. His foresight, however, was limited, and when first he heard the shuffling sound behind him, he was only annoyed that the fellow had seen him enter the alley. Then he was conscious of the increased pace of his pursuer; indeed, all within an instant, it seemed, the fellow was directly behind him.

Could it be?

He turned startled, and looked back.

Out of the alley's darkness came a pair of long thin arms reaching for him with gloved fingers, and behind it came an utterly horrible, soul-searing travesty of a face, whose eyeless sockets seemed to gleam with a hellish light, whose lipless mouth seemed to work in drooling ecstacy.

Bellaman did not have time even to scream.

In the morning Miss Clarice Tregardis received Mr. Bellaman's cheque for a thousand pounds; there was also in her mailbox a well-filled wallet, the contents of which, added to the cheque, made up the precise sum which Miss Tregardis was legally entitled to receive from Mr. Potter's fifty-thousand pound legacy, minus the tax to the Crown.

Bellaman's disappearance was more than a nine day wonder.

The police ultimately got around to discovering that address he had written down and went out to investigate. Being possessed of far more imagination than the late Mr. Bellaman, they proseeded at once to the Upper Leshaway cemetery, and went directly to lot thirty-seven, which presumably had been meant.

So it had. Lot thirty-seven held the grave of one Simeon Brown. Moreover, there was every evidence that the grave had been recently disturbed; so an exhumation order was got and the grave opened.

The grave contained the body of Corbin Bellaman, who had been strangled and otherwise badly mauled, together with the remains of the said Brown, badly decayed and partly skeletal, a tall, thin gentleman apparently, whose bony black-gloved fingers were curiously closed about Bellaman's neck.

It was a ghastly business, even for Scotland Yard. They issued a strongly worded statement in regard to the shocking vandalism accompanying the murder of the late Corbin Bellaman and hinted ominously that the entire mystery would soon be completely explained by the master minds behind the walls of that sacrosanct sanctuary of mysteries.

But, of course, it never was.

The Horror at Red Hook

H. P. LOVECRAFT

"The nightmare horde slithered away, led by the abominable naked phosphorescent thing that now strode insolently bearing in its arms the glassy-eyed corpse of the corpulent old man.
"There are sacraments of evil as well as of good about us, and we live and move to my belief in an unknown world, a place where there are caves and shadows and dwellers in twilight. It is possible that man may sometimes return on the track of evolution, and it is my belief that an awful lore is not yet dead."

—Arthur Machen

I

Not many weeks ago, on a street corner in the village of Pascoag, Rhode Island, a tall heavily built, and wholesome looking pedestrian furnished much speculation by a singular lapse of behaviour. He had, it appears, been descending the hill by the road from Chepachet; and encountering the compact section, had turned to his left into the main thoroughfare where several modest business blocks convey a touch of the urban. At this point, without visible provocation, he committed his astonishing lapse; staring queerly for a second at the tallest of the buildings before him, and then, with a series of terrified, hysterical shrieks, breaking into a frantic run which ended in a stumble and fall at the next crossing. Picked up and dusted off by ready hands, he was found to be conscious, organically unhurt, and evidently cured of his sudden nervous attack. He muttered some shamefaced explanations involving a strain he had undergone, and with downcast glance turned back up the Chepachet road, trudging out of sight without once looking behind him. It was a strange incident to befall so large, robust, normal-featured, and capable-looking a man, and the strangeness was not lessened by the remarks of a bystander who had recognized him as the boarder of a well-known dairyman on the outskirts of Chepachet.

He was, it developed, a New York police detective named Thomas F. Malone, now on a long leave of absence under medical treatment after some disproportionately arduous work on a gruesome local case which accident had made dramatic. There had been a collapse of several old brick buildings during a raid in which he had shared, and something about the wholesale loss of life, both of prisoners and of his companions, had peculiarly appalled him. As a result, he had acquired an acute and anomalous horror of any buildings even remotely suggesting the ones which had fallen in, so that in the end mental specialists forbade him the sight of such things for an indefinite period. A police surgeon with relatives in Chepachet had put forward that quaint hamlet of wooden Colonial houses as an ideal spot for the psychological convalescence; and thither the sufferer had gone, promising never to venture among the brick-lined streets of larger villages till duly advised by the Woonsocket specialist with whom he was put in touch. This walk to Pascoag for magazines had been a mistake, and the patient had paid in fright, bruises, and humiliation for his disobedience.

So much the gossips of Chepachet and Pascoag knew; and so much, also, the most learned specialists believed. But Malone had at first told the specialists much more, ceasing only when he saw the utter incredulity was his portion. Thereafter he held his peace, protesting not at all when it was generally agreed that the collapse of certain squalid brick houses in the Red Hook section of Brooklyn, and the consequent death of many brave officers, had unseated his nervous equilibrium. He had worked too hard, all said, in trying to clean up those nests of disorder and violence; certain features were shocking enough, in all conscience, and the unexpected tragedy was the last straw. This was a simple explanation which everyone could understand, and because Malone was not a simple person he perceived that he had better let it suffice. To hint to unimaginative people of a horror beyond all human conception—a horror of houses and clocks and cities leprous and cancerous with evil dragged from elder worlds—would be merely to invite a padded cell instead of a restful rustication, and Malone was a man of sense despite his mysticism. He had the Celt's far vision of weird and hidden things, but the logician's quick eye for the outwardly unconvincing; an amalgam which had let him far afield in the forty-two years of his life, and set him in strange places for a Dublin University man born in a Georgian villa near Phœnix Park.

And now, as he reviewed the things he had seen and felt and apprehended, Malone was content to keep unshared the secret of what could reduce a dauntless fighter to a quivering neurotic; what could make old brick slums and seas of dark, subtle faces a thing of nightmare and eldritch portent. It would not be the first time his sensations had been forced to bide uninterpreted— for was not his very act of plunging into the polyglot abyss of New York's underworld a freak beyond sensible explanation? What could he tell the prosaic of the antique witcheries and grotesque marvels discernable to sensitive eyes amidst the poison

128

cauldron where all the varied dregs of unwholesome ages mix their venom and perpetuate their obscene terrors? He had seen the hellish green flame of secret wonder in this blatant, evasive welter of outward greed and inward blasphemy, and had smiled gently when all the New Yorkers he knew scoffed at his experiment in police work. They had been very witty and cynical, deriding his fantastic pursuit of unknowable mysteries and assuring him that in these days New York held nothing but cheapness and vulgarity. One of them had wagered him a heavy sum that he could not—despite many poignant things to his credit in the *Dublin Review*—even write a truly interesting story of New York low life; and now, looking back, he perceived that cosmic irony had justified the prophet's words while secretly confuting their flippant meaning. The horror, as glimpsed at last, could not make a story—for like the book cited by Poe's German authority, *"er lässt sich nicht lesen"*—it does not permit itself to be read.

II

To Malone the sense of latent mystery in existence was always present. In youth he had felt the hidden beauty and ecstasy of things, and had been a poet; but poverty and sorrow and exile had turned his gaze in darker directions, and he had thrilled at the imputations of evil in the world around. Daily life had for him come to be a phantasmagoria of *macabre* shadow-studies; now glittering and leering with concealed rottenness as in Aubrey Beardsley's best manner, now hinting terrors behind the commonest shapes and objects as in the subtler and less obvious work of Gustave Doré. He would often regard it as merciful that most persons of high intelligence jeer at the inmost mysteries; for, he argued, if superior minds were ever placed in fullest contact with the secrets preserved by ancient and lowly cults, the resultant abnormalities would soon not only wreck the world, but threaten the very integrity of the universe. All this reflection was no doubt morbid, but keen logic and a deep sense of humour ably offset it. Malone was satisfied to let his notions remain as half-spied and forbidden visions to be lightly played with; and hysteria came only when duty flung him into a hell of revelation too sudden and insidious to escape.

He had for some time been detailed to the Butler Street station in Brooklyn when the Red Hook matter came to his notice. Red Hook is a maze of hybrid squalor near the ancient waterfront opposite Governor's Island, with dirty highways climbing the hill from the wharves to that higher ground where the decayed lengths of Clinton and Court Streets lead off towards the Borough Hall. Its houses are mostly of brick, dating from the first quarter of the middle of the nineteenth century, and some of the obscurer alleys and byways have that alluring antique flavour which conventional reading leads us to call "Dickensian." The population is a hopeless tangle and enigma; Syrian, Spanish, Italian, and Negro elements impinging upon one another, and fragments of Scandinavian and American belts lying not far distant. It is a babel of sound and filth, and sends out strange cries to answer the lapping of oily waves at its grimy piers and the monstrous organ litanies of the harbour whistles. Here long ago a brighter picture dwelt, with clear-eyed mariners on the lower streets and homes of taste and substance where the larger houses line the hill. One can trace the relics of this former happiness in the trim shapes of the buildings, the occasional graceful churches and the evidences of original art and background in bits of detail here and there—a worn flight of steps, a battered doorway, a wormy pair of decorative columns or pilasters, or a fragment of once green space with bent and rusted iron railing. The houses are generally in solid blocks, and now and then a many-windowed cupola arises to tell of days when the households of captains and ship-owners watched the sea.

From this tangle of material and spiritual putrescence the blasphemies of a hundred dialects assail the sky. Hordes of prowlers reel shouting and singing along the lanes and thoroughfares, occasional furtive hands suddenly extinguish lights and pull down curtains, and swarthy, sin-pitted faces disappear from windows when visitors pick their way through. Policemen despair of order or reform, and seek rather to erect barriers protecting the outside world from the contagion.

The clang of the patrol is answered by a kind of spectral silence, and such prisoners as are taken are never communicative. Visible offences are as varied as the local dialects, and run the gamut from the smuggling of rum and prohibited aliens through diverse stages of lawlessness and obscure vice to murder and mutilation in their most abhorent guises. That these visible affairs are not more frequent is not to the neighbourhood's credit, unless the power of concealment be an art demanding credit. More people enter Red Hook than leave it—or at least, than leave it by the landward side—and those who are not loquacious are the likeliest to leave.

Malone found in this state of things a faint stench of secrets more terrible than any of the sins denounced by citizens and bemoaned by priest and philanthropists. He was conscious, as one who united imagination with scientific knowledge, that modern people under lawless conditions tend uncannily to repeat the darkest instinctive patterns of primitive half-ape savagery in their daily life and ritual observances; and he had often viewed with an anthropologist's shudder the chanting, cursing processions of blear-eyed and pock-marked young men which wound their way along in the dark small hours of morning. One saw groups of these youths incessantly; sometimes in leering vigils on street corners, sometimes in doorways playing eerily on cheap instruments of music, sometimes in stupefied dozes or indecent dialogues around cafeteria tables near Borough Hall, and sometimes in whispering converse around dingy taxicabs drawn up at the high stoops of crumbling and closely shuttered old houses. They chilled and fascinated him more than he dared confess to his associates on the force, for he seemed to see in them some monstrous thread of secret continuity; some fiendish, cryptical and ancient pattern utterly beyond and below the sordid mass of facts and habits and haunts listed with such conscientious technical care by the police. They must be, he felt inwardly, the heirs of some shocking and primordial tradition; the sharers of debased and broken scraps from cults and ceremonies older than mankind. Their coherence and definiteness suggested it, and it showed in the singular suspicion of order which lurked beneath their squalid disorder. He had not read in vain such treatises as Miss Murray's Witch Cult in Western Europe; and knew that up to recent years there had certainly survived among peasants and furtive folk a frightful and clandestine system of assemblies and orgies descended from dark religions ante-dating the Aryan World, and appearing in popular legends as Black Masses and Witches' Sabbaths. That these hellish vestiges of old Turanian-Asiatic magic and fertility-cults were even now wholly dead he could not for a moment suppose, and he frequently wondered how much older and how much blacker than the very worst of the muttered tales some of them might really be.

III

It was the case of Robert Suydam which took Malone to the heart of things in Red Hook. Suydam was a lettered recluse of ancient Dutch family, possessed originally of barely independent means, and inhabiting the spacious but ill-preserved mansion which his grandfather had built in Flatbush when that village was little more than a pleasant group of Colonial cottages surrounding the steepled and ivy-clad Reformed Church with its iron-railed yard of Netherlandish gravestones. In this lonely house, set back from Martense Street amidst a yard of venerable trees, Suydam had read and brooded for some six decades except for a period a generation before, when he had sailed for the Old World and remained there out of sight for eight years. He could afford no servants, and would admit but few visitors to his absolute solitude; eschewing close friendships and receiving his rare acquaintances in one of the three ground-floor rooms which he kept in order—a vast, high-ceiled library whose walls were solidly packed with tattered books of ponderous, archaic, and vaguely repellent aspect. The growth of the town and its final absorption in the Brooklyn district had meant nothing to Suydam and he had come to mean less and less to the town. Elderly people still pointed him out on the streets, but to most of the recent population he was merely a queer, corpulent old fellow whose unkempt white hair, stubbly beard, shiny black clothes and gold-headed cane earned him an amused glance and nothing more. Malone did not know him by sight till duty called him to the case, but had heard of him indirectly as a really profound authority on medieval supersition, and had once idly meant to look up an out-of-print pamphlet of his on the Kabbalah and the Faustus legend, which a friend had quoted from memory.

Suydam became a "case" when his distant and only relatives sought court pronouncements on his sanity. Their action seemed sudden to the outside world, but was really undertaken only after prolonged observation and sorrowful debate. It was based on certain odd changes in his speech and habits; wild references to impending wonders, and unaccountable hauntings of disreputable Brooklyn neighbourhoods. He had been growing shabbier and shabbier with the years, and now prowled about like a veritable mendicant; seen occasionally by humiliated friends in subway stations, or loitering on the benches around Borough Hall in conversation with groups of swarthy, evil looking strangers. When he spoke it was to babble of unlimited powers almost within his grasp, and to repeat with knowing leers such mystical words of names as "Sephiroth," "Ashmodai" and "Samael." The court action revealed that he was using up his income and wasting his principal in the purchase of curious tomes imported from London and Paris, and in the maintenance of a squalid basement flat in the Red Hook district where he spent nearly every night, receiving odd delegations of mixed rowdies and foreigners, and apparently conducting some kind of ceremonial service behind the green blinds of secretive windows. Detectives assigned to follow him reported strange cries and chants and prancing of feet filtering out from these nocturnal rites, and shuddered at their peculiar ecstasy and abandon despite the commonness of weird orgies in that sodden section. When, however, the matter came to a hearing, Suydam managed to preserve his liberty. Before the judge his manner grew urbane and reasonable, and he freely admitted the queerness of demeanour and extravagant cast of language into which he had fallen through excessive devotion to study and research. He was, he said, engaged in the investigation of certain details of European tradition which required the closest contact with foreign groups and their songs and folk dances. The notion that any low secret society was preying upon him, as hinted by his relatives, was obviously absurd; and showed how sadly limited was their understanding of him and his work. Triumphing with his calm explanations, he was suffered to depart unhindered; and the paid detectives of the Suydams, Corlears and Van Brunts were withdrawn in resigned disgust.

It was here that an alliance of Federal inspectors and police, Malone with them, entered the case. The law had watched the Suydam action with interest, and had in many instances been called upon to aid the private detectives. In this work it developed that Suydam's new associates were among the blackest and most vicious criminals of Red Hook's devious lanes, and that at least a third of them were known and repeated offenders in the matter of thievery, disorder, and the importation of illegal immigrants. Indeed, it would not have been too much to say that the old scholar's particular circle coincided almost perfectly with the worst of the organized cliques which smuggled ashore certain nameless and unclassified Asian dregs wisely turned back by Ellis Island. In the teeming rookeries of Parker Place—since renamed— where Suydam had his basement flat, there had grown up a very unusual colony of unclassified slant-eyed folk who used the Arabic alphabet but were eloquently repudiated by the great mass of Syrians in and around Atlantic Avenue. They could all have been deported for lack of credentials, but legalism is slow-moving, and one does not disturb Red Hook unless publicity forces one to.

These creatures attended a tumbledown stone church, used Wednesdays as a dance hall, which reared its Gothic buttresses near the vilest part of the waterfront. Clergy throughout Brooklyn denied the place all standing and authenticity, and policemen agreed with them when they listened to the noises it emitted at night. Malone used to fancy he heard terrible cracked bass notes from a hidden organ far underground when the church stood empty and unlighted, whilst all observers dreaded the shrieking and drumming which accompanied the visible services. Suydam, when questioned, said he thought the ritual was some remnant of Nestorian Christianity tinctured with the Shamanism of Tibet. Most of the people, he conjectured, were of Mongoloid stock, originating somewhere in or near Kurdistan—and Malone could not help recalling that Kurdistan is the land of the Yezidees, last survivors of the Persian devil-worshippers. However this may have been, the stir of the Suydam investigation made it certain that these unauthorized newcomers were flooding Red Hook in increasing numbers; entering through some marine conspiracy unreached by revenue officers and harbour police, over-running Parket Place and rapidly spreading up the hill, and welcomed with curious fraternalism by the other assorted denizens of the region. Their squat figures and characteristic squinting physiognomies grotesquely combined with flashy American clothing, appeared more and more numerously among the loafers and nomad gangsters of the Borough Hall section; till at length it was deemed necessary to compute their number, ascertain their sources and occupations, and find if possible a way to round them up and deliver them to the proper immigration authorities. To this task Malone was assigned by agreement of Federal and city forces, and as he commenced his canvass of Red Hook he felt poised upon the brink of nameless terrors, with the shabby, unkempt figure of Robert Suydam as archfiend and adversary.

IV

Police methods are varied and ingenious. Malone, through unostentatious rambles, carefully casual conversations, well-timed offers of hip-pocket liquor, and judicious dialogues with frightened prisoners, learned many isolated facts about the movement whose aspect had become so menacing. The newcomers were indeed Kurds, but of a dialect obscure and puzzling to exact philology. Such of them as worked lived mostly as dockhands and unlicensed peddlers, though frequently serving in Greek restaurants and tending corner news-stands. Most of them, however, had no visible means of support; and were obviously connected with underworld pursuits, of which smuggling and bootlegging were the least indescribable. They had come in steamships, apparently tramp freighters, and had been unloaded by stealth on moonless nights in rowboats which stole under a certain wharf and followed a hidden canal and house Malone could not locate, for the memories of his informants were exceedingly confused, while their speech was to a great extent beyond even the ablest interpreters; nor could he gain any real data on the reasons for their systematic importation. They were reticent about the exact spot from which they had come, and were never sufficiently off guard to reveal the agencies which had sought them out and directed their course. Indeed, they developed something like acute fright when asked the reason for their presence. Gangsters of other breeds were equally taciturn, and the most that could be gathered was that some god or great priesthood had promised them unheard-of powers and supernatural glories and rulerships in a strange land.

The attendance of both newcomers and old gangsters at Suydam's closely guarded nocturnal meetings was very regular, and the police soon learned that the erstwhile recluse had leased additional flats to accommodate such guests as knew his password; at last occupying three entire houses and permanently harbouring many of his queer companions. He spent but little time now at his Flatbush home, apparently going and coming only to obtain and return books; and his face and manners had attained an appalling pitch of wildness. Malone twice interviewed him, but was each time brusquely repulsed. He knew nothing, he said, of any mysterious plots or movements; and had no idea how the Kurds could have entered or what they wanted. His business was to study

134

undisturbed the folk-lore of all the immigrants of the district; a business with which policemen had no legitimate concern. Malone mentioned his admiration for Suydam's old brochure on the Kabbalah and other myths, but the old man's softening was only momentary. He sensed an intrusion, and rebuffed his visitor in no uncertain way; till Malone withdrew disgusted, and turned to other channels of information.

What Malone would have unearthed could he have worked continuously on the case, we shall never know. As it was, a stupid conflict between city and Federal authority suspended the investigation for several months, during which the detective was busy with other assignments. But at no time did he lose interest, or fail to stand amazed at what began to happen to Robert Suydam. Just at the time when a wave of kidnappings and disappearances spread its excitement over New York, the unkempt scholar embarked upon a metamorphosis as startling as it was absurd. One day he was seen near Borough Hall with clean-shaved face, well-trimmed hair, and tastefully immaculate attire, and on every day thereafter some obscure improvement was noticed in him. He maintained his new fastidiousness without interruption, added to it an unwonted sparkle of eye and crispness of speech, and began little by little to shed the corpulence which had so long deformed him. Now frequently taken for less than his age, he acquired an elasticity of step and buoyancy of demeanour to match the new tradition, and showed a curious darkening of the hair which somehow did not suggest dye. As the months passed, he commenced to dress less and less conservatively, and finally astonished his few friends by renovating and redecorating his Flatbush mansion, which he threw open in a series of receptions, summoning all the acquaintances he could remember, and extending a special welcome to the fully forgiven relatives who had lately sought his restraint. Some attended through curiosity, others through duty; but all were suddenly charmed by the dawning grace and urbanity of the former hermit. He had, he asserted, accomplished most of his allotted work; and having just inherited some property from a half-forgotten European friend, was about to spend his remaining years in a brighter second youth which ease, care and diet had made possible to him. Less and less was he seen at Red Hook, and more and more did he move in the society to which he was born. Policemen noted a tendency of the gangsters to congregate at the old stone church and dance-hall instead of at the basement flat in Parker Place, though the latter and its recent annexes still overflowed with noxious life.

Then two incidents occurred—wide enough apart, but both of intense interest in the case as Malone envisaged it. One was

135

a quiet announcement in the *Eagle* of Robert Suydam's engagement to Miss Conelia Gerritsen of Bayside, a young woman of excellent position, and distantly related to the elderly bridegroom-elect; whilst the other was a raid on the dance-hall church by city police, after a report that the face of a kidnapped child had been seen for a second, at one of the basement windows. Malone had participated in this raid, and studied the place with much care when inside. Nothing was found—in fact the building was entirely deserted when visited—but the sensitive Celt was vaguely disturbed by many things about the interior. There were crudely painted panels he did not like—panels which depicted sacred faces with peculiarly worldly and sardonic expressions, and which occasionally took liberties that even a layman's sense of decorum could scarcely countenance. Then, too, he did not relish the Greek inscription on the wall above the pulpit; an ancient incantation which he had once stumbled upon in Dublin college days, and which read, literally translated: "O friend and companion of night, thou who rejoicest in the baying of dogs and spilt blood, who wanderest in the midst of shades among the tombs, who longest for blood and bringest terror to mortals, Gorgo, Mormo, thousand-faced moon, look favourably on our sacrifices!"

When he read this he shuddered, and thought vaguely of the cracked bass organ notes he fancied he had heard beneath the church on certain nights. He shuddered again at the rust around the rim of a metal basin which stood on the altar, and paused nervously when his nostrils seemed to detect a curious and ghastly stench from somewhere in the neighbourhood. That organ memory haunted him, and he explored the basement with particular assiduity before he left. The place was very hateful to him; yet after all, were the blasphemous panels and inscriptions more than mere crudities perpetrated by the ignorant?

By the time of Suydam's wedding the kidnapping epidemic had become a popular newspaper scandal. Most of the victims were young children of the lowest classes, but the increasing number of disappearances had worked up a sentiment of the strongest fury. Journals clamoured for action from the police, and once more the Butler Street station sent its men over Red Hook for clues, discoveries, and criminals. Malone was glad to be on the trail again, and took pride in a raid on one of Suydam's Parker Place houses. There, indeed, no stolen child was found, despite the tales of screams and the red sash picked up in the areaway; but the paintings and rough inscriptions on the peeling walls of most of the rooms, and the primitive chemical laboratory in the attic, all helped to convince the detective that he was on the track of something tremendous. The paintings were appalling hideous monsters of every shape and size, and parodies on human

136

outlines which cannot be described. The writing was in red, and varied from Arabic to Greek, Roman, and Hebrew letters. Malone could not read much of it, but what he did decipher was portentous and cabalistic enough. One frequently repeated motto was in a sort of Hebraized Hellenistic Greek, and suggested the most terrible demon-evocations of the Alexandrian decadence:

HEL. HELOYM. SOTHER. EMMANVEL. SABOATH. AGLA. TETRA-GRAMMATION. AGYROS. OTHEOS. ISCHYROS. ATHANATOS. IEHOVA. VA. ADONAL. SADY. HOMOVSION. MESSIAS. ESCHEREHEYE.

Circles and pentagrams loomed on every hand, and told indubitably of the strange beliefs and aspirations of those who dwelt so squalidly here. In the cellar, however, the strangest thing was found—a pile of genuine gold ingots covered carelessly with a piece of burlap, and bearing upon their shining surfaces the same weird hieroglyphics which also adorned the walls. During this raid the police encountered only a passive resistance from the squinting Orientals that swarmed from every door. Finding nothing relevant, they had to leave all as it was; but the precinct captain wrote Suydam a note advising him to look closely to the character of his tenants and protégés in view of the growing public clamour.

V

Then came the June wedding and the great sensation. Flatbush was gay for the hour about high noon, and pennanted motors thronged the street near the old Dutch church where an awning stretched from door to highway. No local event ever surpassed the Suydam-Gerritsen nuptials in tone and scale, and the party which escorted the bride and groom to the Cunard pier was, if not exactly the smartest, at least a solid page from the Social Register. At five o'clock adieu was waved, and the ponderous liner edged away from the long pier, slowly turned its nose seaward, discarded its tug, and headed for widening water spaces that led to Old World wonders. By night the outer harbour was cleared, and late passengers watched the stars twinkling above an unpolluted ocean.

Whether the tramp steamer or the scream was first to gain attention, no one can say. Probably they were simultaneous, but it is of no use to calculate. The scream came from the Suydam stateroom, and the sailor who broke down the door could perhaps have told frightful things if he had not forthwith gone completely mad—as it is, he shrieked more loudly than the first victims, and thereafter ran simpering about the vessel till caught and put in irons. The ship's doctor who entered the stateroom and turned on the lights a moment later did not go mad, but told nobody what he saw till afterward, when he corresponded with Malone in

137

Chepachet. It was murder—strangulation—but one need not say that the clawmark on Mrs. Suydam's throat could not have come from her husband's or any other human hand, or that upon the white wall there flickered for an instant in hateful red a legend which, later copied from memory, seems to have been nothing less than the fearsome Chaldee letters of the word "LILITH." One need not mention these things because they vanished so quickly— as for Suydam, one could at least bar others from the room until one knew what to think oneself. The doctor has distinctly assured Malone that he did not see IT. The open porthole, just before he turned on the lights, was clouded for a second with a certain phosphorescence, and for a moment there seemed to echo in the night outside the suggestion of a faint and hellish tittering; but no real outline met the eye. As proof, the doctor points to his continued sanity.

Then the tramp steamer claimed all attention. A boat put off, and a horde of swart, insolent ruffians in officers' dress swarmed aboard the temporarily halted Cunarder. They wanted Suydam or his body—they had known of his trip, and for certain reasons were sure he would die. The captain's deck was almost a pandemonium; for at the instant, between the doctor's report from the stateroom and the demands of the men from the tramp, not even the wisest and gravest seaman could think what to do. Suddenly the leader of the visiting mariners, an Arab with a hatefully negroid mouth, pulled forth a dirty, crumpled paper and handed it to the captain. It was signed by Robert Suydam, and bore the following odd message:

In case of sudden or unexpected accident or death on my part, please deliver me or my body unquestionably into the hands of the bearer and his associates. Everything, for me, and perhaps for you, depends on absolute compliance. Explanations can come later—do not fail me now.

Robert Suydam.

Captain and doctor looked at each other, and the latter whispered something to the former. Finally they nodded rather helplessly and led the way to the Suydam stateroom. The doctor directed the captain's glance away as he unlocked the door and admitted the strange seamen, nor did he breathe easily till they filed out with their burden after an unaccountably long period of preparation. It was wrapped in bedding from the berths, and the doctor was glad that the outlines were not very revealing. Somehow the men got the thing over the side and away to their tramp steamer without uncovering it.

The Cunarder started again, and the doctor and ship's undertaker sought out the Suydam stateroom to perform what last services they could. Once more the physician was forced to reticence and even to mendacity, for a hellish thing had happened. When the undertaker asked him why he had drained off all of Mrs. Suydam's blood, he neglected to affirm that he had not done so; nor did he point to the vacant bottle-spaces on the rack, or to the odour in the sink which showed the hasty disposition of the bottles' original contents. The pockets of those men—if men they were—had bulged damnably when they left the ship. Two hours later, and the world knew by radio all that it ought to know of the horrible affair.

VI

That same June evening, without having heard a word from the sea, Malone was very busy among the alleys of Red Hook. A sudden stir seemed to permeate the place, and as if appraised by "grapevine telegraph" of something singular, the denizens clustered expectantly around the dance-hall church and the houses in Parker Place. Three children had just disappeared—blue-eyed Norwegians from the streets towards Gowanus—and there were rumours of a mob forming among the sturdy Vikings of that section. Malone had for weeks been urging his colleagues to attempt a general clean-up; and at last, moved by conditions more obvious to their common sense than the conjectures of a Dublin dreamer, they had agreed upon a final stroke. The unrest and menace of this evening had been the deciding factor, and just about midnight a raiding party recruited from three stations descended upon Parker Place and its environs. Doors were battered in, stragglers arrested, and candle-lighted rooms forced to disgorge unbelievable throngs of mixed foreigners in figured robes, mitres and other inexplicable devices. Much was lost in the mêlée for objects were thrown hastily down unexpected shafts, and betraying odours deadened by the sudden kindling of pungent incense. But spattered blood was everywhere, and Malone shuddered whenever he saw a brazier or altar from which the smoke was still rising.

He wanted to be in several places at once, and decided on Suydam's basement flat only after a messenger had reported the complete emptiness of the dilapidated dance-hall church. The flat, he thought, must hold some clue to a cult of which the occult scholar had so obviously become the centre and leader; and it was with real expectancy that he ransacked the musty rooms, noted their vaguely charnal odour, and examined the curious books, instruments, gold ingots, and glass-stoppered bottles scattered carelessly here and there. Once a lean, black-and-white cat edged between his feet and tripped him, overturning at the same time a beaker half full of red liquid. The shock was severe, and to this day Malone is not certain of what he saw; but in dreams he still

139

pictures that cat as it scuttled away with certain monstrous alterations and peculiarities.

Then came the locked cellar door, and the search for something to break it down. A heavy stool stood near, and its tough seat was more than enough for the antique panels. A crack formed and enlarged, and the whole door gave way—but from the other side; whence poured a howling tumult of ice-cold wind with all the stenches of the bottomless pit, and whence reached a sucking force not of earth of heaven, which, coiling sentiently about the paralyzed detective, dragged him through the aperture and down unmeasured spaces filled with whispers and wails, and gusts of mocking laughter.

Of course it was a dream. All the specialists have told him so and he has nothing tangible to prove the contrary. Indeed, he would rather have it thus; for then the sight of old brick slums and dark foreign faces would not eat so deeply into his soul. But at the time it was all horribly real, and nothing can ever efface the memory of those nighted crypts, those titan arcades, and those half-formed shapes of hell that strode gigantically in silence holding half-eaten things whose still surviving portions screamed for mercy or laughed with madness. Odours of incense and corruption joined in sickening concert, and the black air was alive with the cloudy, semi-visible bulk of shapeless elemental things with eyes. Somewhere dark sticky water was lapping at onyx piers, and once the shivery tinkle of raucous little bells pealed out to greet the insane titter of a naked phosphorescent thing which swam into sight, scrambled ashore, and climbed up to squat leeringly on a carved golden pedestal in the background.

Avenues of limitless night seemed to radiate in every direction, till one might fancy that there lay the root of a contagion destined to sicken and swallow cities, and engulf nations in the fetor of hybrid pestilence. Here cosmic sin had entered, and festered by unhallowed rites had commenced the grinning march of death that was to rot us all to fungus abnormalities too hideous for the grave's holding. Satan here held his Babylonish court, and in the blood of stainless childhood the leprous limbs of phosphorescent Lilith were laved. Incubi and succubæ howled praise to Hecate, and headless mooncalves bleated to the Magna Mater. Goats leaped to the sound of thin accursed flutes, and Ægipans chased endlessly after misshapen fauns over rocks twisted like swollen toads. Moloch and Ashtaroth were not absent; for in this quintessence of all damnation the bounds of consciousness were let down, and man's fancy lay open to vistas of every realm of horror and every forbidden dimension that evil had power to mould. The world and nature were helpless against such assaults from unsealed wells of night, nor could any sign or prayer check the Walpurgissage of horror which had come when a sage with the hateful locked and brimming coffer of transmitted demonlore.

Suddenly a ray of physical light shot through these fantasms, and Malone heard the sound of oars amidst the blasphemies of things that should be dead. A boat with a lantern in its prow darted into sight, made fast to an iron ring in the slimy stone pier, and vomited forth several dark men bearing a long burden swathed in bedding. They took it to the naked phosphorescent thing on the carved gold pedestal, and the thing tittered and pawed the bedding. Then they unswathed it, and propped upright before the pedestal the gangrenous corpse of a corpulent old man with stubby beard and unkempt white hair. The phosphorescent thing tittered again, and the men produced bottles from their pockets and anointed its feet with red, whilst they afterward gave the bottles to the thing to drink from.

All at once, from an arcaded avenue leading endlessly away, there came the demoniac rattle and wheeze of a blasphemous organ, choking and rumbling out of the mockeries of hell in cracked, sardonic bass. In an instant every moving entity was electrified; and forming at once into a ceremonial procession, the nightmare horde slithered away in quest of the sound—goat, satyr, and Ægipan, incubus, succuba, and lemur, twisted toad and shapeless elemental, dog-faced howler and silent strutter in darkness—all led by the abominable naked phosphorescent thing that had squatted on the carved golden throne, and that now strode insolently bearing in its arms the glassy-eyed corpse of the corpulent old man. The strange dark man danced in the rear, and the whole column skipped and leaped with Dionysiac fury, Malone staggered after them a few steps, delirious and hazy, and doubtful of his place in this or any world. Then he turned, faltered, and sank down on the cold damp stone, gasping and shivering as the demon organ croaked on, and the howling and drumming and tinkling of the mad procession grew fainter and fainter.

Vaguely he was conscious of chanted horrors, and shocking croakings afar off. Now and then a wail or whine of ceremonial devotion would float to him through the black arcade, whilst eventually there rose the dreadful Greek incantation whose text he had read above the pulpit of that dance-hall church.

"O friend and companion of night thou who rejoicest in the baying of dogs (here a hideous howl burst forth) and spilt blood (here nameless sounds vied with morbid shriekings), who wanderest in the midst of shades among the tombs (here a whistling sigh occurred), who longest for blood and bringest terror to mortals (short, sharp cries from myriad throats), Gorgo (repeated as response), Mormo (repeated with ecstasy), thousand-faced moon (sighs and flute notes), look favourably on our sacrifices!"

As the chant closed, a general shout went up, and hissing sounds nearly drowned the croaking of the cracked bass organ. Then a gasp as from many throats, and a babel of marked and bleated words—"Lilith, Great Lilith, behold the Bridegroom!"

More cries, a clamour of rioting, and the sharp, clicking footfalls of a running figure. The footfalls approached, and Malone raised himself to his elbow to look.

The luminosity of the crypt, lately diminished, had now slightly increased; and in that devil-light there appeared the fleeing form of that which should not flee or feel or breathe—the glassy-eyed, gangrenous corpse of the corpulent old man, now needing no support, but animated by some infernal sorcery of the rite just closed. After it raced the naked, tittering, phosphorescent thing that belonged on the carven pedestal, and still farther behind panted the dark men, and all the dread crew of sentient loathsomenesses. The corpse was gaining on its pursuers, and seemed bent on a definite object, straining with every rotting muscle towards the carved golden pedestal, whose necromantic importance was evidently so great. Another moment and it had reached its goal, whilst the trailing throng laboured on with more frantic speed. But they were too late, for in one final spurt of strength which ripped tendon from tendon and sent its noisome bulk floundering to the floor in a state of jellyish dissolution, the staring corpse which had been Robert Suydam achieved its object and its triumph. The push had been tremendous, but the force had held out; and as the pusher collapsed to a muddy blotch of corruption the pedestal he had pushed tottered, tipped, and finally careered from its onyx base into the thick waters below, sending up a parting gleam of carved gold as it sank heavily to undreamable gulfs of lower Tartarus. In that instant, too, the whole scene of horror faded to nothingness before Malone's eyes; and he fainted amidst a thunderous crash which seemed to blot out all the evil universe.

VII

Malone's dream, experienced in full before he knew of Suydam's death and transfer at sea, was curiously supplemented by some oddities of the case; though that is no reason why anyone should believe it. The three old houses in Parker Place, doubtless long rotten with decay in its most insidious form, collapsed without visible cause while half the raiders and most of the prisoners were inside; and both of the greater number were instantly killed. Only in the basements and cellars was there much saving of life, and Malone was lucky to have been deep below the house of Robert Suydam. For he really was there, as no one is disposed to deny. They found him unconscious by the edge of the night-black pool, with a grotesquely horrible jumble of decay and bone, identifiable through dental work as the body of Suydam, a few feet away. The case was plain, for it was hither that the smugglers' underground canal led; and the men who took Suydam from the ship had brought him home. They themselves were never found, or identified; and the ship's doctor is not yet satisfied with the certitudes of the police.

Suydam was evidently a leader in extensive man-smuggling operations, for the canal to his house was but one of several subterranean channels and tunnels in the neighbourhood. There was a tunnel from this house to a crypt beneath the dance-hall church; a crypt accessible from the church only through a narrow secret passage in the north wall, and in whose chambers some singular and terrible things were discovered. The croaking organ was there, as well as a vast arched chapel with wooden benches and a strangely figured altar. The walls were lined with small cells, in seventeen of which—hideous to relate—solitary prisoners in a state of complete idiocy were found chained, including four mothers with infants of disturbingly strange appearance. These infants died soon after exposure to the light; a circumstance which the doctors thought rather merciful. Nobody but Malone, among those who inspected them, remembered the sombre question of old Delrio: "*An sint unquan daemones incubi et sucsubœ, et an ex tali, congressu proles nasci queat?*"

Before the canals were filled up they were thoroughly dredged, and yielded forth a sensational array of sawed and split bones of all sizes. The kidnapping epidemic, very clearly, had been traced home; though only two of the surviving prisoners could by any legal thread be connected with it. These men are now in prison, since they failed of conviction as accessories in the actual murders. The carved golden pedestal or throne so often mentioned by Malone as of primary occult importance was never brought to light, though at one place under the Suydam house the canal was observed to sink into a well too keep for dredging. It was choked up at the mouth and cemented over when the cellars of the new houses were made, but Malone often speculates on what lies beneath. The police, satisfied that they had shattered a dangerous gang of maniacs and alien smugglers, turned over to the Federal authorities the unconvicted Kurds, who before their deportation were conclusively found to belong to the Yezidee clan of devil-worshippers. The tramp ship and its crew remain an elusive mystery, though cynical detectives are once more ready to combat its smuggling and rum-running ventures. Malone thinks these detectives show a sadly limited perspective in their lack of wonder at the myriad unexplainable details, and the suggestive obscurity of the whole case; though he is just as critical of the newspapers, which saw only a morbid sensation and gloated over a minor sadist cult when they might have proclaimed a horror from the universe's very heart. But he is content to rest silent in Chepachet, calming his nervous system and praying that time may gradually transfer his terrible experience from the realm of present reality to that of picturesque and semi-mythical remoteness.

Robert Suydam sleeps beside his bride in Greenwood Cemetery. No funeral was held over the strangely released bones, and relatives are grateful for the swift oblivion which overtook the case as a whole.

The scholar's connection with the Red Hook horrors, indeed, was never emblazoned by legal proof; since his death forestalled the inquiry he would otherwise have faced. His own end is not much mentioned, and the Suydams hope that posterity may recall him only as a gentle recluse who dabbled in harmless magic and folk-lore.

As for Red Hook—it is always the same. Suydam came and went; a terror gathered and faded; but the evil spirit of darkness and squalor broods on amongst the mongrels in the old brick houses, and prowling bands still parade on unknown errands past windows where lights and twisted faces unaccountably appear and disappear. Age-old horror is a hydra with a thousand heads, and the cults of darkness are rooted in blasphemies deeper than the well of Democritus. The soul of the beast is omnipresent and triumphant, and Red Hook's legions of blear-eyed, pockmarked youths still chant and curse and howl as they file from abyss to abyss, none knows whence or whither, pushed on by blind laws of biology which they may never understand. As of old more people enter Red Hook than leave it on the landward side, and there are already rumours of new canals running underground to certain centres of traffic in liquor and less mentionable things.

The dance-hall church is now mostly a dance-hall, and queer faces have appeared at night at the windows. Lately a policeman expressed the belief that the filled-up crypt has been dug out again, and for no simple explainable purpose. Who are we to combat poisons older than history and mankind? Apes danced in Asia to those horrors, and the cancer lurks secure and spreading where furtiveness hides in rows of decaying brick.

Malone does not shudder without cause—for only the other day an officer overheard a swarthy squinting hag teaching a small child some whispering patois in the shadow of an areaway. He listened, and thought it very strange when he heard her repeat over and over again:

"O friend and companion of night thou who rejoicest in the baying of dogs and spilt blood, who wanderest in the midst of shades among the tombs, who longest for blood and bringest terror to mortals, Gorgo, Mormo, thousand-faced moon, look favourably on our sacrifices!"

The Triumph of Death

H. RUSSELL WAKEFIELD

"Amelia," said Miss Prunella Pendleham, "I have received a most impertinent letter this morning."

"Yes, Miss Pendleham?"

"It is from some Society, and it has the insolence to suggest that this house is haunted by ghosts. Now you know that to be false, utterly false."

"Yes, Miss Pendleham," said Amelia listlessly.

"Do I detect a hesitant note in your tone? You mean what you say, I trust?"

"Oh, yes, Miss Pendleham."

"Very well. Now this Society actually wished to send down an investigator to examine and report on the house. I have replied that if any such person enters the grounds, he will be prosecuted for trespass. Here is my letter. Take it and post it at once."

"Very well, Miss Pendleham."

"You always seem so glad to get out of the house, Amelia! I wonder why. Now make haste there and back."

A little later Miss Amelia Lornon was hurrying down the drive of Carthwaite Place. But as soon as she knew she was out of eyeshot from its upper windows, she slackened her pace. This she did for two reasons; she was feeling terribly frail and ill that morning, and to be out of that house, even for half an hour, meant a most blessed relief from that anguish which is great fear.

To reach the post office of the little hamlet she had to pass the rectory. Mrs. Redvale, the rector's wife, was glancing out of the drawing-room window at the time.

"There's Amelia," she said to her husband. "I've never seen her looking so ill. Poor creature! It's time you did something about her, Claud, in my opinion."

She was a handsome and determined-looking woman, quite obviously "wearing the trousers," and her voice was sharply authoritative.

"What can I do, my dear?" replied the rector with the plaintive testiness of the conscience-moved weakling.

"You can and must do *something*. You can listen to me for one thing. I've been meaning to have this out with you for some time; ever since I realized what was going on. That sight of her convinces me it must be now, at once. If she dies without our having done a hand's turn to save her, I shall never know a minute's peace again; and I don't think you will either. Come quickly! Here she is going back."

The rector reluctantly went to the window. What he saw brought a look of genuine distress to his kindly, diffident face. "Yes," he sighed, "I can see what you mean only too well."

"Now sit down," ordered his spouse. "I know we're in a difficult position; Miss Pendelham puts two pounds in the plate every Sunday, which is an enormous help to us. 'There are my servant's wages,' she seems to say, as she does it. But she is a very evil old woman; how evil, I don't think either of us fully realizes."

"Yet she *does* come to church," protested the rector.

"Yes, she comes to church," replied his wife sardonically, "and like a great many other people for a quite ulterior motive; she wants to keep *us quiet*, and she bribes us to do so—don't argue —I know I'm right! Now we've been here only six months, but we've learnt quite a lot in that time. We've learnt that the Pendle-ham family have always shown a vicious, inherited streak; drunk-ards, ruthless womanizers, and worse, even criminals—and just occasionally a brilliant exception. This old woman is the last of the line, and it'll be a very good thing when the horrid brood is extinct, in my opinion."

"Of course," said the rector, "we have to trust Miles's opinion for all this, *really*. And we know he's utterly biased against her; he won't even speak to her."

"He's been churchwarden here for forty years; so he ought to know," replied Mrs. Redvale. "Besides, he loses financially by his attitude—she never buys a thing at his shop. He strikes me as a perfectly honest and sincere old man. Don't you think so?"

"I must say I do."

"Well then, what's his story? That she was crossed in love when very young, some other woman, as she believes, stealing her man away. So she made up her mind to have revenge on her sex in her own stealthy, devilish way. He thinks her mind was per-manently tainted at that time; that she is actually, if not technically, insane."

"It all sounds so melodramatic!" murmured the rector.

"Melodramatic doesn't mean impossible," answered his wife sharply; "there's plenty of *real* melodrama in the world. Now Miles says she has had five companions since she marooned herself in that house thirty-five years ago. Three have died there and two escaped quickly, declaring Miss Pendleham was a devil and the house hell. And now there's the sixth, Amelia; and she's dying, too."

"Dying of what?" asked the rector.

"Of terror, if nothing else!"

"She could leave like those other two."

"That's so easy to say! You might say it of a rabbit in a stoat's

146

snare. When you're sufficiently frightened you can neither run nor struggle. And she's in a hopelessly weak position; ageing, penniless, naturally will-less and pliant. She'd never summon up courage to escape on her own."

"But she seems, in a way, to like Miss Pendleham's company!"

"Simply because she dreads being alone in that *foul* house. Now you know it's haunted, Claud."

"My dear Clara, you put me in a most difficult position, because, as you know, I agreed with Miss Pendleham, there were no such entities as ghosts."

"Don't be a humbug, Claud! You said that only out of politeness and a desire to please. You knew it was a lie when you said it."

"My dear!"

"No cant! You remember when we first went there what was looking out of the window on the first floor?"

"There seemed to be something for a moment."

"Was it a small boy with his face covered with blood?"

"I got such a fleeting glimpse, my dear."

"Was it Miss Pendleham or Amelia?"

"No, I suppose not."

"They are the only people living in the house. And I told you what I saw when I went to powder my nose. I can see it now! Do you believe me?"

"I've never known you to tell a *pointless* lie. Yet a bush sometimes closely resembles a bear."

"But a little dead girl doesn't resemble a bush! And you heard that scream?"

"I thought I heard something—a curious cry—it might have been a bird."

"A bird! How would you like to live in that house with that sort of thing! You'd even—like Amelia—prefer Miss Pendleham's company to *Theirs*. It often makes me feel physically sick to think of her there. If we don't do something to save that poor woman, I shall be plagued by remorse till I die!"

"Do me the justice, Clara, to believe that is becoming true of me, also."

"I wonder if you realize it as I do! I'm sensitive to places like that, and always have been. The very motes in the sunbeams there seem to make beastly patterns. I don't wonder Amelia is dying by inches, has been dying for years. She told me, that when *They* are around her, the kettle will not boil. In other words, her brain is going as her body gives up the struggle!"

"Well, what can I do?" exclaimed the rector. "Tell me, Clara! You are wiser than I in the affairs of this world, if I know more about the next."

"And if there is such a place!" rapped Clara.

The rector sighed. "I'm deeply grieved you're such a sceptic, Clara."

147

"Nonsense! Every parson should have an agnostic wife; it keeps his mind alive. Well, we'll both think it over today and discuss it again tomorrow morning. I *mean* tomorrow. My mind is made up. As for that two pounds a week, could you go on taking it if Amelia died? Tomorrow at ten o'clock!"

"You were a long time, Amelia," said Miss Pendleham.

"I was as quick as I could be, Miss Pendleham, but my heart was palpitating so."

"Nonsense! You're perfectly well. Don't imagine things, Amelia!"

Miss Pendleham was one of those apparently timeless spinsters, so leisurely does the process of decay take its way with them. She was very tall and cylindrical in shape, an almost epicene, sexless body. She was invariably dressed in an iridescent grey garment of antique cut and rustling train. About her face, her nose in particular, the rector had made one of his rare jests, by adapting it to a Max Beerbohm pleasantry, "Hints of the Iron Duke at most angles;" and, indeed, that ungainly, craggy feature dominated the rest. Her mouth was small, thin-lipped, dry. Her eyes were quite round—monkey's eyes—and an odd brimstone-yellow, a family stigma. Her hair was a dense grey mass. The face was a mask, as though modelled in wax from a corpse, quite colourless. Her age might have been anything from fifty-five to seventy.

Amelia was about forty-eight. Once upon a time she might have been a bonnie girl, for her features were well enough, but it required a sympathetic and perceptive eye so to scan and reconstruct the past. There are parasites which slowly devour and drain their hosts from within, till nothing is left but a thin, transparent envelope. A puff of wind and it disintegrates. Amelia might have been long entertaining some such greedy guest. Pounds underweight, gaunt and stooping, listless and lifeless of hair and eye, like a prisoner at long last delivered from a dungeon where she had lain neglected and forgotten. Death had his hand on her shoulder and was fast tightening his grip, but to give her her due it had taken nine hard years to bring her to this pass.

"I'll go and cook the luncheon," she said.

"Yes; what is there?"

"Chops."

"I'll have three. Are you hungry?"

"No, Miss Pendleham."

"Then cook four, and let mine be red right through."

Carthwaite Place rose on the northern slopes above Lake Windermere. It was unmistakably Elizabethan: a huge sombre pile of brick with a multitude of mullioned, transomed windows and a flat roof. It had thirty-five bedrooms and one bathroom. It required many thousands spent on it to make it habitable, but that money would never be found; and it was very slowly breaking up and passing. The grounds surrounding it had gone back to a wild, disorderly nature. Miss Pendleham never left it, save to attend matins on Sunday morning. Its one trace of modernity was a telephone, used for ordering her frugal wants from the market town six miles away.

Amelia dragged herself to the great stone vaulted kitchen and raked up the fire. She had begun to tremble again, and never did she glance behind her. Once she paused as though listening, her face revealing the greatest anxiety. Several times her mouth moved as though she were muttering something, but no sound came.

Presently she finished cooking and took the results to the dining-room where Miss Pendleham was already seated. The meal was eaten in dead silence and very quickly, for Miss Pendleham always attacked her food like a starving panther. On the wall facing Amelia was a tattered seventeenth century tapestry. It depicted a company of knights and ladies riding in pairs along a sinister serpentine path. On the left of the path were three rotting corpses in open coffins. The air above them was thronged with vile flying things. Amelia's eyes always flickered around the room trying not to see it. Miss Pendleham watched her covertly. At the end of the meal she said what she always said, "Wash up quickly and come and read to me."

"Very good, Miss Pendleham."

When she got back to the drawing-room, Miss Pendleham handed her a book. It was a translation of the Abbé Boissard's life of Gilles de Rais, realistically illustrated. Amelia had already read it out endless times before. She read well, though the details of the abattoir ritual came oddly from her precise and virginal voice.

Presently Miss Pendelham stopped her. "Something very similar," she said in her high, metallic tone, "is known to have been done here by an ancestor of my own. He killed by torture a number of children, chiefly young girls, and employed their bodies for some such curious ceremonies. It is owing to that, possibly, that the house has acquired its quite *false* repute of being a haunted place. Perhaps I have told you that before?"

"Yes, Miss Pendleham," replied Amelia mechanically.

"I'm going to doze now. Wake me at five with the tea. Sit here till it is time to prepare it."

This was an ordeal Amelia detested, but had long accepted as part of her daily calvary. Was Miss Pendleham asleep, or was she slyly watching her? Were her eyes quite closed?

It was a soaking afternoon, the small dense mountain rain streaming down the windows. There was just that steady rain-purr and the slow beat of the grandfather's clock to break the silence. Miss Pendleham never stirred nor did her breathing change. Slowly the light faded, and Amelia began to ache with stiffness and immobility. Suddenly there came from somewhere in the house a thin high cry of pain. Amelia's eyes went wild and she put her hand to her throat. Miss Pendleham opened her eyes wide and slowly leaned forward, staring at her. "What's the matter, Amelia?" she said slowly.

"Nothing, Miss Pendelham," gulped Amelia, "I'll go and get the tea."

Miss Pendleham glanced after her bowed back. For a moment the mask was raised and she smiled. But the smile merely contorted the lower part of her face, her yellow eyes took no share in it. There came again that remote, agonizing wail. The half-smile vanished, the yellow eyes flickered, the mask came down again.

After tea she played Patience and Amelia was left to her own devices till it was time to cook the supper. Anyone watching Miss Pendleham playing Patience, which is a stark test of virtue, would have decided, that if he ever did business with her, he'd have kept a sharp lawyer at his elbow, for she always cheated when necessary, but never more than necessary.

Anyone who had watched Amelia presently preparing the supper by the light of two candles would have gleamed some understanding of the phrase "mental torture." Those candles threw strange shadows on the bare walls and arched roof. That observer might have caught himself imitating Amelia, glancing up fearfully and furtively at those crowding multi-formed shades, and learned her trick of flinching when she did so. Was that a small body lying prone and a tall figure with its hands to the small one's throat? And did that figure move? Just the flicker of the candle, of course. And yet that observer might well have wished himself away, but would he have had the heart to leave Amelia down there alone?

Supper was again a quite silent meal. Miss Pendleham scraped her well-piled plates tiger-clean. Amelia left half her sparse portions.

After supper Miss Pendleham said, "Fetch my wrap from my bedroom, Amelia; I forgot to bring it down." She said that almost every evening, perhaps because she knew how Amelia dreaded going up those dark stairs, ever since she had that fright four years ago.

Amelia fetched it, washed up, and returned again to the drawing-room. "Now," said Miss Pendleham, "you can read to me for an hour. Get those stories by James."

"Well, Claud," said Clara next morning, "have you been thinking it over?"

"Yes, my dear, but I can't see my way clear, I'm afraid. We say she tortures these women. But *how* does she torture them? She gives them board and lodging, pays them something, I suppose, a pittance, no doubt, but something. She is superficially kind to them. She does not—could not—legally compel them to stay. Who would call that torture, save ourselves?"

"And Mr. Miles!"

"And Mr. Miles, if you like. Suppose I did tackle her. If she didn't at once show me the door, she'd probably call in Amelia and ask her if she had anything to complain about. 'No, Miss Pendleham,' she'd certainly reply; and what sort of fool should I look!"

Mrs. Redvale, like most women in the grip of logic, raised her voice. "You've got to be firm, Claud, and not be fooled by that sort of thing. You must take the offensive. She can neither sack you nor eat you. Tell her straight that you are certain Amelia is dying and must have immediate attention. Remind her three of her companions have already died in the house, and, if there's a fourth, some very awkward questions are bound to be asked. There *is* Amelia again! I'll get her in."

She hurried from the room and out into the street.

"How are you, Miss Lornon?" she asked kindly.

"All right, thank you, Mrs. Redvale."

"You don't look it! Come in a moment."

"Oh, I can't! Miss Pendleham told me to hurry back with the stamps."

"Never mind; it's only for a minute."

Amelia hesitated and then reluctantly followed her in.

The rector scanned her closely as he greeted her.

Mrs. Redvale now assumed her most forcible manner.

"Miss Lornon, you're in a very bad state, aren't you? Don't be afraid to tell me; it will go no further."

Amelia began to cry in the most passive, hopeless way. "I suppose so," she murmured.

"That house is killing you, isn't it?"

"Oh, I can stand it, Mrs. Redvale."

"No, you can't! Have a good cry. You've *got* to get away from it!"

"I can't! Miss Pendleham would never let me go."

"She'll have to! Look here, Amelia—I'm going to call you that —we're determined to help you. In the meantime, remember nothing there can hurt you. They can frighten, they can't *hurt*."

"They can!" she sobbed. "They keep me awake nearly all night. In the summer it's not so bad, because they go away at dawn, but in the long nights it's terrible. I must go now."

"You won't have to stand it much longer! Bear up until we can do something."

"There's nothing to be done, thank you kindly, Mrs. Redvale. Oh, I mustn't say any more. Miss Pendleham would be so cross if she knew I was talking like this!"

"Nonsense! Your health comes before everything!"

But Amelia had hurried from the room.

151

"You see!" exclaimed Clara. "I could strangle that she-devil with my bare hands!"

"There's one thing I've never been sure about," said the rector, "does Miss Pendleham realize there's something the matter with the house? If not, the force of the charge against her is greatly weakened."

"Of course she does!"

"How can you be so sure?"

"I watched her when we heard that ghastly cry. She heard it, too, her demeanour showed it. But it doesn't worry her, she welcomes it as an instrument of that torture. She makes Amelia think, 'I must be going mad if I see and hear things that aren't there.' Can't you see what I mean? Her mind is diseased like that of her foul forbears. Those things are echoes of evil and she is utterly evil too. Did the 'first murderer' frighten the other two? Of course not!"

"Clara, that is a fearful thing to say!"

"You've just seen that wretched woman, haven't you! Look here, Claud, if you don't do something about it I'll lose all respect for you! This is the test of your Christianity and courage. *I'm* an infidel, but I'd do it myself if I thought she'd take any notice of me, but she wouldn't for she hates and despises all women. But you are her spiritual adviser."

"There's no need to be sarcastic, my dear."

"There's need to be something to goad you to action! Will you, Claud?"

"Oh, I suppose so," sighed the rector, "but I wish I could consult the bishop first."

"You'd get nothing but vague boomings. Is your courage at the sticking-point?"

"Yes, I'll do it."

"Then go straight to the phone!"

He left the room and returned after a few moments. "She will see me at half past nine tonight," he said.

"Did you tell her what you wanted to see her about?"

"I just said something of importance."

"And you were under-stating—it's a matter of life and death, and we both know it!"

"Have you been crying, Amelia?"

"Oh no, Miss Pendleham, the cold wind caught my eyes."

"It doesn't seem cold to me. Give me the book of stamps and get luncheon ready."

During the meal Miss Pendleham said, "You see that tapestry, Amelia?"

"Yes, Miss Pendleham."

"You're not looking at it!"

Amelia glanced flinchingly up. She noticed that as each cavalier

152

and his paramour reached the three open coffins, their smiles and lascivious glances changed to looks of loathing and horror. Because, she thought, they are young and happy and haven't learned to long for rest.

"It's called *The Triumph of Death*," said Miss Pendleham.

"Yes, so you've told me."

"That reminds me of something. Have you finished?"

"Yes, Miss Pendleham."

Miss Pendleham led the way into the drawing-room. "Today," she said, "is the anniversary of the death of Miss Davis. She was my companion before you came. She was a foolish, fanciful girl in some ways. Have I told you about her before?"

"Only a little, Miss Pendleham."

"Yes, she was fanciful. She used to fancy she heard and saw strange things in the house and that shows her mind was tainted, does it not?"

"Yes, Miss Pendleham."

"I mean, if the house were haunted, we should both of us see and hear such strange things, should we not?"

"Yes, Miss Pendleham."

"Which we never do?"

"No, Miss Pendleham."

"Of course not. Well, I should, perhaps, have dismissed Miss Davis earlier but I did not like to. Have I told you how she died?"

"No, Miss Pendleham."

"I thought not. I had noticed she was getting thinner, and stranger in her manner, and she told me her sleep was disordered. I should have been warned when she came running to my room one day saying she had seen a child butchered in the kitchen— and she had other hallucinations which revealed her mind was in an abnormal state. One evening I sent her up to fetch my wrap, just as I sometimes send you, and, as she did not reappear, I went in search of her. I found her lying dead in the powder-closet of my room. The doctor said she had died of a heart-attack and asked me if she could have had a fright of some kind. I said not to my knowledge. I think she must have supposed she had seen something displeasing. Look behind you, Amelia!"

Amelia started from her chair with a cry.

"What is the matter with you!" said Miss Pendleham severely. "I merely wanted to draw your attention to the fact that the antimasassar was slipping from your chair. I hope *your* nerves are not giving way. Didn't you imagine you had a fright of some kind a month ago?"

"It was nothing, Miss Pendleham."

"You screamed loudly enough. Bear Miss Davis in mind. Becoming *fanciful* is often the first symptom of brain disease, so the doctor told me; *hearing* things, *seeing* things when there is nothing to see or hear. Now you can read to me."

And this Amelia did; Miss Pendleham presently telling her to stop and *seeming* to doze off, while the windows rattled disconcertingly and, as the light faded and the fire shook out its last flame and sank to its death-glow, something white seemed to dart across the Musicians' Gallery and something follow it as though in pursuit, and there came that thin wail of pain. Amelia went rigid with terror.

"What's the matter, Amelia?" said Miss Pendleham, leaning forward in her chair.

"Nothing, Miss Pendleham. I'll make up the fire and then get tea."

While she was cooking the dinner that night she was thinking over what Miss Pendleham had said about Miss Davis. She had died of what was killing her, of course. She would die soon, now, very soon. She knew it, and then Miss Pendleham would get someone else, and one day that someone would die, too, for the same reason—unless. . . . Suddenly she paused in her work. What was that! Someone was crying in the servants' hall! That was something she'd never heard before. Her heart hammered in her throat, stopped horribly long, then raced away again. A piercing pain ran through her. Who was that crying! She must be brave. It might be someone *real* and not one of Them! She took a candle and tiptoed along the passage of the hall, a bare, desolate place reeking of dirt and vermin, which Amelia dreaded and seldom entered. There was no one there, but the sound of sobbing was louder. "Oh, God," moaned a voice, "I cannot bear it! I cannot bear it!" Then came a laugh, a sly sinister chuckle and the wailing voice rose to a scream. "Oh, God, I cannot bear it!"

As Amelia went back to the kitchen her face twitched violently and uncontrollably. Was that *real* or not? Was it just a sound in her head as Miss Pendleham said it must be; just a *fancy*? If so, she was going mad like Miss Davis. What happened to mad people in that Other World? Were they mad *there*, too, and forever? That didn't bear thinking about. She must die before that happened. She *was* dying; she knew that by the terrible pains in her heart. What would happen when she was dead? Miss Davis had died; she'd just heard her crying. No, that was just a sound in her head. Her face contorted again in the fearful effort to concentrate, to get it *straight* and clear in her mind. Well, she would die, like Miss Davis, and then Miss Pendleham would get someone else to look after her and it would all happen again with the new girl. No, it mustn't. It would not be right. Miss Pendleham was very kind, but she didn't understand about the house. It was all very curious and difficult, but it must not happen again. There was Miss Davis still crying, still crying in her head. But it would happen again unless—unless she was brave. If Miss Pendleham realized what sort of things happened to Miss Davis and her and

154

what they saw and heard, she wouldn't let it happen, of course, but she didn't and so.... Did she hate Miss Pendleham? Of course not; why should she? Again St. Vitus racked her face. But it wouldn't happen again. There was the man and the little girl! She flung up her hands to her ears. A red veil was drawn down before her eyes. She shook her hands from the wrist and stretched and curved her fingers. The expression on her face became at once hard and vacant, like that of a beast at bay. She retained that curious inhuman expression, and Miss Pendleham noticed it when she brought up the meal. It disturbed her and her own eyes went weasel-hard. Presently she said, "Eat your dinner, Amelia; what's the matter with you?"

"Nothing, Miss Pendleham. I'm not very hungry."

"Eat your food! By the way, you haven't been talking to the rector or his wife, have you?"

"I just said good morning to Mrs. Redvale."

"Are you sure that was all?"

"Yes, Miss Pendleham."

And then there was silence for a time till Miss Pendleham rose and remarked, "You can read to me for a while," and Amelia read out a tale about some bedclothes forming into a figure and frightening an old man in the other bed.

"What did you think of that, Amelia?" asked Miss Pendleham.

"Very nice, Miss Pendleham."

"Nice! I don't believe you are paying attention. You read very badly again!"

"I'm sorry, Miss Pendleham. The old man was mad, wasn't he, Miss Pendleham? Like Miss Davis and *me*?"

Miss Pendleham stared at her. "Get my wrap?" she said brutally.

Amelia got up slowly and went through the door leading to the stairs. As she started to climb them she crossed herself and stretched and curved her fingers. A fearful twitch convulsed her face.

Miss Pendleham went to the front door, opened it and left it ajar and went back to the drawing-room. Then, as the minutes passed, she cocked her head as though listening. There came that high torture-wail, and she straightened her head abruptly. The clock ticked, the windows throbbed and hammered in the gale. Presently she got up and went to the foot of the stairs. "Amelia!" she called, her voice cracking oddly. There was no reply. She smiled and ran her thick tongue along her lips. She sent up a few stairs and called again; then fetched a lighted candle from the drawing-room and ascended to the first landing. "Amelia!" she called. A sudden fierce gust of wind spurted down the passage and blew out the candle, leaving her in pitch darkness. She began to grope her way down the corridor, her fingers sliding along the wall. They came to a gap and she turned in to the left, moving forward till her thighs met a bed. "Amelia!" she called, and the

155

echo was hurled hard back at her. She moved across the room, her hands groping out before her, till they found another gap—the powder-closet. This was crammed with her ancient and discarded clothes and stank of stale scent, sweat and decay. She touched a hanging frock and then another, her hands moving along. And then her right hand met something and she drew in her breath with a quickness. The next second she was twisting and writhing and from her lips came a choked scream. As she was ruthlessly drawn in among the reeking stuffs, swinging wildly on their hooks, she struck out blindly with her clenched firsts again and again. At last she leaned forward, buckling at the knees, her arms fell quivering to her sides, there was a long vile rattle from her throat, and she was still.

"It's a quarter past nine," said Clara, "time you were off. You'd better have a drink before you go; it will help you to be firm, and you've got to be very firm." She poured out a stiff whisky which the rector gulped down. Then he picked up his hat and coat and set out.

It had stopped raining, but it was still blowing a full gale and he had to fight his way against it. So soon as he entered the drive through the battered gates screeching on their hinges, he felt his nerves a-tingle. "As one who on a lonely road doth walk in fear and dread." The old lines leaped to his memory. He glanced fearfully up at the over-hanging boughs. Was that a footstep close behind him! He broke into a run. To his surprise he found the front door half-open and went in. He saw a light in the drawing-room, entered and found it empty. He waited a few moments and then called timorously out, "I'm here, Miss Pendleham!" Before the echo of his voice died away there came a long choked scream. "Good God, what was that!" he muttered, and sweat broke out on him. "It came from above I must go up!"

He glanced distractedly around, picked up a candle-stick, lit the candle, and opened the door to the stairs with a quivering hand. As he hurried up the first flight, it seemed to him there was something astir in the house and that the shadows on the wall came from a company of persons following him up, and that others were awaiting him on the landing. He trembled and his breath came fast.

"Miss Pendleham!" he quavered. No sound. He lurched down the corridor till he came to an open door, through which he passed into a huge room. He raised the candle-stick and peered fearfully about him. Ah, there was another door—open—and there was Miss Pendleham.

"Here I am, Miss Pendleham!" he said. What was she doing? He could only see her body from the waist down, the rest was buried in some clothes. He tiptoed into the closet and gingerly pulled the clothes aside. And then he sprang back with a clipped cry, for he was gazing into the battered, dead face of Amelia

Lornon. She was leaning back against the wall, and she had drawn Miss Pendleham's head down on her breast. Her hands clutched her neck so fiercely and the nails were driven in so deep, that the blood was seeping down over her lace collar. The last shred of self-control left him. The candle-stick fell from his hand, and he ran blunderingly from the room and down the stairs. The air seemed full of screams and laughter, something death-cold was pressed against his face, leaping figures ran beside him, till at last he staggered whimpering out into the night.

The Lips

HENRY S. WHITEHEAD

The *Soul Taverner*, blackbirder, Luke Martin, master, up from Cartagena, came to her anchor in the harbour of St. Thomas, capital and chief town of the Danish West Indies. A Martinique barquentine berthed to leeward of her, sent a fully manned boat ashore after the harbour-master with a request for permission to change anchorage. Luke Martin's shore boat was only a few lengths behind the Frenchman's. Martin shouted after the officer whom it landed:

"Tell Lollik I'll change places with ye, an' welcome! What ye carryin'—brandy? I'll take six cases off'n ye."

The barquentine's mate, a French-Island mulatto, nodded over his shoulder, and noted down the order in a leather pocket-book without slackening his pace. It was no joyful experience to lie in a semi-enclosed harbour directly to leeward of a slaver, and haste was indicated despite propitiatory orders for brandy. "Very well, Captain," said the mate, stiffly.

Martin landed as the Martinique mate rounded a corner to the left and disappeared from view in the direction of the harbour-master's. Martin scowled after him, muttering to himself.

"Airs! Talkin' English—language of the islands; thinkin' in French, you an' your airs! An' yer gran'father came outta a blackbird ship like's not! You an' your airs!"

Reaching the corner the mate had turned, Martin glanced after him momentarily, then turned to the right mounting a slight rise. His business ashore took him to the fort. He intended to land his cargo, or a portion of it, that night. The colony was short of field hands. With the help of troops from Martinique, French troops, and Spaniards from its nearer neighbour, Puerto Rico, it had just put down a bloody uprising on its subsidiary island of St. Jan. Many of the slaves had been killed in the joint armed reprisal of the year 1833.

Luke Martin got his permission to land his cargo, therefore, without difficulty, and, being a Yankee bucko who let no grass grow under his feet, four bells in the afternoon watch saw the hatches off and the decks of the *Saul Taverner* swarming with manacled blacks for the ceremony of washing-down.

Huddled together, blinking in the glaring sun of a July afternoon under parallel 18, north latitude, the mass of swart human-

158

ity were soaped, with handfuls of waste out of soft-soap buckets, scrubbed with brushes on the ends of short handles, and rinsed off with other buckets. Boatloads of negroes surrounded the ship to see the washing-down, and these were kept at a distance by a swearing third mate told off for the purpose.

By seven bells the washing-down was completed, and before sundown a row of lighters, each guarded by a pair of Danish *gendarmes* with muskets and fixed bayonets, had ranged alongside for the taking off of the hundred and seventeen blacks who were to be landed, most of whom would be sent to replenish the labourers on to the plantations of St. Jan off the other side of the island of St. Thomas.

The disembarking process began just after dark, to the light of lanterns. Great care was exercised by all concerned lest any escape by plunging overboard. A tally-clerk from shore checked off the blacks as they went over the side into the lighters, and these, as they became filled, were rowed to the landing-stage by other slaves, bending over six great sweeps in each of the stub-bowed, heavy wooden boats.

Among the huddled black bodies of the very last batch stood a woman, very tall and thin, with a new-born child, black as a coal, at her breasts. The woman stood a little aloof from the others, farther from the low rail of the *Sal Taverner's* forward-deck, crooning to her infant. Behind her approached Luke Martin, impatient of his unloading, and cut at her thin ankles with his rhinoceros leather whip. The woman did not wince. Instead, she turned her head and muttered a few syllables in a low tone, in the Eboe dialect. Martin shoved her into the mass of blacks, cursing roundly as he cut a second time at the spindling shins.

The woman turned, very quietly and softly, as he was passing behind her, let her head fall softly on Martin's shoulder and whispered into his ear. The motion was so delicate as to simulate a caress, but Martin's curse died in his throat. He howled in pain as the woman raised her head, and his whip clattered on the deck boarding while the hand which had held it went to the shoulder. The woman, deftly holding her infant, had moved in among the huddling blacks, a dozen or more of whom intervened between her and Martin, who hopped on one foot and cursed, a vicious continuous stream of foul epithets; then, still cursing, made his way in haste to his cabin after an antiseptic, any idea of revenge swallowed up in his superstitious dread of what might happen to him if he did not, forthwith, dress the ghastly wound just under his left ear, where the black woman had caused her firm, white and shining teeth to meet in the great muscle of his neck between shoulder and jaw.

When he emerged, ten minutes later, the wound now soaked in permanganate of potash, and roughly clotted with a clean cloth, the last lighter, under the impetus of its six sweeps, was half-way ashore, and the clerk of the government, from the fort, was awaiting him, with a bag of coin and a pair of *gendarmes* to guard it. He accompanied the government clerk below, where, the *gendarmes* at the cabin door, they figured and added and counted money for the next hour, a bottle of sound rum and a pair of glasses between them.

At two bells, under a shining moon, the *Saul Taverner*, taking advantage of the evening trade wind, was running for the harbour's mouth to stand away for Norfolk, Virginia, whence, empty, she would run up the coast for her home port of Boston, Massachusetts.

It was midnight, what with the care of his ship coming out of even the plain and safe harbour of St. Thomas, before Martin the skipper, Culebra lighthouse off the port quarter, turned in. The wound in the top of his shoulder ached dully, and he sent for Matthew Pound, his first mate, to wash it out with more permanganate and dress it suitably. It was in an awkward place— curse the black slut!—for him to manage it for himself.

Pound went white and muttered under his breath at the ugly sight of it when Martin had removed his shirt, painfully, and eased off the cloth he had roughly laid over it, a cloth now stiff and clotted with the exuding blood drying on its inner surface, from the savage wound.

Thereafter, not liking the look on his mate's face, nor that whitening which the sight of the place in his neck had brought about, Martin dispensed with assistance, and dressed the wound himself.

He slept little that first night, but this was partly for thinking of the bargain he had driven with those short-handed Danes. They had been hard up for black meat to sweat on those hillside canefields over on St. Jan. He could have disposed easily of his entire cargo, but that, unfortunately, was out of the question. He had, what with an exceptionally slow and hot voyage across the Carribean from Cartagena, barely enough of his said cargo left to fulfil his engagement to deliver a certain number of head in Norfolk. But he would have been glad enough to rid his hold of them all— curse them!— and set his course straight for Boston. He was expecting to be married the day after his arrival. He was eager to get home, and even now the *Saul Taverner* was carrying as much sail as she could stand up under, heeling now to the unfailing trade wind of this latitude.

The wound ached and pained, none the less, and he found it well-nigh impossible to settle himself in a comparatively comfortable position on its account. He tossed and cursed far into the warm night. Towards morning he fell into a fitful doze.

The entire side of his neck and shoulder was one huge, searing ache when he awakened and pushed himself carefully upright with both hands. He could not bend his head nor, at first, move it from side to side. Dressing was a very painful process, but he managed it. He wanted to see what the bite looked like, but, as he never shaved during a voyage, there was no glass in his cabin. He bathed the sore place gingerly with bay rum, which hurt abominably and caused him to curse afresh. Dressed at last, he made his way up on deck, past the steward who was laying breakfast in his cabin. The steward, he thought, glanced at him curiously, but he could not be sure. No wonder. He had to walk sidewise, with the pain of his neck, like a crab. He ordered more sail, stuns'ls, and, these set and sheeted home, he returned to the cabin for breakfast.

Mid-afternoon saw him, despite the vessel's more than satisfactory speed and the progress of a long leg towards Boston and Lydia Farnham, in such a devilish temper that everyone on board the ship kept as far as possible out of his way. He took no night watches, these being divided among the three mates, and after his solitary supper, punctuated with numerous curses at a more than usually awkward steward, he went into his stateroom, removed his shirt and singlet, and thoroughly rubbed the entire aching area with coconut oil. The pain now ran down his left arm to the elbow, and penetrated to all the cords of his neck, the muscles of which throbbed and burned atrociously.

The embrocation gave him a certain amount of relief. He remembered that the woman had muttered something. It was *not* Eboe, that jargon of *lingua franca* which served as a medium for the few remarks necessary between slavers and their human cattle. It was some outlandish coastal or tribal dialect. He had not caught it, sensed its meaning; though there had resided in those few syllables some germ of deadly meaning. He remembered vaguely, the cadence of the syllables, even though their meaning had been unknown to him. Swearing, aching, depressed, he turned in, and this time, almost immediately, he fell asleep.

And in his sleep, those syllables were repeated to him, into his left ear, endlessly, over and over again, and in his sleep he knew their meaning; and when he awoke, a swaying beam of pouring moonlight coming through his porthole, at four bells after midnight, the cold sweat had made his pillow clammy wet and stood dankly in the hollows of his eyes and soaked his tangled beard.

Burning from head to foot, he rose and lit the candle in his binnacle-light, and cursed himself again for a fool for not acquiring a mirror through the day. Young Summer, the third mate, shaved. One or two of the fo'c'sle hands, too. There would be mirrors on board. He must obtain one tomorrow. What was it the woman had said—those syllables? He shuddered. He could not remember. Why should he remember? Gibberish—niggertalk! It was nothing. Merely the act of a bestial black. They were all alike. He should have taken the living hide off the wench. To bite him! Well, painful as it was, it should be well healed before he got back to Boston, and Lydia.

Laboriously, for he was very stiff and sore all along the left side, he climbed back into his bed, after blowing out the binnacle-light. That candlewick! It was very foul. He should have wet his thumb and finger and pinched it out. It was still smoking.

Then the syllables again, endlessly—over and over, and, now that he slept, and, somehow, knew that he slept and could not carry their meaning into the next waking state, *he knew what they meant*. Asleep, drowned in sleep, he tossed from side to side of his berth-bed, and the cold sweat ran in oily trickles down into his thick beard.

He awakened in the early light of morning in a state of horrified half-realization. He could not get up, it seemed. The ache now ran all through his body, which felt as though it had been beaten until flayed. One of the brandy bottles from the Martinique barquentine, opened the night of departure from St. Thomas, was within reach. He got it, painfully, drew the cork with his teeth, holding the bottle in his right hand, and took a long, gasping drink of the neat spirit. He could feel it through him like liquid, golden fire. Ah! that was better. He raised the bottle again, set it back where it had been, half empty. He made a great effort to roll out of the berth, failed, sank back well-nigh helpless, his head humming and singing like a hive of angry bees.

He lay there, semi-stupefied now, vague and dreadful things working within his head, his mind, his body; things brewing, seething, there inside him, as though something had entered into him and was growing there where the focus of pain throbbed, in the great muscles of his neck on the left side.

There, an hour later, a timid steward found him, after repeated and unanswered knocks on the stateroom door. The steward had at last ventured to open the door a mere peeping-slit, and then, softly closing it behind him, and white-faced, hastened to find Pound, the first mate.

Pound, after consultation with the second mate, Summer, accompanied the steward to the stateroom door, opening off the captain's cabin. Even there, hard bucko that he was, he hesitated. No one aboard the *Saul Taverner* approached Captain Luke Martin with a sense of ease or anything like self-assurance. Pound repeated the steward's door-opening, peeped within, and there-after entered the cabin, shutting the door.

Martin lay on his right side, the bedclothes pushed down to near his waist. He slept in his singlet, and the left side of his neck was uppermost. Pound looked long at the wound, his face like chalk, his hands and lips trembling. Then he softly departed, shutting the door behind him a second time, and went thought-fully up on deck again. He sought out young Sumner and the two spoke together for several minutes. Then Sumner went below to his cabin, and, emerging on the deck, looked furtively all around him. Observing the coast clear, he drew from beneath his drill jacket something twice the size of his hand, and, again glancing about to make sure he was not observed, dropped the article overboard. It flashed in the bright morning sun as it turned about in the air before the waters received it foreever. It was his small cabin shaving-mirror.

At four bells in the forenoon, Pound again descended to the captain's cabin. This time Martin's voice, a weak voice, answered his discreet knock and at its invitation he entered the stateroom. Martin now lay on his back, his left side away from the door.

"How are you feeling, sir?" asked Pound.

"Better," murmured Martin; "this damned thing!" He indicated the left side of his neck a motion of his right thumb. "I got some sleep this morning. Just woke up, just now. It's better—the worst of it over, I reckon."

A pause fell between the men. There seemed nothing more to say. Finally, after several twitches and fidgeting, Pound mentioned several details about the ship, the surest way to enlist Martin's interest at any time. Martin replied, and Pound took his departure.

Martin had spoken the truth when he alleged he was better. He had awakened with a sense that the worst was over. The wound ached abominably still, but the unpleasantness was distinctly lessened. He got up, rather languidly, slowly pulled on his deck clothes, called for coffee through the stateroom door.

Yet, when he emerged on his deck ten minutes later, his face was drawn and haggard, and there was a look in his eyes that kept the men silent. He looked over the ship professionally, the regular six bells morning inspection, but he was preoccupied and his usual intense interest in anything concerned with his ship was this day merely perfunctory. For, nearly constantly now that the savage pain was somewhat allayed and tending to grow less as the deck exercise cleared his mind and body of their poisons, those last syllables, the muttered syllables in his left ear when the black woman's head had lain for an instant on his shoulder, those syllables which were not in Eboe, kept repeating themselves to him. It was as though they were constantly reiterated in his physical ear rather than merely mentally; vague syllables, with one word, "*l'kundu*," standing out and pounding itself deeper and deeper into his consciousness.

"Hearin' things!" he muttered to himself as he descended to his cabin on the conclusion of the routine morning inspection a half-hour before noon. He did not go up on deck again for the noon observations. He remained, sitting very quietly there in his cabin, listening to what was being whispered over and over again in his left ear, the ear above the wound in his neck muscle.

It was highly unusual for this full-blooded bucko skipper to be quiet as his cabin steward roundly noted. The explanation was, however, very far from the steward's mind. He imagined that the wound had had a devastating effect upon the captain's nerves,

163

and so far his intuition was a right one. But beyond that the steward's crude psychology did not penetrate. He would have been sceptical, amused, scornful, had anyone suggested to him the true reason for this unaccustomed silence and quietude on the part of his employer. Captain Luke Martin, for the first time in his heady and truculent career, was frightened.

He ate little for his midday dinner, and immediately afterward retired to his stateroom. He came out again, almost at once, however, and mounted the cabin ladder to the after deck. The *Saul Taverner*, carrying a heavy load of canvas, was spanking along at a good twelve knots. Martin looked aloft, like a sound sailor-man, when he emerged on deck, but his preoccupied gaze came down and seemed to young Sumner, who touched his hat to him, to look inward. Martin was addressing him.

"I want the lend of your lookin'-glass," said he in quiet tones.

Young Sumner started, felt the blood leave his face. This was what Pound had warned him about; why he had thrown his glass over the side.

"Sorry, sir. It ain't along with me this v'yage, sir. I had it till we lay in St. Thomas. But now it's gone. I couldn't shave this mornin', sir." The young mate made an evidential gesture, rubbing a sun-burned hand across his day's growth of beard on a weak but not unhandsome face.

He expected a bull-like roar of annoyance from the captain. Instead Martin merely nodded absently, and walked forward. Sumner watched him interestedly until he reached the hatch leading to the crew's quarters below decks forward. Then:

"Cripes! He'll get one from Dave Sloan!" And young Sumner ran to find Pound and tell him that the captain would probably have a looking-glass within a minute. He was very curious to know the whys and wherefores of his senior mate's unusual request about his own looking-glass. He had obeyed, but he wanted to know; for here, indeed, was something very strange. Pound had merely told him the captain mustn't see that wound in his neck, which was high enough up so that without a glass he could not manage to look at it.

"What's it like, Mr. Pound," he ventured to inquire.

"It's wot you'd name kinder livid-like," returned Pound, slowly. "It's a kind of purplish. Looks like—nigger lips!"

Back in his stateroom, Martin, after closing the door leading to the cabin, started to take off his shirt. He was half-way through this operation when he was summoned on deck. He hastily re-adjusted the shirt, almost shamefacedly, as though discovered in some shameful act, and mounted the ladder. Pound engaged him for twenty minutes, ship matters. He gave his decisions in the same half-hearted voice which was so new to those about him, and descended again.

The bit of mirror-glass which he had borrowed from Sloan in

the fo'c'sle was gone from his washstand. He looked, painfully, all over the cabin for it, but it was not there. Ordinarily such a thing happening would have elicited a very tempest of raging curses. Now he sat down, almost helplessly, and stared about the stateroom with unseeing eyes. But not with unheeding ears! The voice was speaking English now, no longer gibberish syllables grouped about the one clear word, "*l'kundu.*" The voice in his left ear was compelling, tense, repetitive. "Over the side," it was repeating to him, and again, and yet again, "Over the side!"

He sat there a long time. Then, at last, perhaps, an hour later, his face, which there was no one by to see, now pinched, drawn and grey in the bold challenging afternoon light in the white-painted stateroom, he rose, slowly, and with almost furtive motions began to pull off his shirt.

He got it off, laid it on his berth, drew off the light singlet which he wore under it, and slowly, tentatively, with his right hand, reached for the wound in his neck. As his hand approached it, he felt cold and weak. At last his hand, fingers groping, touched the sore and tender area of the wound, felt about, found the wound itself. . . .

It was Pound who found him, two hours later, huddled in a heap on the cramped floor of the stateroom, naked to the waist, unconscious.

It was Pound, hard old Pound, who laboriously propped the captain's great bulk—for he was a heavy-set man, standing six feet in height—into his chair, pulled the singlet and then the discarded shirt over his head and then poured brandy between his bluish lips. It required half an hour of the mate's rough restoratives, brandy, chafing of the hands, slapping the limp, huge wrists, before Captain Luke Martin's eyelids fluttered and the big man gradually came awake.

But Pound found the monosyllabic answers to his few, brief questions cryptic, inappropriate. It was as though Martin were answering someone else, some other voice.

"I will," he said, wearily, and again, "Yes, I will!"

It was then, looking him up and down in considerable puzzlement, that the mate saw the blood on the fingers of his right hand, picked up the great, heavy hand now lying limply on the arm of the stateroom chair.

The three middle fingers had been bleeding for some time. The blood from them was now dry and clotted. Pound, picking up the hand, examining it in the light of the lowering afternoon sun, saw that these fingers had been savagely cut, or, it looked like, *sawed*. It was as though the saw-teeth that had ground and torn them had grated along their bones. It was a ghastly wound.

Pound, trembling from head to foot, fumbling about the medicine case, mixed a bowl of permanganate solution, soaked the unresisting hand, bound it up. He spoke to Martin several times, but Martin's eyes were looking at something far away, his ears deaf to his mate's words. Now and again he nodded his head acquiescently, and once more, before old Pound left him, sitting there, limply, he muttered, "Yes, yes!—I will, I will!"

Pound visited him again just before four bells in the early evening, supper time. He was still seated, looking, somehow, shrunken, apathetic.

"Supper, Captain?" inquired Pound tentatively. Martin did not raise his eyes. His lips moved, however, and Pound bent to catch what was being said.

"Yes, yes, yes," said Martin, "I will, I will—yes, I will!"

"It's laid in the cabin, sir," ventured Pound, but he got no reply, and he slipped out, closing the door behind him.

"The captain's sick, Maguire," said Pound to the little steward. "You might as well take down the table and all that, and then go forward as soon as you're finished."

"Aye, aye, sir," replied the wondering steward, and proceeded to unset the cabin table according to these orders. Pound saw him through with these duties, followed him out on deck, saw that he went forward as directed. Then he returned, softly.

He paused outside the stateroom door, listened. There was someone talking in there, someone besides the skipper—a thick voice, like one of the negroes, but very faint; thick, guttural, but light; a voice like a young boy's or—a woman's. Pound, stupefied, listened, his ear now directly against the door. He could not catch, through that thickness, what was being said, but it was in form, by the repeated sounds, the captain's voice alternating with the light, guttural voice, clearly a conversation, like question and answer, question and answer. The ship had no boy. Of women there was a couple of dozen, but all of them were battened below, under hatches, black women, down in the stinking manhold. Besides, the captain—there could not be a woman in there with him. No woman, no one at all, could have got in. The stateroom had been occupied only by the captain when he had left it fifteen minutes before. He had not been out of sight of the closed door all that time. Yet—he listened the more intently, his mind now wholly intrigued by this strange riddle.

He caught the cadence of Martin's words, now, the same cadence, he knew instinctively, as that of the broken sentence he had been repeating to him in his half-dazed state while he was binding up those gashed fingers. Those fingers! He shuddered. The *Saul Taverner* was a hell-ship. None was better aware of that than he, who had largely contributed, through many voyages in her, to that sinister reputation she bore, but—this! This was something like real hell.

"Yes, yes—I will, I will, I will——" that was the swing, the tonal cadence of what Martin was saying at more or less regular intervals in there; then the guttural, light voice—the two going

166

on alternately, one after the other, no pauses in that outlandish conversation.

Abruptly the conversation ceased. It was as though a sound-proof door had been pulled down over it. Pound straightened himself up, waited a minute, then knocked on the door.

The door was abruptly thrown open from inside, and Captain Luke Martin, his eyes glassy, unseeing, stepped out, Pound giving way before him. The captain paused in the middle of his cabin, looking about him, his eyes still bearing that "unseeing" look. Then he made his way straight towards the companion ladder. He was going up on deck, it seemed. His clothes hung on him now, his shirt awry, his trousers crumpled and seamed where he had lain on the floor, sat, huddled up, in the small chair where Pound had placed him.

Pound followed him up the ladder.

Once on deck, he made his way straight to the port rail, and stood, looking, still as though "unseeingly," out over the billowing waves. It was dark now; the sub-tropic dusk had lately fallen. The ship was quiet save for the noise of her sharp bows as they cut through the middle North Atlantic swell on her twelve-knot way to Virginia.

Suddenly old Pound sprang forward, grappled with Martin. The captain had started to climb the rail—suicide, that was it, then—those voices!

The thwarting of what seemed to be his purpose aroused Martin at last. Behind him lay a middle-aged man's lifetime of command, of following his own will in all things. He was not accustomed to being thwarted, to any resistance which, aboard his own ship, always went down, died still-born, before his bull-like bellow, his truculent fists.

He grappled in turn with his mate, and a long, desperate, and withal a silent struggle began there on the deck, lighted only by the light from the captain's cabin below, the light of the great binnacle-lamp of whale oil, through the skylights set above-decks for daytime illumination below.

In the course of that silent, deadly struggle, Pound seeking to drag the captain back from the vicinity of the rail, the captain laying about him with vicious blows, the man became rapidly dishevelled. Martin had been coatless, and a great swath of his white shirt came away in the clutching grip of Pound, baring his neck and left shoulder.

Pound slackened, let go, shrank and reeled away, covering his eyes lest they be blasted from their sockets by the horror which he had seen.

For there, where the shirt had been torn away and exposed the side of Martin's neck, stood a pair of blackish-purple, perfectly formed, blubbery lips; and as he gazed, appalled, horrified, the lips had opened in a wide yawn, exposing great, shining African

167

teeth, from between which, before he could bury his face in his hands away from this horror, a long, pink tongue had protruded and licked the lips. . . .

And when old Pound, shaking now to his very marrow, cold with the horror of this dreadful portent there on the deck warm with the pulsing breath of the trade wind, had recovered himself sufficiently to look again towards the place where the master of the *Saul Taverner* had struggled with him there against the railing, that place stood empty and no trace of Luke Martin so much as ruffled the phosphorescent surface of the *Saul Taverner*'s creaming wake.

A Piece of Linoleum

DAVID H. KELLER

It was a plain case of suicide. The coroner absolutely refused to consider any other verdict. And Mrs. Harker had the profound sympathy of her neighbours.

"I can't explain it at all," she whispered to two of her friends. "Just why John had to do a thing like that, when we were so happy, is beyond me.

"It would have been different if I hadn't been a kind, loving wife to him. I was more than a wife: I was a helpmate. Take this house, for example. Do you suppose for one moment it would belong to us, and every cent paid on the mortgage, if John Harker had been left to do it? Not in a hundred years. The first few weeks we were married and I found he was stopping at the station to buy flowers for the house on his way home, I knew what my duty was as a loving wife, and I lost no time doing it. From that time on I handled the pay cheque. Of course, I gave him some spending money every week, and saw to it that he had his evening paper after supper, but I wouldn't let him buy the paper on his way home, because he always mussed it so on the train and it never was fit to put on the shelves afterwards; but when I gave it to him after supper and spoke to him now and then about wrinkling it, it hardly got mussed at all.

"If we had had children, I wouldn't have been able to take such good care of him and the house and the furniture, but before we married the doctor told me I was delicate and better off without the responsibility of maternity. He was so sweet about it, when he said I could look on my future husband as my baby. Of course, it was hard for John to understand, so many men do not have the feminine viewpoint, but he finally submitted to the inevitable, though he always failed to see why I decorated his bedroom in pink.

"Being alone all day gave me lots of time for sewing, and in a few years I was making all my own clothes and most of John's. He used to ask me to buy his shirts, told me I was too busy to spend time on them, but I told him I just loved to do things like that for him, and that he was all the baby I had; so by and by, he stopped talking about it.

"I studied his health. Even sent to Washington for special books on invalid feeding, and if, in the twenty years of our sweet married life John Harker ever ate a spoonful of anything that was not pure and wholesome and fit for a man of his weight and digestive peculiarities, he must have bought it at a restaurant, he never ate it at his own table.

"I was always careful about his health. Every morning the same thing. Remind him of his umbrella, be sure he had his rubbers on, and the right weight of underwear. If it was clear in the morning and damp at night, I would meet his car with a raincoat and overshoes. Nothing was too much trouble for me.

"And I kept a clean house for him. That wasn't easy to do with a man in it. What he did not know, I taught him, patiently, just as you would a little child. It took over two years to train him to come in the back door, take off his shoes in the woodshed and put on his carpet slippers before he came into the house. But patience and love and repetition finally helped him to form the habit.

"We had lovely carpets, beautiful things that would last three generations if properly cared for, and when I found out how careless he was I put squares of linoleum around where he was in the habit of sitting, and when his friends came in, and he would forget himself and ask them to smoke, I would always run and put a piece of linoleum under them so the ashes wouldn't get on the floor. I was delicate and nervous after I was thirty; the dear doctor thought it was the change of life working on me; so I suggested that John save me by washing the supper dishes every night; but, do you know, he was so careless that I had to put several pieces of linoleum where he was working or he would get drops of soapy water on the beautiful waxed floor?

"I let him have his recreation. Once a year I insisted on his attending a meeting of his lodge of Lofty Pine Trees, even though he would smell of cigar smoke when he came back, but I was patient with him and never threw it up to him how hard I had to work to get the smell out of his best suit. At last I used lavender and heliotrope alternately and, finally, when he wore the suit to church, you could not smell anything but the perfume. It seems that the lodge appreciated what kind of loving wife John Harker had because the floral piece they sent to the funeral was perfectly lovely. Perhaps you ladies noticed it? I placed it in a conspicuous place at the head of the coffin. It was a large pillow made of little daisies with the words '*At Peace*' worked out in violets.

"But, of course, you want to know just how it happened. You realize that in my delicate health we always had separate bedrooms. But, as the dear doctor said, every husband has his rights, and so I never once shut the door between the rooms at night. I will say this, that John was a gentleman, and never once took advantage of my kindness. You see, I told him right after we were married just what the doctor said, about any sudden shock being likely to kill me, and of course, he, realized how delicate I was, didn't want to have my death on his conscience.

"I had his room decorated in pink, and on the wall facing the bed, just where he could see it the last thing at night and the first thing in the morning, I had an enlarged picture of us on our first trip to Atlantic City. Me on a chair and he in back, standing, holding an umbrella over me to protect my complexion from the sun. You know how sacred such experiences are during the first weeks of matrimony. He had a nice single bed and kept it and the room scrupulously clean. There was a piece of linoleum by the side of the bed, and on it I had a china spittoon hand-painted with tea roses. I gave it to him before we were married. Of course, he wasn't vulgar enough to chew or smoke, though goodness knows, he might have formed such habits had he been married to any other kind of woman; but he was fond of chewing gum, so every night I let him have one stick and the instructions were for him to put the wad in the spittoon just before he went to sleep. When I was well I used to turn the light out for him, but the nights of my martyrdom from headaches I made him put himself to bed.

"The dear doctor says that just as soon as I change the headaches will stop and I hope they do. No one who isn't married knows just what a terrible thing it is to be a woman.

"This night I went over his weekly allowance with him, and explained how, by drinking chicory instead of coffee, I had saved three dollars and had spent it for a new piece of art linoleum for his bedroom. It had the loveliest design on it—a Cupid, shooting an arrow at a trembling deer, symbolic of married life, I told him, and explained that it was a female deer, and that was why it was trembling. He did not say much, but later on his light went out and he said, 'Good night'. I knew right away there was something wrong, because I had always taught him to say, 'Good night, Dear', with the loving emphasis on the last word. Later on I heard a drip, drip, drip and I knew right away that either a tap was leaking or that it was raining a little, and I called, 'John, did you turn off the tap tight in the bathroom?' and he just laughed, and told me everything was all right and to go to sleep and not worry.

"The drip, drip, drip kept on, but fainter, so I went to sleep. When I went into his room to wake him, so he could go down and get breakfast, for that was the way we divided the work and it gave me a half hour more of necessary rest every day, I found the poor man had cut his wrist with a safety razor blade and was dead. What I heard dripping during the night was his life's blood.

"The doctor explained it all to me. He said that he was psychotic; that no man who had a loving, tender wife like John Harker would do a thing like that if he were not insane. That must be the explanation. One thing I am sure of: during all the twenty years of our sweet married life he never learned to appreciate my efforts to give him a nice, clean home. Even at the end he was careless. If he had just moved down in bed eight inches he could have bled on the linoleum, instead of on the lovely ingrain carpet."

The Seed from the Sepulchre

CLARK ASHTON SMITH

"Yes, I found the place," said Falmer. "It's a queer sort of place, pretty much as the legends describe it." He spat quickly into the fire, as if the act of speech had been physically distasteful to him, and, half averting his face from the scrutiny of Thone, stared with morose and sombre eyes into the jungle-matted Venezuelan darkness.

Thone, still weak and dizzy from the fever that had incapacitated him for continuing their journey to its end, was curiously puzzled. Falmer, he thought, had undergone an inexplicable change during the three days of his absence; a change that was too elusive in some of its phases to be fully defined or delimited.

Other phases, however, were all too obvious. Falmer, even during extreme hardship or illness, had heretofore been unquenchably loquacious and cheerful. Now he seemed sullen, uncommunicative, as if preoccupied with far-off things of disagreeable import. His bluff face had grown hollow—even pointed—and his eyes had narrowed to secretive slits. Thone was troubled by these changes, though he tried to dismiss his impressions as mere distempered fancies due to the influence of the ebbing fever.

"But can't you tell me what the place was like?" he persisted.

"There isn't much to tell," said Falmer, in a queer grumbling tone.

"Just a few crumbling walls and falling pillars."

"But didn't you find the burial pit of the Indian legend, where the gold was supposed to be?"

"I found it . . . but there was no treasure," Falmer's voice had taken on a forbidding surliness; and Thone decided to refrain from further questioning.

"I guess," he commented lightly, "that we had better stick to orchid-hunting. Treasure trove doesn't seem to be in our line. By the way, did you see any unusual flowers or plants during the trip?"

"Hell, no," Falmer snapped. His face had gone suddenly ashen in the firelight, and his eyes had assumed a set glare that might have meant either fear or anger. "Shut up, can't you? I don't want to talk. I've had a headache all day; some damned Venezuelan fever coming on, I suppose. We'd better head for the Orinoco tomorrow. I've had all I want of this trip."

173

James Falmer and Roderick Thone, professional orchid hunters, with two Indian guides, had been following an obscure tributary of the upper Orinoco. The country was rich in rare flowers; and, beyond its floral wealth, they had been drawn by vague but persistent rumours among the local tribes concerning the existence of a ruined city somewhere on this tributary; a city that contained a burial pit in which vast treasures of gold, silver, and jewels had been interred together with the dead of some nameless people. The two men had thought it worth while to investigate these rumours. Thone had fallen sick while they were still a full day's journey from the site of the ruins, and Falmer had gone on in a canoe with one of the Indians, leaving the other to attend to Thone. He had returned at nightfall of the third day following his departure.

Thone decided after a while, as he lay staring at his companion, that the latter's taciturnity and moroseness were perhaps due to disappointment over his failure to find the treasure. It must have been that, together with some tropical infection working in the man's blood. However, he admitted doubtfully to himself, it was not like Falmer, to be disappointed or downcast under such circumstances.

Falmer did not speak again, but sat glaring before him as if he saw something invisible to others beyond the labyrinth of fire-touched boughs and lianas in which the whispering, stealthy darkness crouched. Somehow, there was a shadowy fear in his aspect. Thone continued to watch him, and saw that the Indians, impassive and cryptic, were also watching him, as if with some obscure expectancy. The riddle was too much for Thone, and he gave it up after a while, lasping into restless, fever-turbulent slumber from which he awakened at intervals, to see the set face of Falmer, dimmer and more distorted each time with the slowly dying fire and the invading shadows.

Thone felt stronger in the morning: his brain was clear, his pulse tranquil once more; and he saw with mounting concern the indisposition of Falmer, who seemed to rouse and exert himself with great difficulty, speaking hardly a word and moving with singular stiffness and sluggishness. He appeared to have forgotten his announced project of returning towards the Orinoco, and Thone took entire charge of the preparations for departure. His companions' condition puzzled him more and more: apparently there was no fever and the symptoms were wholly ambiguous. However, on general principles, he administered a stiff dose of quinine to Falmer before they started.

The paling saffron of sultry dawn sifted upon them through the jungle tops as they loaded their belongings into the dug-outs and pushed off down the slow current. Thone sat near the bow of one of the boats, with Falmer in the rear, and a large bundle of orchid roots and part of their equipment filling the middle. The

174

two Indians occupied the other boat, together with the rest of the supplies.

It was a monotonous journey. The river wound like a sluggish olive snake between dark, interminable walls or forest, from which the goblin faces of orchids leered. There were no sounds other than the splash of paddles, the furious chattering of monkeys, and petulant cries of fiery-coloured birds. The sun rose above the jungle and poured down a tide of torrid brilliance.

Thone rowed steadily looking back over his shoulder at times to address Falmer with some casual remark or friendly question. The latter, with dazed eyes and features queerly pale and pinched in the sunlight, sat dully erect and made no effort to use his paddle. He offered no reply to the queries of Thone, but shook his head at intervals with a sort of shuddering motion that was plainly involuntary. After a while he began to moan thickly, as if in pain or delirium.

They went on in this manner for hours. The heat grew more oppressive between the stifling walls of jungle. Thone became aware of a shriller cadence in the moans of his companion. Looking back, he saw that Falmer had removed his sun-helmet, seemingly oblivious of the murderous heat, and was clawing at the crown of his head with frantic fingers. Convulsions shook his entire body, and the dug-out began to rock dangerously as he tossed to and fro in a paroxysm of manifest agony. His voice mounted to a high un-human shrieking.

Thone made a quick decision. There was a break in the lining palisade of sombre forest, and he headed the boat for shore immediately. The Indians followed, whispering between themselves and eyeing the sick man with glances of apprehensive awe and terror that puzzled Thone tremendously. He felt that there was some devilish mystery about the whole affair; and he could not imagine what was wrong with Falmer. All the known manifestations of malignant tropical diseases rose before him like a rout of hideous fantasms; but, among them, he could not recognize the thing that had assailed his companion.

Having got Falmer ashore on a semicircle of liana-latticed beach without the aid of the Indians, who seemed unwilling to approach the sick man, Thone administered a heavy hypodermic injection of morphine from his medicine chest. This appeared to ease Falmer's suffering, and the convulsions ceased. Thone, taking advantage of their remission, proceeded to examine the crown of Falmer's head.

He was startled to find, amid the thick dishevelled hair, a hard and pointed lump which resembled the tip of a beginning horn, rising under the still unbroken skin. As if endowed with erectile and resistless life, it seemed to grow beneath his fingers.

At the same time, abruptly and mysteriously, Falmer opened his eyes and appeared to regain full consciouness. For a few

175

minutes he was more his normal self than at any time since his return from the ruins. He began to talk, as if anxious to relieve his mind of some oppressing burden. His voice was peculiarly thick and toneless, but Thone was able to follow his mutterings and piece them together.

"The pit! the pit!" said Falmer—"the infernal thing that was in the pit, in the deep sepulchre! . . . I wouldn't go back there for the treasure of a dozen El Dorados. . . . I didn't tell you much about those ruins, Thone. Somehow it was hard—impossibly hard—to talk."

"I guess the Indian knew there was something wrong with the ruins. He led me to the place . . . but he wouldn't tell me anything about it; and he waited by the riverside while I searched for the treasure.

"Great grey walls there were, older than the jungle—old as death and time. They must have been quarried and reared by people from some lost planet. They loomed and leaned, at mad, unnatural angles, threatening to crush the trees about them. And there were columns too: thick, swollen columns of unholy form, whose abominable carvings the jungle had not wholly screened from view.

"There was no trouble finding that accursed burial pit. The pavement above had broken through quite recently, I think. A big tree had pried with its boa-like roots between the flagstones that were buried beneath centuries of mould. One of the flags had been tilted back on the pavement, and another had fallen through into the pit. There was a large hole, whose bottom I could see dimly in the forest-strangled light. Something glimmered palely at the bottom; but I could not be sure what it was.

"I had taken along a coil of rope, as you remember. I tied one end of it to a main root of the tree, dropped the other through the opening, and went down like a monkey. When I got to the bottom I could see little at first in the gloom, except the whitish glimmering all around me, at my feet. Something that was unspeakably brittle and friable crunched beneath me when I began to move. I turned on my flashlight, and saw that the place was fairly littered with bones. Human skeletons lay tumbled everywhere. They must have been removed long ago. I groped around amid the bones and dust, feeling pretty much like a ghoul, but couldn't find anything of value, not even a bracelet or a finger ring on any of the skeletons.

"It wasn't until I thought of climbing out that I noticed the real horror. In one of the corners—the corner nearest to the opening in the roof—I looked up and saw it in the webby shadows. Ten feet above my head it hung, and I had almost touched it, unknowing, when I descended the rope.

"It looked like a sort of white lattice work at first. When I saw that the lattice was partly formed of human bones—a complete skeleton very tall and stalwart, like that of a warrior. A pale, withered thing grew out of the skull, like a set of fantastic antlers ending in mydriads of long and stringy tendrils that had spread upward till they reached the roof. They must have lifted the skeleton, or body, along with them as they climbed.

"I examined the thing with my flashlight. It must have been a plant of some sort, and apparently it had started to grow in the cranium. Some of the branches had issued from the cloven crown, others through the eye holes, the mouth, and the nose hole, to flare upward. And the roots of the blasphemous thing had gone downward, trellising themselves on every bone. The very toes and fingers were ringed with them, and they dropped in writhing coils. Worst of all, the ones that had issued from the toe ends *were rooted in a second skull*, which dangled just below, with fragments of the broken-off root system. There was a litter of fallen bones on the floor in the corner. . . .

"The sight made me feel a little weak, somehow, and more than a little nauseated—that abhorrent, inexplicable mingling of the human and the plant. I started to climb the rope, in a feverish hurry to get out, but the thing fascinated me in its abominable fashion, and I couldn't help pausing to study it a little more when I had climbed half way. I leaned towards it too fast, I guess, and the rope began to sway, bringing my face lightly against the leprous, antler-shaped boughs above the skull.

"Something broke—possibly a sort of pod on one of the branches. I found my head enveloped in a cloud of pearl-grey powder, very light, fine, and scentless. The stuff settled on my hair, it got into my nose and eyes, nearly choking and blinding me. I shook if off as well as I could. Then I climbed on and pulled myself through the opening. . . ."

As if the effort of coherent narration had been too heavy a strain, Falmer lapsed into disconnected mumblings. The mysterious malady, whatever it was, returned upon him, and his delirious ramblings were mixed with groans of torture. But at moments he regained a flash of coherence.

"My head! my head!" he muttered. "There must be something in my brain, something that grows and spreads; I tell you, I can feel it there. I haven't felt right at any time since I left the burial pit.

". . . My mind has been queer ever since. . . . It must have been the spores of the ancient devil-plant. . . . The spores have taken root . . . the thing is splitting my skull, going down into my brain—a plant that springs out of a human cranium—as if from a flower pot!"

The dreadful convulsions began once more, and Falmer writhed uncontrollably in his companion's arms, shrieking with agony. Thone, sick at heart, and shocked by his sufferings, abandoned all effort to restrain him and took up the hypodermic. With much difficulty, he managed to inject a triple dose, and

Falmer grew quiet by degrees, and lay with open glassy eyes, breathing stertorously. Thone, for the first time, perceived an odd protrusion of his eyeballs, which seemed about to start from their sockets, making it impossible for the lids to close, and lending the drawn features an expression of mad horror. It was as if something were pushing Falmer's eyes from his head.

Thone, trembling with sudden weakness and terror, felt that he was involved in some unnatural web of nightmare. He could not, dared not, believe the story Falmer had told him, and its implications. Assuring himself that his companion had imagined it all, had been ill throughout with the incubation of some strange fever, he stooped over and found that the horn-shaped lump on Falmer's head had now broken through the skin.

With a sense of unreality, he stared at the object that his prying fingers had revealed amid the matted hair. It was unmistakably a plant-bud of some sort, with involuted folds of pale green and bloody pink that seemed about to expand. The thing issued from above the central suture of the skull.

A nausea swept upon Thone, and he recoiled from the lolling head and its baleful outgrowth, averting his gaze. His fever was returning, there was a woeful debility in all his limbs, and he heard the muttering voice of delirium through the quinine-induced ringing in his ears. His eyes blurred with a deathly and miasmal mist.

He fought to subdue his illness and impotence. He must not give way to it wholly; he must go on with Falmer and the Indians and reach the nearest trading station, many days away on the Orinoco, where Falmer could receive aid.

As if through sheer volition, his eyes cleared, and he felt a resurgence of strength. He looked around for the guides, and saw, with a start of uncomprehending surprise, that they had vanished. Peering further, he observed that one of the boats—the dug-out used by the Indians—had also disappeared. It was plain that he and Falmer had been deserted. Perhaps the Indians had known what was wrong with the sick man, and had been afraid. At any rate, they were gone, and they had taken much of the camp equipment and most of the provisions with them.

Thone turned once more to the supine body of Falmer, conquering his repugnance, with effort. Resolutely he drew out his clasp knife, and, stooping over the stricken man, he excised the protruding bud, cutting as close to the scalp as he could with safety. The thing was unnaturally tough and rubbery; it exuded a thin, sanious fluid; and he shuddered when he saw its internal structure, full of nerve-like filaments, with a core that suggested cartilage. He flung it aside, quickly, on the river sand. Then, lifting Falmer in his arms, he lurched and staggered towards the remaining boat. He fell more than once, and lay half swooning across the inert body. Alternately carrying and dragging his burden, he reached the boat at last. With the remainder of his failing strength, he contrived to prop Falmer in the stern against the pile of equipment.

His fever was mounting apace. After much delay, with tedious, half-delirious exertions, he pushed off from the shore and got the boat into midstream. He paddled with nerveless strokes, till the fever mastered him wholly and the oar slipped from oblivious fingers. . . .

He awoke in the yellow glare of dawn, with his brain and his senses comparatively clear. His illness had left a great languor, but his first thought was of Falmer. He twisted about, nearly falling overboard in his debility, and sat facing his companion.

Falmer still reclined, half sitting, half lying, against the pile of blankets and other impediments. His knees were drawn up, his hands clasping them as if in tetanic rigor. His features had grown as stark and ghastly as those of a dead man, and his whole aspect was one of mortal rigidity. It was not this, however, that caused Thone to gasp with unbelieving horror.

During the interim of Thone's delirium and his lapse into slumber, the monstrous plant bud, merely stimulated, it would seem, by the act of excision, had grown again with preternatural rapidity, from Falmer's head. A loathsome pale-green stem was mounting thickly, and had started to branch like antlers after attaining a height of six or seven inches.

More dreadful than this, if possible, similar growths had issued from the eyes, and their stems, climbing vertically across the forehead, had entirely displaced the eyeballs. Already they were branching like the thing from the crown. The antlers were all tipped with pale vermillion. They appeared to quiver with repulsive animations, nodding rhythmically in the warm, windless air. . . . From the mouth, another stem protruded, curling upward like a long and whitish tongue. It had not yet begun to birfucate.

Thone closed his eyes to shut away the shocking vision. Behind his lids, in a yellow dazzle of light, he still saw the cadaverous features, the climbing stems that quivered against the dawn like ghastly hydras of tomb-etiolated green. They seemed to be waving towards him, growing and lengthening as they waved. He opened his eyes again, and fancied, with a start of new terror, that the antlers were actually taller than they had been a few moments previous.

After that, he sat watching them in a sort of baleful hypnosis. The illusion of the plant's visible growth and freer movement— if it were illusion—increased upon him. Falmer, however, did not stir, and his parchment face appeared to shrivel and fall in, as if the roots of the growth were draining his blood, were devouring his very flesh in their insatiable and ghoulish hunger.

Thone wrenched his eyes away and stared at the river shore. The stream had widened and the current had grown more sluggish.

179

He sought to recognize their location, looking vainly for some familiar landmark in the monotonous dull-green cliffs of jungle that lined the margin. He felt hopelessly lost and alienated. He seemed to be drifting on an unknown tide of madness and nightmare, accompanied by something more frightful than corruption itself.

His mind began to wander with an odd inconsequence, coming back always, in a sort of closed circle, to the thing that was devouring Falmer. With a flash of scientific curiosity, he found himself wondering to what genus it belonged. It was neither fungus nor pitcher plant, nor anything that he had ever encountered or heard of in his explorations. It must have come, as Falmer had suggested, from an alien world: it was nothing that the earth could conceivably have nourished.

He felt, with a comforting assurance, that Falmer was dead. That at least, was a mercy. But, even as he shaped the thought, he heard a low, gutteral moaning, and peering at Falmer in a horrible startlement, saw that his limbs and body were twitching slightly. The twitching increased, and took on a rhythmic regularity, though at no time did it resemble the agonized and violent convulsions of the previous day. It was plainly automatic, like a sort of galvanism; and Thone saw that it was timed with the languorous and loathsome swaying of the plant. The effect on the watcher was insidiously mesmeric and somnolent; and once he caught himself beating the detestable rhythm with his foot.

He tried to pull himself together, groping desperately for something to which his sanity could cling. Ineluctably, his illness returned: fever, nausea, and revulsion worse than the loathliness of death. But, before he yielded to it utterly, he drew his loaded revolver from the holster and fired six times into Falmer's quivering body. . . . He knew that he had not missed, but, after the final bullet, Falmer still moaned and twitched in unison with the evil swaying of the plant, and Thone, sliding into delirium, heard still the ceaseless, automatic moaning.

There was no time in the world of seething unreality and shoreless oblivion through which he drifted. When he came to himself again, he could not know if hours or weeks had elapsed. But he knew at once that the boat was no longer moving; and lifting himself dizzily, he saw that it had floated into shallow water and mud and was nosing the beach of a tiny, jungle-tufted isle in midriver. The putrid odour of slime was about him like a stagnant pool; and he heard a strident humming of insects.

It was either late morning or early afternoon, for the sun was high in the still heavens. Lianas were drooping above him from the island trees like uncoiled serpents, and epiphytic orchids, marked with ophidian mottlings, leaned towards him grotesquely from lowering boughs. Immense butterflies went past on sumptuously spotted wings.

180

He sat up, feeling very giddy and lightheaded, and faced again the horror that accompanied him. The thing had grown incredibly: the three-antlers stems, mounting above Falmer's head, had become gigantic and had put out masses of ropy feelers and tossed uneasily in the air, as if searching for support—or new provender. In the topmost antlers, a prodigious blossom had opened—a sort of fleshy disc, broad as a man's face and white as leprosy.

Falmer's features had shrunken till the outlines of every bone were visible as if beneath tightened paper. He was a mere death's head in a mask of human skin; and beneath his clothing the body was little more than a skeleton. He was quite still now, except for the communicated quivering of the stems. The atrocious plant had sucked him dry, had eaten his vitals and his flesh.

Thone wanted to hurl himself forward in a mad impulse to grapple with the growth. But a strange paralysis held him back. The plant was like a living and sentient thing—a thing that watched him, that dominated him with its unclean but superior will. And the huge blossom, as he stared, took on the dim, unnatural semblance of a face. It was somehow like the face of Falmer but the lineaments were twisted all awry, and were mingled with those of something wholly devilish and nonhuman. Thone could not move—he could not take his eyes from the blasphemous abnormality.

By some miracle, his fever had left him; and it did not return. Instead, there came an eternity of frozen fright and madness, in which he sat facing the mesmeric plant. It towered before him from the dry, dead shell that had been Falmer, its swollen, glutted stems and branches swaying gently, and huge flower leering perpetually upon him with its impious travesty of a human face. He thought that he heard a low, singing sound, ineffably sweet, but whether it emanated from the plant or was a mere hallucination of his overwrought senses, he could not know.

The sluggish hours went by, and a gruelling sun poured down its beams like molten lead from some titanic vessel of torture. His head swam with weakness and the fetor-laden heat, but he could not relax the rigor of his posture. There was no change in the nodding monstrosity, which seemed to have attained its full growth above the head of its victim. But after a long interim Thone's eyes were drawn to the shrunken hands of Falmer, which still clasped the drawn-up knees in a spasmodic clutch. From the ends of the fingers, tiny white rootlets had broken and were writhing slowly in the air—groping, it seemed, for a new source of nourishment. Then, from the neck and chin, other tips were breaking, and over the whole body the clothing stirred in a curious manner, as if with the crawling and lifting of hidden lizards.

At the same time the singing grew louder, sweeter, more imperious, and the swaying of the great plant assumed an indescribably seductive tempo. It was like the allurement of voluptuous sirens, the deadly languor of dancing cobras. Thone felt an irresistible compulsion: a summons was being laid upon him, and his drugged mind and body must obey it. The very fingers of Falmer, twisting viperishly, seemed beckoning to him. Suddenly he was on his hands and knees in the bottom of the boat.

Inch by inch, with terror and fascination contending in his brain, he crept forward, dragging himself over the disregarded bundle of orchid-plants—inch by inch, foot by foot, till his head was against the withered hands of Falmer, from which hung and floated the questing roots.

Some cataleptic spell had made him helpless. He felt the root-lets as they moved like delving fingers through his hair and over his face and neck, and started to strike in with agonizing, needle-sharp tips. He could not stir, he could not even close his lids. In a frozen stare he saw the gold and carmine flesh of a hovering butterfly as the roots began to pierce his pupils.

Deeper and deeper went the greedy roots, while new filaments grew out to enmesh him like a witch's net. . . . For a while, it seemed that the dead and the living writhed together in leashed convulsions. . . . At last Thone hung supine amid the lethal, ever-growing web; bloated and colossal, the plant lived on; and in its upper branches, through the still, stifling afternoon, a second flower began to unfold.

Canavan's Back Yard

JOSEPH PAYNE BRENNAN

I first met Canavan over twenty years ago, shortly after he had emigrated from London. He was an antiquarian and a lover of old books and so he quite naturally set up shop as a second-hand book dealer after he settled in New Haven.

Since his small capital didn't permit him to rent premises in the centre of the city, he engaged combined business and living quarters in an isolated old house near the outskirts of town. The section was sparsely settled, but since a good percentage of Canavan's business was transacted by mail, it didn't particularly matter.

Quite often, after a morning spent at my typewriter, I walked out to Canvan's shop and spent most of the afternoon browsing among his old books. I found it a great pleasure, especially because Canavan never resorted to high-pressure methods to make a sale. He was aware of my precarious financial situation; he never frowned if I walked away empty-handed.

In fact he seemed to welcome me for my company alone. Only a few buyers called at his place with regularity, and I think he was often lonely. Sometimes when business was slow, he would brew a pot of English tea and the two of us would sit for hours, drinking tea and talking about books.

Canavan even looked like an antiquarian book dealer—or the popular caricature of one. He was small of frame, somewhat stoop-shouldered, and his blue eyes peered out from behind archaic spectacles with steel rims and square-cut lenses.

Although I doubt if his yearly income ever matched that of a good paperhanger, he managed to "get by" and he was content. Content, that is, until he began noticing his back yard.

Behind the ramshackled old house in which he lived and ran his shop, stretched a long desolate yard overgrown with brambles and high brindle-coloured grass. Several decayed apple trees, jagged and black with rot, added to the scene's dismal aspect. The broken wooden fences on both sides of the yard were all but swallowed up by the tangle of coarse grass. They appeared to be literally sinking into the ground. Altogether the yard presented an unusually depressing picture and I often wondered why Canavan didn't clean it up. But it was none of my business; I never mentioned it.

183

One afternoon when I visited the shop, Canavan was not in the front display room and I therefore walked down a narrow corridor to a rear storeroom where he sometimes worked, packing and unpacking book shipments. When I entered the storeroom, Canavan was standing at the window, looking out at the back yard.

I started to speak and then for some reason didn't. I think what stopped me was the look on Canavan's face. He was gazing out at the yard with a peculiar intense expression, as if he were completely absorbed by something he saw there. Varying, conflicting emotions showed on his strained features. He seemed both fascinated and fearful, attracted and repelled. When he finally noticed me, he almost jumped. He stared at me for a moment as if I were a total stranger.

Then his old easy smile came back and his blue eyes twinkled behind the square spectacles. He shook his head. "That back yard of mine sure looks funny sometimes. You look at it long enough, you think it runs for miles!"

That was all he said at the time, and I soon forgot about it, but had I only known, that was just the beginning of the horrible business.

After that, whenever I visited the shop, I found Canavan in the rear storeroom. Once in a while he was actually working, but most of the time he was simply standing at the window looking out at that dreary yard of his.

Sometimes he would stand there for minutes completely oblivious to my presence. Whatever he saw appeared to rivet his entire attention. His countenance at these times showed an expression of fright mingled with a queer kind of pleasureable expectancy. Usually it was necessary for me to cough loudly, or shuffle my feet, before he turned from the window.

Afterward, when he talked about books, he would seem to be his old self again, but I began to experience the disconcerting feeling that he was merely acting, that while he chatted about incunabula, his thoughts were actually still dwelling on that infernal back yard.

Several times I thought of questioning him about the yard but whenever words were on the tip of my tongue, I was stopped by a sense of embarrassment. How can one admonish a man for looking out of a window at his own back yard? What does one say and how does one say it?

I kept silent. Later I regretted it bitterly.

Canavan's business, never really flourishing, began to diminish. Worse than that, he appeared to be failing physically. He grew more stooped and gaunt, and though his eyes never lost their sharp glint, I began to believe it was more the glitter of fever than the twinkle of healthy enthusiasm which animated them.

One afternoon when I entered the shop, Canavan was nowhere to be found. Thinking he might be just outside the back door engaged in some household chore, I leaned up against the rear window and looked out.

I didn't see Canavan, but as I gazed out over the yard I was swept with a sudden inexplicable sense of desolation which seemed to roll over me like the wave of an icy sea. My initial impulse was to pull away from the window, but something held me. As I stared out over that miserable tangle of briars and brindle grass, I experienced what for want of a better word I can only call *curiosity*. Perhaps some cool, analytical, dispassionate part of my brain simply wanted to discover what had caused my sudden sense of acute depression. Or possibly some feature of that wretched vista attracted me on a subconscious level which I had never permitted to crowd up into my sane and waking hours.

In any case, I remained at the window. The long dry brown grass wavered slightly in the wind. The rotted black trees reared motionless. Not a single bird, not even a butterfly, hovered over that bleak expanse. There was nothing to be seen except the stalks of long brindle grass, the decayed trees and scattered clumps of low-growing briary bushes.

Yet there was something about that particular isolated slice of landscape which I found intriguing. I think I had the feeling that it presented some kind of puzzle and that if I gazed at it long enough, the puzzle would resolve itself.

After I had stood looking out at it for a few minutes, I experienced the odd sensation that its perspectives were subtly altering. Neither the grass nor the trees changed and yet the yard itself seemed to expand its dimensions. At first I merely reflected that the yard was actually much longer than I had previously believed. Then I had an idea that in reality it stretched for several acres. Finally I became convinced that it continued for an interminable distance and that if I entered it, I might walk for miles and miles before I came to the end.

I was seized by a sudden almost overpowering desire to rush out the back door, plunge into that sea of wavering brindle grass and stride straight ahead until I had discovered for myself just how far it did extend. I was, in fact, on the point of doing so—when I saw Canavan.

He appeared abruptly out of the tangle of tall grass at the near end of the yard. For at least a minute he seemed to be completely lost. He looked at the back of his own house as if he had never in his life seen it before. He was dishevelled and obviously excited. Briars clung to his trousers and jacket and pieces of grass were stuck in the hooks of his old-fashioned shoes. His eyes roved around wildly; he seemed about to turn and bolt back into the tangle from which he had just emerged.

I rapped loudly on the window pane. He paused in a half turn, looked over his shoulder and saw me. Gradually an expression of normalcy returned to his agitated features. Walking in a weary slouch, he approached the house. I hurried to the door and let him in. He went straight to the front display room and sank down in a chair.

He looked up when I followed him into the room. "Frank," he said in a half whisper, "would you make some tea?"

I brewed tea and he drank it scalding hot without saying a word. He looked utterly exhausted; I knew he was too tired to tell me what had happened.

"You had better stay indoors for a few days," I said as I left. He nodded weakly, without looking up, and bade me good day.

When I returned to the shop the next afternoon, he appeared rested and refreshed but nevertheless moody and depressed. He made no mention of the previous day's episode. For a week or so it seemed as if he might forget about the yard.

But one day when I went into the shop, he was standing at the rear window and I could see that he tore himself away only with the greatest reluctance. After that, the pattern began repeating itself with regularity and I knew that that weird tangle of brindle grass behind his house was becoming an obsession.

Because I feared for his business, as well as for his fragile health, I finally remonstrated with him. I pointed out that he was losing customers; he had not issued a book catalogue in months. I told him that the time spent in gazing at that witch's half acre he called his back yard would be better spent in listing his books and filling his orders. I assured him that an obsession such as his was sure to undermine his health. And finally I pointed out the absurd and ridiculous aspects of the affair. If people knew he spent hours in staring out his window at nothing more than a miniature jungle of grass and briars, they might think he was actually mad!

I ended by boldly asking him exactly what he had experienced that afternoon when I had seen him come out of the grass with a lost bewildered expression on his face.

He removed his square spectacles with a sigh. "Frank," he said, "I know you mean well. But there's something about that back yard—some secret—that I've got to find out. I don't know what it is exactly—something about distance and dimensions and perspectives, I think. But whatever it is, I've come to consider it—well, a challenge. I've got to get to the root of it. If you think I'm crazy, I'm sorry. But I'll have no rest until I solve the riddle of that piece of ground."

He replaced his spectacles with a frown. "That afternoon," he went on, "when you were standing at the window. I had a strange and frightening experience out there. I had been watching at the window and finally I felt myself drawn irresistibly outside. I plunged into the grass with a feeling of exhilaration, of adventure, of expectancy. As I advanced into the yard, my sense of elation quickly changed to a mood of black depression. I turned around, intending to come right out—but I couldn't. You won't believe this, I know—but I was lost! I simply lost all sense of direction and couldn't decide which way to turn. That grass is taller than it looks! When you get into it, you can't see anything beyond it.

"I know this sounds incredible—but I wandered out there for an hour. The yard seemed fantastically large once I got into that tangle of grass. It almost seemed to alter its dimensions as I moved, so that a large expanse of it lay always in front of me. I must have walked in circles. I swear I trudged miles!"

He shook his head. "You don't have to believe me. I don't expect you to. But that's what happened. When I finally found my way out, it was by the sheerest accident. And the strangest part of it is that once I got out, I felt suddenly terrified without the tall grass all around me and I wanted to rush back in again! This in spite of the ghastly sense of desolation which the place aroused in me.

"But I've got to go back. I've got to figure the thing out. There's something out there that defies the laws of earthly nature as we know them. I mean to find out what it is. I think I have a plan and I mean to put it into practice."

His words stirred me strangely and when I uneasily recalled my own experience at the window that afternoon, I found it difficult to dismiss his story as sheer nonsense. I did—half-heartedly—try to dissuade him from entering the yard again, but I knew even as I spoke that I was wasting my breath.

I left the shop that afternoon with a feeling of oppression and foreboding which nothing could remove.

When I called several days later, my worst fears were realized —Canavan was missing. The front door of the shop was unlatched as usual but Canavan was not in the house. I looked in every room. Finally, with a feeling of infinite dread. I opened the back door and looked out towards the yard.

The long stalks of brown grass slid against each other in the slight breeze with dry sibilant whispers. The dead trees reared black and motionless. Although it was late summer, I could hear neither the chirp of a bird nor the chirr of a single insect. The yard itself seemed to be listening.

Feeling something against my foot, I glanced down and saw a thick twine stretching from inside the door, across the scant cleared space immediately adjacent to the house and thence into the wavering wall of grass. Instantly I recalled Canavan's mention of a "plan". His plan, I realized immediately, was to enter the yard trailing a stout cord behind him. No matter how he twisted and turned, he must have reasoned, he could always find his way out by following back along the cord.

It seemed like a workable scheme and I felt relieved. Probably Canavan was still in the yard. I decided I would wait for him to come out. Perhaps if he were permitted to roam around in the

187

yard long enough, without interruption, the place would lose its evil fascination for him, and he would forget about it.

I went back into the shop and browsed among the books. At the end of an hour I became uneasy again. I wondered how long Canavan had been in the yard. When I began reflecting on the old man's uncertain health, I felt a sense of responsibility.

I finally returned to the back door, saw that he was nowhere in sight, and called out his name. I experienced the disquieting sensation that my shout carried no further than the very edge of that whispering fringe of grass. It was as if the sound had been smothered, deadened, nullified as soon as the vibrations of it reached the border of that overgrown yard.

I called again, and again, but there was no reply. At length I decided to go in after him. I would follow along the cord, I thought, and I would be sure to locate him. I told myself that the thick grass undoubtedly did stifle my shout and possibly in any case Canavan might be growing slightly deaf.

Just inside the door, the cord was tied securely around the leg of a heavy table. Taking hold of the twine, I crossed the cleared area back of the house and slipped into the rustling expanse of grass.

The going was easy at first, and I made good progress. As I advanced, however, the grass stems became thicker, and grew closer together, and I was forced to shove my way through them.

When I was no more than a few yards inside the tangle, I was overwhelmed with the same bottomless sense of desolation which I had experienced before. There was certainly something uncanny about the place. I felt as if I had suddenly veered into another world—a world of briars and brindle grass whose ceaseless half-heard whisperings were somehow alive with evil.

As I pushed along, the cord abruptly came to an end. Glancing down, I saw that it had caught against a thorn bush, abraded itself and subsequently broken. Although I bent down and poked in the area for several minutes, I was unable to locate the piece from which it had parted. Probably Canavan was unaware that the cord had broken and was now pulling it along with him.

I straightened up, cupped my hands to my mouth and shouted. My shout seemed to be all but drowned in my throat by that dismal wall of grass. I felt as if I were down at the bottom of a well, shouting up.

Frowning with growing uneasiness, I tramped ahead. The grass stalks kept getting thicker and tougher and at length I needed both hands to propel myself through the matted growth.

I began to sweat profusely; my head started to ache, and I imagined that my vision was beginning to blur. I felt the same tense, almost unbearable oppression which one experiences on a stifling summer's day when a storm is brewing and the atmosphere is charged with static electricity.

188

Also, I realized with a slight qualm of fear that I had got turned around and didn't know which part of the yard I was in. During an objective half-minute in which I reflected that I was actually worried about getting lost in someone's back yard, I almost laughed—almost. But there was something about the place which didn't permit laughter. I plodded ahead with a sober face.

Presently I began to feel that I was not alone. I had a sudden hair-raising conviction that someone—or something—was creeping along in the grass behind me. I cannot say with certainty that I heard anything, although I may have, all at once I was firmly convinced that some creature was crawling or wriggling a short distance in my rear.

I felt that I was being watched and that the watcher was wholly malignant.

For a wild instant, I considered headlong flight. Then, unaccountably, rage took possession of me. I was suddenly furious with Canavan, furious with the yard, furious with myself. All my pent-up tension exploded in a gust of rage which swept away fear. Now, I vowed, I would get to the root of the weird business. I would be tormented and frustrated by it no longer.

I whirled without warning and lunged into the grass where I believed my stealthy pursuer might be hiding.

I stopped abruptly; my savage anger melted into inexpressible horror.

In the faint brassy sunlight which filtered down through the towering stalks of brindle grass, Canavan crouched on all fours like a beast about to spring. His glasses were gone, his clothes were in shreds and his mouth was twisted into an insane grimace, half smirk, half snarl.

I stood petrified, staring at him. His eyes, queerly out of focus, glared at me with concentrated hatred and without any faint glimmer of recognition. His grey hair was matted with grass and small sticks; his entire body, in fact, including the tattered remains of his clothing, was covered with them, as if he had grovelled or rolled on the ground like a wild animal.

After the first throat-freezing shock, I finally found my tongue. "Canavan!" I screamed at him. "Canavan, for God's sake don't you know me?"

His answer was a low throaty snarl. His lips twisted back from his yellowish teeth and his crouching body tensed for a spring.

Pure terror took possession of me. I leaped aside and flung myself into that infernal wall of grass an instant before he lunged.

The intensity of my terror must have given me added strength. I rammed headlong through those twisted stalks which before I had laboriously pulled aside. I could hear the grass and briar

189

bushes crashing behind me and I knew that I was running for my life.

I pounded on as in a nightmare. Grass stalk snapped against my face like whips and thorns gashed me like razors but I felt nothing. All my physical and mental resources were concentrated in one frenzied resolve: I must get out of that devil's field of grass and away from the monstrous thing which followed swiftly in my wake.

My breath began coming in great shuddering sobs. My legs felt weak and I seemed to be looking through spinning saucers of light. But I ran on.

The thing behind me was gaining. I could hear it growling and I could feel it lunge against the earth only inches back of my flying feet. And all the time I had the maddening conviction that I was actually running in circles.

At last, when I felt that I must surely collapse in another second, I plunged through a final brindle thicket into the open sunlight. Ahead of me lay the cleared area at the rear of Canavan's shop. Just beyond was the house itself.

Gasping and fighting for breath, I dragged myself towards the door. For no reason that I could explain, then or afterwards, I felt absolutely certain that the horror at my heels would not venture into the open area. I didn't even turn around to make sure.

Inside the house I fell weakly into a chair. My strained breathing slowly returned to normal, but my mind remained caught up in a whirlwind of sheer horror and hideous conjecture.

Canavan, I realized, had gone completely mad. Some ghastly shock had turned him into a ravening bestial lunatic thirsting for the savage destruction of any living thing that crossed his path. Remembering the oddly-focused eyes which had glared at me with a glaze of animal ferocity, I knew that his mind had not been merely unhinged—it had been totally destroyed. Death could be the only possible release.

But Canavan was still at least the shell of a human being, and he had been my friend. I could not take the law into my own hands.

With many misgivings I called the police and an ambulance.

What followed was more madness, plus an inquisitorial session of questions and demands which left me in a state of near nervous collapse.

A half dozen burly policemen spent the better part of an hour tramping through that wavering brindle grass without locating any trace of Canavan. They came out cursing, rubbing their eyes and shaking their heads. They were flushed, furious—and ill at ease. They announced that they had seen nothing, and heard nothing except some sneaking dog which stayed always out of sight and growled at them at intervals.

190

When they mentioned the growling dog, I opened my mouth to speak, but thought better of it and said nothing. They were already regarding me with open suspicion, as if they believed my own mind might be breaking.

I repeated my story at least twenty times and still they were not satisfied. They ransacked the entire house. They inspected Canavan's files. They even removed some loose boards in one of the rooms and searched underneath.

At length they grudgingly concluded that Canavan had suffered total loss of memory after experiencing some kind of shock and that he had wandered off the premises in a state of amnesia shortly after I had encountered him in the yard. My own description of his appearance and actions they discounted as lurid exaggeration. After warning me that I would probably be questioned further and that my own premises might be inspected, they reluctantly permitted me to leave.

Their subsequent searches and investigations revealed nothing new and Canavan was put down as a missing person, probably afflicted with acute amnesia.

But I was not satisfied, and I could not rest.

Six months of patient, painstaking, tedious research in the files and stacks of the local University Library finally yielded something which I do not offer as an explanation, nor even as a definite clue, but only as a fantastic near-impossibility which I ask no one to believe.

One afternoon, after my extended research over a period of months had produced nothing of significance, the Keeper of Rare Books at the University Library triumphantly bore to my study niche a tiny, crumbling pamphlet which had been printed in New Haven in 1695. It mentioned no author and carried the stark title, *Deathe of Goodie Larkins, Witche*.

Several years before, it revealed, an ancient crone, one Goodie Larkins, had been accused by neighbours of turning a missing child into a wild dog. The Salem madness was raging at the time and Goodie Larkins had been summarily condemned to death. Instead of being burned, she had been driven into a marsh deep in the woods where seven savage dogs, starved for a fortnight, had been turned loose on her trail. Apparently her accusers felt that this was a touch of truly poetic justice.

As the ravening dogs closed in on her, she was heard by her retreating neighbours to utter a frightful curse:

"*Let this lande I fall upon lye alle the way to Hell!*" she had screamed. "*And they who tarry here be as these beastes that rende me dead!*"

A subsequent inspection of old maps and land deeds satisfied me that the marsh in which Goodie Larkins was torn to pieces by the dogs after uttering her awful curse—originally occupied the

191

same lot or square which now enclosed Canavan's hellish back yard!

I say no more. I returned only once to that devilish spot. It was a cold desolate autumn day and a keening wind rattled the brindle stalks in that unholy acre. I cannot say what urged me back; perhaps it was some lingering feeling or loyalty towards the Canavan I had known. Perhaps it was even some last shred of hope. But as soon as I entered the cleared area behind Canavan's boarded-up house, I knew I had made a mistake.

As I stared at the stiff waving grass, the bare trees and the black ragged briar bushes, I felt as if I, in turn, were being watched. I felt as if something alien and wholly evil were observing me, and though I was terrified, I experienced a perverse, insane impulse to rush headlong into that whispering expanse. Again I imagined I saw that monstrous landscape subtly alter its dimensions and perspectives until I was staring towards a stretch of blowing brindle grass and rotted trees which ran for miles. Something urged me to enter, to lose myself in the lovely grass, to roll and grovel at its roots, to rip off the foolish encumbrances of cloth which covered me and run howling and ravenous, on and on, on and on. . . .

Instead, I turned and rushed away. I ran through the windy autumn streets like a madman. I lurched into my rooms and bolted the door.

I have never gone back since. And I never shall.

The Shuttered Room

H. P. LOVECRAFT and AUGUST DERLETH

I

At dusk, the wild, lonely country guarding the approaches to the village of Dunwich in north central Massachusetts seems more desolate and forbidding than it ever does by day. Twilight lends the barren fields and domed hills a strangeness that sets them apart from the country around that area; it brings to everything a kind of sentient, watchful animosity—to the ancient trees, to the brier-bordered stone walls pressing close upon the dusty road, to the low marshes with their myriads of fireflies and their incessantly calling whip-poor-wills vying with the muttering of frogs and the shrill songs of toads, to the sinuous windings of the upper reaches of the Miskatonic flowing among the dark hills seaward, all of which seem to close in upon the traveller as if intent upon holding him fast, beyond all escape.

On his way to Dunwich, Abner Whateley felt all this again, as once in childhood he had felt it and run screaming in terror to beg his mother to take him away from Dunwich and Grandfather Luther Whateley. So many years ago! He had lost count of them. It was curious that the country should affect him so, pushing through all the years he had lived since then—the years at the Sorbonne, in Cairo, in London—pushing through all the learning he had assimilated since those early visits to grim old Grandfather Whateley in his ancient house attached to the mill along the Miskatonic, the country of his childhood, coming back now out of the mists of time as were it but yesterday that he had visited his kinfolk.

They were all gone now—Mother, Grandfather Whateley, Aunt Sarey, whom he had never seen but only knew to be living somewhere in that old house—the loathsome cousin Wilbur and his terrible twin brother few had ever known before his frightful death on top of Sentinel Hill. But Dunwich, he saw as he drove through the cavernous covered bridge, had not changed; its main street lay under the looming mound of Round Mountain, its gambrel roofs as rotting as ever, its houses deserted, the only store still in the broken-steepled church, over everything the unmistakable aura of decay.

He turned off the main street and followed a rutted road up along the river, until he came within sight of the great old house with the mill wheel on the river-side. It was his property now, by the will of Grandfather Whateley, who had stipulated that he must settle the estate and "take such steps as may be necessary to bring about that dissolution I myself was not able to take." A curious proviso, Abner thought. But then, everything about Grandfather Whateley had been strange, as if the decadence of Dunwich had infected him irrevocably.

And nothing was stranger than that Abner Whateley should come back from his cosmopolitan way of life to heed his grandfather's adjurations for property which was scarcely worth the time and trouble it would take to dispose of it. He reflected ruefully that such relatives as still lived in or near Dunwich might well resent his return in their curious inward growing and isolated rustication which had kept most of the Whateleys in this immediate region, particularly since the shocking events which had overtaken the country branch of the family on Sentinel Hill.

The house appeared to be unchanged. The river-side of the house was given over to the mill, which had long ago ceased to function, as more and more of the fields around Dunwich had grown barren; except for one room above the mill wheel—Aunt Sarey's room—the entire side of the structure bordering the Miskatonic had been abandoned even in the time of his boyhood, when Abner Whateley had last visited his grandfather, then living alone in the house except for the never seen Aunt Sarey who abode in her shuttered room with her door locked, never to move about the house under prohibition of such movement by her father, from whose domination only death at last had freed her.

A veranda, fallen in at the corner of the house, circled that part of the structure used as a dwelling; from the lattice-work under the eaves great cobwebs hung, undisturbed by anything save the wind for years. And dust lay over everything, inside as well as out, as Abner discovered when he had found the right key among the lot the lawyer had sent him. He found a lamp and lit it, for Grandfather Whateley had scorned electricity. In the yellow glow of light, the familiarity of the old kitchen with its nineteenth century appointments smote him like a blow. Its spareness, the hand-hewn table and chairs, the century-old clock on the mantel, the worn broom—all were tangible reminders of his fear-haunted childhood visits to this formidable house and its even more formidable occupant, his mother's aged father.

The lamplight disclosed something more. On the kitchen table lay an envelope addressed to him in handwriting so crabbed that it could only be that of a very old or infirm man—his grandfather. Without troubling to bring the rest of his things from the car, Abner sat down to the table, blowing the dust off the chair and sufficiently from the table to allow him a resting place for his elbows, and opened the envelope.

The spidery script leapt out at him. The words were as severe as he remembered his grandfather to have been. And abrupt, with no term of endearment, not even the prosaic form of greeting.

194

"GRANDSON:

"When you read this, I will be some months dead. Perhaps more, unless they find you sooner than I believe they will. I have left you a sum of money—all I have and die possessed of—which is in the bank at Arkham under your name now. I do this not alone because you are my own and only grandson but because among all the Whateleys—we are an accursed clan, my boy— you have gone forth into the world and gathered to yourself learning sufficient to permit you to look upon all things with an inquiring mind ridden neither by the superstition of ignorance nor the superstition of science. You will understand my meaning.

"It is my wish that at least the mill section of this house be destroyed. Let it be taken apart, board by board. *If anything in it lives, I adjure you solemnly to kill it. No matter how small it may be. No matter what form it may have, for if it seem to you human it will beguile you and endanger your life and God knows how many others.*

"Heed me in this.

"If I seem to have the sound of madness, pray recall that worse than madness has spawned among the Whateleys. I have stood free of it. It has not been so of all that is mine. There is more stubborn madness in those who are unwilling to believe in what they know not of and deny that such exists, than in those of our blood who have been guilty of terrible practices, and blasphemy against God, and worse.

"YOUR GRANDFATHER, LUTHER S. WHATELEY."

How like Grandfather! thought Abner. He remembered, spurred into memory by this enigmatic, self-righteous communication, how on one occasion when his mother had mentioned her sister Sarah, and clapped her fingers across her mouth in dismay, he had run to his grandfather to ask,

"Grandpa, where's Aunt Sarey?"

The old man had looked at him out of eyes that were basilisk and answered, "Boy, we do not speak of Sarah here."

Aunt Sarey had offended the old man in some dreadful way— dreadful, at least, to that firm disciplinarian—for from that time beyond even Abner Whateley's memory, his aunt had been only the name of a woman, who was his mother's older sister, and who was locked in the big room over the mill and kept forever invisible within those walls, behind the shutters nailed to her windows. It had been forbidden both Abner and his mother even to linger before the door of that shuttered room, though on one occasion Abner had crept up to the door and put his ear against it to listen to the snuffling and whimpering sounds that went on inside, as from some large person, and Aunty Sarey, he had decided, must be as large as a circus fat lady, for she devoured so much, judging by the great platters of food—chiefly meat, which she must have prepared herself, since so much of it was raw—carried to the room twice daily by old Luther Whateley himself, for there were no servants in that house, and had not been since the time Abner's mother had married, after Aunt Sarey had come back, strange and mazed, from a visit to distant kin in Innsmouth.

He refolded the letter and put it back into the envelope. He would think of its contents another day. His first need now was to make sure of a place to sleep. He went out and got his two remaining bags from the car and brought them to the kitchen. Then he picked up the lamp and went into the interior of the house. The old-fashioned parlour, which was always kept closed against that day when visitors came—and none save Whateleys called upon Whateleys in Dunwich—he ignored. He made his way instead to his grandfather's bedroom; it was fitting that he should occupy the old man's bed now that he, and not Luther Whateley, was master here.

The large, double bed was covered with faded copies of the *Arkham Advertiser*, carefully arranged to protect the fine cloth of the spread, which had been embossed with an armigerous design, doubtless a legitimate Whateley heritage. He set down the lamp and cleared away the newspapers. When he turned down the bed, he saw that it was clean and fresh, ready for occupation; some cousin of his grandfather's had doubtless seen to this, against his arrival, after the obsequies.

Then he got his bags and transferred them to the bedroom, which was in that corner of the house away from the village; its windows looked along the river, though they were more than the width of the mill from the bank of the stream. He opened the only one of them which had a screen across its lower half, then sat down on the edge of the bed, bemused, pondering the circumstances which had brought him back to Dunwich after all these years.

He was tired now. The heavy traffic around Boston had tired him. The contrast between the Boston region and this desolate Dunwich country depressed and troubled him. Moreover, he was conscious of an intangible uneasiness. If he had not had need of his legacy to continue his research abroad into the ancient civilizations of the South Pacific, he would never have come here. Yet family ties existed, for all that he would deny them. Grim and forbidding as old Luther Whateley had always been, he was his mother's father, and to him his grandson owed the allegiance of common blood.

Round Mountain loomed close outside the bedroom; he felt its presence as he had when a boy, sleeping in the room above. Trees, for long untended, pressed upon the house, and from one of them at this hour of deep dusk, a screech owl's bell-like notes dropped into the still summer air. He lay back for a moment, strangely lulled by the owl's pleasant song. A thousand thoughts crowded upon him, a myriad memories. He saw himself again as the little boy he was, always half-fearful of enjoying himself in these fore-boding surroundings, always happy to come and happier to leave.

But he could not lie here, however relaxing it was. There was so much to be done before he could hope to take his departure that he could ill afford to indulge himself in rest and make a poor beginning of his nebulous obligation. He swung himself off the bed, picked up the lamp again, and begun a tour of the house.

He went from the bedroom to the dining-room, which was sit-uated between it and the kitchen—a room of stiff, uncomfortable furniture, also hand-made—and from there across to the parlour, the door of which opened upon a world far closer in its furniture and decorations to the eighteeneth century than to the nineteenth, and far removed from the twentieth. The absence of dust testified to the tightness of the doors closing the room off from the rest of the house. He went up the open stairs to the floor above, from bedroom to bedroom—all dusty, with faded curtains, and showing every sign of having remained unoccupied for many years even before old Luther Whateley died.

Then he came to the passage which led to the shuttered room —Aunt Sarey's hideaway—or prison—he could now never learn what it might have been, and, on impulse, he went down and stood before that forbidden door. No snuffling, no whimpering greeted him now—nothing at all, as he stood before it, remem-bering, still caught in the spell of the prohibition laid upon him by his grandfather.

But there was no longer any reason to remain under that adjur-ation. He pulled out the ring of keys, and patiently tried one after another in the lock, until he found the right one. He unlocked the door and pushed; it swung protestingly open. He held the lamp high.

He had expected to find a lady's boudoir, but the shuttered room was startling in its condition—bedding scattered about, pillows on the floor, the remains of food dried on a huge platter hidden behind a bureau. An odd, ichthyic smell pervaded the room, rushing at him with such musty strength that he could hardly repress a gasp of disgust. The room was a shambles; moreover, it wore the aspect of having been in such wild disorder for a long, long time.

Abner put the lamp on a bureau drawn away from the wall, crossed to the window above the mill wheel, unlocked it, and raised it. He strove to open the shutters before he remembered that they had been nailed shut. Then he stood back, raised his foot, and kicked the shutters out to let a welcome blast of fresh damp air into the room.

He went around to the adjoining outer wall and broke away the shutters from the single window in that wall, as well. It was not until he stood back to survey his work that he noticed he had broken a small corner out of the pane of the window above the mill wheel. His quick regret was as quickly repressed in the memory of his grandfather's insistence that the mill and this room above it be torn down or otherwise destroyed. What mattered a broken pane!

He returned to take up the lamp again. As he did so, he gave the bureau a shove to push it back against the wall once more. At the same moment he heard a small, rustling sound along the baseboard, and, looking down caught sight of a long-legged frog or toad—he could not make out which—vanishing under the bureau. He was tempted to rout the creature out, but he reflected that its presence could not matter—if it had existed in these locked quarters for so long on such cockroaches and other insects as it had managed to uncover, it merited being left alone.

He went out of the room, locked the door again, and returned to the master bedroom downstairs. He felt, obscurely, that he had made a beginning, however trivial; he had scouted the ground, so to speak. And he was twice as tired for his brief look around as he had been before. Though the hour was not late, he decided to go to bed and get an early start in the morning. There was the old mill yet to be gone through—perhaps some of the machinery could be sold, if any remained—and the mill wheel was now a curiosity, having continued to exist beyond its time.

He stood for a few minutes on the veranda, marking with surprise the welling stridulation of the crickets and katydids, and the almost overwhelming choir of the whip-poor-wills and frogs, which rose on all sides to assault him with a deafening insistence of such proportion as to drown out all other sounds, even such as might have risen from Dunwich. He stood there until he could tolerate the voices of the night no longer; then he retreated, locking the door, and made his way to the bedroom.

He undressed and got into bed, but he did not sleep for almost an hour, bedevilled by the chorus of natural sounds outside the house and from within himself by a rising confusion about what his grandfather had meant by the "dissolution" he himself had not been able to make. But at last he drifted into a troubled sleep.

II

He woke with the dawn, little rested. All night he had dreamed of strange places and beings that filled him with beauty and wonder and dread—of swimming in the ocean's depths and up the Miskatonic among fish and amphibia and strange men, half batrachian in aspect—of monstrous entities that lay sleeping in an eerie stone city at the bottom of the sea—of utterly *outré* music as of flutes accompanied by weird ululations from throats far, far from human—of Grandfather Luther Wheatley standing accusingly before him and thundering forth his wrath at him for having dared to enter Aunt Sarey's shuttered room.

198

He was troubled, but he shrugged his unease away before the necessity of walking into Dunwich for the provisions he had neglected to bring with him in his haste. The morning was bright and sunny; pewees and thrushes sang, and dew pearled on leaf and blade reflected the sunlight in a thousand jewels along the winding path that led to the main street of the village. As he went along, his spirits rose; he whistled happily, and contemplated the early fulfilment of his obligation, upon which his escape from this desolate, forgotten pocket of ingrown humanity was predicted.

But the main street of Dunwich was no more reassuring under the light of the sun than it had been in the dusk of the past evening. The village huddled between the Miskatonic and the almost vertical slope of Round Mountain, a dark and brooding settlement which seemed somehow never to have passed 1900, as if time had ground to a stop before the turn of the last century. His gay whistle faltered and died away; he averted his eyes from the buildings falling into ruin; he avoided the curiously expressionless faces of passers-by, and went directly to the old church with its general store, which he knew he would find slovenly and ill-kept, in keeping with the village itself.

A gaunt-faced storekeeper watched his advance down the aisle, searching his features for any familiar lineament.

Abner strode up to him and asked for bacon, coffee, eggs and milk.

The storekeeper peered at him. He made no move. "Ye'll be a Whateley," he said at last. "I dun't expeck ye know me. I'm yer cousin Tobias. Which one uv 'em are ye?"

"I'm Abner—Luther's grandson." He spoke reluctantly.

Tobias Whateley's face froze. "Libby's boy—Libby, that married cousin Jeremiah. Yew folks ain't back—back at Luther's? Yew folks ain't a-goin' to start things again?"

"There's no one but me," said Abner shortly. "What things are you talking about?"

"If ye dun't know, tain't fer me to say."

Nor would Tobias Whateley speak again. He put together what Abner wanted, took his money sullenly, and watched him out of the store with ill-concealed animosity.

Abner was disagreeably affected. The brightness of the morning had dimmed for him, though the sun shone from the same unclouded heaven. He hastened away from the store and main street, and hurried along the lane towards the house he had but recently quitted.

He was even more disturbed to discover, standing before the house, an ancient rig drawn by an old work-horse. Beside it stood a boy, and inside it sat an old, white-bearded man, who, at sight of Abner's approach, signalled to the boy for assistance, and by the lad's aid, laboriously descended to the ground and stood to await Abner.

As Abner came up, the boy spoke, unsmiling. "Great-grampa'll talk to yew."

"Abner," said the old man quaveringly, and Abner saw for the first time how very old he was.

"This here's Great-grampa Zebulon Whateley," said the boy. Grandfather Luther Whateley's brother—the only living Whateley of his generation. "Come in, sir," said Abner, offering the old man his arm.

Zebulon Whateley took it.

The three of them made slow progress towards the veranda, where the old man halted at the foot of the steps, turning his dark eyes upon Abner from under their bushy white brows, and shaking his head gently.

"Naow, if ye'll fetch me a cheer, I'll set."

"Bring a chair from the kitchen, boy," said Abner.

The boy sped up the steps and into the house. He was out as fast with a chair for the old man, and helped to lower him to it, and stood beside him while Zeublon Whateley caught his breath.

Presently he turned his eyes full upon Abner and contemplated him, taking in every detail of his clothes, which, unlike his own, were not made by hand.

"Why have ye come, Abner?" he asked, his voice firmer now.

Abner told him, as simply and directly as he could.

Zebulon Whateley shook his head. "Ye know no more'n the rest, and less'n some," he said. "What Luther was abaout, only God knowed. Naow Luther's gone, and ye'll have it do dew. I kin tell ye, Abner, I vaow afur God, I dun't know why Luther took on so and locked hisself up and Sarey that time she come back from Innsmouth—but I kin say it was suthin' turrible, turrible—and the things what happened was turrible. Ain't nobody left to say Luther was to blame, nor poor Sarey—but take care, take care, Abner."

"I expect to follow my grandfather's wishes," said Abner.

The old man nodded. But his eyes were troubled, and it was plain that he had little faith in Abner.

"How'd you find out I was here, Uncle Zebulon?" Abner asked.

"I had the word ye'd come. It was my bounden duty to talk to ye. The Whateleys has a curse on 'em. Thar's been them naow gone to graoun' has had to dew with the devil, and thar's some what whistled turrible things aout o' the air, and thar's some what had to dew with things that wasn't all human nor all fish but lived in the water and swum oaut—way oaut—to sea, and thar's some what growed in on themselves and got all mazed and queer —and thar's what happened on Sentinel Hill that time—Lavinny's Wilbur—and that other one by the Sentinel Stone—Gawd, I shake when I think on it. . . ."

"Now, Grandpa—don't ye git yer dander up," chided the boy.

"I wun't, I wun't," said the old man tremulously. "It's all died

200

away naow. It's forgot—by all but me and them what took the signs daown—the signs that pointed to Dunwich, sayin', it was too turrible a place to know abaout. . . ." He shook his head and was silent.

"Uncle Zebulon," said Abner. "I never saw my Aunt Sarah."

"No, no, boy—she was locked up that time. Afore you was borned, I think it was."

"Why?"

"Only Luther knowed—and Gawd. Now Luther's gone, and Gawd dun't seem like He knowed Dunwich was still here."

"What was Aunt Sarah doing in Innsmouth?"

"Visitin' kin."

"Are there Whateleys there, too?"

"Not Whateleys. Marshes. Old Obed Marsh that was Pa's cousin. Him and his wife that he faound in the trade—at Ponape, if ye know whar that is."

"I do."

"Ye dew? I never knowed. They say Sarey was visitin' Marsh kin—Obed's son or grandson—I never knowed which. Never heerd. Dun't care. She was thar quite a spell. They say when she come back she was different. Flighty. Unsettled. Sassed her pa. And then, not long after, he locked her up in that room till she died."

"How long after?"

"Three, four months. And Luther never said what fer. Nobody saw her again after that till the day she wuz laid aout in her coffin. Two year, might be three year ago. Thar was that time nigh onto a year after she come back from Innsmouth thar was sech goins-on here at this house a-fightin' and a-screamin' and a-screechin'—most everyone in Dunwich heerd it, but no one went to see whut it was, and next day Luther he said it was only Sarey took with a spell. Might be it was. Might be it was suthin' else. . . ."

"What else, Uncle Zebulon?"

"Devil's work," said the old man instantly. "But I fergit—ye're the eddicated one. Ain't many Whateleys ever bin eddicated. Thar was Lavinny—she read them turrible books what was no good for her. And Sarey—she read some. Them as has only a little learnin' might's well have none—they ain't fit to handle life with only a little learnin', they're fitter with none a-tall."

Abner smiled.

"Dun't ye laugh, boy!"

"I'm not laughing, Uncle Zebulon. I agree with you."

"Then ef ye come face to face with it, ye'll know what to dew. Ye wun't stop and think—ye'll jest dew."

"With what?"

"I wisht I knowed, Abner. I dun't. Gawd knows. Luther knowed. Luther's dead. It comes on me Sarey knowed, too.

201

Sarey's dead. Now nobody knows whut turrible thing it was. Ef I was a prayin' man, I'd pray you dun't find oaut—but ef ye dew, dun't stop to figger it aout by eddication, jest dew whut ye have to dew. Yer Grandpa kep' a record—look fer it. Ye might learn whut kind a people the Marshes was—they wasn't like us—suthin' turrible happened to 'em—and might be it reached aout and tetched Sarey. . . ."

Something stood between the old man and Abner Whateley—something unvoiced, perhaps unknown; but it was something that cast a chill about Abner for all his conscious attempt to belittle what he felt.

"I'll learn what I can, Uncle Zebulon," he promised.

The old man nodded and beckoned to the boy. He signified that he wished to rise, to return to the buggy. The boy came running.

"Ef ye need me, Abner, send word to Tobias," said Zebulon Whateley. "I'll come—ef I can."

"Thank you."

Abner and the boy helped the old man back into the buggy. Zebulon Whateley raised his forearm in a gesture of farewell, the boy whipped up the horse, and the buggy drew away.

Abner stood for a moment looking after the departing vehicle. He was both troubled and irritated—troubled at the suggestion of something dreadful which lurked beneath Zebulon Whateley's words of warning, irritated because his grandfather, despite all his adjurations, had left him so little to act upon. Yet this must have been because his grandfather evidently believed there might be nothing untoward to greet his grandson when at last Abner Whateley arrived at the old house. It could be nothing other by way of explanation.

Yet Abner was not entirely convinced. Was the matter one of such horror that Abner should not know of it unless he had to? Or had Luther Whateley laid down a key to the riddle elsewhere in the house? He doubted it. It would not be grandfather's way to seek the devious when he had always been so blunt and direct.

He went into the house with his groceries, put them away, and sat down to map out a plan of action. The very first thing to be accomplished was a survey of the mill part of the structure, to determine whether any machinery could be salvaged. Next he must find someone who would undertake to tear down the mill and the room above it. Thereafter he must dispose of the house and adjoining property, though he had a sinking feeling of futility at the conviction that he would never find anyone who would want to settle in so forlorn a corner of Massachusetts as Dunwich.

He began at once to carry out his obligations.

His search of the mill, however, disclosed that the machinery which had been in it—save for such pieces as were fixed to the running of the wheel—had been removed, and presumably sold. Perhaps the increment from the sale was part of that very legacy

202

Luther Whateley had deposited in the bank at Arkham for his grandson. Abner was thus spared the necessity of removing the machinery before beginning the planned demolition. The dust in the old mill almost suffocated him; it lay an inch thick over everything, and it rose in great gusts to cloud about him when he walked through the empty, cobwebbed rooms. Dust muffled his footsteps and he was glad to leave the mill to go around and look at the wheel.

He worked his way around the wooden ledge to the frame of the wheel, somewhat uncertain, lest the wood give way and plunge him into the water beneath; but the construction was firm, the wood did not give, and he was soon at the wheel. It appeared to be a splendid example of middle nineteenth century work. It would be a shame to tear it apart, thought Abner. Perhaps the wheel could be removed, and a place could be found for it either in some museum or in some one of those buildings which were forever being reconstructed by wealthy persons interested in the preservation of the American heritage.

He was about to turn away from the wheel, when his eye was caught by a series of small wet prints on the paddles. He bent closer to examine them, but, apart from ascertaining that they were already in part dried, he could not see in them more than marks left by some small animal, probably batrachian—a frog or a toad —which had apparently mounted the wheel in the early hours before the rising of the sun. His eyes, raising, followed the line of the wheel to the broken out shutters of the room above.

He stood for a moment, thinking. He recalled the batrachian creature he had glimpsed along the baseboard of the shuttered room. Perhaps it had escaped through the broken pane? Or, more likely, perhaps another of its kind had discovered its presence and gone up to it. A faint apprehension stirred in him, but he brushed it away in irritation that a man of his intelligence should have been sufficiently stirred by the aura of ignorant, superstitious mystery clinging to his grandfather's memory to respond to it.

Nevertheless, he went around and mounted the stairs to the shuttered room. He half expected, when he unlocked the door, to find some significant change in the aspect of the room as he remembered it from last night, but, apart from the unaccustomed daylight streaming into the room, there was no alteration.

He crossed to the window.

There were prints on the sill. There were two sets of them. One appeared to be leading out, the other entering. They were not the same size. The prints leading outward were tiny, only half an inch across. Those leading in were double that size. Abner bent close and stared at them in fixed fascination.

He was not a zoologist, but he was by no means ignorant of zoology. The prints on the sill were like nothing he had ever seen before, not even in dreams. Save for being or seeming to be webbed, they were the perfect prints in miniature of human hands and feet.

Though he made a cursory search for the creature, he saw no sign of it, and finally, somewhat shaken, he retreated from the room and locked the door behind him, already regretting the impulse which had led him to it in the first place and which had caused him to burst open the shutters which for so long had walled the room away from the outer world.

III

He was not entirely surprised to learn that no one in Dunwich could be found to undertake the demolition of the mill. Even such carpenters as those who had not worked for a long time were reluctant to undertake the task, pleading a variety of excuses, which Abner easily recognized as a disguise for the superstitious fear of the place under which one and all laboured. He found it necessary to drive into Aylesbury, but, though he encountered no difficulty in engaging a trio of husky young men who had formed a partnership to tear down the mill, he was forced to wait upon their previous commitments and had to return to Dunwich with the promise that they would come "in a week or ten days."

Thereupon he set about at once to examine into all the effects of Luther Whateley which still remained in the house. There were stacks of newspapers—chiefly the *Arkham Advertiser* and the *Aylesbury Transcript*—now yellowing with age and moulder- ing with dust, which he set aside for burning. There were books which he determined to go over individually in order that he might not destroy anything of value. And there were letters which he would have burned at once had he not happened to glance into one of them and caught sight of the name "Marsh", at which he read on.

"Luther, what happened to cousin Obed is a singular thing. I do not know how to tell it to you. I do not know how to make it credible. I am not sure I have all the facts in this matter. I can- not believe but that it is a rigmarole deliberately invented to con- ceal something of a scandalous nature, for you know the Marshes have always been given to exaggeration and had a pronounced flare for deception. Their ways are devious. They have always been.

"But the story, as I have it from cousin Alizah, is that when he was a young man Obed and some others from Innsmouth, sailing their trading ships into the Polynesian Islands, encountered there a strange people who called themselves the 'Deep Ones' and who had the ability to live either in the water or on the earth. Amphibians, they would then be. Does this sound credible to you? It does not to me. What is most astonishing is that Obed and some others married women of these people and brought them home to live with them.

"Now that is the *legend*. Here are the *facts*. Ever since that

204

time, the Marshes have prospered mightily in the trade. Mrs. Marsh is never seen abroad, save on such occasions as she goes to certain closed affairs of the Order of Dagon Hall. 'Dagon' is said to be a sea god. I know nothing of these pagan religions, and wish to know nothing. The Marsh children have *a very strange* look. I do not exaggerate, Luther, when I tell you that they have such wide mouths and such chinless faces and such large staring eyes that I swear they sometimes look more like frogs than human beings! They are not, at least, so far as I can see, *gilled*. The 'Deep Ones' are said to be possessed of gills, and to belong to Dagon or to some other deity of the sea whose name I cannot even pronounce, far less set down. No matter. It is such a rigmarole as the Marshes might well invent to serve their purposes, but by God, Luther, judging by the way the ships Captain Marsh has in the East India trade keep afloat without a smitchin of damage done to them by storm or wear—the brigantine *Columbia*, the barque *Sumatra Queen*, the brig *Hetty* and some others—it might almost seem that he has made some sort of bargain with Neptune himself!

"Then there are all the doings off the coast where the Marshes live. Night swimming. They swim way out off Devil Reef, which, as you know, is a mile and a half out from the harbour here at Innsmouth. People keep away from the Marshes—except the Martins and some such others among them who were also in the East India trade. Now that Obed is gone—and I suppose Mrs. Marsh may be also, since she is no longer seen anywhere—the children and the grandchildren of old Captain Obed follow in his strange ways."

The letter dwindled down to commonplaces about prices—ridiculously low figures seen from this vantage of over half a century later, for Luther Whateley must have been a young man, unmarried, at the time this letter had been written to him by Ariah, a cousin of whom Abner had never heard. What it had to say of the Marshes was nothing—or all, perhaps, if Abner had had the key to the puzzle of which, he began to believe with mounting irritation, he held only certain disassociated parts.

But it Luther Whateley had believed this rigmarole, would he, years later, have permitted his daughter to visit the Marsh cousins? Abner doubted it.

He went through other letters—bills, receipts, trivial accounts of journeys made to Boston, Newburyport, Kingsport—postcards, and came at last to another letter from Cousin Ariah, written, if a comparison of dates was sufficient evidence, immediately after the one Abner had just read. They were ten days apart, and Luther would have had time to reply to that first.

Abner opened it eagerly.

The first page was an account of certain small family matters pertinent to the marriage of another cousin, evidently a sister of

Ariah's; the second a speculation about the future of the East India trade, with a paragraph about a new book by Whitman—evidently Walt; but the third was manifestly in answer to something Grandfather Whateley had evidently written concerning the Marsh branch of the family.

"Well, Luther, you may be right in this matter of race prejudice as responsible for the feeling against the Marshes. I know how people here feel about other races. It is unfortunate, perhaps, but such is their lack of education that they find much room for such prejudices. But I am not convinced that it is *all* due to race prejudice. I don't know what kind of race it is that would give the Marshes after Obed that strange *look*. The East India people—such as I have seen and recall from my early days in the trade—have features much like our own, and only a different colour to the skin—copper, I would call it. Once I did see a native who had a similiar appearance, but he was evidently not typical, for he was shunned by all the workers around the ships in the harbour where I saw him. I've forgotten now where it was, but I think Ponape.

"To give them their due, the Marshes keep pretty much to themselves—or to those families living here under the same cloud. And they more or less run the town. It may be significant—it may have been accident—that one selectman who spoke out against them was found drowned soon after. I am the first to admit that coincidences more startling than this frequently occur, but you may be sure that people who disliked the Marshes made the most of this.

"But I know how your analytical mind is cold to such talk; I will spare you more of it."

Thereafter not a word. Abner went through bundles of letters in vain. What Ariah wrote in subsequent letters dealt scrupulously with family matters of the utmost triviality. Luther Whateley had evidently made his displeasure with mere gossip clear; even as a young man, Luther must have been strictly self-disciplined. Abner found but one further reference to any mystery at Innsmouth—that was a newspaper clipping dealing in very vague terms, suggesting that the reporter who sent in the story did not really know what had taken place, with certain Federal activity in and near Innsmouth in 1928—the attempted destruction of Devil Reef, and the blowing up of large sections of the waterfront, together with wholesale arrests of Marshes and Martins and some others. But this event was decades removed from Ariah's early letters.

Abner put the letters dealing with the Marshes into his pocket, and summarily burned the rest, taking the mass of material he had gone through out along the riverbank and setting fire to it. He stood guarding it, lest a chance wind carry a spark to surrounding grass, which was unseasonably dry. He welcomed the smell of the smoke, however, for a certain dead odour lingered along the river bank, rising from the remains of fish upon which some animal had feasted—an otter, he thought.

As he stood beside the fire his eyes roved over the old Whateley building, and he saw, with a rueful reflection that it was high time the mill were coming down, that several panes of the window he had broken in the room that had been Aunt Sarey's, together with a portion of the frame, had fallen out. Fragments of the window were scattered on the paddles of the mill wheel.

By the time the fire was sufficiently low to permit his leaving it, the day was drawing to a close. He ate a meagre supper, and, having had his fill of reading for the day, decided against attempting to turn up his grandfather's "record" of which Uncle Zebulon Whateley had spoken, and went out to watch the dusk and the night in from the veranda, hearing again the rising chorus of the frogs and whip-poor-wills.

He retired early, unwontedly weary.

Sleep, however, would not come. For one thing, the summer night was warm; hardly a breath of air stirred. For another, even above the ululation of the frogs and the demoniac insistence of the whip-poor-wills, sounds from within the house invaded his consciousness—the creaks and groans of a many-timbered house settling in for the night; a peculiar scuffling or shuffling sound, half-drag, half-hop, which Abner laid to rats, which must abound in the mill section of the structure—and indeed, the noises were muffled, and seemed to reach him as from some distance; and, at one time, the cracking of wood and the tinkle of glass, which, Abner guessed, very probably came from the window above the mill wheel. The house was virtually falling to pieces about him; it was as if he served as a catalytic agent to bring about the final dissolution of the old structure.

This concept amused him because it struck him that, willy-nilly, he was carrying out his grandfather's adjuration. And, so bemused, he fell asleep.

He was awakened early in the morning by the ringing of the telephone, which he had had the foresight to have connected for the duration of his visit in Dunwich. He had already taken down the receiver from the ancient instrument attached to the wall before he realized that the call was on a party line and not intended for him. Nevertheless, the woman's voice that leapt out at him, burst open his ear with such screaming insistence that he remained frozen to the telephone.

"I tell ye, Mis' Corey, I heard things las' night—the graoun' was a-talkin' agen, and along abaout midnight I heerd that scream—I never figgered a caow'd scream that way—jest like a rabbit, only deeper. That was Lutey Sawyer's coaw—they faoun' her this morning—more 'n haff et by animals. . . ."

"Mis' Bishop, you dun't s'pose . . . it's come back?"

"I dun't know. I hope t' Gawd it ain't. But it's the same as the las' time."

"Was it jest that one caow took?"

"Jest the one. I ain't heerd abaout no more. But that's how it begun the las' time, Mis' Corey."

Quietly, Abner replaced the receiver. He smiled grimly at this evidence of the rampant superstitions of the Dunwich natives. He had never really known the depths of ignorance and superstition in which dwellers in such out-of-the-way places as Dunwich lived, and this manifestation of it was, he was convinced, but a mild sample.

He had little time, however, to dwell upon the subject, for he had to go into town for fresh milk, and he strode forth into the morning of sun and clouds with a certain feeling of relief at such brief escape from the house.

Tobias Whateley was uncommonly sullen and silent at Abner's entrance. Abner sensed not only resentment, but a certain tangible fear. He was astonished. To all Abner's comments Tobias replied in muttered monosyllables. Thinking to make conversation, he began to tell Tobias what he had overheard on the party line.

"I know it," said Tobias, curtly, for the first time gazing at Abner's face with naked terror.

Abner was stunned into silence. Terror vied with animosity in Tobias's eyes. His feelings were plain to Abner before he dropped his gaze and took the money Abner offered in payment.

"Yew seen Zebulon?" he asked in a low voice.

"He was at the house," said Abner.

"Yew talk to him?"

"We talked."

It seemed as if Tobias expected that certain matters had passed between them, but there was that in his attitude that suggested he was puzzled by subsequent events, which seemed to indicate that Zebulon had not told him what Tobias had expected the old man to tell him, or else that Abner had disregarded some of his Uncle's advice. Abner began to feel completely mystified; added to the superstitious talk of the natives on the telephone, to the strange hints Uncle Zebulon had dropped, this attitude of his cousin Tobias filled him with utter perplexity. Tobias, no more than Zebulon, seemed inclined to come out frankly and put into words what lay behind his sullen features—each acted as if Abner, as a matter of course, should know.

In his bafflement, he left the store, and walked back to the Whateley house determined to hasten his tasks as much as he could so that he might get away from this forgotten hamlet with its queer, superstition-ridden people, for all that many of them were his relatives.

To that end, he returned to the task of sorting his grand-father's things as soon as he had had his breakfast, of which he ate very little, for his disagreeable visit to the store had dulled the appetite which he had felt when he had set out for the store earlier.

It was not until late afternoon that he found the record he

sought—an old ledger, in which Luther Whateley had made certain entries in his crabbed hand.

<h1 style="text-align:center">IV</h1>

By the light of the lamp, Abner sat down to the kitchen table after he had had a small repast, and opened Luther Whateley's ledger. The opening pages had been torn out, but, from an examination of the fragments of sheets still attached to the threads of the sewing, Abner concluded that these pages were purely of accounts, as if his grandfather had taken up an old, not completely used account book for a purpose other than keeping accounts, and had removed such sheets as had been more prosaically utilized.

From the beginning, the entries were cryptic. They were undated, except for the day of the week.

"This Saturday Ariah answered my inquiry. S. was seen sev times with Ralsa Marsh. Obed's great-grandson. *Swam* together by night."

Such was the first entry, clearly pertaining to Aunt Sarey's visit to Innsmouth, about which Grandfather had plainly inquired of Ariah. Something had impelled Luther to make such inquiry. From what he knew of his grandfather's character, Abner concluded that the inquiry had been made after Sarey had returned to Dunwich.

Why?

The next entry was pasted in, and was clearly part of a typewritten letter received by Luther Whateley.

"Ralsa Marsh is probably the most repellent of all the family. He is almost *degenerate* in his looks. I know you have said that it was Libby of your daughters who was the fairest; even so, we cannot imagine how Sarah came to take up with someone who is so repulsive as Ralsa, in whom all those recessive characteristics which have been seen in the Marsh family after Obed's strange marriage to the Polynesian woman—(the Marshes have denied that Obed's wife was Polynesian, but of course, he was trading there at the time, and I don't credit those stories about that uncharted island where he was supposed to have dallied)—seem to have come to fullest fruit.

"As far as I can now ascertain—after all, it is over two months —close to four, I think—since her return to Dunwich—they were constantly together. I am surprised that Ariah did not inform you of this. None of us here had any mandate to halt Sarah's seeing Ralsa, and, after all, they are cousins and she was visiting at Marshes—not here."

Abner judged that this letter had been written by a woman, also a cousin, who bore Luther some resentment for Sarah's not having been sent to stay with her branch of the family. Luther had evidently made inquiry of her regarding Ralsa.

The third entry was once again in Luther's hand, summarizing a letter from Ariah.

"Saturday. Ariah maintains Deep Ones a sect or quasi-religious group. Sub-human. Said to live in the sea and worship Dagon. Another God named Cthulhu. Gilled people. Resembling frogs or toads more than fish, but eyes ichthyic. Claims Obed's late wife was one. Holds that Obed's children all bore the marks. Marshes gilled? How else could they swim a mile and a half to Devil Reef, and back? Marshes eat sparingly, can go without food and drink a long time, diminish or expand in size rapidly." (To this Luther had appended four scornful exclamation marks.)

"Zadok Allen swears he saw Sarah swimming out to Devil Reef. Marshes carrying her along. All *naked*. Swears he saw Marshes with tough, warty skin. Some with *scales*, like fish! Swears he saw them chase and eat fish! Tear them apart like animals."

The next entry was again a portion of a letter, patently a reply to one from Grandfather Whateley.

"You ask who is responsible for those *ridiculous* tales about the Marshes. Well, Luther, it would be impossible to single out any one or a dozen people over several generations. I agree that old Zadok Allen talks too much, drinks, and may be romancing. But he is only one. The fact is this legendry—or *rigmarole* as you call it,—has grown up from one generation to the next. Through three generations. You have only to look at some of the descendants of Captain Obed to understand why this could have come about. There are some Marsh offspring said to have been too horrible to look upon. Old wives' tales? Well, Dr. Rowley Marsh was too ill to attend one of the Marsh women one time; so they had to call Dr. Gilman, and Gilman always said that what he delivered was less than human. And nobody ever saw that particular Marsh, though there were people later who claimed to have seen *things moving on two legs that weren't human*."

Following this there was but a brief but revealing entry in two words: "Punished Sarah."

This must then mark the date of Sarah Whateley's confinement to the room above the mill. For some time after this entry, there was no mention of his daughter in Luther's script. Instead, his jottings were not dated in any way, and, judging by the difference in the colour of the ink were made at different times though run together.

"Many frogs. Seem to bear in on the mill. Seem to be more than in the marshes across the Miskatonic. Sleeping difficult. Are whip-poor-wills on the increase, too, or is this imagination? . . . Counted thirty-seven frogs at the porch steps tonight."

There were more entries of this nature. Abner read them all, but there was no clue in them to what the old man had been getting at. Luther Whateley had thereafter kept book on frogs, fog, fish and their movements in the Miskatonic—when they rose and leaped from the water, and so on. This seemed to be unrelated data, and was not in any way connected to the problem of Sarah.

There was another hiatus after this series of notes, and then came a single underscored entry.

"*Ariah was right!*"

But about what had Ariah been right? Abner wondered. And how had Luther Whateley learned that Ariah had been right? There was no evidence that Ariah and Luther had continued their correspondence, or even that Ariah desired to write to the crotchety Luther without a letter of direct inquiry from Luther.

There followed a section of the record to which newspaper clippings had been pasted. These were clearly unrelated, but they did establish for Abner the fact that somewhat better than a year had passed before Luther's next entry, one of the most puzzling Abner found. Indeed, the time hiatus seemed to be closer to two years.

"R. out again."

If Luther and Sarah were the only people in the house, who was "R."? Could it have been Ralsa Marsh come to visit? Abner doubted it, for there was nothing to show that Ralsa Marsh harboured any affection for his distant cousin, or certainly he would have pursued her before this.

The next notation seemed to be unrelated.

"Two turtles, one dog, remains of woodchuck. Bishop's—two cows, found on the Miskatonic end of the pasture."

A little further along, Luther had set down further such data.

"After one month a total of 17 cattle, 6 sheep. Hideous alterations; size commensurate with amt. of food. Z. over. Anxious about talk going around."

Could Z. stand for Zebulon? Abner thought it did. Evidently then Zebulon had come in vain, for he had left him, Abner, with only vague and uncertain hints about the situation at the house when Aunt Sarey was confined to the shuttered room. Zebulon, on the evidence of such conversation as he had shared with Abner, knew less than Abner himself did after reading his grandfather's record. But he did know of Luther's record; so Luther must have told him he had set down certain facts.

These notations, however, were more in the nature of notes for something to be completed later; they were unaccountably cryptic, unless one had the key of basic knowledge which belonged to Luther Whateley. But a growing sense of urgency was clearly manifest in the old man's further entries.

"Ada Wilkerson gone. Trace of scuffle. Strong feeling in Dunwich. John Sawyer shook his fist at me—safely across the street, where I couldn't reach him."

"Monday. Howard Willie this time. They found one shoe, with the foot still in it!"

The record was now near its end. Many pages, unfortunately, had been detached from it—some with violence—but no clue remained as to why this violence had been done to Grandfather Whateley's account. It could not have been done by anyone but Luther himself; perhaps, thought Abner, Luther felt he had told too much, and intended to destroy anything which might put a later reader on the track of the true facts regarding Aunt Sarey's confinement for the rest of her life. He had certainly succeeded.

The next entry once again referred to the elusive "R."

"R. back at last."

Then, "Nailed the shutters to the windows of Sarah's room."

And at last: "Once he has lost weight, he must be kept on a careful diet and to a controllable size."

In a way, this was the most enigmatic entry of them all. Was "he" also "R."? If so, why must he be kept on a careful diet, and what did Luther Whateley mean by controlling? There was no ready answer to these questions in such material as Abner had read thus far, either in this record—or the fragmentary account still left in the record—or in letters previously perused.

He pushed away the record-book, resisting an impulse to burn it. He was exasperated, all the more so because he was uneasily aware of an urgent need to learn the secret embalmed within this old building.

The hour was now late; darkness had fallen some time ago, and the ever-present clamour of the frogs and the whip-poor-wills had begun once more, rising all around the house. Pushing from his thoughts briefly the apparently unconnected jottings he had been reading, he called from his memory the superstitions of the family, representing those prevalent in the countryside—associating frogs and the calling of whip-poor-wills and owls with death, and from this meditation progressed readily to the amphibian link which presented itself—the presence of the frogs brought before his mind's eye a grotesque caricature of one of the Marsh clan of Innsmouth, as described in the letters Luther Whateley had saved for so many years.

Oddly, this very thought, for all that it was so casual, startled him. The insistence of frogs and toads on singing and calling in the vicinity was truly remarkable. Yet, batrachia had always been plentiful in the Dunwich vicinity, and he had no way of knowing for how long a period before his arrival they had been calling about the old Whateley house. He discounted the suggestion that his arrival had anything at all to do with it; more than likely, the proximity of the Miskatonic and a low, swampy area immediately across the river on the edge of Dunwich, accounted for the presence of so many frogs.

His exasperation faded away; his concern about the frogs did likewise. He was weary. He got up and put the record left by Luther Whateley carefully into one of his bags, intending to carry

212

it away with him, and to puzzle over it until some sort of meaning came out of it. Somewhere there must exist a clue. If certain horrible events had taken place in the vicinity, something more in the way of a record must exist than Luther Whateley's spare notes. It would do no good to inquire of Dunwich people; Abner knew they would maintain a close-mouthed silence before an "outsider" like himself, for all that he was related to many of them.

It was then that he thought of the stacks of newspapers, still set aside to be burned. Despite his weariness, he began to go through packs of the *Aylesbury Transcript*, which carried, from time to time, a Dunwich feature.

After an hour's hasty search, he found three vague articles, none of them in the regular Dunwich columns, which corroborated entries in Luther Whateley's ledger. The first appeared under the heading: *Wild Animal Slays Stock Near Dunwich*.

"Several cows and sheep have been slain on farms just outside Dunwich by what appears to be a wild animal of some kind. Traces left at the scenes of the slaughter suggest some large beast, but Professor Bethnall of Miskatonic University's anthropology department points out that it is not inconceivable that packs of wolves could lurk in the wild hill country around Dunwich. No beast of the size suggested by the traces reported was ever known to inhabit the eastern seaboard within the memory of man. County officials are investigating."

Search as he might, Abner could find no follow-up story. He did, however, come upon the story of Ada Wilkerson.

"A widow-lady, Ada Wilkerson, 57, living along the Miskatonic out of Dunwich, may have been the victim of foul play three nights ago. When she failed to visit a friend by appointment in Dunwich, her home was visited. No trace of her was found. However, the door of her house had been broken in, and the furniture had been wildly thrown about, as if a violent struggle had taken place. A very strong musk is said to have pervaded the entire area. Up to press time today, Mrs. Wilkerson has not been heard from."

Two subsequent paragraphs reported briefly that authorities had not found any clue to Mrs. Wilkerson's disappearance. The account of a "large animal" was resurrected, lamely, and Professor Bethnall's beliefs on the possible existence of a wolf-pack, but nothing further, for investigation had disclosed that the missing lady had neither money nor enemies, and no one would have had any motive for killing her.

Finally, there was the account of Howard Willie's death, headed: *Shocking Crime at Dunwich*.

"Some time during the night of the twenty-first Howard Willie, 37, a native of Dunwich, was brutally slain as he was on his way home from a fishing trip along the upper reaches of the Miskatonic.

Mr. Willie was attacked about half a mile past the Luther Whateley property, as he walked through an arbored lane. He evidently put up a fierce fiight, for the ground is badly torn up in all directions. The poor fellow was overcome, and must have been literally torn limb from limb, for the only physical remains of the victim consisted of his right foot, still encased in its shoe. It had evidently been cruelly torn from his leg by a great force.

"Our correspondent in Dunwich advises us that people there are very sullen and in a great rage of anger and fear. They suspect many of their number of being at least partly to blame, though they stoutly deny that anyone in Dunwich murdered either Willie or Mrs. Wilkerson, who disappeared a fortnight ago, and of whom no word has since been heard."

The account concluded with some data about Willie's family connections. Thereafter, subsequent editions of the *Transcript* were distinguished only for the lack of information about the events which had taken place in Dunwich, where authorities and reporters alike apparently ran up against blank walls in the stolid refusal of the natives to talk or even speculate about what had happened. There was, however, one insistent note which recurred in the comments of investigators, relayed to the Press, and that was that such trail or track as could be seen appeared to have disappeared into the waters of the Miskatonic, suggesting that if an animal were responsible for the orgy of slaughter which had occurred at Dunwich, it may have come from and returned to the river.

Though it was now close to midnight, Abner massed the discarded newspapers together and took them out to the river bank, where he set them on fire, having saved only torn pages relative to the occurrences at Dunwich. The air being still, he did not feel obliged to watch the fire, since he had already burned a considerable area, and the grass was not likely to catch on fire. As he started away, he heard suddenly above the ululation of the whip-poor-wills and frogs, now at a frenzied crescendo, the tearing and breaking sound of wood. He thought at once of the window of the shuttered room, and retraced his steps.

In the very dim light flickering towards the house from the burning newspapers, it seemed to Abner that the window gaped wider than before. Could it be that the entire mill part of the house was about to collapse? Then, out of the corner of his eye, he caught sight of a singularly formless moving shadow just beyond the mill wheel, and a moment later heard a churning sound in the water. The voices of the frogs had now risen to such a volume that he could hear nothing more.

He was inclined to dismiss the shadow as the creation of the wild flames leaping upward from the fire. The sound in the water might well have been that of the movement made by a school of fish, darting forward in concert. Nevertheless, he thought, it would do no harm to have another look at Aunt Sarey's room.

He returned to the kitchen, took the lamp, and mounted the stairs. He unlocked the door of the shuttered room, threw open the door, and was almost felled by the powerful musk which pushed hallward. The smell of the Miskatonic, of the marshes, the odour of that slimy deposit left on the stones and sunken debris when the Miskatonic receded to its low water stage, the cloying pungence of some animal lairs—all these were combined in the shuttered room.

Abner stood for a moment, wavering on the threshold. True, the odour in the room could have come in through the open window. He raised the lamp so that more of its light fell upon the wall above the mill wheel. Even from where he stood, it was possible to see that not only was all the window itself now gone, but so was the frame. Even at this distance it was manifest that the frame had been broken out *from inside!*

He fell back, slammed the door shut, locked it, and fled down stairs with the shell of his rationalizations tumbling about him.

V

Downstairs, he fought for self-control. What he had seen was but one more detail added to the proliferating accumulation of seemingly unrelated data upon which he had stumbled ever since his coming to his grandfather's home. He was convinced now that however unlikely it had at first seemed to him, all these data must be related. What he needed to learn was the one basic fact or element which bound them together.

He was badly shaken, particularly because he had the uneasy conviction that he did indeed have all the facts he needed to know, that it was his scientific training which made it impossible for him to make the primary assumption, to state the premise which the facts before him would inevitably prove. The evidence of his senses told him that something laired in that room—some bestial creature; it was folly to assume that odours from outside could so permeate Aunt Sarey's old room and not be noticeable outside the kitchen and at the windows of his own bedroom.

The habit of rational thinking was strong in him. He took out Luther Whateley's final letter to him once more and read it again. That was what his grandfather had meant when he had written "you have gone forth into the world and gathered to yourself learning sufficient to permit you to look upon all things with an inquiring mind ridden neither by the superstition of ignorance nor the superstition of science." Was this puzzle, with all its horrible connotations, beyond rationalization?

The wild ringing of the telephone broke in upon his confused thoughts. Slipping the letter back into his pocket, he strode rapidly to the wall and took the receiver off the hook.

A man's voice screamed over the wire, amid a chaos of inquiring voices as everyone on the line picked up his receiver as if they waited, like Abner Whateley himself, for word of another tragedy. One of the voices—all were disembodied and unidentifiable for Abner—identified the caller.

"It's Luke Lang!"

"Git a posse up an' come quick," Luke shouted hoarsely over the wire. "It's jest aoutside my door. Snifflin' araoun'. Tryin' the door. Feelin' at the winders."

"Luke, what is it?" asked a woman's voice.

"Oh, Gawd! It's some unairthly thing. It's a hoppin' raoun' like it was too big to move right—like jelly. Oh, hurry, hurry, afore it's too late. It got my dog. . . ."

"Git off the wire so's we can call fer help," interrupted another subscriber.

But Luke never heard in his extremity. "It's a-pushin' at the door—it's a-bowin' the door in. . . ."

"Luke! Luke! Git off'n the wire!"

"It's a-tryin' the winder naow." Luke Lang's voice rose in a scream of terror. "There goes the glass. Gawd! Gawd! Hain't yew comin'? Oh, that hand! That turr'ble arm! Gawd! That face. . . !"

Luke's voice died away in a frightful screech. There was the sound of breaking glass and rending wood—then all was still at Luke Lang's, and for a moment all was still along the wire. Then the voice burst forth again in a fury of excitement and fear.

"Git help!"

"We'll meet at Bishops' place."

And someone put in, "It's Abner Whateley done it!"

Sick with shock and half paralysed with a growing awareness, Abner struggled to tear the receiver from his ear, to shut off the half-crazed bedlam on the party line. He managed it with an effort. Confused, upset, frightened himself, he stood for a moment with his head leaning against the wall. His thoughts seethed around but one central point—the fact that the Dunwich rustics considered him somehow responsible for what was happening. And their conviction, he knew intuitively, was based on more than the countryman's conventional distrust of the stranger.

He did not want to think of what had happened to Luke Lang —and to those others. Luke's frightened, agonized voice still rang in his ears. He pulled himself away from the wall, almost stumbling over one of the kitchen chairs. He stood for a moment beside the table, not knowing what to do, but as his mind cleared a little, he thought only of escape. Yet he was caught between the desire to get away, and the obligation to Luther Whateley he had not yet fulfilled.

But he had come, he had gone through the old man's things —all save the books—he had made arrangements to tear down

216

the mill part of the house—he could manage its sale through some agency; there was no need for him to be present. Impulsively, he hastened to the bedroom, threw such things as he had unpacked, together with Luther Whateley's note-filled ledger, into his bags, and carried them out to his car.

Having done this, however, he had second thoughts. Why should he take flight? He had done nothing. No guilt of any kind rested upon him. He returned to the house. All was still, save for the unending chorus of frogs and whip-poor-wills. He stood briefly undecided; then he sat down at the table and took out Grandfather Whateley's final letter to read it once more.

He read it over carefully, thoughtfully. What had the old man meant when, in referring to the madness that had spawned among the Whateleys, he had said "It has not been so of all that is mine" though he himself had kept free of that madness? Grandmother Whateley had died long before Abner's birth; his Aunt Julia had died as a young girl; his mother had led a blameless life. There remained Aunt Sarey. What had been her madness then? Luther Whateley could have meant none other. Only Sarey remained. What had she done to bring about her imprisonment unto death?

And what had he intended to hint at when he adjured Abner to kill anything in the mill section of the house, anything that lived? *No matter how small it may be. No matter what form it may have.* . . . Even something so small as an inoffensive toad? A spider? A fly? Luther Whateley wrote in riddles, which in itself was an affront to an intelligent man. Or did his grandfather think Abner a victim to the superstition of science? Ants, spiders, flies, various kinds of bugs, millers, centipedes, daddy-long-legs—all occupied the old mill; and doubtless in its walls were mice as well. Did Luther Whateley expect his grandson to go about exterminating all these?

Behind him suddenly something struck the window. Glass fragmented to the floor, together with something heavy. Abner sprang to his feet and whirled around. From outside came the sound of running footsteps.

A rock lay on the floor amid the shattered glass. There was a piece of "store paper" tied to it by common store string. Abner picked it up, broke the string, and unfolded the paper.

Crude lettering stared up at him. "Git out before ye git kilt!" Store paper and string. It was not meant so much a threat as a well-intentioned warning. And it was clearly the work of Tobias Whateley, thought Abner. He tossed it contemptuously to the table.

His thoughts were still in turmoil, but he had decided that precipitate flight was not necessary. He would stay, not only to learn if his suspicions about Luke Lang were true—as if the evidence of the telephone left room for doubt—but also to make a final attempt to fathom the riddle Luther Whateley had left behind.

He put out the light and went in darkness to the bedroom where he stretched out, fully clothed, upon the bed.

Sleep, however, would not come. He lay probing the maze of his thoughts, trying to make sense out of the mass of data he had accumulated, seeking always the basic fact which was the key to all the others. He felt sure it existed; worse, he was positive that it lay before his eyes—he had but failed to interpret it or to recognize it.

He had been lying there scarcely half an hour, when he heard, rising above the pulsating choir of the frogs and whip-poor-wills, a splashing from the direction of the Miskatonic—an approaching sound, as if a large wave were washing up the banks on its seaward way. He sat up, listening. But even as he did so, the sound stopped and another took its place—one he was loath to identify, and yet could define as no other than that of someone trying to climb the mill wheel.

He slid off the bed and went out of the room.

From the direction of the shuttered room came a muffled, heavy falling sound—then a curious, choking whimpering that sounded, horribly, like a child at a great distance trying to call out—then all was still, and it seemed that even the noise and clamour of the frogs diminished and fell away.

He returned to the kitchen and lit the lamp.

Pooled in the yellow glow of light, Abner made his way slowly up the stairs towards the shuttered room. He walked softly, careful to make no sound.

Arriving at the door, he listened. At first he heard nothing—then a susurration smote his ears.

Something in that room—*breathed!*

Fighting back his fear, Abner put the key in the lock and turned it. He flung open the door and held the lamp high.

Shock and horror paralysed him.

There, squatting in the midst of the tumbled bedding from that long-abandoned bed, sat a monstrous, leathery-skinned creature that was neither frog nor man, one gorged with food, with blood still slavering from its batrachian jaws and upon its webbed fingers—a monstrous entity that had strong, powerfully long arms, grown from its bestial body like those of a frog, and tapering off into a man's hands, save for the webbing between the fingers....

The tableau held for only a moment.

Then, with a frenzied growling sound—"*Eh-ya-ya-ya-yaah-aah—ngh'aaa—h'yuh, h'yuh—*" it rose up, towering, and launched itself at Abner.

His reaction was instantaneous, born of terrible, shattering knowledge. He flung the kerosene-filled lamp with all his might straight at the thing reaching towards him.

218

Fire enveloped the thing. It halted and began to tear frantically at its burning body, unmindful of the flames rising from the bedding behind it and the floor of the room, and at the same instant the calibre of its voice changed from a deep growling to a shrill, high wailing—"*Mama-mama—ma-aa-ma-aa-ma-aah!*"

Abner pulled the door shut and fled.

Down the stairs, half falling, through the rooms below, with his heart pounding madly, and out of the house. He tumbled into the car, almost bereft of his senses, half-blinded by the perspiration of his fear, turned the key in the ignition, and roared away from that accursed place from which the smoke already poured, while spreading flames in that tinder-dry building began to cast a red glow into the sky.

He drove like one possessed—through Dunwich—through the covered bridge—his eyes half-closed, as if to shut out forever the sight of that which he had seen, while the dark, brooding hills seemed to reach for him and the chanting whip-poor-wills and frogs mocked him.

But nothing could erase that final, cataclysmic knowledge seared into his mind—the key to which he had had all along and not known it—the knowledge implicit in his own memories as well as in the notes Luther Whateley had left—the chunks of raw meat he had childishly supposed were going to be prepared in Aunt Sarey's room instead of to be *eaten raw*, the reference to "R." who had come "back at last" after having escaped, back to the only home "R." knew—the seemingly unrelated references also in his grandfather's hand to missing cows, sheep, and the remains of other animals—the hideous suggestion clearly defined now in those entries of Luther Whateley's about R.'s "size commensurate with amt. of food," and "he must be kept on a careful diet and to a controllable size"—like the Innsmouth people! —controlled to nothingness after Sarah's death, with Luther hoping that foodless confinement might shrivel the thing in the shuttered room and kill it beyond revival, despite the doubt that had led him to adjure Abner to kill "anything in it that lives,"—*the thing Abner had unwittingly liberated when he broke the pane and kicked out the shutters, liberated to seek its own food and its hellish growth again, at first with fish from the Miskatonic, then with small animals, then cattle, and at last human beings—the thing that was half-batrachian, half-human, but human enough to come back to the only home it had ever known and to cry out in terror for its Mother in the face of the fatal holocaust—the thing that had been born to the unblessed union of Sarah Whateley and Ralsa Marsh, spawn of tainted and degenerate blood, the monster that would loom forever on the perimeter of Abner Whateley's awareness —his cousin Ralsa, doomed by his grandfather's iron will, instead of being released long ago into the sea to join the Deep Ones among the minions of Dagon and great Cthulhu!*

219

Bibliographical Notes

DONALD WANDREI (1908-   ) is a native and resident of St. Paul, Minnesota, though an inveterate traveller. He is the author of many published stories, as well as of two collections of poetry—*Ecstasy* and *Dark Odyssey*, a collection of short stories, *The Eye and the Finger*, and a novel, *The Web of Easter Island*. A second collection, *Strange Harvest*, is forthcoming.

JOHN METCALFE is one of that distinguished group of British authors who have dominated the genre of the macabre. Though not a prolific writer, such tales of his as *The Smoking Leg, The Bad Lands, Brenner's Boy* and a few others have been widely anthologized. His work is not limited to the fantastic; he has written such novels as *Arm's-Length, Spring Darkness, Foster-Girl, All Friends Are Strangers, My Cousin Geoffrey*, and others. His uncanny tales have been collected into *Judas and Other Stories* and *The Smoking Leg and Other Stories*. He is currently living in the United States, where he is writing and teaching in New York City.

FRANK BELKNAP LONG (1903-   ) is a New Yorker by birth and inclination. He was an early recruit to the Lovecraft Circle—that group of writers engaged in contributing to Lovecraft's Cthulhu Mythos. His first book was a collection of verse, *A Man from Genoa and Other Poems*. His work has been widely published and almost as frequently anthologized. He has contributed to all the magazines in the domain of fantasy, and under his own and various pen names has written many books, of which the most important are *The Hounds of Tindalos*, a collection of his best stories, and a novel, *The Horror from the Hills*.

GEORGE HITCHCOCK (1914-   ) lives in California, where he is stage director for the San Francisco Conservatory of Music and serves as an editor of the *San Francisco Review*, after having worked as a seaman, gardener, logger, smelterman, etc. He has been an actor. He writes plays, prose and poetry, and has been published in the *Northwest Review, Paris Review, Chelsea, Story*, and many other magazines. He is the author of a volume of poetry.

STEPHEN GRENDON (1909-   ) is the pen name of a well-known American writer, whose work in the domain of the macabre has been sparingly published and widely viewed on the television screen. His first collection, *Mr. George and Other Odd Persons*, is forthcoming.

VIRGINIA LAYEFSKY was born in Seattle, Washington, and has spent many years studying music at the Julliard School of Music. She is the wife of a violinist in the Pittsburgh, Pennsylvania symphony orchestra. She spends her time between Pittsburgh and the Virgin Island. *Moonlight—Starlight* is one of her first stories.

CARL JACOBI (1908-   ) is a native resident of Minnesota, where he is at present employed as a journalist. He was launched upon a writing career when he won a short story contest at the University of Minnesota with his fine macabre tale, *Mive*. His short fiction has appeared in *Ghost Stories*, *Amazing Stories*, *Weird Tales*, *The Toronto Star*, *Strange Stories*, *MacLean's Magazine*, *Wonder Stories*, etc.; the best of them have been collected into two volumes, *Revelations in Black*, and the forthcoming *Portraits in Moonlight*.

ROBERT BLOCH (1914-   ) began to write in his teens, and virtually all his work has been published in magazines belonging to the fantastic genre. He belongs to that small group of writers known as the Lovecraft Circle, and contributed to the Cthulhu Mythos. He is unusually prolific, and publishes under several pen names, both in magazine and book form. While the majority of his work is entertainment only, he has achieved certain heights in the macabre, particularly with his widely-read novel, *Psycho*, made into an even more widely-seen film by Alfred Hitchcock. His novels include such works as *The Scarf* and *The Dead Beat*, among others, and his best short stories have been collected into *The Opener of the Way* and *Pleasant Dreams*. He lives in California, where he writes teleplays and cinema scripts.

SIMON WEST (1908-   ) is one of the pen names of one of the most prolific and versatile writers in the world. Under his own and several pen names, he has published in approximately 500 magazines throughout the world. He is the author of more than 100 books, only a minority of them in the vein of the fantastic.

HOWARD PHILLIPS LOVECRAFT (1890-1937) has taken rank, in the quarter century since his untimely death, as one of the minor masters of the macabre among American writers, past and present. A lifelong resident of Providence, Rhode Island, he was a pronounced Anglophile, and his influences were predominantly British—Arthur Machen, Lord Dunsany, Algernon Blackwood, and others. He was not widely published among American magazines during his lifetime, contributing primarily to *Weird Tales*, but since his death his work has been collected into two major omnibus volumes—*The Outsider and Others* and *Beyond the Wall of Sleep*—and several lesser collections: *Marginalia*, *Something About Cats and Other Pieces*, *The Shuttered Room and Other Pieces*, *Collected Poems*—and his unfinished manuscripts have been completed and published in two volumes—*The Lurker at the Threshold* and *The Survivor and Others*, as by H. P. Lovecraft and August Derleth. He has been more widely translated and published abroad than any other modern writer in the genre of the macabre. *The Horror at Red Hook* was the result of two years of living in Brooklyn and the city milieu he much disliked.

H. RUSSELL WAKEFIELD (1890-   ), the son of Bishop Wakefield of Birmingham, was educated at Marlborough College and Oxford, where he took Second Class Honours in Modern History. Though he was for a time Secretary to Lord Northcliffe, and in service in both World Wars, he has been a writer for most of his life. He is the author of five outstanding collections of macabre tales—*They Return at Evening, Others Who Returned, Imagine a Man in a Box, The Clock Strikes Twelve*, and *Strayers from Sheol*—as well as such remarkable mystery novels as *Hearken to the Evidence, Belt of Suspicion*, and *Hostess to Death*—and such studies in criminology as *Landru* and *The Green Bicycle Case*. His supernatural stories have been widely anthologized. Mr. Wakefield lives and writes in London, where he writes for the B.B.C. and turns out tele-plays in addition to his occasional ghost stories.

HENRY ST. CLAIR WHITEHEAD (1882-1932) was an Episcopalian minister. A native of New England, where he spent most of his life, he lived for a time in the West Indies and spent his last years in Florida. The material for his stories was gathered principally in the Virgin Islands; they were published in such magazines as *Adventure, Strange Tales, Weird Tales*, etc. His books include on the one hand volumes for the lay Christian—*The Invitations of Our Lord, Neighbours of the Early Church*, etc., and on the other two notable collections of his supernatural stories—*Jumbee and Other Uncanny Tales* and *West India Lights*.

DAVID H. KELLER (1880-   ) is a doctor, now retired from a long experience in the U.S. armed services, with the rank of Lieutenant-Colonel. More importantly, he was one of the earliest American writers in the domain of science-fiction, in the vein of social satire made popular by H. G. Wells. His work appeared most frequently in *Amazing Stories, Weird Tales, Les Premieres, Tales of Wonder*, and less often in many other magazines. He is the author of many books, among them *Tales from Underwood, The Homonculus. The Eternal Conflict, The Devil and the Doctor, The Sign of the Burning Hart*. He lives in Pennsylvania, where he is still actively writing, putting to good use not only his flair for science-fiction but also his training in psychiatry.

CLARK ASHTON SMITH (1893-1961) was one of America's foremost fantasts. He was associated with Ambrose Bierce, George Sterling, and H. P. Lovecraft, to whose Cthulhu Mythos he contributed many features in his tales. He spent his life in California, where he wrote poems and short stories, and carved out of minerals and rocks the strange sculptures which were his *forte*. His work appeared widely in magazines ranging from *Poetry* to *The London Mercury*, *The Black Cat* to *Weird Tales*, from *The Yale Review* to *Smart Set*. One of the most effective lyric poets of his time, he collected his verse into seven books, from *The Star-Treader and Other Poems* to *Spells and Philtres*, and prepared his forthcoming *Selected Poems* before his death. His remarkable macabre fiction has been widely anthologized and collected into four published books—*Out of Space and Time*, *Lost Worlds*, *Genius Loci and Other Tales*. *The Abominations of Yondo*—and one forthcoming book, *Tales of Science and Sorcery*.

JOSEPH PAYNE BRENNAN (1918-   ) has been on the staff of *Theatre News*, is currently working at the Yale Library, and editing two little reviews—*Essence* and *Macabre*. He is primarily a poet, the author of three collections—*Heart of Earth*, *The Humming Stair*, and *The Wind of Time*. He has contributed to many magazines, including *The American Scholar*, *The Chicago Review*, *The Carolina Quarterly*, *The New York Times*, *The Beloit Poetry Journal*, *Weird Tales*, *Esquire*, etc., and is the author of two collections of macabre tales—*Nine Horrors and a Dream* and *The Dark Returners*.

AUGUST DERLETH (1909-   ) undertook to complete unfinished Lovecraft stories in 1945, when his publishing house, Arkham House, published the novel, *The Lurker at the Threshold*, next to which, the present story is the longest posthumous collaboration. Both belong to Lovecraft's Cthulhu Mythos.

A SELECTION OF FINE READING
AVAILABLE IN CORGI BOOKS

Novels

☐ 552 08651 7	THE HAND-REARED BOY	*Brian W. Aldiss*	25p
☐ 552 07938 3	THE NAKED LUNCH	*William Burroughs*	37½p
☐ 552 08562 6	GOD'S LITTLE ACRE	*Erskine Caldwell*	25p
☐ 552 08734 3	GRETTA	*Erskine Caldwell*	25p
☐ 552 08668 1	GO NAKED IN THE WORLD	*Tom Chamales*	35p
☐ 552 08700 9	THE BLIND MILLER	*Catherine Cookson*	35p
☐ 552 08653 3	THE MENAGERIE	*Catherine Cookson*	30p
☐ 552 08440 9	THE ANDROMEDA STRAIN	*Michael Crichton*	35p
☐ 552 08702 5	THERE WAS A FAIR MAID DWELLING	*R. F. Delderfield*	35p
☐ 552 08736 X	IMMORTAL WIFE	*Irving Stone*	50p
☐ 552 08125 6	CATCH-22	*Joseph Heller*	35p
☐ 552 08585 5	THE PHILANDERER	*Stanley Kauffmann*	30p
☐ 552 08652 5	THY DAUGHTER'S NAKEDNESS	*Myron S. Kaufmann*	62½p
☐ 552 08632 0	MICHAEL AND ALL ANGELS	*Norah Lofts*	30p
☐ 552 08349 6	THE LOST QUEEN	*Norah Lofts*	30p
☐ 552 08442 5	THE AU PAIR BOY	*Andrew McCall*	30p
☐ 552 08701 7	THE SAND PEBBLES	*Richard McKenna*	40p
☐ 552 08467 0	ALMOST AN AFFAIR	*Nan Maynard*	30p
☐ 552 08124 8	LOLITA	*Vladimir Nabokov*	30p
☐ 552 08491 3	PRETTY MAIDS ALL IN A ROW	*Francis Pollini*	35p
☐ 552 08582 0	RAMAGE AND THE FREEBOOTERS	*Dudley Pope*	35p
☐ 552 07954 5	RUN FOR THE TREES	*James Rand*	35p
☐ 552 08597 9	PORTNOY'S COMPLAINT	*Philip Roth*	40p
☐ 552 08713 0	POOR NO MORE	*Robert Ruark*	50p
☐ 552 08372 0	LAST EXIT TO BROOKLYN	*Hubert Selby Jr*	50p
☐ 552 08716 5	THE LONG VALLEY	*John Steinbeck*	25p
☐ 552 08633 9	RUSTY	*Joyce Stranger*	25p
☐ 552 07807 7	VALLEY OF THE DOLLS	*Jacqueline Susann*	40p
☐ 552 08523 5	THE LOVE MACHINE	*Jacqueline Susann*	40p
☐ 552 08013 6	THE EXHIBITIONIST	*Henry Sutton*	37½p
☐ 552 08217 1	THE CARETAKERS	*Dariel Telfer*	35p
☐ 552 08091 8	TOPAZ	*Leon Uris*	40p
☐ 552 08384 4	EXODUS	*Leon Uris*	40p
☐ 552 08676 2	EXODUS REVISITED (illustrated)	*Leon Uris*	50p
☐ 552 08735 1	WINTER OF THE WITCH	*Julia Watson*	30p

Science Fiction

☐ 552 08744 0	NEW WRITINGS IN S.F.19	*ed. John Carnell*	25p
☐ 552 08675 4	TALES OF TEN WORLDS	*Arthur C. Clarke*	25p
☐ 552 08661 4	DECISION AT DOONA	*Anne McCaffrey*	25p
☐ 552 08709 2	THREE TO THE HIGHEST POWER	*ed. William Nolan*	25p
☐ 552 08708 4	DIGITS AND DASTARDS	*Frederick Pohl*	25p

Crime

☐ 552 08687 8	CYNTHIA	*E. V. Cunningham*	25p
☐ 552 08739 4	TRAITOR'S EXIT	*John Gardner*	25p
☐ 552 08690 8	THE TOFF TAKES SHARES	*John Creasey*	25p
☐ 552 08705 X	GOODBYE, FRIEND	*Sebastien Japrisot*	25p
☐ 552 08640 1	RED FILE FOR CALLAN	*James Mitchell*	25p
☐ 552 08697 5	DAY OF THE GUNS	*Mickey Spillane*	25p
☐ 552 08698 3	ME, HOOD!	*Mickey Spillane*	25p

All these books are available at your book shop or newsagent; or can be ordered direct from the publisher. Just tick the titles you want and fill in the form below.

- -

CORGI BOOKS, Cash Sales Department, P.O. Box 11, Falmouth, Cornwall.

Please send cheque or postal order. No currency and allow 5 p per book to cover he cost of postage and packing in the U.K. and overseas.

NAME ....

ADDRESS ....

(JULY, '71) ....